LOVE THE STRANGER

ALSO BY THE AUTHOR

Tower of Babel

LOVE THE STRANGER

MICHAEL SEARS

SOHO
CRIME

Published by Soho Press, Inc.
227 W 17th Street
New York, NY 10011

Library of Congress Cataloging-in-Publication Data
Sears, Michael, 1950– author.
Love the stranger / Michael Sears.
New York, NY : Soho Crime, [2024] Series: The Queens mysteries ; 2

ISBN 978-1-64129-545-1
eISBN 978-1-64129-546-8

LCSH: Murder–Investigation–Fiction. | Queens (New York,
N.Y.)–Fiction. | LCGFT: Detective and mystery fiction. | Novels.
LCC PS3619.E2565 L68 2024 | DDC 813'.6–dc23/eng/20240617
LC record available at https://lccn.loc.gov/2024012296

Interior design by Janine Agro

Printed in the United States of America

10 9 8 7 6 5 4 3 2 1

as always, to Ruby

WHEN TED MOLLOY WAS a boy, he had been told that there were over a hundred languages spoken in Astoria. At the time, Greek may have led the list, as the next Mediterranean wave replaced the early Italians. Today first place was no doubt a hipster version of English, as gentrification had captured one block after another, building by building. People with a little bit of money, who loved living in a diverse community, moved in and their friends followed. A generation later, bearded men with man buns pushed fifteen-hundred-dollar baby strollers past a store offering religious goods for Hasidim, Greek Orthodox, Coptic Christians, and followers of Brazilian Spiritism—among others. Newcomers ambled through local markets that offered goat meat and camel milk, mangosteen and breadfruit, cases of Limca and Guaraná, and now such additions as gluten-free pasta, vegan cheese, and local rooftop-harvested honeys.

Queens was not a melting pot. It was a kaleidoscope of colors, classes, and ethnicities. Home to dreamers, strivers, con men, and crooks. A haven for many, Ted Molloy being one.

TUESDAY

-1-

HAIDIR WAS ON HIS knees in aisle 7 unpacking a box of Swad Coriander Chutney when Eber Lopez careened around the corner and tripped over him. Eber tucked and rolled and came up on all fours. Jars spewed across the floor, spinning and clattering.

"ICE, asshole," Eber said in a harsh whisper. He scrambled forward, got his footing, and bolted for the back of the store.

Haidir reacted without thinking.

He and his mother had refugee status. And she had won her citizenship two years ago. His stepfather told him repeatedly that if he stayed out of trouble, he would soon be a citizen, too. "You keep your face clean, and you will walk tall, like a man. You will not be afraid of the police, the *migra*. You run? They will chase you. That's what they do."

But Haidir was fourteen and like many of his contemporaries, he had been arrested multiple times. Twice for shoplifting, though when he was searched at the precinct with his mother present, nothing was found. The storekeeper regularly called the police whenever three or more kids were in the shop at the same time. Once for public intoxication, though the brown bag he carried held nothing but a mandarin Jarritos, and though the lying arresting officer swore he smelled vodka in the bottle, the ADA had sent Haidir home. And once for jaywalking. Jaywalking. In New York City. Another free ride to the station. They hadn't bothered calling his mother that time, they simply brought him in the back door, and let him out the front.

It was a game. A cruel game, designed to introduce young people of all colors—though black, brown, and tan seemed to be predominant—to the hierarchy of the street. The police were cold, brusque, and both rigid and capricious—but they weren't terrifying. There was a predictability to their actions—a perverse logic. You went with the flow and as long as you weren't carrying a weapon or drugs—and Haidir would never have held either—you were released the same day. The police operated under the fiction that as long as no jail time resulted, an arrest was an inconvenience, nothing more, especially for juvies.

ICE, on the other hand, took people and they never came back. Like that waiter everybody talked about. Twenty-four years he worked at that diner. He had two teenage children. They arrested him and put him on a plane. He never even got to say goodbye. Everyone feared *la migra*.

Pulse pounding in his ears, Haidir ran.

Ahead of Haidir, Eber skidded around a pyramid of Hellmann's Mayonnaise—Real, Homestyle, 1/2 the Fat, and Avocado Oil—that the two of them had stacked the previous day. Feet churning, he barely missed a slow-moving shopping cart guided by a grim-faced Chinese woman, and finally burst through the double swinging doors between the fresh fish display and the prepackaged meat section.

The woman saw Haidir coming and braced herself for contact.

"Aeeyah! *Migra!*" Shouts behind him spurred him on. He grabbed the cart and swung it out of his way and darted for the doors. Another brown-skinned man from the produce department slipped through in front of him.

Haidir followed. The warehouse area in the back of the Walmart-sized Manny Singh's Fruit & Produce held a meat locker, a freezer room, a kitchen, and rows of shelves stacked to the twelve-foot ceiling. And Manny's office.

The walls around the outside of the office reached a full twelve feet, but inside there was a drop-panel ceiling eight feet off the ground. Beyond the ceiling, there was a four-foot-high space—four feet wide and six feet long—that, in a pinch, could hold a half dozen crouching men or women. Everyone who worked for Manny knew it was there, though Haidir had never seen it before. He'd never been through an ICE raid before.

He ducked in the office door and took a quick look back. No one was behind him. He closed the door quietly and began to climb the staggered pallets of canned soda toward a gap in the ceiling where a panel had been removed.

"Get the light, *ese*," a voice hissed.

He dashed back to the door, flicked the switch, and felt his way back to the pyramid of carbonation. A soft light came from overhead. One of the men there had his cell phone aimed down, providing enough illumination for Haidir to make his way up.

"*Rápido*," the voice ordered.

Haidir knew better. The plastic wrapping was slick. One slip and he could fall, knocking cans to the floor to roll and clatter, giving them all away.

He made it to the top tier, reached into the recess over his head, and felt his arms grabbed and hoisted. For a brief moment he had a view of his surroundings—four men balanced on the rafters of the dropped ceiling. Then the light went out. Someone replaced the panel, and they all hunkered in silence.

Haidir slowed his breathing and tried to make himself comfortable straddling the two-by-sixes. He strained to hear anything beyond the walls of their hideaway.

A minute crawled by.

"What are you doing here, *niño?*" a husky Latino voice whispered.

Haidir didn't answer. He didn't recognize the voice. Now that he was here in the sanctuary, he was asking himself that same question. He had run out of fear, not because he had a plan, or believed he needed one.

"You think the police care about you?" The man sneered.

"Sssst," Eber warned. "*Silencio, pendejo.*"

In the absence of sight, Haidir's other senses worked harder. He could smell the man who had been dissing him, recognizing him as one of the countermen from the fish department. He felt the coarse asbestos dust—fallen from the fire retardant overhead—under his hands. And he heard the movement of men filing through the aisles of the warehouse.

"Clear," one voice called.

"Clear," another answered.

Haidir heard the click and clink of metal on metal, a sound he would always associate with police. And he heard his heart pounding at double speed, a sound so loud he could not believe it didn't carry—an audible magnet for the police to uncover them all in that dark claustrophobic space. His teeth threatened to chatter; he squeezed his face into a painful grimace.

And he felt the urge to piss.

"Oh, Allah," he prayed silently. "I beg you for the blessing of *Afiyah*. Do not let me be caught. And do not let me piss in my pants in front of these men." He briefly worried the last thought might be blasphemous, but all-knowing, all-forgiving Allah would understand.

Below, the office door opened, banging against the wall. The sound threatened to release Haidir's bladder on the spot. He gripped his crotch and the spasm passed.

The light in the office came on, casting thin shafts up through a field of cracks and gaps in the ceiling panels. Haidir could see his fellow refugees. Ali, who worked on the loading dock, a recent immigrant from Somalia—tall and thin. Jorge from produce—a Colombian who spoke English but mumbled so badly he couldn't be understood in any language. The fish man—Jorge's cousin. And Eber. All four looked as frightened as he was.

"Clear," a deep voice called.

Other voices approached. He heard Mr. Singh. Sri Singh. And two other men. One had the gruff, belligerent voice of a policeman. He spoke over the other two.

"Look, Mr. Singh, we *know* he works here, all right? Be a good citizen and take a look at the picture." The words were polite, but the tone was condescending.

"I have looked." Haidir heard Singh bring the two policemen into his office. "As you can see there is no one here. Are we done?"

"You're not trying. We want to see your employee books. This guy uses multiple aliases."

"I do not believe the firm's books are covered by your warrant."

The third man spoke. A softer voice. Respectful. Firm but apologetic. "I can assure you they are."

"I want to hear that from my lawyer," Singh said.

The bigger voice rode over him. "Why do you want to make trouble for yourself? Failing to obey a lawful order is a crime. We can arrest you."

"It is a misdemeanor, is it not? I am calling my lawyer now. You may have a seat while we wait."

Haidir's bladder did not want to wait. Neither did he. None of them did. The longer this stretched out, the more likely something would give them away. Someone would get a cramp and have to move. Or pee.

Only Eber looked unperturbed. His face was an unreadable, impenetrable rock.

The second officer spoke again. He projected reason rather than might. "Hold up. You recognize the picture, Mr. Singh. I can see it in your face. You may know this man as Angelo Castillo, or Eber Lopez, or Emo Mendez. Or another name entirely. Let me tell you about him. He is wanted in El Salvador for kidnapping and sexual assault on a minor. In Texas he killed a man. I'm not interested in shaking down a few random illegals—all of us came from somewhere, didn't we? But this is a bad guy."

Silence.

Crammed together in that ill-lit, dusty space, Haidir could not help but feel the burning tension emanating from Eber Lopez. He'd been named.

Eber turned his head in a slow arc, daring each one of them to call out or to make any threatening movements. No one took him up.

He was a killer. Haidir could see it in his eyes. He could smell it in the man's perspiration. He could hear it in every hoarse breath he took.

"I'm calling my lawyer," Singh said. "I'll leave it on speaker."

The tension in the loft abated in tiny increments. Eber no longer looked like a demon; he was one more frightened pilgrim faking bravado in the face of overwhelming odds. Maybe he wasn't the same Eber Lopez; it was not an uncommon name. Maybe he wasn't the man they sought. The murderer. The raper of children.

Haidir stared at Eber. He was sure the man was all that and worse.

The outgoing ring of the phone reached them. On the fourth ring a no-nonsense female voice announced, "Rogers and Fuchs. Hold, please."

The hearty cop cleared his throat—loudly—but it was the soft-voiced one who spoke. "This isn't really necessary, Mr.

Singh. We'll go. Let me remind you—and I'm sure your lawyer will make it clear—that harboring a fugitive is also a crime. You have a good day now."

Singh had called them on their threats. And won.

The female voice came back on the speaker. "Rogers and Fuchs. How may I direct your call?"

"We're going," the cop said.

Haidir's heart surged with pride for the strength and wisdom of the Sikh man below him. It was like watching Riyad Mahrez do his "*La spéciale*" when he played for the Algerian football team.

"I am sorry for taking your time," Singh said to the voice on the phone. "Goodbye, officers."

In the loft, anxiety levels plummeted. The immediate threat was over. Haidir was not going to be arrested, nor would he have to explain to his stepfather why he ignored his instructions not to run. The police only wanted one man and would have paid no mind to a beardless teenager. He felt foolish. Drained. Exhausted. His nose itched from the dust. He was nauseated from the fear and adrenaline, and the sour smell of five frightened men cooped up in an airless cave. And he still needed to piss.

The door closed behind the cops and every man up there— and one almost-a-man—let out a collective pent-up breath. Some smiled in relief. Eber did not.

"Who is up there?" Singh said in a conversational tone that easily reached them. "You should come down and get back to work now."

Ali lifted up the panel. They shuffled along the rafters, doubled over and bent-kneed, until, one by one, they dropped down onto the pyramid of soda and into the starkly lit office.

Haidir was second to last down. Eber came last. Sri Singh was standing at the door, arms crossed over his chest. He looked taller to Haidir. More authoritative. There was a glint of anger in his eyes.

All of them bowed their heads in humble gratitude. Ali bowed so low he looked like he was bent in half. Jorge and the man from the fish counter had been through all this before—these raids had been more frequent in years past as political winds blew—but this was a first for Ali and Haidir. And, he imagined, for Eber, as well.

"I want to speak to the two of you," Singh said, indicating Haidir and Eber. He stepped aside, swung the door open, and waved the other three men out. The moment they were gone he shut it again.

Haidir saw a sheet of paper on Singh's desk. A photo of Eber, looking angry. And guilty. It was a mug shot—an arrest photo—printed on plain paper with a description beneath and a list of aliases. There was no doubt this was Eber.

"What are you doing here, young man?" Singh asked, fixing his eyes on Haidir. "Explain yourself. What were you thinking?"

Haidir bridled. "You're not my father."

"No. I'm your employer. Answer me."

"ICE take people for no reason." Haidir tried for defiant, but even to his ears he sounded like a foolish child, rebelling for no reason. As soon as he heard himself, he wanted the words back.

Sri Singh sighed. "You were afraid," he said in a voice of infinite patience. "That is understandable. But your fear threatens all of us. I will talk to your mother about this. Go stack the shelves and if you broke any of those jars, it will come out of your paycheck." He opened the door and stood aside.

Haidir dashed out. The door slammed closed behind him. His bladder reminded him that he was in urgent need of a bathroom.

There was one toilet at Manny Singh's Fruit & Produce Market used by all employees, regardless of gender or seniority. Remarkably, it was, by communal effort, kept spotlessly clean. Anything less would have led to chaos. Haidir was already pulling down his zipper as he rushed into the small room.

Relief was so intense he forgot for the moment his anger and shame. He remembered to thank Allah for his deliverance and the further blessing of not having pissed his pants. He worried again that this could be sacrilege. Whom could he ask? A boy might ask an uncle or a male cousin about something like this, but he had neither.

He bent forward to flush the toilet and heard a muffled voice come through the wall. He stopped. Two voices. Both angry. Loud, but not screaming. He pressed his ear to the wall.

"Come back when you have cleared your name." It was Singh.

"*Quién? Quién les dijo?* Someone gave that name to ICE. *Quién?* That *maldito abogado. Chinga mentiroso.*"

"I cannot have DHS and Immigration here. Or the NYPD. Too many depend upon me. They will shut me down if they find you here. You have to go."

Eber rattled off something else, all in Spanish. Haidir, like most people who grew up in Queens, spoke a little bit. "*No tengo dinero*" was something one learned in grade school. A "*mentiroso*" was a liar. In fourth grade he had been grounded for a week for saying "*chinga*" in front of his mother. But Eber spoke too fast. Haidir missed most of what he said. Most. He understood the phrase "*te mataré.*"

"Go, and do not come back." Singh sounded unafraid and strong.

But Haidir had heard something in Eber's tone that maybe Sri Singh had not. Eber meant it. He would most certainly kill if given the chance.

2

LESTER YOUNG MCKINLEY WAS wearing a double-breasted charcoal-gray wool suit with a pale lavender chalk stripe, two-tone oxfords, and a silk tie so deeply purple it had to have been dyed in a vat of plum juice. He was closing in on seventy, with his silver-dusted hair and newly seated dental implants. The overall effect was over-the-top and eye-catching, and reeked of new wealth. Had he gone for a facial? His dark brown skin radiated good health and frequent moisturizing. Ted Molloy—seated in the back booth at Gallagher's Pub, which doubled as his satellite office—thought his partner looked great.

Eighteen months earlier they'd begun working together after Ted's previous researcher, a hopeless con man named Richie, had bumbled his way into a vast real estate conspiracy involving a megalomaniac developer, crooked politicians, Russian gangsters, a defrauded multimillionaire suffering from dementia, money launderers, at least one corrupt judge, and a pair of unlikely lovers. Richie hadn't survived the encounter. He'd been murdered.

Lester had been beaten, losing some teeth in the process. Ted's girlfriend, a fiery community activist named McKenzie Zielinski, a.k.a. Kenzie, had been violently attacked twice. And Ted was there at the final bullet-strewn showdown on the courthouse steps. When it was over, there were plenty of bodies. Ted had been forced to trade his silence about what he knew, to ensure the future health and safety of Kenzie and other innocents he cared about.

Ted and Lester had gone on to form a working unit as Ted resurrected his once-stellar law career. Ted recognized that his fall was partly the result of his own arrogance. He was the child of an alcoholic father who had finally done one good act—he left—and a tired, beaten mother who passed away before Ted's rising star fizzled and crashed. Though Ted and his wife had remained friendly for some time, he had few other friends, and he'd lost her affections when he'd failed to protect the woman who'd replaced him in her life.

But Ted was, above all, a survivor. He devised a strategy and soldiered on. As he now concentrated on his single big case—working with Kenzie and the organization she ran to halt the construction of a behemoth, community-destroying project in the heart of Corona—he delegated other business matters to Lester, who took on the daily operations of their various commercial real estate dealings. Much of this work entailed research in county files and negotiations with broken, bankrupt, or otherwise miserably unhappy individuals whose dreams of financial success had been destroyed by divorce, mismanagement, fraud, or an over-reliance on rose-colored glasses in lieu of hard-nosed bookkeeping. Lester was both the face of the business and the daily manager, overseeing a small group of independent researchers who picked up a few extra hours when title work got slow.

The responsibility had done wonders for Lester's self-assurance—he looked ten years younger, and the increase in income, for Lester, at least, was paying off both in wardrobe and living quarters. He'd recently moved out of the one-room SRO with hot plate and community bathroom down the hall, and into a third-floor two bedroom in Hollis where he hoped to have his granddaughters visit as soon as he got a bit further along in patching the holes in his relationship with his daughter. Lester had not completely given up his forty-year love affair with vodka, but they now only dated on weekends and kept the hard-partying to a minimum. Like an ill-matched old married couple, they maintained.

Lester dumped a pile of manila folders on the table and took a seat on the opposite side of the booth from Ted, elbows planted, hands propping up his graying head. Each folder represented an open case needing some review or action on Ted's part to speed the slow-moving cogs of the legal system in the direction of completion—and a payday for them both.

At nine in the morning, the bar was empty, save for the near-permanent fixture of Paulie McGirk nursing his first beer of the day. Ted and Lester squeezed their business meetings into the hours before lunch or late in the afternoon before happy hour.

The most recent bar owner had saved the decaying eighty-some-year-old institution from bankruptcy by expanding the menu to better reflect the changing demographics, adding a weekend dim sum brunch and pan-Asian specials through the week. He had also replaced the mostly crooked staff with cousins, nieces, and nephews recently arrived from his homeland in northern China. Business improved significantly, and though not all the new staff were equally up to the challenges of restaurant service, the overall increase in efficiency was a welcome change. Lily, Gallagher's assistant manager and day shift bartender and a first cousin, was busy layering green bottles of beer with shaved ice in preparation for the day's work. The sound of ice cascading over glass punctuated both the background murmur from the television above the backbar, and the competing seventies classics coming through the satellite music system. There was no one to eavesdrop on Lester and Ted's conversation.

"How's the new guy in Brooklyn? I don't see anything here," Ted said.

"I'm afraid Brooklyn's been picked over. Suppose we try him up on the Concourse."

"I don't know the Bronx. Slip him a little something to keep him happy. I don't want to give up yet."

Lily boosted the volume on the music and was doing a solo dance as she restocked the beer. The oldie drowned out the talking head on CNN. " . . . *de lime in de coconut* . . ."

"Any movement on the Lefferts case?" Lester asked.

"The judge is sitting on it." What should have been a straight up surplus money retrieval for the estate of the previous owner had become a long-term project thanks to a disinterested judge. Ted had agreed to cut their fee by ten percent to win the deal, but it was still a lot of money. "But it'll happen. We must practice patience, oh great one."

"I want to put in a dishwasher," Lester said.

"Houseproud," Ted replied. "Order the dishwasher. From what I hear they're all backordered for six months or more. You'll have the money before the dishwasher."

Paulie McGirk suddenly burst into song. "*One is the lone-liest number* . . ." Three Dog Night had been doing fine on their own.

"Shut up, Paulie, or I'll cut you off," Lily cried, popping the cap on a Budweiser and planting it in front of the man.

Paulie shut up and Lily turned the music back down.

A familiar voice emanated from the television. Channel 1. New York's all news, weather, transit station. The camera was focused on Ron Reisner, chief executive of La Bella Casa, the umbrella conglomerate that included LBC International, La Bella Casa Hotels, and, Ted's nemesis, the LBC Development Corporation. It was an obviously staged appearance in front of an empty lot. A once-tall, handsome man, Ron Reisner looked smaller, weaker, pained, though his well-moisturized bald pate still gave off a glow.

"The man's not aging well," Lester said.

Reisner had been shot a year and some months ago. His son had been killed in the same incident. Grief combined with physical pain was wearing the real estate developer down. Ted felt no sympathy. Reisner had been ruthless—and still was.

"And because we are being held back by these frivolous and illegal actions in court, this blight continues . . ." Despite the aging, the camera liked Reisner. He went on complaining but managed to make himself sound both abused and amused by these legal problems. Ted was responsible for more than a few of them.

"Who's with him? They look like bodyguards." Though both men were wearing suits, they had the pumped-up build of steroid users and the piercing eyes of raptors.

"Oh, we know those boys," Lester said. "Reisner hired Collins Guards as security for both family and the business."

Ted did not bother to note that, for Reisner, there was no differentiation between the two.

Lester went on. "The one with the Pancho Villa mustache is named Ford. He runs the detail. Ex–Navy SEAL, I heard. I see him at the courthouse whenever Reisner has to appear."

Ted hadn't seen the man before. Reisner rarely showed up in court. He paid lawyers to do that.

"And the other?"

Lester shrugged. "Muscle. Collins Guards does everything from heavy lifting to cyber warfare. Judging by the guns on that hombre, I'd say he's a lifter."

The television cut away to a scene of a Santa Muerte festival in Corona.

Paulie waddled past on his way to the restrooms in back. "How ya doon, Eddie?" He leaned in as though expecting to join them.

Ted had on occasion paid for a beer or two for Paulie.

Paulie never forgot an easy touch, though he was not as good at remembering names.

"Forget where you were headed? The bathroom's thataway," Ted said.

"You're a good man, Eddie." Paulie continued on his trek.

Lester watched him, shaking his head sadly. At one point in his life, that could have been him.

"We good here?" Ted asked, gathering the files into a single stack.

Lester nodded. "Come see the new digs," he said.

Ted had to be in court later that morning to argue for Reisner's firm to provide certain documents—emails, memos, reports. The lawyers would resist and delay until forced to comply. Then they'd bury him in paper and demand he immediately respond. It was standard behavior. In his previous role as junior partner at a prestigious Manhattan law practice, he'd used the exact same tactics.

But he didn't have to be there until eleven. "Quick trip. I'll call Mohammed." A Yemeni refugee who had recently stepped up from driving a rented gypsy cab to being an Uber driver in his own car. Ted liked him. Lester was terrified of him.

"Mohammed is driving your lovely lady today—all day. She's busy."

Of course Kenzie was busy. Over breakfast, she'd had that preoccupied air that made him feel like an obstruction rather than a beloved roomie. She had told him her plans for the day, only he had immediately forgotten everything she'd said.

He opened the Uber app. The tail end of rush hour. Closest claimed to be thirty minutes away, making a drop.

Damn. "Lily," he yelled. "Call us a cab."

3

LESTER'S APARTMENT WAS A third-floor walk-up and had only one
window that actually allowed in any sunlight. The rooms were
all small, save the kitchen, which held a footed tub in addition
to the standard fixtures. The fresh paint smell failed to entirely
camouflage an aroma of fried onions, which was muted at the
moment, but which, Ted was sure, would become predominant in a July heat spell in the un-air-conditioned space. But
he kept all such reservations to himself. Lester was proud and
Ted was happy for him.

"You've done well for yourself, my friend. It's a nice place."
Ted's last apartment hadn't had any windows. The recently
resectioned three-family he shared with Kenzie had lots of
light. No room, but plenty of sunlight. Typical New York City
real estate trade-offs.

"Not yet. But it's gonna be." Lester was looking for something, opening the few—empty—cupboards and looking under
the sink. "A little furniture. Something on the walls. First up
is some way to play music. But yeah, thanks. It'll get there."
He stood under the archway leading to the bedrooms, arms
akimbo, head swiveling.

Other than two large cardboard boxes, the only items in
the living room were a metal folding chair and a spindly two-
tiered bookcase that now held a half dozen well-thumbed
paperbacks by Walter Mosley and James McBride. Ted recognized the names but hadn't read either. "Maybe a trip to
IKEA?" he suggested. "I'm known for my skills at putting
together IKEA furniture."

Lester gave him a skeptical look. "Okay? What's your secret?"

"When all else fails, read the instructions."

A sudden light came into Lester's eyes. He came into the living room and tore at the tape on one of the two large cardboard boxes. "We were lucky, when I was a kid. Everything we owned was a hand-me-down. My folks never bought on credit. Something broke, my daddy fixed it. Or we did without." The packing tape finally gave way. "I'm not talking about appliances. Furniture. Like that." He pulled a plastic basket filled with plastic dishes out of the box and began to empty it onto the counter. Two dinner plates, two soup bowls, two mugs. "When we had to clean out that apartment after he didn't come back from the VA, there was nobody who wanted any of that old stuff. We couldn't give it away. Everybody wants new, even if it's crap. Even if it costs like precious metals and they have to sign away their whole future." He placed the dishes in the sink. "Tell you what, you let me know if you see some old table and chairs on the street. I'll be there." With the now-empty basket under one arm, he headed for the door.

"You look like you're going somewhere." Ted looked pointedly at his watch. "I've got to be in court."

"I'm washing sheets. I just want to get them out of the dryer and we can go." He waved the basket.

"You're doing laundry?" Ted dropped off a bag at the laundromat every Thursday morning, and picked it up, cleaned and folded, every Thursday evening. He'd never asked, but he assumed his girlfriend did the same.

"There's washers and dryers in the basement. I am now a man of substance and no longer need to pay immigrant women to fold my boxers for me. Can you call a cab?"

Hollis was a primarily Black community. Ted wasn't sure he could get a cab to make the pickup. "I'll get us an Uber."

Lester raised his eyes heavenward. "Uber comes to Hollis. It's a brave new world."

"Go get your sheets."

Lester paused and looked back. "Make sure you tell 'em not to try and come down Ninetieth Avenue—"

"Because Ninetieth doesn't go all the way through. I know." The Uber app was close to perfect, but they'd both been passengers when the directions had led to minor disasters.

Laundry basket under his arm, Lester hustled out the door, letting it swing shut behind him.

Ted gave his attention to finding them a ride. He tapped his phone, submitted his request, and waited. Not much happened at first. It was now well after rush hour, there should have been multiple takers. In the twenty-first century, in the most ethnically diverse city in the world, racist microaggressions were still a constant.

Success. Eighteen minutes out. Acceptable. He'd be at the courthouse in plenty of time. He responded with a warning about Ninetieth Street. All clear. Tariq in sixteen.

He made use of the toilet and sink in the bathroom, noting that the shower stall was three times the size of the one he and Kenzie shared. He wouldn't tell her.

There was a loud knocking at the door. Had Lester forgotten his key?

Ted came out of the bathroom wiping his hands dry on the seat of his pants—Lester apparently had taken towels as well as sheets to the basement.

"Hold on!" he called, coming down the narrow hallway. He checked his phone. Tariq was coming down Francis Lewis Boulevard. He took the right turn at Ninetieth Avenue.

"Goddamnit!" he yelled as he reached the front door, realizing that he'd cautioned the driver about Ninetieth Street rather than Avenue. A tourist's mistake.

"Delivery," a nasal voice called out.

The Uber was accelerating this way on Ninetieth. In another few blocks he'd hit a dead end and have to reroute. "Idiot," Ted mumbled. He grabbed the door and swung it open.

A youngish, overly muscled deliveryman stood there. He wore the brown uniform. Despite the season—mid-November—the kid was wearing the summer shirt—short sleeved. It had to be to accentuate his biceps.

The delivery guy was accompanied by a slightly taller, heavyset older man with a broken nose and plenty of scar tissue on his forehead and around his eyes. He'd been a boxer at one time, but not a particularly good one. He wore an expensive-looking gray suit—spread collar, lightning-white dress shirt, and no tie. He was carrying a dusty brown padded moving blanket like the ones you'd get with a U-Haul van. Ted registered all this in half a second. Then the blanket came up and swirled over his head.

"Aaaah!" he squawked, ducking quickly and dropping the phone. Ted had wrestled all through middle and high school, and with a full four-year scholarship at St. John's. That was almost twenty years ago. But instincts and muscle memory took charge. He ducked the blanket, grabbed the ex-boxer around the calf, and came up fast. The boxer went down on the landing with a resounding slam.

The young bodybuilder was strong and quick, but he lacked training. He threw himself at Ted, using his strength and mass rather than any technique, and locked his arms around Ted's shoulders. Ted waited a split second for the man to get comfortable, letting him think he was truly in charge of the situation, then he took the man's elbows and pushed up while abruptly squatting, sliding down and out of the iron grip. He thrust upward and continued to push on one elbow, turning the man away from him.

But the first guy was up and moving. He closed in and jabbed at Ted's back, landing a punch to his right kidney. The pain felt like an electric jolt. Ted's knees sagged and the bodybuilder swung away from him. Ted had the bitter realization that he was losing this fight.

He opened his mouth to scream and felt another slam to his back. All the air in his lungs rushed out and the best he was able to accomplish was a soft "Unnnngggh."

The blanket came down over his head. Someone kicked his ankles and he fell to the floor. He tried to roll away but one of the thugs dropped on his abdomen and he was done. He gasped for air, but his solar plexus was paralyzed; his diaphragm was a single cramped knot of pain. Something heavy and hard slammed into the side of his head and black curtains came down.

4

MCKENZIE ZIELINSKI—ACTIVIST, COMMUNITY ORGANIZER, and constant irritant to the real estate developers trying to turn the patchwork charm of Queens into one huge shopping mall—looked at the trays of homemade sugar cookies and the neat rows of clear plastic cups filled with red or blue Kool-Aid and sighed. She hadn't had time for dinner—again. She'd given the same talk the week before at the Korean church in Bayside where, after the service and her short speech, there had been a buffet large enough to feed a small army. And the parishioners had taken full advantage. Of course, the Golden Jubilee Church of Christ made a point of celebrating the best of this world as well as the next—the sermon, in English, Korean, and American Sign Language, argued that the achievement of great wealth in this world was testament to the Lord's goodwill, and guaranteed a front-row seat for the heavenly choir when one made the transition.

Here in South Jamaica, at the Holy Spirit Community Temple, poverty was a given. A constant. Any aspirations for the accumulation of wealth were temptations of the devil. Reverend McNaughton ministered to families fighting the effects of alcoholism, addiction, disease, and multigenerational unemployment and dysfunction. The goal was to survive. Rewards in this world were spiritual, not material.

"There is love in those cookies," a man's hoarse voice reminded Kenzie. A friend. A sixtysomething street preacher whom she'd known for years. He had approached her when she was first struggling to marshal community support for her protests. He was tall, thin, Black, somewhat disheveled, with a long white beard and a serene but serious demeanor. She was white, redheaded, and more prone to exhibiting her anger and impatience with those who tried to brush her aside. The odd couple.

Kenzie and the Preacher often worked as a team. The Preacher had the contacts; Kenzie provided the story of how Stop the Spike was fighting to maintain the integrity of neighborhoods throughout the borough, but particularly in Corona where Ron Reisner wanted to build a mammoth testament to his own ego. Together they managed to perform at these gatherings—usually sponsored by churches, but not exclusively so—three or four times a month. The object was less about fundraising—Kenzie didn't take money from those who couldn't afford it—than simply spreading the word.

"I hear you," Kenzie replied. "But a little protein would go a long way to restoring my youthful glow." Kenzie was always hyperaware of her whiteness at these gatherings. Her fiery red halo of hair made her stand out even in a crowd of Irish Catholics. But it was her obvious good health that always made her feel most disconnected and alone in any group of those less fortunate, less privileged. In the neighborhoods she most frequently visited, poverty often meant obesity, asthma, diabetes, arthritis, and worse. Canes, crutches, and wheelchairs were common.

"We can stop for a bucket of wings soon as we're done."

Tall, stooped, and with a basso voice that never seemed to tire, the Right Reverend Abidan McNaughton stepped forward, taking both of Kenzie's hands in his large, long-fingered grasp. His skin had the cool softness of frequent use of conditioning lotion and he gave off a faint scent of lavender.

"I want to thank you again for your inspiring words, miss.

My people cannot offer much more than prayer to help your cause, but that they will give abundantly."

"No need for thanks, Reverend. I need to thank you. Our mutual friend here," she nodded in the Preacher's direction, "speaks highly of you and the work you do. If you and your parishioners can join us in front of the courthouse some morning, that will be a huge help in getting the community engaged and getting the politicians to take some notice. If that tower gets built, it will affect us all."

"As you said, miss. We will do our best."

The Preacher slipped between them, allowing Kenzie to rescue her hands from the reverend's grasp, and made leaving sounds of excuses, promises, and appreciation. Then he took her arm and whisked her down the aisle between the rows of folding chairs and out onto the street.

"Where is he?" Kenzie said.

Mohammed, their fast-talking—and fast driving—chauffeur, had sworn to wait for them, half parked in front of the fire hydrant a few steps down the block. He and his car were not there.

"He will return," the Preacher said with the absolute assurance of a man of the cloth—or a lying politician.

Kenzie did not have the same level of confidence. "This is becoming a regular thing with him." Mohammed did always show up, it was true, but not with the alacrity and dependability she was used to—and expected.

"He is a troubled man," the Preacher said.

"Five minutes and I call an Uber," she said. Then, hearing the bite in her voice and realizing it had more to do with exhaustion, hunger, and the adrenaline drop she always felt after giving one of her talks, she softened her tone and said, "I haven't been paying attention. What's got him in a twist?"

"Problems with his stepson."

"Haidir," Kenzie said with a nod. The problems weren't new.

Mohammed had married a fellow refugee that winter, a twenty-nine-year-old divorcée with a fourteen-year-old son. The two refugees had come to the States almost a decade ago and for years had shared an apartment with a pair of older Yemeni women. The women ran a successful bodega in Astoria. Mohammed had moved in, and the boy was having a hard time adjusting to a man in the house. Kenzie could only imagine how hard.

"They need to get a place of their own," she said, and instantly regretted it. A reasonably priced apartment in an acceptable neighborhood was the Holy Grail of the five boroughs, so rare as to be mythical. Seekers shared tales over Chinese takeout of friends who knew people who had heard of a guy who had supposedly found such a thing, but verification was always hazy. "I sound like a bitch." It was neither an apology nor an explanation, but it served for both. "I'm hungry," she added for clarification.

The street was empty of traffic and for a moment Kenzie heard what New Yorkers called silence—the low hum of the city, never completely at rest. Then her brain adjusted and began to sort through the components: the rumble of car and truck tires on the Van Wyck a half dozen blocks to the west; the throb of air conditioner compressors behind the CTown Supermarket, pumping away despite the cool of the fall evening; the low jumble of voices and music from televisions emanating from open windows, punctuated at regular intervals by the hilarity of canned laughter.

It calmed her. Centered her. Allowed her to relax and find her bearings again. "I'm not myself tonight," she said. "There were good people there tonight. They asked questions. They cared. And all I saw was a blur of poor people. I feel like a shit."

"You treated them with respect," the Preacher said.

"By force of habit," she replied. "Inside I was a racist. A class supremacist. An educated white liberal lady who knows better than you how to run your life. God, I am so sick of myself."

"I have a feeling that this goes deeper than being tired and hungry."

She laughed—a release in response to the comfort of being understood by a good friend. "Ted is pissing me off. And I know I'm pissing him off. We're both busy, doing what we love. Only we're doing it all the frigging time. We live together, but we barely have time to talk to each other."

"He may be a good man, but he is not an easy one," the Preacher said.

"Change the 'man' to 'woman' and you've got a good description of me."

A car horn blasted a block or two away.

"That will be Mohammed," the Preacher said.

Kenzie checked the time on her phone. "Four minutes and counting."

5

TED CAME ROUND SUDDENLY. One moment he was blissfully unaware of his pain and discomfort, the next it was all thrust upon him once more. The vortex was centered in the side of his skull but it radiated, pulsing with every heartbeat. A secondary source of agony was located in his upper abs. There was bruising there, he could feel it, but no broken ribs. He hoped. There wasn't much you could do for broken ribs but tape them up and hope they knit. He might as well hope his were unbroken.

But he was alive. And whoever these guys were, and whatever it was they wanted, they hadn't murdered him. Yet. That was a very good sign. There was room to negotiate, and he would do so when given the opportunity.

His hands were bound. Behind him. A plastic zip tie. He'd watched a YouTube video once where an athletic man in sweatpants and a sleeveless gym shirt curled himself into a ball, stepped backward through the restraint, and then broke free with one slashing movement of his upper body. Ted didn't think he was up to it.

He was wrapped head to shins in double or triple layers of the padded blanket, so even if he had felt more like a superhero, he wouldn't have been able to execute any of the preliminary movements. He was trapped.

It became apparent from the various sounds, smells, and sensations that he was in the trunk of a large automobile, traveling on a straight, smooth roadway. There weren't many such sections of highway in Queens. The Jackie Robinson was all curves, the Belt was all potholes, and traffic never moved on the Van Wyck.

The car braked suddenly and veered to the side. Ted could do nothing to protect himself as he rolled forward, his head slamming into the raised wheel well. The pain was a fresh attack on his halting consciousness and he faded away again. Back to the place of no pain. His refuge.

Hands were pulling at the blanket when next he returned to the land of pain. The last layer was pulled away and the dust-laden petroleum scent of the padding was replaced by a glorious wash of salty fresh air. Before he knew anything else, he knew he was near the ocean. Sunlight blinded him, but he could make out the vague form of a man leaning over him. Then the trunk lid slammed down, and he was back in total darkness.

But he could hear.

"Who the fuck is this? Who the fuck is this? I'm asking you two. Somebody start talking to me."

The man wasn't screaming, but it was close. More than yelling. There was a hint that the speaker could lose control at any moment if events slid in a certain direction. No one answered him. Ted didn't blame them. He wouldn't have either.

"I'm sorry. Carmine. I'm sorry. I got no right talkin' a you like that. You have been solid with me as long as I live." The same voice, but now suddenly soothing. Reasonable. Contrite. And yet, there was still an undercurrent of barely controlled fury.

Carmine fell for it. He spoke in a deep bass rumble with a touch of hoarseness, as though he might have taken a punch to his larynx once upon a time. "Lester McKinley. That's who you said. We went to his apartment. This guy opened the door. There was nobody else there. We took him."

Ted heard the simple logic of these statements. Carmine had done his best. He must be the older one in the suit. Ted doubted the other one could have strung together more than two complete sentences without assistance.

"Is that what happened? You. Yeah, I'm asking you, gym rat. Is that how you saw it?" The manic edge had crept back into his voice.

There was an indeterminate tenor mumble in reply.

"You fuckin' *stunads*! What'd I tell you? 'Pick up the old man.' Isn't that what I said?"

No one answered. "Somebody talk to me, goddamnit. Didn't I tell you to pick up the old man?"

A bass mumble.

"I did. That's what I said. Thank you. Lester McKinley is a juicer coming up on seventy and what else? What the fuck else?"

No answer.

"He's *melanzan'*. Did you see this guy? Of course you did. You brought him here. Maybe you noticed, he's not Black. Did you see that? Did either of you fuckin' geniuses see that?"

There was a long deep mumble. Ted couldn't catch most of it, but the tone was respectful, yet also somewhat aggrieved.

In a voice dripping with venomous sarcasm, the angry man replied. "Carmine, you are right. Thank you, my friend, for pointing that out. I sent you to Hollis, which is almost exclusively occupied by people of color and told you to bring me 'that old *schwartze*,' but I neglected to mention that the person I wanted was of the Black persuasion. My bad."

Ted was not at all surprised that a mobster from Queens had used a Yiddishism to describe a Black person. Ted was of Irish extraction—with some German thrown in for depth—but growing up on the streets of the world's most culturally and ethnically diverse 178 square miles, he'd picked up words and phrases in a dozen languages by the time he started middle school. But neither was he surprised that another mobster from Queens did not recognize the word—the third- and fourth-generation Italians in Howard Beach belonged to an intensively insular community—not unlike many other immigrant clusters in the city. Queens was not so much a melting pot as it was a stone soup of distinct ingredients.

"Whaddya want us to do with him?" High-pitched and whiney. Axl Rose in his comeback years. The bodybuilder.

"Who the fuck is he? Either of you know?" A silent pause. "I didn't think so."

Something heavy and metallic banged on the trunk hood. Ted imagined a handgun.

"You there. I know you're awake, fella, because I saw you squint when I looked in. So answer me. You got a name?"

There was nothing to be gained by being secretive. "Ted Molloy. I'm a lawyer. Mostly real estate."

"Never heard of you."

"I'm not surprised."

"What were you doing in Lester McKinley's apartment? That's where my associates found you, isn't that right?"

"He's a business acquaintance. We invest in foreclosures together. Sometimes we broker hard money loans."

The man laughed. It wasn't a funny sound. It was a scary laugh. One step this side of unhinged. "I don't fuckin' believe this shit. Do you know who I am?"

"Under the circumstances, I think it's better that I don't."

"What'd he say? I didn't hear him. Get him out of there, but don't take that blanket off. I don't want him to see your faces."

Ted had already seen their faces, but he would gladly forget them, given the chance.

As neither the boxer nor the bodybuilder owned up to having been seen by him back at Lester's apartment, this put Ted in the uncomfortable position of coconspirator allied against the angry man giving all the orders.

The hood of the trunk popped open with a blast of cool, salty air and a piercing lance of sunlight that managed to enter through a single uncovered eye, make an almost immediate right turn, and slam into the bruised area of his temple, triggering another explosion of pain. If he'd been standing, he would have fallen to the ground.

"Get him out. Now."

Hands grabbed his legs and lifted. Ted grunted as his weight shifted and centered on the crook of his neck.

"Gently, for the love of Christ."

Arms wrapped around Ted's shoulders. There was the smell of a musky cologne. Expensive, but way too much of it. The boxer.

"That's better." The man's voice was now gentle, concerned.

"On three," the deep voice said, almost in his ear. "One, two, and UP."

Ted soared up easily, out of the trunk, and down onto the ground. Hard. Despite the man's instructions, Ted hit hard enough to awaken a host of pains from head to toe. A gasp found its way past his clenched teeth.

Asphalt. He could smell it. He wriggled his head and his view improved. He was lying in the middle of a vast empty parking lot. A sand dune, partially covered in brown and green vegetation, rose in the distance.

Jones Beach. That's why the road had been so smooth and so straight. Ocean Parkway. A hand grabbed the edge of the blanket and pulled it down, obscuring the scene but allowing some light to come through.

"Carmine! What did you hit this guy with? You see that lump on his head?" Then in a softer tone, "Molloy? Is that right? You need to get that looked at. Seriously."

"I'll do that," Ted said, though he wasn't sure whether his words carried through the blanket. "Just as soon as we're done here."

"Right. So, here's the story. I expected to be talking directly to Lester—I know you're only the lawyer. He's got a default case against my uncle for a property on Pitkin. It's coming before the judge next week. The family is going through a major cash crunch."

The way he spoke the word "family" gave Ted a chill. It had a special meaning for this man.

"I mean, we're good for it, but not right away. So, I wanted to bring Lester out here to talk things over someplace with no witnesses, and where no one could hear him if we needed to use persuasion. You understand. Nothing personal, but he can be a hardhead."

Lester was only a hardhead over the phone. He would have agreed to any plan to keep from getting hurt. But now that they'd dragged Ted here—in Lester's place—might they now apply the same methods on him? Ted was ready to negotiate.

"All I want is for him to give us six months and we'll make him whole."

Ted knew the case. Lester had contacted the owner and negotiated the loan—$350,000 for three years at 9 percent. Half what the city charged for delinquent taxes. There was plenty of equity; the building had to be worth three times that amount. Ted had found the lender—someone he knew from law school—who, for his own reasons (tax avoidance being high on the list, Ted thought) had not wanted his name on the documents. Lester's name was on everything.

But things went toes-up when the uncle failed to make

a single interest payment—he was now a year and a half in arrears—and refused to take any of Lester's calls. The only recourse had been the courts—slow but with infinite inevitability.

The man was ripe for negotiating. "Lester's going to need more than your word."

"I know. I know. That's why I brought a peace offering." He snapped an order. "Hey, Morey. There's a paper bag on the front seat of my car. Get it for me."

Ted heard sneakered feet scuffing through the off-season loose sand on the parking lot.

"Here's what I got," the angry man went on. "I brought six months of the vig. Fifteen thou, seven fifty. In cash. You give that to Lester. I'm buying those six months."

What Ted heard was desperation.

"It's not enough."

"What the fuck?" the man exploded. "Don't tell me that shit. That's the deal. Take it or I fuckin' shoot you in the asshole. You hear me?"

Ted was prepared for this. He did not want to get shot, or beaten, but neither could he appear to give in too quickly. This was a negotiation, and the man would have expectations. Ted needed to maintain a strong front. They wouldn't shoot him while they were talking.

"Why yell at me? I'm only telling you what Lester's going to say. He's gonna want at least a full year's worth of interest."

"It's cash, asshole. Cash! He'll take it."

"Not enough. By the way, this is kind of awkward, I don't even know your name."

"Fuck you. That's my name. Cause I'm gonna fuck you if you don't make this happen. There's close to sixteen grand here."

"Double it."

"Fuck you, double it."

"I am advising you, sir. Mr. McKinley is a hard man."

"Fuck you. Fuck him."

"Then we'll see you in court." Which was funny as in addition to not knowing the man's name, Ted had also not seen his face.

"Kid! Kid, get my briefcase. I've got another ten grand. And that's all. That's twenty-five, seven fifty. That's ten months vigorish."

"Almost ten months."

"It's all I got."

Ted didn't believe him, but he saw no reason to push it. If the uncle came up with the full outstanding balance in six months, so be it. If not? Back in court and nothing lost. Interest and penalties continued to accrue. Their lender would get his money back eventually.

He heard the scrape of sneakers approaching, then the snap of briefcase locks. A rustle of paper. The briefcase closed again.

"There. Fuckin' done. Twenty-six grand. It's all in the paper bag."

They were done. A kidnapping, a bound and blinded trip to a deserted beach, threats of violence—of death. And then nothing. The guy had handed over the cash without much more than a few loud threats. "Nice working with you guys," Ted said.

If anyone else saw the humor in the situation, they weren't laughing.

"We're leaving now. When we're down the road, I'll call you an Uber."

"No, wait. Call this number," Ted said, rattling it off. "The guy's name is Mohammed. Tell him I'm here. He'll come get me."

"And get that head looked at. I wouldn't be surprised if you got a concussion there."

"Thank you."

"No. Thank you. You take care of this, and my uncle will owe you one. That's a good place to be."

Ted lay there and waited. It was only long after the car had left—and he was beginning to feel the cold seeping through the padding—that he remembered. Mohammed was driving Kenzie all day.

6

MOHAMMED ROLLED UP SECONDS before Kenzie's five minutes ran out. He waved impatiently for her to get in the car. He appeared to be talking—earnestly and with great concentration—to himself, though when he shook his head at words only he could hear, Kenzie saw the Bluetooth bud in his ear. She hopped in the back and slid over to give the Preacher room.

"Last stop," the Preacher said, "Corona, and then you may take the lady home."

Mohammed waved to show he'd heard, but his attention was still on his phone. "I am hanging you up now. I am working," Mohammed said, though he made no indication that he was about to disconnect. "No. No. No." The noes came without pause, each as clear and sharp as a gunshot. "I come to you tomorrow." This time he did hit the big red dot. He jammed the gearshift into drive and pulled away from the curb. "Sorry, my friends. Sorry. I know I keep you waiting. Not long? Ah, I see in your face. Long. Long. Sorry. What do I say?"

All of this was addressed to Kenzie in his rearview mirror as he barreled down the street toward the expressway. Kenzie would have preferred he kept his eyes focused on the road, especially as he approached the intersection.

"More problems with the boy?" the Preacher asked.

"That boy is a man. But, no. Problems with that slyster lawyer."

Shyster, Kenzie mentally corrected, though on reflection "slyster" was more descriptive.

"He takes money and does nothing."

Kenzie had heard Mohammed complain about this lawyer many times before. When Almeda, the woman who was now Mohammed's wife, came to the United States, she had been sponsored by an organization that provided legal aid. But later, she hired this lawyer to help with her son's path to citizenship. Almeda got a work permit, a green card, and eventually became a citizen. But her son's case dragged on. And now Mohammed's application process also seemed to be stuck in neutral. The system was broken—everyone admitted this—but the legal bills kept coming.

"He's helping you, isn't he?" Kenzie asked. She thought Mohammed's refugee application should be a slam dunk. He came from a war-torn country where members of his own family were waiting to kill him, having already murdered an uncle and a cousin.

"I hope so. I pay him." Mohammed often joked that Yemen had once produced crude oil and khat, but now refugees were the primary export. Khat was still number two. "But he did nothing for Haidir. Nothing."

"Hold up," Kenzie said. "His mother's a citizen. That makes him a citizen too. It's an automatic. I don't know much about immigration law, but I know that much."

"Automatic," Mohammed said. It sounded dirty the way he said it. He hit the horn in two long blasts though there was no other vehicle moving in sight. "Fucking lawyer."

No matter what country they came from, or what age, gender, or background, Kenzie thought, *that is their first curse word in English.*

Mohammed was approaching the Van Wyck at a speed, and with an intensity, that could prove disastrous in that concrete gorge filled—at any hour—with barely moving traffic.

"Brother, I see you have a heavy heart—and the lady is hungry. Can we find her sustenance before we get on the highway? And that would offer an opportunity for you to share your burden with us."

To Kenzie's surprise—and great relief—Mohammed agreed. "Popeyes?" he suggested.

Kenzie did not normally eat chain food on moral principles—profits left the community rather than remaining with local entrepreneurs who stayed and supported others—but her stomach was growling, and Mohammed was hurting. "There's got to be one near here," she said.

7

KENZIE WAS HUMBLY REASSESSING her opinion of chain food. Or of Popeyes at any rate. The fried breast was juicy, light tasting, with a subtle piquant kick at the end. The dirty rice was earthy and strong. A little sexy. She had no opinion on the biscuit, and as a native New Yorker she would not have allowed herself to pass judgment. New Yorkers did bread brilliantly, from pizza dough to bagels to croissants to loaves of seeded rye. However, she freely admitted they did not do biscuits. Was it the water? The flour?

Even before finishing her meal, she felt a glow replacing her doubts, complaints, and nitpicking comments. The world was a better place when the observer was fed. She would have to point this out to Ted at the next chance.

The Preacher and Mohammed were working their way through the rest of the sixteen-piece family meal bucket. Mohammed seemed to be enjoying himself, assuring them all that the bacon in the green beans was, in fact, turkey, not pork. He avoided the dirty rice, for which Kenzie applauded him. The rice was delicious, but the bits of meat, no matter what animal they might have come from, were certainly not halal.

"Are you ready to talk about it?" she asked.

The Preacher gave her a skeptical look. Did he think she was rushing things? Pressuring Mohammed? She didn't think so and plunged ahead.

"Is the lawyer the problem? Or is it the boy?"

Mohammed glowered. "The lawyer is maybe not so good.

But he is very busy. He handles many cases from the neighborhood."

Most immigration lawyers specialized in one or two ethnic populations because the problems were often similar, and the constantly shifting rules were at least close to uniform for any given country of origin.

"But this boy. He is angry. Always he is angry."

Kenzie was not at all surprised that a fourteen-year-old boy, having grown up in a house full of women, constantly treated like the chosen one, the next messiah, might act out a bit when his mother brought an older man into their lives. It wasn't culture, it was human nature.

"He complains. He says he wants to go back to Yemen and live with his father. Feh! His father does not want him. Why would anyone want to leave Bay Ridge for Aden? He is an idiot."

"I'm a little concerned, Mohammed," Kenzie said. "This lawyer should have been on it. There's no reason for him not to have made the boy's application before now."

The Preacher hummed by way of introducing his opinion. Conversation halted while Kenzie and Mohammed waited for him to speak. "Unless the lawyer wants to collect a greater fee," he finally said.

Kenzie put her chicken down. She was slipping, she thought. She should have come up with that. "What do you think, Mohammed?"

Mohammed stared down at the collection of bones on his tray. "I don't know, miss. I think maybe this man is not so good."

WEDNESDAY

8

IT WAS AFTER MIDNIGHT before Lester extricated Ted from the grips of the Mount Sinai South ER in Oceanside. On a routine drive-by at the beach, looking for teenage trysters or underage drinkers armed with a twelve-pack of Bud and another dozen of Fireball nips, a lone Nassau County policeman had instead discovered Ted shivering on the windswept blacktop. He was still wrapped in the moving blanket, which had no doubt saved his life as the temperature had plummeted once the early-November sun had dropped below the horizon.

"Where the hell is Mohammed?" Ted asked once they were in the Uber from the hospital and headed home. He was cold, in pain, and cranky, yet relieved at being rescued, not murdered, and that the policeman had not checked the contents of the mobster's briefcase. Ted had explained the whole episode to the cop as a bachelor party prank, though he suspected that his delivery had been less than successful.

"He's got problems."

"Tell me about it," Ted scoffed.

"And he's not answering his phone."

"How does he get fares?"

"It's an app," Lester said, raising one eyebrow.

"Of course it is." Everything was an app these days. He was nearing forty and some days felt like eighty.

"And he drove for Kenzie all day."

Kenzie was safe and had Mohammed to ferry her to and from her meetings—while Ted with battered head and zip-tied limbs lay freezing his balls off in Jones Beach Parking Lot 4. "So, why isn't he answering his phone?"

"As I understand the situation," Lester said with a dubious sniff, "he's being pursued by a car dealer who keeps demanding he extend his automobile warranty."

"That's a scam, Lester. Everybody knows that."

"I don't think 'everybody' includes Mohammed." He dug in his jacket pocket and produced Ted's phone. "You dropped this, I think."

"Thank you," Ted said. He checked the charge. Red zone. "And Kenzie's okay?"

"Worried, but otherwise good. I didn't know what to think. I come back with a basket full of laundry and you're gone and the door is wide open."

"Sorry, I'd have locked up, but those guys were in a hurry and I was unconscious."

"Nice to see you've still got your sense of humor."

"And a bump on my head. One of the cops thought it was a sap. He said his father always carried one as a detective."

"Blackjack."

"Same thing. Very effective. But no permanent damage. No fracture. They gave me Tylenol."

"We could make a stop if you need something stronger."

"Thank you, no. I will suffer soberly."

"I was thinking more like CVS," Lester said.

"Here," Ted said, handing over the briefcase. "Put this in the bank."

Lester snapped open the catch and stared at the field of green. "In small deposits, over a week or so."

"So, are you going to tell me about these guys? How did we end up lending money to wiseguys?"

"I'm as surprised as you."

"Not quite."

9

"I CAN EXPLAIN," LESTER said, selling it hard.

Kenzie wasn't buying. "You lent money to the mob. The two of you?"

"We structured it," Ted answered. "It's not our money." Was that supposed to make it sound better? "But it's well collateralized."

A lawyer's response. She wanted to scream.

"I'll be sure to remember that when your body floats up in Jamaica Bay."

She had begun with compassion, care, and concern. She'd checked his wound—a blossoming purple bruise, but little swelling, and no sign of bleeding. She'd offered tea, wrapped him in a blanket on the sofa, kissed him gently but warmly, and asked what had happened. It was soon after that the conversation made a dramatic turn and her sympathy took a back seat to increasing alarm.

There was a single light on in the living room, possibly the only internal light going on the street. Lester and Ted were sprawled on the couch, Kenzie facing them in Ted's office chair. The couch was the main piece of furniture in the room that served both as their living/dining room and the waiting room—and sometime conference room—for Ted's law practice. There was one chair, in case they had a guest, a two-shelved bookcase loaded with retired library copies of paperback crime novels from late in the last century, all donated by Kenzie's mother, and a twenty-nine-inch television perched on the wall over it, a housewarming gift from her father. The apartment had been carved out of one quarter of a two-family house—now three—in Richmond Hill, equidistant from the courts where Ted spent time and Ridgewood where Kenzie's Stop the Spike offices were headquartered—in a church basement they rented from the Korean-born Catholic priest, Father Byun.

Ted's office was in what was advertised as the "second bedroom," an alcove off the far side of the living room. The sole bathroom was reached through a pocket door behind the metal circular staircase that led up to their bedroom. Through an archway was a galley-sized kitchen. Outside the off-street kitchen door—the only entrance—was a rack where Kenzie locked the frame of her bicycle—both wheels having been stolen the night they moved in. The apartment had no closets and little charm, but it was cheap and had enough windows on each floor to qualify as "sunlit" for any realtor. And it was available when they needed it. Ted had been forced out of his old place by a landlord who objected to Russian gangsters trashing the apartment and scaring his secretary.

It was their first home together. And they were now sitting in it discussing gangsters.

"Can I say something?" Lester asked, bravely attempting to deflect her anger—most of which had been directed at Ted so far.

"It was you they were looking for," Kenzie snapped.

"Six months ago," Lester began, and then stopped for a second to clear his throat. "Six months ago, I was checking for tax liens at the county clerk."

Kenzie rolled her eyes in a silent *where-the-hell-is-this-going.*

"Patience is a virtue," Ted said, taking another sip of red wine. Kenzie had tried to get him to have hot tea, but he elected to finish the last glass in the bottle.

"So is getting to the point," she shot back. Lester had accepted the tea, but hadn't drunk any, gripping the warm mug in two hands.

Lester bravely plowed ahead with his tale. "There's only two computers for the public. They're ancient. Green screens. And the software hasn't been updated since the Koch administration. It's not what most people these days think of as user-friendly."

Kenzie gritted her teeth. Trying to rush Lester when he had the floor was a losing proposition. She'd listen. But she didn't have to do it patiently. "Moving right along," she said.

"There was this woman trying to work the program. Tall, blonde—bottle blonde, but not cheap—wearing an expensive-looking skirt and blouse and dripping with gold jewelry. Bracelets, rings, a necklace, all with little sparklers. Some not so little. In other words, she didn't fit. She didn't belong there. And she was having a miserable time getting what she wanted out of that machine."

"So you offered to help her."

Lester sighed at this bit of understanding. "Exactly. And she jumped at it. Thanked me and showed me a list of properties. She said she was checking on unpaid taxes on her brother's buildings because he was in trouble. What she didn't mention was that her brother was in MCC waiting on trial in federal court." Manhattan Correctional Center was where the bad guys were held pending trial.

"This is Scarduzio's sister you're talking about." Kenzie was appalled. And pissed. Peter Scarduzio. "The Gent," according to the *New York Post*. "Mafia boss," per the *Daily News*. "She's the one on TV. *Married to the Mob* or something, right? Holy hell."

"I don't have a television." Lester raised his voice at the injustice.

"What's her name? Jeanine Something."

"Gerhart," Ted answered. "Her husband runs a string of car washes."

Kenzie glared at him. "Car washes. I imagine that's important."

Lester came to his rescue again. "She seemed like a nice lady, and she was having trouble with the machine. I was being polite."

"She's a very attractive woman," Kenzie said pointedly.

"I try not to let such things influence me," Lester answered.

Ted laughed. Kenzie gave him the death stare once more. He stopped laughing. She turned to Lester. "Go on."

"All told, there's a little over a quarter mil in unpaid taxes and water on eight buildings. I thought it would make a nice hard money loan for one of Ted's investors."

Kenzie whirled on Ted again. "Where do you find these people? Somebody just writes a check for hundreds of thousands? Who the hell do you know with that kind of disposable income? That's a small fortune."

"For us, yes. For them, not so much." Ted met her ferocity with his usual calm.

His calm made her crazy. He knew it. So did she.

"Who? Jill's family?"

That was a cheap shot. Unwarranted, but it popped out before she knew she was forming the words. Ted's ex-wife. The family had money. Big money. And power. Lots of power. Ted claimed they had not spoken in well over a year. Kenzie believed him but had to remind herself of that fairly often. Jill's presence was like the aroma of Valentine's Day flowers left in the vase until the water went bad.

"Those people want nothing to do with me," Ted said. "I promise." He wanted her to believe. Was he trying to convince himself as well?

"So why does this mob guy need to borrow from you? Or whoever is putting up the cash?"

Ted let a long sigh escape. "Technically, the money went to the brother-in-law. It's his name on the corporate papers."

"But . . ." Lester said.

Ted nodded. "But Mr. Scarduzio is in federal custody. He needs money to pay his lawyers." Ted looked tired—exhausted. He wasn't going to last much longer. She felt her anger softening.

Lester continued to explain. "Only all of his accounts are frozen. And he can't use the property as collateral until he cleans up the tax liens. That's where we come in."

"You're helping a mob guy stand off a federal prosecutor? Do I have that right?"

The two men looked at each other.

"Yes," Lester said.

"No," Ted said at the same moment.

"I see why you didn't want the cops to know you'd been kidnapped. This is so going to come back and bite you in the ass."

"I wasn't kidnapped."

"What do you call it? They tied you up, beat you, threatened you with a gun, and left you to freeze to death." She heard herself sounding like a harpy. She needed to listen, not rush to the attack.

"We were negotiating. The younger Mr. Scarduzio was impatient for results."

"Why not go to the Feds and dump the whole thing in their lap?"

"Ahhh, because the Feds would go after our lender, put

liens on the property, and probably begin investigating us. Nightmare. On the other hand, if we hold off on the foreclosure and wait patiently, our client gets his money, plus interest, in six months, and everybody's happy."

"And some mobster gets to walk."

"Unless convicted. That's the American way."

10

KENZIE HAD TRIED TO get Lester to spend the night on their couch, arguing that it would be close to impossible to find a car service at that hour. Ted stayed out of it until, driven by exhaustion and exasperation, he pulled out his phone and found an Uber four minutes away.

"Let him go and sleep in his own bed. Right now, that's all any of us want."

Kenzie smiled at that—a tired smile, but a gracious one. She gave Lester a hug as she ushered him out. "Thank you for rescuing my guy."

"I'm sure he'd do the same," Lester said.

"I would," Ted said. "But not right now."

There was an awkward moment after Lester left. Ted and Kenzie stared at each other across the living room. Ted spoke first.

"We okay?"

She nodded. "We have very different views on some things."

"Truth," he said.

"But we're good. Let's get some sleep." She came to him and hugged him tightly.

He hugged back and kissed the silver streak in her hair, a remnant of having been attacked by a pair of murderous Russian thugs eighteen months ago. She sighed once and gently patted his chest. "You're a good man," she said, and started up the spiral stairs.

Ted had no idea why he had been given that appraisal, but he took it. He followed.

Kenzie changed into her flannel leggings and an oversized gray T-shirt that read STOLEN FROM NEW YORK CITY FOOTBALL CLUB while Ted took care of brushing his teeth and splashing lukewarm water over his tired face, careful to avoid rubbing too intently at the egg-shaped bump at his hairline. He popped two Extra Strength Tylenol, then ceded the tiny bathroom to her and got into bed.

He listened to the comforting sounds of Kenzie brushing her teeth and gargling with mouthwash. Then he caught the familiar faint aroma of her moisturizer. His eyes snapped open, and he realized he'd been asleep—fully unconscious. How long? Seconds, maybe? Despite his utter exhaustion, he made himself stay awake to bestow a good night kiss before surrendering to the void.

Kenzie came out of the bathroom and sat on the edge of the bed. And sighed.

It was a signal.

Ted could not do this now. His brain was already shutting down.

"I have to ask you something."

"What?"

"It's Mohammed. He needs help."

Connecting the words so that they made any kind of sense was taking a monumental amount of mental energy. He wouldn't be able to keep it up.

"Why are we talking about Mohammed?"

"I'm worried about him."

"I've had a hell of a day."

"I know." She touched his cheek. "He needs your help."

There was nothing for it. Kenzie needed to talk about it and nothing short of an alien invasion would dissuade her. Ted sat up, plumped the pillow behind his back, and rubbed his face with both hands. His brain was no clearer, but he was now capable of appearing to be awake. "Okay. I'm listening. Tell me about Mohammed."

"His lawyer sounds like a crook."

"Immigrants and their lawyers. Mutual distrust." He successfully swallowed a yawn.

"And I know he's worried about his son—stepson. Haidir."

"What does Mohammed think?"

"He wants to believe the guy is going to come through for them—somehow. But he's not happy. He's already paid him a lot of money and owes him a lot more."

Ted exhaled through pursed lips. "Haidir's mother has her citizenship—she was sponsored. Fast-tracked, but that's a joke. The paperwork still took years. But, yes, her son is an automatic."

"Guaranteed automatic?" she asked, demanding an absolute response.

Absolutes were rare in his world, but he gave her what assurance he could. "His lawyer would need to file the paperwork in a timely manner, but yes. Automatic."

"And Mohammed?"

"He's married to a US citizen. They may give him a runaround, but someday he will be fast-forwarded too. We can celebrate their citizenship with strong tea and *bint al-sahn*. If we're lucky we'll get to see a *baraa* dance."

"That's not some kind of 'seven veils' thing, I hope."

"No. It's all men and they carry knives."

"Would you look into it for him? Mohammed is frantic."

"I hear he's also afraid his extended car warranty is expiring."

"Please. Be serious. The lawyer's name is Spitzer. Howard Spitzer. Just talk to him. See if he's on the level."

He was fully awake now. "Tomorrow I've got a full dance card—most of it pro bono, by the way. All for the cause. First, in a few hours I've got to grovel and beg both judge and opposing counsel to forgive me for blowing off a hearing today—I don't think they'll buy a story about being waylaid by pirates, do you? The sharks were supposed to show cause why LBC should not be held in contempt for failure to provide certain documents pertaining to the traffic pattern study, so it was kind of important that I be there. Are you following this?" He did not wait for her to answer but continued with his calm, reasoned rant. "But now the judge is going to be pissed off at me for not showing up and I won't get the contempt citation." He was done. Finished. Aggrieved. And suddenly ravenous.

"Well, thank you. I'm sure there's a lot I don't understand about all that." She fluttered a hand, indicating general distaste for all legal maneuvering. "I'm not asking for much. I only want you to talk to this guy."

He wasn't going to sleep again anytime soon. "Do we have anything to eat? If we're going to do this, I need sustenance."

"There's always leftovers."

She followed him down to the kitchen.

"I'll get you his address," she said, hovering behind as he stared into the refrigerator.

Clear plastic boxes from the Korean market. Half a Greek salad with wrapped fig leaves that were now an unlikely brown. California rolls. There were three left. The wasabi was all gone. Kenzie loved wasabi.

Bamboo boxes from that new Turkish place. He didn't look. It had been a week and a half since he'd brought that home.

The Balkan *pasulj*, a smoked beef and bean stew, was the most appetizing, but it would require heating in the microwave—which sat on top of the refrigerator in their miniscule kitchen—and *that* would require at least a minimum of thought and patience to get out a bowl, cover it, and clean up afterward. He couldn't deal with all that.

He looked around the tiny space. They used the stove to boil water. The colander in the drying rack had been there since the last time they cooked pasta—frozen ravioli three weeks ago.

"You want to take a cooking class? Together, I mean. This is New York City. There must be classes in cooking anything." He took the sushi and the two mini packets of soy sauce. Almost as an afterthought, he took the lone bottle of Dogfish IPA.

"What?! No! I'm talking about Mohammed. He's a friend and he's in trouble. And all I want you to do is find out if this lawyer of his is a total scumbag."

He stepped around her and took his foragings to the living room. "Okay. I hear you. But I have no experience in immigration law. Any advice I might give to Mohammed could get me in deep shit. I'm talking disbarred deep shit. I wouldn't even know who to ask." The surimi in the California roll had held up, surprisingly. It still didn't taste like crab, but he didn't think it was going to kill him.

"I'm not asking you to take his case. Talk to the guy and get a feel for whether he's really doing his best for Mohammed and his son."

"Stepson." He survived another death glare. "I wouldn't even know what questions to ask."

"But you're the lawyer," she cried. "You can do things. You helped that health aide, didn't you? Anora? Wasn't that her name?"

A year or so ago, Ted had cut his devil's bargain with the spokesmen for the Tower cabal, Judge Fitzmaurice, trading his silence—and a large chunk of his integrity—in exchange for Kenzie's safety—and she must never know. But a side benefit had been the acquisition of a green card for a key witness, Anora.

"I didn't do anything but make a call. Someone owed me a favor. It wouldn't work twice."

"It's not that you're too busy, right? You tell me every day how busy you are."

"I am busy. I am too busy. Between filings for the case against LBC and glad-handing for donations, I barely have enough time to meet with Lester and work on projects that actually make us money." They were both too busy. Work fills the time allotted to it. Was all this busyness simply a distraction to mask his reluctance to take the relationship any further? That was much too big a question for three in the morning.

Capitulation—partial and possibly temporary—was the wise move at this hour.

"Okay. Okay. I will ask around, but I am not going to confront this guy. That's not how I work."

Direct confrontation was exactly how Kenzie worked. People felt her passion and followed her to the ramparts or retreated in confusion. Sometimes it paid off.

"You'll ask around?" Her voice was alarmingly neutral.

He held back from releasing the sigh in his chest. "Did you know that something like two-thirds of the calories in imitation crab come from added sugars and other carbohydrates? You think you're eating some high-protein omega-3 booster, but you might as well be having a Twinkie."

"Good night," she said, giving him a quick peck of a kiss on the undamaged side of his head. Before he had a chance to reply she was up the stairs and had turned off the light.

11

KENZIE ADMITTED TO HERSELF that she could be a pest. It was what made her good at her job. People who valued polite persuasion over political effectiveness were not drawn to the role of community activist. She knew how to hammer and felt no shame in it. Mohammed needed help. Ted could provide it. She was a pest. So be it.

But Ted Molloy was a jerk.

Could she have found a better time to ask for his help? Probably. But if she hadn't brought it up then she'd have fretted about it for the rest of the night.

Should she have tried another approach? Something softer, less demanding? No. She was who she was. She would not be false. Could not. It would have cheapened them both.

"McKenzie? Got a minute?"

Deepa, her hard-nosed office manager, was standing over her, one hand on hip, the other holding a single sheet of paper. A sturdily built woman draped in an unseasonable pale yellow sari, Deepa oversaw an ever-changing group of volunteers.

Kenzie's work as a community organizer had blossomed. The one-person office she had been using at the church a few blocks from her parents' home had grown and now took over the basement. Stop the Spike was no longer merely a slogan about preventing the construction of a community-destroying skyscraper in the middle of Corona, Queens; it was a political organization with over two hundred members who could be counted on to help the cause. Volunteers worked at phones and laptops raising funds, exhorted fellow citizens to show up for rallies, and networked with other like-minded groups throughout the city. Afternoons and evenings were their busy times, but Deepa was always first to arrive and last to leave.

"What's up?" Kenzie shook off her ruminations on Mohammed's problems and the shortcomings of her partner. "How's the preparations for our little soiree?"

The little soiree, which they'd been planning for some months, was the biggest fundraiser they had attempted. A donor was throwing an invite-only cocktail party at his duplex penthouse in Long Island City. The guest list represented more wealth than the GDP of many small nations.

"The RSVPs are coming in. Let's hope for a clear night."

The party was primarily Deepa's responsibility. Kenzie needed only to show up in the appropriate dress—chic, elegant, but also expressing humility and need, confident yet not aggressive. She did not own such a dress and she hated spending money they didn't have. The chances of finding what she needed at T.J. Maxx were slim to none. Maybe she could ask her mother to find something for her. They wore the same size.

The idea was to get these wealthy would-be patrons in the east-facing thirty-eighth-floor penthouse to watch the moonrise. Then, with graphics provided by a local print shop, to point out to them how the view would be ruined by the proposed LBC tower. And, finally, to fleece the group as gracefully as possible.

Which meant a presentation, which was also her responsibility. She could do the standard begging speech on automatic but had a feeling that this crowd was going to need something more. Different. Eye-opening for a crowd that had heard it all.

Which is what she should have been preparing instead of staring at her laptop while mentally cursing her partner.

"Please tell me something nice and not too complicated," she begged.

"I got a weird one. Some kid wants to intern." Deepa had a touch of a Queens bray in her voice that made people underestimate her—to their everlasting regret. She was smart and could be tough. She had recently retired from running her husband's dentist office after he hired a sleek thirtysomething dental technician who made no secret of the fact that she was sleeping with her boss. Deepa got the house, alimony, and child support for the three of their six children who were still living at home.

"Not really a kid, I guess." Deepa went on scanning the paper as she spoke. "Twenty-three. Law student. She's specializing in Environmental Law and Urban Planning. She's looking for 'real-world experience,' says here."

"Well, look at us," Kenzie grinned. "Ain't we something?"

"Interns. What next?"

"Six months ago it was just you and me, in an office the size of a closet."

"And now we rule the whole basement," Deepa said, waving her arm to include the vastness of the space they shared with a hissing, knocking, pinging, gasping boiler.

"What'll we do with her?" Kenzie said, laughing with delight.

Deepa looked stunned. "I have no idea."

"Where's she go to school?"

"NYU."

"Seriously? NYU? And she wants to come work in a basement in Ridgewood, Queens? Now, I'm a skeptic."

"Computer skills. Fundraising experience," Deepa said, continuing to read from the letter.

"At twenty-three? Probably stuffing envelopes. We can't put an intern from a top-tier law school in charge of printing flyers."

"She's gonna want to do legal stuff. Hands on."

And possibly there was a need for just that. Despite Ted's concerns about missing yesterday's hearing, she was confident that eventually he would prevail. And then there would be an ocean of documents to be reviewed and an impossible deadline. "I'll see if Ted can put her to work."

She realized that she was no longer angry with him. He had his strengths and his own moral compass. It didn't always point the direction she'd like, but in his way, he was as driven as she to do what he believed was right. He was an invaluable member of the Stop the Spike team. And as committed to their success as she.

But "asking around" about Mohammed's lawyer wasn't going to cut it. If she wanted something done, she'd have to do it herself. The new dress could wait. She checked the address for the lawyer. Spitzer. Howard Spitzer. On Steinway.

"I'm out, Deepa. I've got to run an errand. I might be a couple of hours." She pocketed her phone and slung her bag over her shoulder.

12

WHEN TED FINALLY WOKE up, Kenzie was already gone. He was not surprised—relieved, actually, in a small way. He had a lot to do and a lot to think about. She was unquestionably annoyed with him, but that could wait. He'd make some calls about this guy Spitzer—later—when he'd taken care of more immediate business.

There was coffee in the pot when he came downstairs and judging by his first sip it had not been sitting for long. It was strong, but not stale or so concentrated that he needed to start over.

His phone was charged, and it was time to start picking up the pieces from yesterday. He scrolled through. Eight calls from opposing counsel—oddly most of them were from *before* he was due in court. No messages. Two calls from Lester, the second with a breathless message that he had found Ted's phone. Another two from Kenzie. Texts from them both. The last from Kenzie: Are you all white? Damn. All right. There was a heart emoji attached. She must have been seriously worried; she hadn't bothered to edit—and she did not usually use emojis. He was touched that she'd been concerned, but also that she'd sent a heart. He sent her an explosion of hearts in response.

And there was one call from Sammi, the judge's clerk.

Life lessons. Do the hard thing first.

Eighteen months ago, Ted had unearthed a scheme involving a major real estate developer with ties to a corrupt city councilman and a Russian banker who laundered money for members of an organized crime syndicate. The tip-off had been the murder—both brutal and unnecessary—of Ted's assistant, who had discovered a comparatively penny-ante fraud committed against a nonagenarian woman fighting the early stages of dementia. Ted had found himself pitted against a conspiracy that included the most powerful men in New York—city and state—and his ex-wife's family. More people died before it was over and few of the truly guilty were punished.

But he had not agreed to give up the fight.

The evildoers had won the first round, but Ted had inflicted some damage.

A year later, Ted, Kenzie, and supporters had watched on television as politicians posed with real estate developer Ron Reisner, CEO of LBC, breaking ground for the monster tower to be built in Corona. But three weeks later, Ted, acting as sole counsel for the community group opposing the tower, won a ruling in court to halt the project until a more comprehensive environmental impact study focusing on traffic patterns could be done—the earlier study having been done during the Covid lockdown when the streets were empty. Rather than let the new study go forward, Reisner's lawyers chose to fight it in court. The issue was not yet resolved. Even if he eventually lost on the original motion, Ted had won a delay of half a year—so far. Ted had thought the filing was a Hail Mary. The ruling had seemed like a fluke. And may have been. Judge Bagdasian, a dark-browed, stern man who sometimes showed an ironic side, may have recognized the motion to block the study as the mistake it was. The judge had a reputation for being fair and that was the best Ted could hope for.

Most of Ted's strategy centered on delay. The only real hope he could offer of stopping the project permanently was for the developer to give up and move on. Delay cost money and market demand fluctuated. He had no slingshot to take

down this Goliath, only a dogged perseverance and the possibility of a sympathetic judge.

And he was afraid he may have lost that.

He dialed the clerk.

"So what happened to you?" Sammi asked when finally
on the line.

She sounded remarkably relaxed. Normally, the judge's
displeasure would be communicated in the tone and delivery
of every syllable from the clerk.

"I'll tell you straight up," Ted said. "I don't have a good
excuse. What did I miss? Did LBC agree to provide the documents or are they going to fight it?"

"Well, a little of each. They walked in and immediately
requested a continuance—though they are sending you some
files this week. Judge Bagdasian gave them one week to show
cause or demonstrate full compliance. We were out of there
in minutes."

A hundred pounds of anxiety that he hadn't even been
aware of lifted off Ted's chest.

"What do I need to do?"

"Nothing really. The judge didn't make a big deal of it.
You're not a chronic. You don't waste his time."

"I should buy a lotto ticket today."

"Tell you what, shoot me an email apologizing for being late
and I'll make sure he sees it. Case closed. See you next week."

Not only had he escaped retribution from an angry judge,
he'd been granted another delay. It was only after he had
disconnected and sat savoring his luck that he realized he'd
also learned something valuable. The lawyers wanted that
time because they were concerned that there was something
compromising in those documents. There was something there
they did not want him to see.

Therefore, they needed to delay until they identified it.

Once they did so, there would be a request to withhold, which would be denied as a matter of course, but for which Ted should be prepared. Then they would hit him with another avalanche of paper, hoping that a lone attorney would have no chance of finding the gem in the dross in a reasonable amount of time. And that was a problem because they'd be right. He couldn't possibly read all of it in depth.

But this fortuitous development had one immediate effect. He could now devote some time to asking around about Mohammed's lawyer. He would like to have something concrete to offer Kenzie when next he saw her.

Having no idea where to begin, he called Lester.

"How's the head?" Lester asked.

"Tender. But I'll live."

"Are we still in the doghouse for lending money to the mob?"

"That issue has been eclipsed. And I don't think you were ever in danger of being blamed—for anything. You were just in the wrong place at the right time."

"So what's on today's agenda?" Lester asked.

"Stop by Judge Bagdasian's chambers and bring Sammi some flowers."

"Not flowers. Oreos. Double Stuf."

"You're the expert." Ted switched gears. "I've got an assignment from Kenzie. She wants me to check out Mohammed's attorney. She thinks he's not on the level."

"I'm enough of a curmudgeon to believe that every man has his price, but there is no amount of money you could offer me to work a week as an immigration lawyer."

"Amen."

But Lester wasn't done. "I'll haul trash, clean public toilets, sell magazine subscriptions door-to-door, but I will not sit and try to explain to some mother and her kids why the strongest country in the world finds it necessary to send Daddy back to someplace in Central America where the local cartel will cut off his nuts before they set him on fire. All because he got arrested for not keeping his bottle of Tecate hidden in a paper bag."

"Lester."

"I'm done ranting. What's this guy's name?"

Ted had no trouble remembering. "Spitzer. Howard Spitzer. He's got an office in Corona."

"Never heard of him. But I don't travel in those circles. My people weren't technically immigrants."

"Do we know anyone who might be able to point me in the right direction?"

"You do."

"I do?"

"Your old landlord, there. Israel Ortiz. He did immigration."

"I didn't think of him." Or think much of him. "But he doesn't really specialize in immigration law. He mostly helps Spanish-speaking people fill out government forms." He did taxes, driver's license applications, school enrollment forms, or any other bewildering governmental document his clients put before him. Israel was also a landlord, a travel agent, a notary, and a tax advisor. He handled no-fault divorces for $400 plus court costs. He arranged wire transfers to Central and South America. His secretary did palm readings and sold Santeria beads and candles.

"He may not know Spitzer, but he'll have heard of him."

Ted did not want to talk to Israel Ortiz but he would. He reminded himself this was for Mohammed. And Kenzie.

13

THE OFFICES OF HILLYER & Spitzer were located on the second floor of a three-story commercial on Steinway Street over a halal butcher shop and the Providence Nail Salon. Kenzie stood outside the door to the upstairs offices staring at the buzzers. Second floor for the lawyers. The third-floor tag looked like it had been scratched out by someone with anger management issues.

She gave the buzzer a quick poke. There was no response. But then, she hadn't heard a sound. She couldn't tell whether it was working or not. She tried again. Nada.

Kenzie stepped back and looked up. The windows to either side were covered with identical posters of a smiling, brown-skinned family all holding right hand to heart and gazing with adoration at the Stars and Stripes waving in the breeze. The window over the door had a sign advertising the law firm and their specialties. *Problemas de Inmigracion? Llámanos Ahora!* A telephone number followed. The sign continued in English. Hillyer and/or Spitzer were prepared to represent you for everything from estate planning to capital murder, though immigration issues were in bold lettering. The telephone number was repeated at the bottom. She dialed it.

Eventually—eight long rings later—a female voice that could only have been produced by a computer came on and informed her that she was welcome to leave a message after the tone. Beep.

She tried the door. To her surprise, it was not locked.

Kenzie stepped inside, to be greeted by a smorgasbord of

aromas—none pleasant, but none overwhelming, either. Nail polish remover, a potent blast of ammonia at war with a pine-scented cleaning agent, and a touch of something she did not recognize at first. Then it hit her. A memory. The Fall Harvest Festival at Notre Dame Academy when she was in third grade. A bake sale, with pumpkins and apples and cider. And straw. Bales of straw. A pyramid of straw bales to climb on and over and the smell of straw dust in her hair, her clothes, her nose. Straw dust and ammonia, that's what she was smelling.

Ahead was a double-wide staircase with a narrow hallway beside it leading to the back of the building. There was a door with sunlight coming through a mesh-coated, frosted glass window. The building was surprisingly shallow. The backyard had to be huge.

Halfway to the next floor was a broad landing where she paused and listened. The smell was less pungent here. The building was eerily quiet, but she heard a voice from the next floor. She paused and listened. A woman's voice, cultured, well-modulated, warm but lacking strong emotion. She knew that voice, or had heard it before, at any rate. And then it was gone, replaced by the sound of a violin, and Kenzie belatedly recognized the velvet voice of the midday announcer on WQXR, the classical music station.

She didn't know the piece that was playing, but that was not unusual. Kenzie's knowledge of classical music did not extend much beyond the playlist for pledge week on PBS. The violin soared, crescendoed, and fell away. A faint flute line began.

Kenzie blocked out all other senses and strained to hear any sound beyond the music. And it came to her. Through the painted-over window behind her there was a soft but constant chatter of birds. Kenzie didn't know if she had ever heard the sound of live chickens, outside of a televised farm visit on

Sesame Street twenty-five years ago, but she knew immediately that's what she was hearing. Chickens. There were chickens in the backyard. And from the nonstop chatter, she thought there must be a lot of them.

There were scratches in the paintwork where others had presumably attempted to view the yard below. Kenzie pressed her face to the window, but the glass had been painted on both sides and all she could see was a gray translucent blur.

Now that she could hear the chickens, she could not unhear them. Music was the antidote. Without it, one would soon go mad.

A door creaked and hurriedly closed on the floor above.

Kenzie called out. "Mr. Spitzer?" She paused. "Mr. Hillyer." She climbed the steps to the next landing. To her left, the stairs continued to the third and final floor. A much-faded arrow-shaped sign read KRZYSZTOF AGENCJA TALENTOW. She did not read or speak Polish—nor did her third-generation American father—but she could easily translate the words. The sign was so old it could have been there when Astoria was the East Coast film capital—a hundred years ago. Though why a Polish-specific talent agency was needed was a mystery.

The double doors to the law offices were straight ahead. HILLYER & SPITZER in gold on solid black enameled wood doors. She knocked. No response. She knocked again and tried the doorknob. Like the downstairs door, it opened easily, demonstrating the firm's unusual disregard for security. She stepped into a large anteroom with doors on either side. Bruce Hillyer to the left, Howard Spitzer to the right—both marked with brass plaques. Between them was a large oak desk with a monitor, phone, and other office accoutrements. Behind the desk was the window she had seen from the street. The signs advertising the firm's expertise were faded from too many years of direct sunlight, sagging from being propped up against the glass, fraying along the edges as the poster board deteriorated. Chest-high file cabinets bracketed the desk. A jungle of potted plants sat atop the cabinets all vying for the stray rays of sunshine that made it through the smog-coated window. But there was no one there.

She called again. And again, there was no reply.

Which presented an opportunity Kenzie would not pass up. The monitor was lit and the computer was running. A momentary flash of guilt held her back. This was snooping, and she generally frowned upon anything that resembled snooping, lying, or cheating. She was capable of all three, given the right circumstances, though the hurdle was always there. But here was an opportunity that might never appear again. Besides, detecting was not snooping. This was for Mohammed, not herself. She stepped around the desk, waving away a snaking yellow tendril from the plants.

The screen saver was a portfolio of family photos. A very American family. A too-thin teenaged girl in a flowered sun-dress with mom and dad with matching graying ponytails outside the Noguchi Museum. A handsome square-jawed man in his late thirties in Marine dress blues. A frazzled-looking woman of about the same age at Disney World with two grinning preteen girls hanging on her waist.

She looked around, her hand hovering over the mouse pad. She could almost believe she was alone here.

"Hello?" she called, waited; and when after a third time there was still no response, she tapped the mouse. The faces disappeared and a spreadsheet took over.

Kenzie's experience of bookkeeping statements—billing, receivables, income, expense, and so on—was limited to the nonprofit sector. She had never worked for an entity that had to show earnings. But she understood cash flow. Money in. Money out. It wasn't rocket science. She clicked and opened a file.

Billing. Streams of names and numbers. She scrolled through, not sure at first what she was looking for. Mahdi. That was Mohammed's last name. She went to the Ms, and found him.

Mahdi, Mohammed Al Fazal. She clicked on his name and a file appeared.

Current billings. 3.2 hrs. $640.00. The lawyer was billing in twelve-minute increments at $200 an hour. Not egregious. And, it appeared, he was actively working Mohammed's file.

Balance 90 days. $2,340. Kenzie had no idea whether that was high, low, or fair, so she left herself a mental prompt to ask Ted.

Outstanding. The square was blank. No value at all. She stared at this for a moment. The soothing voice came back on the radio. Far in the background she could hear the ongoing cacophony of the chickens. She slid the mouse over the empty square and waited. A moment later the cursor began to pulse. The cell held another file. She clicked on it.

The second file blossomed immediately.

And things got interesting.

Payments. A column followed showing regular monthly deposits of $200 each, going back almost two years. Not long after Mohammed arrived in the US. How the man had been able to maintain those payments on what he made driving a cab was a testament to Mohammed's work ethic, sense of honor, and self-reliance. But it barely made a dent in what he owed.

Balance 90 days and greater. $30,885. Holy hell!

Interest and Late Fees. Another column of gradually increasing figures.

Kenzie was no math wizard—for all she could tell, the individual amounts might be reasonable, but the accumulated figure at the bottom was horrifying:

$11,779. And below it:

TOTAL OWED. $42,664. The damn interest and late fees were accumulating faster than Mohammed could pay. If through some miracle, Mohammed could continue making those meager payments forever and at the same time could stop the lawyer from doing anything to further his case—anything that might generate even an hour's worth of billing, anything that might get Mohammed closer to having his refugee status approved—he would still die owing more to his lawyer than he did right now.

Kenzie had come to the offices expecting to appeal to the lawyer's empathy—or reason, as it was apparent that Mohammed would never have the resources to pay all that was owed. But she could see now that she had been dreaming. The man was a cannibal, feeding on his clients.

Somewhat in shock, she returned to the previous screen to search for Mohammed's wife. She momentarily blanked on Almeda's last name. Not Mahdi, she knew that much. She scrolled up slowly and came upon it by accident. A half dozen lines above Mohammed's file was an Almeda Khalil. That was it. Khalil. Her father's name. She had kept it through both marriages.

Kenzie opened the file and was amazed to see a zero balance. Then she remembered that Almeda had come to the States through the efforts of a refugee assistance program run by a religious group. It appeared that they had paid for the work of getting Almeda both her green card and, finally, citizenship. The woman was one of the fortunate few. She waited until the screen saver returned before stepping away from the desk. Other than the radio and the muffled clamor of chickens, there had not been a sound behind either of the two doors. It was time to investigate before someone came in and discovered her snooping. Hillyer or Spitzer? Hillyer won the toss for the simple reason that the door was slightly ajar. She knocked. And again. Loudly. She put her ear to the door and heard nothing. Taking the lack of response for a cleverly disguised invitation, she pushed. The door swung open on well-oiled hinges. She walked into the room.

No one lurked there. It was dark, the only light source a strip on the ceiling that illuminated the near wall. Framed diplomas were surrounded by photos of a grimly smiling man with angry eyes shaking hands with politicians—a senator, two mayors, and a Queens borough president. Kenzie had met—and argued with—all but the senator.

Across the room was a desk and behind it a low bookcase. Kenzie could make out two silver pens standing at attention in a holder on the desk, but there was not a single piece of paper to be seen. The laptop there was closed. An American flag hung like a dark shroud from a standing pole. A pair of three-foot-tall brass, or bronze, sculptures stood on the bookcase: the Washington Monument and the Eiffel Tower. They looked like they came from the world's tackiest gift shop.

The air held the aroma of frequently—or recently—smoked cigars. She felt Hillyer's presence. He was not there but he had been not long ago. She felt like an invader.

She was about to creep back out of the room when she heard a sound on the far side of the suite. Someone was there. She ducked behind the door without thinking.

Movement. Someone had left the other room and was moving, almost silently, for the exit and the stairway.

She peeked through the crack between door and frame and saw a man in a dark hoodie, dark pants, and dark shoes, which could have been blue, black, or gray, cross to the double doors, slip out, and close them quietly behind him.

Kenzie had barely glimpsed the person; why had she automatically assumed it was a man?

She was relieved at not being discovered and yet the furtive, rushed movements of the young man concerned her. Young? Another impression, but she was sure she was right. He had moved like a young man. A young man bearing a load of guilt.

Should she follow, to get a possibly better look? No, she most wanted to remain invisible.

He was gone. She crossed the room and knocked at the door, knowing that there would be no answer. She knocked again. The door swung slowly inward, revealing a large book-lined office. In front of her was a small sofa, coffee table, and two chairs.

A brass version of the Empire State Building stood on the table. The Statue of Liberty lay on the carpet in the middle of the room—covered in blood.

"Mr. Spitzer?" she called. "Hello? Anyone here?" She took a hesitant step in and looked to her left.

A man was seated in a comfortable-looking leather executive chair, slumped forward, his arms cradling his head on the desktop in front of him. She stepped closer.

The man's skull was turned at an impossible angle. There was a lot of blood. The room felt warm. The air dense and unmoving. And there was that smell you get on your fingers when you've been rolling old pennies.

Kenzie knew from personal experience that head wounds bled ferociously and that this alone was not necessarily a sign of severity. But the boneless slump of the man's shoulders and the thoroughly awkward aspect of his head told her he was dead.

A mad explosion of sound from the chickens briefly overwhelmed a lone cello. Then both faded away. She took out her phone and dialed.

A voice answered. "Nine-one-one. What's the address of the emergency?"

14

PHATEENA WAS GUARDING THE fort, and she took her duties seriously.

"You are not welcome here," she mouthed through the glass door, shaking her head in a wide arc to accentuate her meaning. "And Israel's not here."

Ted had been both a client and tenant of her employer until a pair of Russians had trashed his apartment and scared the bejesus out of Israel and Phateena, who was not one to surrender a grudge easily.

It was raining. Not a heavy rain, but enough to warrant an umbrella. Ted's umbrella was bone-dry back at the apartment, standing upright in the empty metal ice bucket by the door. He would never use it. It was a present from Kenzie and Ted would not risk leaving it somewhere.

"I have an appointment," Ted mouthed back at her. A forgivable stretch of the truth. Israel had not answered when Ted called so he'd left a message with his estimated time of arrival. He'd gotten a one-letter reply via text, K. "He'll be here soon, so you can let me in." He felt a cold trickle on the back of his neck as a drop of rain fell from his hat and slid beneath his collar.

"No way. No how. I don't let nobody in when Israel's not here."

Both Phateena's attitude and use of the English language were quite fluid, adapting to the needs of the client and the situation. Currently she was demonstrating her "Don't Even Think about It" mode, normally reserved for panhandlers and deadbeat clients.

He checked his watch. Seven minutes—if Israel arrived on time. Ted needed a dry place to stand while he waited. He looked over his shoulder. The sign over the Honduran bodega was dark. For years, they had sold him his breakfast, and now they were gone. His rational brain said there could be no connection between his having moved away and the demise of the establishment, but his heart felt a pang of loss. There was a new Mexican restaurant across the street—Comidas de Ciudad—that was experiencing a rush of day laborers huddled under the awning, already queuing up for an early lunch. Ted with his briefcase, dressed in suit, tie, fedora, and raincoat, would be an intrusion. He looked like a lawyer, and a lawyer was rarely good news for those guys.

The rain came a little harder. Not yet a torrent, but beyond a shower. He tucked his briefcase under his coat and ran for the funeral home at the end of the block. Romero Memorial Chapel had a long, wide awning that stretched from the curb to the double-wide doors. Ted made it there in seconds. Not bad, he thought, for an overworked desk jockey who recently celebrated his thirty-ninth birthday—not for the first time.

The torrent arrived. A clear plastic dry cleaning bag floated by in the sudden rush of water in the gutter. It got sucked into the sewer grate and the water began to back up immediately. Ted debated making a grab for it, but the water level rose too quickly, slopping over the curb onto the sidewalk. As he stood there dithering, a black SUV—an Uber, he was sure—sped by, sending a wave of New York City rainwater and accumulated effluents and detritus six feet into the air. A good bit of it landed on Ted.

The door of the funeral home opened, and Israel Ortiz stepped out. He stopped and looked about, obviously surprised at the intensity of the downpour. Then he saw Ted.

"What are you doing standing out here in the rain?"

Ted refrained from pointing out that he was, in fact, standing under an awning. As he was wet from head to toe, he did not argue the case.

"I'm waiting for you," Ted said. Despite the rocky moments in their shared past, the two men had maintained a cautious but mutual respect.

Israel gave him a wide-eyed stare. "Why not wait in my store?"

"Phateena won't let me in. I think she's still afraid."

Israel choked a laugh. "Naw, she just doesn't like you. She thinks that foreclosure stuff you do is preying on the poor."

"She reads palms. Tells fortunes. For money."

"Yeah, well, she's a believer." He opened a black golf umbrella. "Come on. We'll get you a cuppa hot tea."

Phateena unlocked the door and let them in, and then disappeared into the back room leaving a scowl behind for Ted's benefit. Israel poured two steaming mugs of hot water, swirled each, and emptied them both down the sink. Then he filled them again. "The girl says she doesn't *do* dishes."

Ted was willing to bet that Israel did not refer to Phateena as "the girl" when she was in the room.

"I got Earl Grey and some herbal chai thing that she drinks," Israel said.

"Earl Grey, thanks."

"Good choice." He dropped in the teabags and handed a mug to Ted. "So, tell me. Whaddya got?"

Ted examined his cup for any random floating debris. "I need you to tell me what you know about an immigration lawyer named Howard Spitzer."

"I thought that case was all taken care of. You know, the girl from the islands. Anora-something."

As with most secrets, a lot of people knew a little bit of the story.

"This is something else. I can't go back to the same source." The pact he had made with Judge Fitzmaurice would not survive a further visit.

"Burned your bridges? That's a shame. A good lawyer can't afford to do that."

Ted had burned bridges, torn up tracks, and blown up tunnels in the course of his legal career. There was no looking back.

"A friend has asked me to look into the guy. He's paid a lot of money and there doesn't seem to be much happening."

Israel leaned back in his chair and sipped his tea, but his eyes were moving the whole time, focusing everywhere but on Ted.

"It's the Gray Wall thing, you know?"

"I'm afraid I don't," Ted said.

"You know, like the cops. The Blue Wall of Silence. We lawyers got the same thing. The Gray Wall."

Ted recognized the ploy. Most lawyers he'd known would sue their own mother if there was a fee to be earned. He took his billfold from his jacket, removed the fifty-dollar bill he kept for emergencies such as this, and slid it across the desk in Israel's direction. But he never took his hand off it.

"A retainer," he said. "I would never ask you to work for nothing."

Israel didn't move. "I would need at least two of those to violate my unspoken oath to the Gray Wall."

Ted didn't have two. He guessed he had a few twenties, maybe a ten, and some singles. When buying someone's reluctant cooperation, it's best to avoid looking like you're doing it with your spare change. "Tell you what. If what you know is worth it, I'll go for the other fifty. But not up front."

Israel thought about it for a minute, his eyes focused on the ceiling. Then, his hand came forward and U. S. Grant disappeared.

"Immigration work can be like that. You get a complicated case, and it can take years. Years of sitting in the back of the courtroom, waiting for a judge who's going to ask you all the same things he asked last time, and when you think you're done and ready for a ruling, he asks one more thing and you've got to ask to come back at a future date. I don't take complicated cases."

"Are you saying this Spitzer is legit? He takes complicated cases?"

"No and yes. I know who he is. And let's say he doesn't take the easy ones. Most immigration lawyers specialize by country. They work the basics. I kinda fell into working with people from Honduras. They tell their cousin, their friend from work, and I get a new client. But anything more than helping them fill out the forms, I take a pass. I tell 'em that up front and I give them a referral if they want it. I don't make a lot of money off it, but it keeps my success rate up there and clients keep showing up."

"Spitzer doesn't work that way?"

"No. He's a referral guy. He takes anything. The messier the better."

"And how's his success rate?"

"About what you'd expect. Terrible. The deck is stacked. Cases are backed up forever. There're not enough judges. Rules change constantly. It's an unholy mess. And when ICE is threatening, people get desperate. They'll say anything. They'll take bad advice. And they'll assume the whole system is broken—which is true—and can be bought—which isn't true at all, though that's the way things always worked back wherever they came from. So, they throw money at it—even money they don't have. And that's why they keep going to guys like Howard Spitzer."

"But is he any good?"

He shrugged. "He charges like he is. But I stopped sending him cases. A man's gotta eat, but he's gotta be able to sleep, too."

"What do I tell my friend?"

"It's time to move on."

Ted dug out two twenties and a ten. "Anything else I should know?"

"The guy's a goddamn snake. Everybody hates him. His clients, his partner, his wife. I'd bet his mother hates him. Tell your friend I'll find him somebody much better."

"For a referral fee?" Ted asked.

Israel smiled. "God bless America."

15

KENZIE WAITED FOR THE police outside the office, where she tried to convince herself that finding a murder victim lying in a puddle of blood was not a traumatic event. Waiting inside was out of the question.

She heard the street door open. No buzzer. Someone had a key. Therefore, it was someone who worked here.

It was not the police coming up the stairs. There was only one person and in New York, policemen always arrived in twos. Kenzie heard heavy shoes. Boots? It was early in the season for boots. For women. Why did she think it was a woman? From the drag of her steps, she was tired. She was walking very slowly.

She appeared on the lower landing. A thin young woman with dyed pitch-black hair, a face so pale she had to be either a vampire or a vegan, with glints of rings in her eyebrows, ears, and nose. She had on a black suit jacket and billowing black skirt, and boots. Black, lug soled, chunky heel, lace-up mid-calf boots that would have served to prevent snakebite while she marched cross-country. Kenzie guessed that beneath the veneer the girl was barely out of her teens. She was carrying a white take-out bag from Bareburger—a good hike.

"Who are you?" the woman said, looking up and taking note of Kenzie. It sounded more like an accusation than an offer of assistance.

Wash away the powder, ditch the facial jewelry—and the scowl—and she was obviously the daughter in the family pictured on the screen saver—having grown five years or so. She worked here. That anteroom was her domain. The computer was her workstation.

"I came to talk to Mr. Spitzer."

The girl's eyes widened in a cartoonish display of disbelief. The overdone mascara gave the look a raccoon quality. Kenzie imagined that she did not fit the profile of a typical client, but this goth girl's attitude was beginning to piss her off. And right now, with her nerves on fire, she might have a very short fuse.

"You have an appointment?" the goth girl—GeeGee, Kenzie named her—asked sharply, trudging up the final flight of stairs. "He's with a client."

He was alone now. Kenzie waited until GeeGee reached the landing before replying. "I wouldn't go in just yet. I called the police."

GeeGee was huffing slightly and did not speak for a moment. But her eyes narrowed to slits. "You did what?" There was a sneer in every word she spoke.

"There's a dead man in there," Kenzie said, choosing cold truth over a heated response.

It took a second for the words to register. The girl's immediate response was total blankness. She simply stared. Then she dropped her purse and the lunch bag and sighed like the whole world was allied against her. "Fuck. I can't handle this shit today."

The buzzer sounded. Kenzie heard it in stereo—inside the law office and above. An answering buzz opened the downstairs door.

"I hate this fucking job. I hate this fucking job." GeeGee had a glazed look in her eyes and went on mumbling to herself.

Two sets of heavy footsteps tromped in and started up the stairs. The police had arrived.

At that moment, another voice came down from the Polish Talent Agency upstairs.

"Who's there? Who's there?" a man cried in a deep phlegmy rasp. He may have been asleep, or suffering the effects of late-season allergies, but Kenzie thought the most likely reason for the harshness of his voice was a touch of alcohol applied internally.

"It's the police," Kenzie answered, though she had not yet seen them. Accuracy took a back seat to the desire to stop the repeated cries.

"Who's that? What? The police? The police?" he yelled. He had a thick accent and the word came out as *"politzi."*

"Ms. DuPre? Ms. DuPre? What are the police doing here? Looking for one of those bums you call clients?" As his outrage found a target, his voice modulated and shifted across the continent. Now he was closer to Oxford than Warsaw.

"Shuuut uuup," GeeGee yelled up at him in a long whine. She was focused again and seemingly over her initial zombie response.

Two uniformed cops appeared on the landing and continued up the stairs. At the same time the man from upstairs began a shuffling descent.

He was a vision. Kenzie pegged him at eighty plus. The plus could easily have been a decade. He had a half dozen strands of silver hair combed back and plastered to his otherwise bald pate. He wore a violet pin-striped shirt with a deep purple bow tie, loose-fitting high-waisted slacks, purple-framed rose-tinted glasses, and fuzzy pink slippers.

"Why are you here?" he demanded from the third step up. He was now facing—and looking down on—Kenzie, GeeGee, and the two cops. His authority was undercut by the police, who paid no attention to him.

The older of the two cops had a sagging face and the

sloping shoulders of a man who'd long ago lost the ability to be surprised. It wasn't something he missed.

"Which of you two is Swarovski?" he asked.

"Zielinski?" Kenzie replied.

He shrugged. "Sounds right."

"A good name," the talent agent interjected. He now sounded like Benedict Cumberbatch with a sore throat.

The cop turned to the other woman. "And that makes you . . . ?"

"Jennifer DuPre. I work for the lawyers. I just got here."

"That right?" the second cop asked Kenzie. He was young, fit, good-looking in a bland kind of way, and he spoke softly as though they shared some secret.

Kenzie recognized the routine right away, though this was her first interaction with the police as a witness. She had been a victim once, and a target—suspected perp—more than a dozen times. Annoying arrests were a constant for a community activist. But she knew the drill. Keep the witnesses talking and a little off-center. Don't let them get comfortable. And verify whenever possible.

"Can we see some ID?" the young cop asked. He managed to hit the thin border between polite request and official demand.

Kenzie produced her NYC ID. The cop copied her information into a small notebook.

Jennifer DuPre was still rummaging through her purse.

"And you, ma'am?" the cop said.

She stopped rummaging and shot him a dark look. "Workin' on it." A second later she produced a New York State driver's license.

The cop examined it and frowned. "This says Guinevere."

"It's pronounced *Jennifer*."

"According to who?"

She shrugged. "Take it up with my parents." She put out her hand demanding the return of the ID.

The cop scribbled the information into his book. "Tell me what happened."

"I have no idea. Mrs. Hillyer sent me to pick up lunch for Mr. Spitzer. I just got back."

"Where's this Mrs. Hillyer?"

"I'd guess she went home."

The cop squinted at her, obviously no better informed.

"I'm the one who called it in," Kenzie said, addressing both cops. "Gee . . ." she stopped herself. "The girl got here a minute ago." She pointed with her chin at the vision on the stairs. "And he got here the same time as you."

"I knew you were Polish the moment I saw you," the old man said to Kenzie with a twinkle.

"Ridgewood," she answered, hoping the truth would double as a brush-off. She turned back to the cops. "The dead man is in the office on the right. I saw someone duck out of that room."

"That's Spitzer's office," GeeGee said, sounding bored.

"You told dispatch it was a murder." The older cop had lost the momentum of his questioning. He now loomed over Kenzie and raised his voice a touch too loudly. GeeGee did her eye-widening thing—which, this time, almost caused Kenzie to grin—and the old man raised one eyebrow. The cop took a deep breath and began again. "What made you think the man was murdered?"

"Take a look," Kenzie said.

"Is there anyone else here?"

"I told the dispatcher I saw someone leave. They're long gone now."

"Tell me," the old cop said.

"Male. I think. Taller than me, but not by much. He wore a

hoodie. Up, I mean. I'm not much help, am I?" Kenzie noted that GeeGee had retreated into zombie mode again, but her fingers were busy scratching away her black nail polish.

"White? Black? Asian? Latino?"

Kenzie shook her head. "I never saw his face and he went by so quickly."

"Anything distinctive about his clothes?"

She had a sudden realization. "Really, I can't swear it was a man." The thought stunned her and for a moment she felt lightheaded.

"Shoes?" the younger cop asked in his smooth voice.

"Shoes? No." Why would she remember shoes? And as that question formed in her mind, an image appeared. "Wait."

It was the right question. She was surprised she remembered. She could now picture them against the beige carpet. "Black Adidas with the three seams. Not stripes."

"Stan Smiths?"

Who? Or what? She ignored the question. "So, yeah, it was most likely a guy."

"Women always notice the shoes," he said to his partner. Turning back to her, "Half the kids on the street wear those these days."

GeeGee had completely bared one thumbnail. The pink skin revealed was a relative blast of color.

The older cop took over again. "I want you two ladies to wait here with my partner while I take a look around inside." He turned to the aging talent agent. "And you may go about your business. Leave your name in case we need to get in touch."

The old man looked somewhat put out to be so dismissed. "You haven't asked whether I saw the young man."

This got him the full attention of everyone there.

"Okay," the sad-faced cop said with an overly patient expression. "What can you tell us?"

The talent agent smiled and then projected. "He was not a Black man. I would call him swarthy." He swelled his chest and turned his head to present his profile. Center stage. "Mediterranean, possibly. Or Latino. Young. Possibly very young. A teenager or early twenties at most."

"How'd you see him?"

"I was expecting a client and came out onto the landing to see." He drew himself up again. "May I continue?" He did not wait for a reply. "I caught only a glimpse of his face. Slight build. Very fast on his feet, but not graceful. Stiff in the hips. Not an athlete or a dancer. I only saw him as he ran down the first flight of stairs."

"That's very good. But how can you be so sure if you only saw him for a second?"

The eyebrow rose again, and the voice dripped with disdain. "It is my business to know the difference between a person who can move gracefully and a plodder. Though swift, he was a plodder." He managed to leave the impression—without actually saying so—that he considered the cop to be a plodder also. "And I have an eye for detail."

16

TED COULD HAVE WALKED from Elmhurst to Ridgewood faster than the car service drove it, but he would have arrived wet, cold, and thoroughly annoyed. As it was, he got there thoroughly annoyed.

As they passed under the Long Island Expressway, his phone announced a call from Lester.

"Howard Spitzer? That's the name, am I right?"

"That's what she said. Why? What've you got?"

"I just left Sammi. I mentioned the name and it was like shooting fireworks. The guy is famous."

"For what?"

"Mostly being an asshole. He's a player. Sorry. He *thinks* he's a player."

A preteen boy riding a green scooter shot out from the curb immediately in front of them, crossing against the westbound Grand Avenue traffic. Somehow, he made it to the center island without being killed. Ted's driver never even bothered to tap the brakes.

"Israel knew the name, too." Ted had a flash of panic. Was this too easy? "Could there be two of them?"

Lester chuckled. "Two asshole lawyers in Queens, both named Howard Spitzer? The mind boggles."

"Right," Ted said. "As my mother often said, 'Son, get a grip.' What did Sammi say?"

"Spitzer hit on Bagdasian's wife."

"Not a well-thought-out career move."

"At Judge Nathan's memorial service."

"Nobody liked Judge Nathan, but, what the hell?"

Lester gave a harrumph. "He hits on everybody's wife whenever he's had a glass or two. Which is often. Too often. That's fact. You want rumors too?"

"I'm not usually a fan, but under the circumstances, please proceed."

"Sammi says he's been doin' the nasty with his law partner's old lady. That's why the partnership is on the rocks."

"An assistant DA once told me, 'There's no such thing as an honest immigration lawyer.' I'm on my way to tell Kenzie she's right; we've got to get Mohammed and his family away from this guy." If even half of all this were true, it explained why Israel said the man was universally hated.

"By the way, it's Deepa."

"What's Deepa?"

"The manager at Kenzie's office. You ask me her name every time you go over there."

17

THE YOUNGER OF THE two cops walked Kenzie out to the landing, where she was sure he was going to ask for her number, but he surprised her by comforting her instead. He thanked her for the little information she had provided and cautioned her about dwelling on what she had seen. Meanwhile the police were through with her "for now . . ." and he gave her a guarantee that a detective would contact her "within a day or so . . ."

Kenzie waited for the wrap-up and the pitch. The pitch. All the young cops did it.

She'd been arrested. It was part of the job, after all. Some cops were bullies and enjoyed inflicting pain or injury but after the initial takedown, most cops were polite about it as soon as they realized she wasn't putting up resistance. Some of the older ones apologized and helped her to her feet after they'd put the cuffs on her. But the young guys all gave it a try. It must work for them sometimes, right? Otherwise, they'd stop. If it weren't so goddamn annoying, she might feel sorry for them. New York must be a tough town for cops trying to get dates.

"I was wondering," she heard him say.

She was wrung out. Not at all sleepy, but incapable of exerting herself for anything more energetic than the trip back to the apartment, where she would make a cup of tea, wrap herself in a blanket, and watch an episode or two of *Parks and Recreation*, a guilty pleasure that she kept exceedingly private, even from Ted.

"I think I might be sick," she lied, putting a hand over her mouth and faking a gurgling cough.

"Hey! Hey! Who? What?"

A man was coming up the stairs. Forties, fair complexion, blue suit, red tie, white shirt, and from where she stood a half floor above, a bald spot on his crown.

"What's going on?" he yelled.

"Who are you?" the cop responded.

"Why are the police here?"

Kenzie took an immediate dislike to the man. She had that reaction often to men who strode into any given situation with the attitude that they were rightfully in charge. She did not have that response to women who did this, and often used the tactic herself. Resentment? Possibly. Prejudice? Most likely. But she owned up to the feelings and was at peace with herself. She didn't like him. She didn't have to.

"Jennie!" he yelled. "What in hell is going on here?" He had arrived at the landing and looked as though he was prepared to walk directly through either the cop or Kenzie, who held her ground and waited to see what he would do. She was surprised when the young cop stepped out of the man's way.

Ms. DuPre's voice came from the other side of the door. "It's Mr. Spitzer, Mr. H. Somebody killed him."

He ignored her brief but accurate response to his question and continued to bellow. "What's happened?" he demanded of the young cop.

"Your name, sir?"

"Hillyer. This is my office."

"I'm going to have to ask you to remain out here. This is a crime scene."

"I'm a lawyer."

"I understand," the cop said without rolling his eyes at

the man. "There's been a death. We're waiting on detectives. They'll want to speak with you."

Hillyer was a tall man and he pulled himself up to look down at the cop. The cop didn't cringe. "Will this take long?"

It was a stunningly heartless question. He showed no interest in the who, how, or why of his partner's death. Kenzie couldn't stop herself from letting a touch of her disgust escape.

"Asshole," she said, though she did say it quietly.

Hillyer looked at her as though committing her features to memory for some future lineup of possible perpetrators. And then recognition came over him. Unpleasantly. "I know you. You're the lady who keeps getting up Ron Reisner's nose."

He hadn't reacted to being called an asshole to his face. Kenzie assumed that it was not an unusual event in his life— personal or professional.

"McKenzie Zielinski," she said, and pointedly offered a hand.

He ignored it. "Someday he's gonna notice you and sweep you out of his way." He addressed the cop again. "Who's in charge here?"

The cop chose to ignore him and spoke to Kenzie again. "You can go. The detectives will be in touch."

"Before I go, Mr. Hillyer, I'd be interested to know, what's your connection to Reisner?"

Hillyer glared at her. "None. But I admire a man who gets things done."

She turned away and started down the stairs. Tea, blanket, television. She might have to add a square of dark chocolate.

18

A BLOCK BEFORE REACHING the church Ted ducked into a store-front, where he ordered a spinach and cheese *burek* from the dark-eyed, mustached woman at the counter. She obviously recognized him, anticipating his order the moment he came through the door, sliding the still-steaming slice of rolled *burek* onto a paper plate as he reached for a plastic tray. Ted didn't know when he had become a regular but was already afraid to change his order. The woman never spoke but smiled when she handed him his change.

It was the perfect meal for a cold, wet November lunch, the dough light and flaky, the spinach and cheese dark and warming, filling without being heavy. He put aside all other thoughts and concentrated on enjoying his lunch and a few minutes with nothing to do but eat and breathe—when he became aware that he was being watched.

A young woman stood out from the other diners. She was the only person there dressed in a blue business suit. And she was surreptitiously watching Ted with a questioning look on her face. Questioning? No. Surprised. And amused.

She must have realized that she had been caught staring and suddenly looked down at her tomato and cucumber salad.

Ted did not think of himself as the kind of man that young women might stare at—whether surprised, amused, attracted, or even repelled. He was in good health, reasonably fit, and possessed of no hideous scars or other disfigurements. But he was not movie star handsome. Unlike the sometime bus driver on the Q43 who often drew double-takes due to his extraordinary resemblance to Idris Elba, Ted did not look like anyone famous. And he had been assured by his ex-wife, in a gentle, confiding manner, that his resting charisma and normal animal magnetism were muted. Most appreciated by those who knew him well and loved him dearly, but not generally noticed by the passing throngs.

He was, therefore, suspicious of this young woman.

He could see her blurred reflection if he cocked his head at a certain angle. From her point of view he was staring out at the street and the passing midday pedestrians. She did not look up again. He was distracted for a moment by a man going by the window dressed in a white T-shirt, fashionably ripped blue jeans, and bright orange basketball sneakers, an ensemble odd only in that it was still raining and the temperature was approaching the low forties. The man looked cold.

When Ted checked up on the young woman again, she was eating and apparently no longer interested in him. He finished his lunch and left, taking a brief second, as he dumped the used plate and napkin into the trash receptacle, to look back one last time.

She was digging into her purse, ignoring him, but he had the odd feeling that she'd been watching him leave a moment earlier. He stepped out onto the street.

The rain had let up, leaving a cold mist that threatened to seep into his bones. His forehead still throbbed where he'd been smacked. He quick-walked to the church, cut through the open gate, and stepped down to the basement door. He hit the buzzer, looked up at the camera with an expectant grin, and heard the lock open.

"Good afternoon," he called. "How's everybody today? Staying dry?"

Four pair of eyes swung in his direction. Three of the women were on their phones, laptops open in front of them, talking or listening with earnest expressions of concentration. The fourth woman gave him a scowl by way of a greeting. She had a phone plastered to her ear.

Deepa, he thought with an internal nod of thanks to Lester.

"You are looking lovely today, Deepa. A new sari?" Ted may or may not have seen the yellow garment a dozen times before, but he found that a simple compliment often had the effect of softening her natural aggressiveness.

"I can't talk to you. The flower service is trying to cancel."

Ted understood immediately. The fundraiser. Deepa's show. "But I thought all that was being handled by the host."

"That is who I am talking to."

"Oh" was all he could say. She didn't appear to be talking at all.

She scowled again. "I am on hold."

"Ah," he said, trying a different tack.

"Ms. Zielinski wants ya to meet the new volunteer. She's in law school."

"Is she here? Kenzie? I was hoping to find her."

"She went out."

Though she was brusque with men in general, distrusting of most women, and protective of Kenzie to a fault, Deepa at times maintained a modicum of respect for Ted. That didn't mean she liked him. She appreciated his work on behalf of Stop the Spike. She was one of the true believers, hating LBC, Ron Reisner, and the bought politicians who were his enablers. She was also a tireless worker, organized and efficient, and a champion of all the volunteers. But she liked Ted best when he wasn't around.

"Shall I wait for her?" Ted asked. The germ of a presentiment began to grow in the back of his mind.

"Can't tell ya when she'll be back. The intern should be here at two." She checked her phone. "Any minute."

"Intern?" Ted asked, distracted by the previously unheard-of title in this environment.

"The volunteer. The law student." She was still on hold. Deepa searched through a loose stack of papers on the table and handed him a letter.

"Yes," he said, his mind already returning to the question of where Kenzie might have gone. The lawyer? Spitzer. Had she decided to bring the conflict to the man in his den?

"You can talk to her upstairs if you want. You'll have some privacy." She gestured at the near empty expanse of the basement. The only private spot was behind the ancient boiler.

"Has Kenzie checked her out already?"

"Not yet. Ms. Zielinski says you can use the help."

As he headed up the stairs, he heard her phone conversation recommence. "You know I am still holding. I am not not holding. I am holding."

The mountain of documents would be arriving any day. He needed an assistant. Or a team of assistants. People with some legal training who would know what they were looking at. He needed a team of free lawyers. And that was not going to happen. A law-student intern, however, might be a heaven-sent second best. He made his way up the back stairway and into the church.

The gray skies outside allowed little light to filter through the stained-glass windows, and the only electric-generated light came from over the altar. He scanned the document Deepa had given him, gathering a few facts. A single votive candle flickered, an offering probably left over from morning mass. Ted thought about looking for the lighting panel and making the nave less ghostly, but let the semidarkness take him.

He and Lester had spent a night there while evading a pair of Russian mobsters. For a moment he found himself revisiting the anger and fear he had felt then. He plunked down in a pew and told himself to focus on the here and now. They'd come a long way since then. They were safe.

A short, rueful laugh escaped him. "Safe" was a subjective concept. He'd been assaulted only yesterday—by accident. By misidentification. A mistake. The utter absurdity of chance. Despite his daily struggles to order his life and to create a refuge for himself and his loved ones, chaos had intervened. He laughed again.

"Hi," a voice said with some hesitancy. "Is this a bad time?"

He looked up. A pale face stared back at him. "Sorry?" he asked.

"Well, I find you sitting here in a dark church, laughing, with no one else around, and I thought maybe I'm interrupting some private moment or something."

It was the young woman from the *burek* takeout place. The one who'd been watching him. Or looking at him. Was she following him as well?

"Something," he said. "Can I help you?"

"I hope so. Deepa sent me to talk to you. I'm Ashley Parker."

The cloud of reminiscence lifted. "You're the law student," he said.

"And you're the guy taking on Ron Reisner and his hired guns. I like that."

"You don't like Ron Reisner? Something personal?"

"No. I'm capable of rational thought."

He laughed again, the sense of the absurd still on him. "We're here just trying to plug the hole in the dyke."

She looked perplexed. The reference obviously escaped her. "You're Edward Molloy."

"Ted. I saw you eating lunch. I had the feeling you were watching me."

"I recognized you."

"Really?"

She flashed an embarrassed smile. "I wanted to prepare for the interview, so I googled you."

Of course she did. Everyone googled everyone. Privacy was so twentieth century. What was unusual was that she so freely owned up to it. Of course, he and Lester tracked people all the time, using much more intrusive search engines. Not everyone who'd gone bankrupt welcomed being found. He found he didn't much like it himself.

"I was eating my lunch. I looked up and there you were." She said this with the awe usually reserved for Penn & Teller exhibitions.

"And here I thought I had a stalker." It was a lame joke, mostly because there was a hint of truth in it. He found he was predisposed not to like her. Or trust her?

Again, a touch of confusion passed over her face before she answered. "I'm specializing in both Urban Planning and Environmental Law."

He lit the flashlight on his phone and quickly read the letter.

"At NYU," he said. Law students at top-ten schools usually came with a touch of arrogance. They were the elite and they knew it. Ted had worked with many such in the past. This one didn't have it for some reason. He liked that.

"Oh, gosh, no. Oh, shoot. People make that mistake all the time. No, I'm at New York Law School. Sorry."

New York Law was not a top-ten school. It was not a top-one-hundred school. Ted's alma mater, St. John's, was not top ten either. He found he immediately liked her better. A fellow striver. He needed a striver. Someone who would bust her ass on a mind-numbing assignment because the ability to work hard was all she had. Like him.

Her approach was ballsy. He liked that. But he'd keep an eye on her.

It wasn't like he had a choice.

"I need someone to go through thousands of documents and tell me which ones I have to read. Can you do that?"

"How long have I got?"

He liked that she asked before making a commitment. She was eager but no fool. "A week. Two? More or less. The first boxes should get here this week. Maybe as soon as tomorrow. There'll be more coming. We'll have plenty to keep us busy." He heard himself use the word "us." He'd already made his decision.

She smiled. She'd heard it too.

He'd been suspicious of Lester at first. He, too, had appeared at a highly coincidental moment. And Lester was now a full partner. There was a lesson there.

She spoke again, still selling herself. "I've done fundraising before. I can help there, too. And tech."

Kenzie's realm, not his. "I'll mention that to the boss."

Ashley met his gaze, as though she were assessing him. He felt a little uncomfortable.

She smiled again.

In another setting, he would have thought the smile was a touch of flirtation. He pushed the thought away. She wasn't interviewing for a top-tier law firm; she was donating her time and energy to a shoestring forlorn hope with a 90 percent chance of failure. Cut her a break.

"Welcome aboard, Ms. Parker."

"Ashley," she said.

19

KENZIE DREAMED OF A bathtub. She didn't need pulsing jets, room for two, or—god forbid—a walk-in. But there were times, not always, when she did want to lie back in scented hot water and luxuriate. A shower in a space the size of a refrigerator box was a poor substitute. In fact, it wasn't even in the same universe of experience.

She wanted the smell of a dead man out of her nostrils, her hair, her skin.

And as she approached the apartment, she felt an unreasonable anger at Ted. Not just unreasonable, but irrational. She admitted it. None of this was in any way his fault, but he might have listened and accompanied her to the lawyer's office. She would still feel dirty, violated, and much too aware of the concept of mortality, but she would be sharing those feelings with someone she trusted and loved. She needed a bath. Then the tea, blanket, etc.

But she did not want to get merely clean, she needed to soak.

She turned in to the alley and stopped. A man in dark sunglasses and a light blue fabric mask was standing at her door. He was in uniform. A gray one-piece coverall with neon-yellow vest and a blue helmet. He looked very official, and yet she had the feeling she'd never seen someone dressed like that before. Not at the entrance to her apartment.

"Can I help you?" she called out, keeping enough distance that she'd have a good head start if needed.

He turned to face her, looking neither furtive nor concerned at having been discovered. He had a laughably huge mustache, like that *Looney Tunes* character who was always shooting off his revolvers, peeking out around his mask.

"Textron," he said.

Or something like it. It didn't sound like a word. "And?" she asked.

"Checking for gas leaks."

"I see. You're with the gas company. I thought our gas company was . . ." She paused. Ted paid the utility bills, she paid the rent. They went fifty-fifty on everything, but the responsibility for actually making the payments was shared. Kenzie had to admit she didn't know who their gas company was. "Con Ed," she said, feeling the dishonesty lurking behind the surety in her voice.

"Tacidon," the man said again, though not exactly again. "We're providers."

Maybe she should have paid greater attention to the vendors of the utilities, but there was nothing for it now. He looked legit. Her immediate distrust probably had more to do with his build and manner. He was bulked up and she thought the bodybuilding fraternity both frivolous and vain. Lacking in intelligence, grace, or empathy. Another prejudice on her part, of course.

Or was she just having a really bad day?

And she still needed to find a dress for Friday night.

"The meters are around the back." She waved a hand to indicate where "back" was in case he had any doubts.

"I need to get inside." He waved a metal tube. It could have been a natural gas sensor. Or not. She certainly wouldn't have known one even if it came with a label.

She didn't want him to come inside. She wanted a shower. There was no leak—or hadn't been when she left that morning.

"The dog doesn't like strangers. And he's a rotty. Come back when my husband gets home. It's his dog."

There was no dog, of course, but she was proud of herself for both the quick thinking and her confident delivery.

Above the mask, his eyes crinkled. He was smiling, the shit. He didn't believe her, and she resented that. She'd been lying, but she'd done it well. He should believe her.

"I'm good with dogs," he said. "You have to be. It's part of the job. I'll only be a minute."

For some reason that decided her. From cable guys to Amazon delivery drivers to plumbers to the Jehovah's Witnesses, she had never met anyone who would come into her parents' house until her mother had locked the dog in the spare room. And that dog was a female golden retriever who loved everybody.

"You know what? Have your office call and make an appointment. I can't deal with this today."

He did not like that response. But from the swelling of his chest and his combative stance she could read that what he didn't like was a woman standing up to him, whether he had to return another day or not.

He fought to keep his cool. "It could be an emergency." He took two long steps in her direction.

"There's no leak," she said with a surety she didn't feel.

She was acutely aware that they were alone and separated by a few long strides. She was a fast runner, but he looked like he'd have the stamina for an extended pursuit. If she hollered at the top of her lungs, she could wake her landlord—who worked shifts for Transit—but that was a last resort. He didn't like being awakened during the day.

"I'm sorry if I seem rude, but I've had a hard day and I would like for you to leave. Now, please."

For a brief moment, she was sure she'd gone too far. She'd used the boss voice. Men never liked the boss voice. He glowered.

But the capitulation came so quickly that afterward she couldn't understand why she'd been afraid.

"Certainly, ma'am. I'll have the office call. Is there a good time to reach you?" He rolled his shoulders, releasing tension, exuding trustworthiness. Liar.

"We both work," she said.

"And there's the dog," he replied.

"Have them call Mr. Molloy."

"Will do." He nodded.

She stood aside and he walked away.

He never looked at the meter, she thought. Nor did he check any other building. But it had been an atrocious day and she wanted a shower. Maybe they should get a dog.

20

"**I WAS NEVER IN** any danger, Ted. Give it a rest. And, yes, I *would* like a glass of wine." Kenzie was wearing a path in the threadbare carpet, pacing like a caged leopard. A red-haired, pale-skinned leopard.

Ted had not yet offered to get Kenzie a glass, but he recognized a thinly disguised order when he heard it. He got the screw-top sauvignon blanc out of the refrigerator and filled a juice glass to the brim. "I'm trying hard not to be reactive," he said as he handed her the wine. "But did you or did you not tell me that you saw the murderer?"

"I said I saw a person." She stopped pacing and looked at the ceiling for a moment. "Well, almost saw them. Him. But I have no idea who he was or why he was there." She gulped down a few ounces of wine. "And thank you." The pacing started up again.

"The police think you saw the murderer."

"Yes. That assumption is for their convenience," she said. "It would make their job considerably easier. I tried to make that clear to them, but I don't think they cared."

"Hey. Take a minute. Sit down. You had a horrible experience. You might want to relax and let your mind process."

"That sounds suspiciously like 'Calm down, little lady.'"

"Comfort food. I'll call for Chinese. More wine. Ice cream for later. We can watch *Shadow of the Thin Man*."

"Ted. Not all problems can be solved by old black-and-white movies."

Ted thought he could make a brilliant counter-argument,

but scoring debate points might leave him sleeping on the sofa. "Peking House?"

"You know what I want? Adana."

Turkish food. Not his favorite. "Great." He grabbed his phone from the charger. "Tell me what you want."

"I haven't even looked at the menu," she said, holding out the empty juice glass.

Ted took it and poured another generous serving.

"Get the shrimp. I'll get the bronzini. We can share both."

"Not the shrimp. Deepa was telling me the other day about the bycatch. It's like strip-mining for seafood."

Before Ted could point out that there was also farmed shrimp, Kenzie saved him from self-immolation by saying, "It's the weirdest thing, but when I try to picture the guy I saw leaving Spitzer's office, I keep putting Mohammed's face on him. I mean I know that's not possible because I already asked him, and he said he was waiting on an arrival at JFK that came in two hours late. So, it couldn't have been him. And besides, the old guy from upstairs is sure it was a teenager he saw."

"The salmon?"

"I don't know. Can we get a pizza? They do pizza, don't they?"

Like all native New Yorkers, Ted acknowledged the primacy of Brooklyn pizza. Queens was competitive in everything else, but not in pizza. In the land of exquisite empanadas and heavenly pupusas, why eat pizza with an average crust or a too-sweet sauce?

Because Kenzie wanted pizza, and she'd had a really awful day.

"Pizza it is," he said. "But let me see if I can get Dani's to deliver." He could. He added an order of calamari for the protein and, as a last thought, a garden salad. The salad always came with bread and good bread could be found in all five boroughs.

Kenzie, by this time, had finally planted herself on the sofa, her eyes drifting over the wall-mounted television across the room. The TV was off. Ted filled her glass and wrapped her legs in the throw blanket. Then he got himself a beer, checked the level in the growler of Red IPA from Finback and reminded himself he must replenish soon. He plunked down next to her.

"Do you want to talk about it? Or would you rather turn on *Jeopardy?*"

She sipped her wine and with the other hand reached out for his. She squeezed once and then closed her eyes.

He thought about getting out plates and silverware but decided they could wait. He stayed next to her.

"I think I know why I keep putting Mohammed's face on that guy." She stopped and stared into space.

He waited to hear her insight—and was disappointed.

"I mean, I really never *saw* his face. After seeing Spitzer lying there dead with blood all over, I was in shock. Only, I wasn't. And I'm pretty sure I saw the guy before I found the body."

Another pause.

"Pretty sure. Isn't it funny? This happened only a few hours ago and already I'm doubting my memories."

"Criminal Law 101," he said. "The police and the DA want the jury to believe that their eyewitness has an infallible imprint in her brain of indisputable, ironclad facts. The defense knows better. Memory is fiction. You begin rewriting and editing immediately and keep it up every time you go over it in your head."

"Are you saying you don't believe me?"

"What? No. More wine?"

"Because I saw Spitzer with his blood all over him, his desk, the floor. Do you suppose my mind invented all of that?"

"Not at all. I'm saying that the brain, like nature, abhors a vacuum. It fills in the cracks automatically, adding a bit of color here and there, until you have a coherent story. But it's fiction."

She emptied the glass and handed it to him. "Just a half this time."

"A half it is," he said, not stopping until it was two-thirds full.

She sipped it. And again. "I think that I'm afraid the person I saw was Mohammed's stepson—whom I have met exactly twice. There is an excellent chance that I wouldn't know him if he showed up delivering our pizza tonight."

"And why are you afraid of that?"

"Because Mohammed said the boy is mad at the lawyer." She took his hand again and gave another squeeze. "I'm afraid for Mohammed. This is bad and it isn't over."

"And I'm afraid for you. You were the first person to arrive at a murder scene. That's a scary place to be."

"I'm not frightened about that at all."

Had Kenzie in fact seen the murderer? Or was the man she'd glimpsed himself a witness?

Or had the murderer seen her? Ted didn't want her scared, but he did wish she would be cautious. Kenzie was both brave and impulsive—that gave her a risk profile well above his own.

"The police are going to want to talk to you again," he said.

"When's dinner getting here?" she asked.

Dani's was usually quick on a weeknight. "Soon."

"I looked at his records," she said, avoiding his eyes.

"Oh?" She obviously had a story to tell, and just as obviously felt some guilt about it. That made it interesting.

"The computer was on. There was no one around." She paused. "I mean, I *thought* there was no one. I looked."

"Congratulations," Ted said. "Both for your audacity, and for overcoming your better nature. What did you find?"

"I don't know. Numbers." Kenzie paused between each small revelation. It was disconcerting, but Ted understood. She didn't—couldn't—know what was important but wanted to be sure nothing was left out. "Files. Bookkeeping files. I found Mohammed. His wife. It looks like he owes the firm a lot of money."

Ted stopped her. "Take it slow. I want as many details as you can remember."

"Okay," she said. She hadn't yet mentioned the gas leak guy. She sighed. Priorities.

THURSDAY

21

KENZIE DID NOT REMEMBER finishing the bottle of wine, but the evidence was clear. The empty was still on the coffee table in front of her, all sounds were elevated to an unbearable volume, her head hurt, her eyeballs throbbed, and she craved water no matter how much she drank. Not ten feet away, Ted was in the alcove they called a kitchen, humming as he fixed his breakfast of sausage and eggs. She didn't know which was worse—the tuneless drone or the smell of fried pork. She felt murderous.

"Can I fix you an egg sandwich? I found some cheddar that's not turned woody, and I can use the rest of the Italian bread that came with the salads last night. I'll even toast it in the oven if you want."

He sounded so cheery, so considerate, and so loving she was sure a jury would understand and acquit her.

"I got hold of Mohammed," Ted said. "He's going to stop by in a little while. I asked him to see if he could find the Preacher and bring him along. I thought you might like to have his input."

One, possibly two men were coming to her home in "a little while." She had not yet showered and was wearing her usual sleep attire—a long T-shirt and nothing else. Normally a visit from either man would be welcomed and a touch of the Preacher's streetwise advice might be invaluable after her experience, but today was special. Today she didn't want to see anyone.

"Brilliant," she tried to say, layering the word with as much venom as she could summon. To her dismay, the phlegm in the back of her throat refused to make way for communication and the sound that came out of her mouth was more like a cough than a withering witticism.

She cleared her throat—noisily. "I need a shower," she said, standing up and staggering back upstairs to the bathroom.

"So that's a no on the egg sandy?" Ted called after her.

Half an hour later, showered, dressed in jeans and a men's white button-down with the cuffs turned up, she came back down the stairs, feeling much better. She was looking forward to seeing Mohammed and the Preacher. And she was willing to give Ted a second chance as long as he dropped the perky, pleasant act and provided her with a cup of strong coffee flavored with silence.

The Preacher, dressed in his usual long black overcoat and well-used sneakers, stood and she shook his hand. She smiled at Mohammed. The two men shared the sofa. Ted stuck his head out of the alcove kitchen, and she rewarded him with a quick kiss on the cheek. She opted for her seat at the tiny café table where they usually ate dinner.

"Coffee all 'round?" Ted asked. "I've got a fresh pot brewing."

He might be allowed to live.

"Did Ted tell you why he asked you here? Or is he being all mysterious?"

Mohammed shook his head, but the Preacher spoke first. "He said that you two have been looking into this Spitzer lawyer."

"What are you talking?" Mohammed blurted out. "Why would you do this? Mr. Spitzer is my business."

"Take a moment, brother," the Preacher said. "Let us hear what they have to say."

Ted, in an unusual display of polite hosting—and with unprecedented impeccable timing—arrived with a tray holding a full pot of coffee, four cups, a measuring cup holding a pale white liquid with the telltale blueish tinge of non-fat milk, and a handful of sugar cubes which might have been left in the cabinet by the previous tenant, as neither Ted nor Kenzie used sugar on anything. Kenzie was both touched to see this domestic side of her man, and suspicious of it.

The Preacher took both milk and sugar. Mohammed took no milk but a startling four cubes of sugar. Kenzie thought he might have taken more had she not gasped as the fourth cube dropped into his cup.

"Kenzie has the bigger news," Ted said, handing her a cup. "So why don't you go first." He smiled encouragingly in her direction.

All eyes were now on her. She wanted to fold and go back to bed. She did not want to revisit the offices of Mr. Spitzer and what she had found there. But she would not allow herself to fail in front of these three men, all of whom she knew respected her tenacity.

"I asked Ted," she began, only it came out with such a back-of-the-throat catarrh she might have been speaking Yiddish. She held up a finger and took a deep slug of coffee, feeling an immediate release in her larynx. She began again. "I asked Ted to look into your Mr. Spitzer, Mohammed, and . . ." She stopped again, realizing that she had been about to describe Ted's unwillingness to help as "dismissive." "But he wasn't sure when he'd be able to find the time. So, as I was in the neighborhood, I stopped into Spitzer's offices myself."

Mohammed showed immediate agitation. His head jerked two or three times and his free hand fluttered over his face. He almost spilled his coffee. "No. Please. I am not wanting you to do this."

"I'm with you there," Ted said, "but let her finish."

Kenzie took another fortifying sip of black coffee. "I

thought if I confronted Spitzer, he'd see that we were onto his games and maybe do the right thing."

"Ah, please, no. He is slow at his work. Yah, I know."

Kenzie could detect a number of conflicting emotions coming from Mohammed. Bruised pride and fear produced anger and resentment. But there was more.

"And I can be excited," he went on. "My wife tell me this is so. So, maybe this is not such a good combination. But he is my lawyer and he works for me."

"Well, not anymore," Ted said.

"What?" Mohammed swung around to face him, a look of guilt followed almost immediately by shock, and ending in confusion?

Kenzie was hungover enough to doubt her own perceptions, but shouldn't the shock have come first? Or the confusion. Had she imagined the initial guilt? No one else seemed to have noticed.

"Can we all take this a little slower?" the Preacher said. "Mohammed, I was there the other night. You sounded very much like a man in need of assistance. McKenzie is not the sort of person who can hear a cry for help and do nothing."

Kenzie needed to relay the rest of her story before this escalated further. "You're going to have to find a new lawyer, Mohammed."

Mohammed emitted a sigh of infinite patience. "Miss McKenzie Zielinski, you are a friend, I know. But 'enter not houses not your own.' Only evil comes of it."

"Evil got there first. Spitzer was dead when I arrived." There. It was out—most of it.

Mohammed appeared to have a moment of confusion before the precise meaning of the words hit. Then he yelled something in Arabic that did not need translation. His grief, anger, and surprise all came through.

"I'm sorry, Mohammed. But it was horrible. I found him. He'd been murdered." She didn't need to wait for an official announcement; she'd seen the body and the murder weapon.

He recovered quickly. "I see and am so sorry for your pain, my friend." He dropped his head to his chest and for a moment there was silence.

"May I tell you what happened?" Kenzie asked. As no one replied she took this as assent.

She described the whole experience, the chickens in the backyard, the man who ran, the goth paralegal, the Polish talent agent, ending with the arrival of the police. For some reason, she held back her confrontation with Hillyer. She had not liked him at all.

"The man you saw," the Preacher said. "What did he look like? How good a look did you get?"

"I'm not even sure it was a man. I was afraid. He, she, or they were there for less than a second." And as she now tried to picture the figure, her mind was filling in the picture with the talent agent's descriptions. Maddening. "The police wanted me to be sure, but when I hesitated, they acted like I was a suspect."

"And you might be," the Preacher said. "The police will focus on the last person to see the victim alive."

"I never saw him alive." Kenzie was drained and defeated. None of it made much sense to her. She wanted to climb back into bed and sleep until Tuesday. Or next Friday.

"Preacher is right," Ted said. "Be prepared. And if you think they're headed down that alley, call me. In fact, you should call me the moment you hear from them."

Mohammed had his head down and was muttering something that might have been a prayer. The Preacher listened for a moment and then translated, "There is neither power nor strength except from Allah."

"Inshallah," Mohammed said.

"I'm sorry we're the bearers of bad news," Ted began, but then made a slight turn. "But your grief surprises me. I was under the impression you thought this lawyer was screwing you."

"I want him to make my case faster. I don't want him dead."

Kenzie thought this made perfect sense, but her wine-sodden brain kept putting a brown face on the man she had seen. Or not seen. She needed more coffee.

"Before we get too far along in mourning for this guy, I should tell you what I know—and what I think I know," Ted said. He put down his cup and placed a hand on each thigh as though summoning strength for an ordeal. "There are so many issues I'm not sure where to start. Can I ask you something first? How did you pay Mr. Spitzer?"

Mohammed was calmer now. Ted's words and tone had done their work. "He was a good person. He knew we could not pay so good, so he gave a big discount for cash. Half. Like BOGO."

The Preacher raised an eyebrow. "BOGO?"

"Like at the Dollar Store. Buy one, get one."

"You paid cash," Ted said. "Did he give you a receipt?"

"No, boss. I did not need one. He kept it all in a book. He show me."

"How much did you still owe him?"

Mohammed bristled again.

Kenzie thought Ted's approach much too lawyerly. Mohammed was a proud man. Expecting him to publicly announce his indebtedness was insensitive—rude. "You don't have to answer that, Mohammed. Ted's on your side, but he doesn't need to pry."

Showing no teeth, and no pleasure, Ted smiled at her.

"No problem," Mohammed said. And turning to Ted he announced proudly, "Nada. Nothing. Sip."

"Zip?" Ted asked.

"Zip? Okay. I pay one hundred dollars—cash—every week for almost two years. Mr. Spitzer put it in the book."

Ted nodded, but he was barely paying attention. His eyes had drifted, and he was thinking hard.

Kenzie waited a beat for him to respond. When it became apparent that he was somewhere else and wasn't returning as soon as she would like, she spoke for him. "Ted spoke to another attorney. He had some strong opinions regarding Mr. Spitzer. He may have been milking you."

Mohammed's eyes opened wide.

"Taking advantage," Kenzie explained.

"But . . . half off for cash," Mohammed argued.

Ted was tuned in again. She gave him a questioning look, but he did not respond.

"Refugee status isn't easy. It can take time. But you're now married to a citizen. That changes things. It can still take forever because the system is a mess, but he shouldn't keep billing you just because the bureaucracy is slow. As for Haidir, his case is a layup. The lawyer has to file before the boy turns sixteen, but then it's simply a matter of waiting."

"Haidir is not patient. He is young."

"And angry?" Ted asked.

"He thinks his parents are fools."

The Preacher chuckled. "All American teenagers believe that."

Mohammed shook his head. "All peoples are the same."

22

NOT ONE OF THE volunteers acknowledged her presence, but Kenzie could feel the slight surge of energy from the group. It was a comforting feeling. These women worked hard with real focus, not to impress or curry favor, but because they wanted the project to succeed. They wanted the tower stopped. Without them, Ron Reisner would have torn up whole neighborhoods, displacing thousands of residents, their businesses, their communities—and still might. All for the glory of branding this monstrosity with his company letters, LBC. And profit. Never forget profit. But these women believed in Kenzie's battle to save Queens. Her goals were theirs. She was not an interruption but an inspiration.

She unpacked her tote bag at the school desk in the corner that served as her office. Water bottle, coffee cup, a small bag of almonds, a Gala apple, laptop, phone charger, notepad, pens. Her sweater went around the back of the chair, the bulky jacket on a hook by the door.

Here there was order. She had control. There were no bodies, no blood, no overbearing cops, and no scary mustache-wearing guys trying to get into her apartment. She didn't believe that story about the gas leak, but then what had the guy wanted? She reminded herself again to tell Ted.

The egg sandwich Ted had finally persuaded her to eat rumbled in her stomach like a gathering storm, but it was doing its work in subtler ways. She felt both energized and centered. The coffee, a liter of water, two ibuprofen, and another hour-long nap had also helped. The vow to never do anything like that to herself again was already fading from memory. Prepared now for anything, she took a minute to greet individually and by name each of the three long-term volunteers.

"The flowers canceled," Deepa said in her version of a whisper, which managed to reach the far end of the room.

"Reisner got to him," Kenzie guessed. She didn't know how it had happened, but she was sure it had.

Deepa nodded. "But I got this. Hunt's Point will deliver, and I and a couple of the girls will make the arrangements. Disaster averted."

"Do we need flowers?"

Deepa let out a deep belly laugh. "Without flowers, the aroma of all that money would knock you on your butt."

Kenzie allowed herself to smile and relax just a bit. "What else?"

"That intern has been here," Deepa said in a voice that warned of unforeseen events. "She's run out on some errand and is due back any minute."

Kenzie didn't want to meet anyone. She wanted to call her mother about the damned dress and then get to work on the double-damned speech. "I thought she was going to work with Ted."

"He okayed her. We're waiting on documents."

"Can I not meet her?"

"She's already been busy," Deepa said.

A young, dark-haired woman in a sensible suit came through the door carrying a pizza box from Patsy's. She saw Kenzie and her face brightened into an excited grin.

"Good morning, McKenzie. I'm really excited. I hope you are, too."

This was something of a non sequitur and Kenzie gave Deepa a quick glance for clarification.

"Ashley has shown some initiative. She's managed to get

you booked on WBAI Friday morning." Deepa's voice registered no excitement. Flat. Informational.

"Next Friday?" Kenzie asked. It was already looking to be
a busy week.

"No. This Friday. Tomorrow." Again, Deepa delivered
the alarming information with all the emotional strength of
reading a shopping list.

"Oh. Whoops," Ashley said. "I thought Deepa would have
told you already."

Kenzie refused to be overwhelmed. She could do this,
couldn't she? She could be gracious, complimentary, and
display amazing self-control. She could scream when she got
home. "Welcome, Ashley. Parker, isn't it? We're glad to have
you helping out. I'm McKenzie Zielinski." The woman was
not exactly what Kenzie had expected. She carried herself with
some authority, which made her appear a little older than a
typical first-year law student.

"I know. I googled you. Anyway, I made some calls and
lucked out."

Kenzie had been on WBAI, the relentlessly progressive
radio station in New York, more than a few times. She was
usually grouped with other community activists from the
outer boroughs, all of whom were vying to make their own
projects sound most important and worthy of donations and
political support. The headache was back.

"What time?" she asked.

Ashley looked a little less proud of herself. Deepa squinted
as she answered. "Six to half-past."

Kenzie didn't have to ask. A.M.

"Oh, good. The morning commute." At least it wasn't the
5 A.M. slot. "Can I phone it in or are we supposed to show up
at the studio?" There was one woman from the Bronx who
particularly got on her nerves and Kenzie would be happy

not to have to share a claustrophobia-inducing studio with her before dawn.

"It's a phone-in," Ashley said, obviously relieved at having further good news.

"Well, thank you." Kenzie managed to put a little enthusiasm into her delivery, reminding herself for perhaps the thousandth time that overseeing an all-volunteer staff had challenges not found in the for-profit world. "Be sure to run anything like this by Deepa before you commit, okay? There may be conflicts and I'd hate to have to cancel."

"Oh, I checked your calendar first."

Kenzie shot a questioning look at Deepa who winced silently in reply.

"It's okay, isn't it?" Ashley said.

Kenzie kept two calendars on her phone and computer. One was strictly for organization business and it made sense for Deepa to have access to it. The other was personal and merged with Ted's. But as their personal and professional lives intersected so regularly, Kenzie had given Deepa access to all.

"Deepa?" Kenzie asked, leaving as much room as needed for an explanation.

"I have now made clear that though we're informal around here, there is a chain of command. But, it's not bad, what she did. You might like it."

"Your schedule will be on the internal message board, so everybody can know when you'll be here," Ashley said.

And where I'll be when I'm not, Kenzie thought. And when I'm skipping Pilates, and when Ted drags me to a Mets game, and where Ted is meeting Lester for lunch and when. She felt her last dregs of privacy running out the drain.

"Also, I upgraded some things. It's all password protected now."

"Password protected sounds good." She was not, as a rule, subject to panic attacks, but this perky young woman with all her improvements might cause her to make an exception.

"Excuse us." Her hangover had robbed her of her ability—and willingness—to talk to Ashley further.

Ashley took her pizza and offered to share it with the other volunteers.

Kenzie guided Deepa away. "Am I losing it? I feel like we rescued an orphan who's now running the show."

"She needs to slow down, that's all. But we need an energy boost. She's already making friends with the volunteers."

Blame it on the hangover. "Fine. But keep an eye on her."

"Will do," Deepa said, looking somewhat chagrined.

They discussed the details of the party for a few minutes. Kenzie allowed herself to feel a touch of guilt. Deepa had all the stress and Kenzie couldn't manage to get her comparatively easy tasks completed. There was also some delicacy demanded by the fact that very few of the volunteers would be invited to attend, and those few would be there to work—getting signatures and recording pledges. Further complicating affairs, the host had insisted on a caterer for the event, which, to many, seemed an unnecessary expense—despite the fact that the host was paying for it. The staff were used to the potluck contributions of their friends and colleagues. To some it felt like a snub.

"If it's a success, we'll throw a staff party at the end of the month," Kenzie suggested. "We'll all feel more comfortable—and have a lot more fun with something to celebrate." Having accomplished all she could for now to promote world peace, she plunked down at her desk and began to review her schedule for upcoming talks and meetings. For a brief moment she was put off by the amount of information on the organization's calendar. It was accessible to anyone who had the password, hopefully a limited group, but far from what she considered private or privileged. She took a deep breath.

What was best for the organization? The fact that she was uncomfortable having her life plastered on the screen was not important. This was password protected after all. The distribution list would be limited.

And then she could see the beauty in it. Ted's court dates, filing deadlines, and so on were all there. No longer would there be any excuse for overlap with community meetings, fundraisers, or strategy sessions. Deepa would be able to coordinate things easily. Future planning for all of them would be so much simpler.

Kenzie mentally kicked herself. She'd been less than welcoming to the newbie. Ashley was merely being enthusiastic. After all, shaking things up was supposed to be what Stop the Spike was all about.

Then it occurred to her. How had Ashley merged Ted's calendar into the general schedule? Kenzie had access to Ted's account but had to put in a password every time she accessed it. She'd never checked before—first, because the situation had never come up; and second, she had a horror of not respecting her partner's privacy—but what more than calendar dates might there be? Notes on cases? His work with Lester? She grabbed her phone and speed-dialed Ted.

The phone rang four times and went to voicemail. No way was she going to talk about this in a voicemail. She texted.

Can I access your case files?

WHAT? No.

Not May I. Can I.

NO.

Good.

??

Later.

She shut down the phone and looked up.

Deepa was standing over her with an expression of extreme fretfulness, a most unlikely state for that hardheaded woman.

Kenzie tried smiling into the woman's discomfort. "What's up, Deepa?"

"There's two cops here. Detectives. They want to speak to you."

23

TWO BEEFY MEN IN suits stood by the door at the far end of the basement. She had expected some follow-up from the NYPD, but the sudden appearance at her humble office was a surprise. And it felt intimidating.

"Police? Well, they don't look so scary." They did. "Ask them in. Get them chairs."

This show of bravado would not convince Deepa, but it might remind her to put up a brave front herself. The volunteers were watching, and in this community even those with family on the force were wary of the police. Any police.

"Welcome, guys," Kenzie said when Deepa presented them. "How can I help you?" She extricated herself from the little desk and offered a hand. "What you see is what we've got, so if it's okay with you, we'll talk right here." Kenzie waited while Deepa dragged over two folding chairs. "Take a seat."

After a brief handshake the two men sat. Both were tall and well-built, though carrying some extra weight around their middles. The gray-haired Black man exuded a quiet serenity that invited confidences. His partner had a heavy face and a natural scowl as though he'd seen all the world had to offer and was disappointed.

"My name is Duran," the Black detective said. He had a deep, clear voice. She was surprised to realize she immediately trusted him. "And this is my partner, Detective

Kasabian. I don't suppose you remember us, McKenzie Zielinski."

He was right; she did not recognize either man. But something was triggered because she felt a sudden stab of pain in her scalp along the scar from the attack more than a year ago. She'd been nearly run down by a pair of Russian gangsters in a stolen car. The doctors had induced a coma to stem the swelling in her brain. She didn't remember anything from that period.

"You weren't there yesterday," she said.

"No, ma'am. We're with the major case unit. You came to our attention last year because of your involvement in a gang-related assault. The system alerts us now whenever your name pops up in relation to any violent felony."

She flashed on Ted's warning about talking to the police but dispelled the thought. She had this, and Ted wasn't available anyway. And she was surprised to realize she wanted to help this Detective Duran.

"Is that like a 'watch list'? Should I be flattered? Who else is on it? Oh, wait, you can't tell me. Right? It's a 'secret' list."

Duran gave the kind of patient smile that indicates the person understands you were trying to be funny even though you have failed to provoke laughter. "Can you describe the man you saw leaving the offices? I've got what you told the patrolmen yesterday, but maybe something else has come to you."

She thought this safe ground. "I didn't see much."

"No, I understand. How tall would you put the man? Take a guess."

"My height or maybe a couple of inches taller."

"That's good. Now, think. I know you didn't see his face, but maybe you saw his hands. Take your time. What color were his hands? White? Black? Yellow? Brown? Light or dark?"

The detective was good, she thought. Parsing the moment this way was stimulating her memory. And he was easy to talk to. "Brown," she said. "Dark brown." The word "swarthy" flashed through her mind. An old person's word. Was she remembering what she'd seen or what the old man upstairs had said? "I think."

Duran didn't give her time to equivocate. "Did he move like a young person or an old one?"

"Young. Definitely."

"Heavy? Skinny? Average?"

Not heavy. Average? No. "Slight," she said.

"I know you didn't see the face, but if you had to guess, what color were his eyes?"

"But I—"

"I know. I know. You didn't see his face. But tell me what pops into your head when I ask?"

What popped into her head was an image of Mohammed's stepson, Haidir. Basically a typical teenage American boy who happened to have been born halfway around the world.

The rhythm was broken. She was afraid of what her mind had done. Did she really think she'd seen Haidir running from a murder scene? Or was her mind creatively filling in blanks, as Ted had warned? She reminded herself to be cautious.

"No idea," she said. "I didn't see him."

Duran nodded a few times. "You did great. Thanks for your help."

Now, Kenzie didn't want to have helped him. Not if Haidir could become a suspect. "I think it's time for you guys to let me get back to work."

Duran looked for a moment as though he was about to agree, but Kasabian jumped in. "I've got a question or two for you. Tell me about you and Mr. Spitzer," he said.

"Whoa, there," Kenzie said. "There is no me and Mr. Spitzer. I never met the man. I'm just the unlucky one who found him dead."

"Then I don't get it," the dour-faced detective asked. "What were you doing snooping around his office? Checking out his files."

Alarms went off. Ted's warning was sounding in her head like a siren. She had been snooping, but that wasn't why she was there. Nor was it relevant to the man's death. Duran had lulled her into complacency. She was an idiot.

"A year or so ago, I was a victim. This time I'm a witness. But you guys are here because you think I'm a perp. Have I got this right?" The volunteers were all watching without any attempt at subterfuge while Deepa had her head down. The young Ms. Parker was transfixed. Kenzie knew she was getting loud—but she'd had it with these two.

"It's a murder case. We'd like to hear your side." Duran made it sound like an invitation to confess.

She didn't fall for it. "My side? My side! I went to talk to a lawyer and found him dead. What 'side' am I supposed to have?"

Kasabian cut in again. "How did you know the deceased? Was there a personal relationship?"

"Lawyer," she said. "Or better yet, leave."

"Easy," Duran said. "Why would you need a lawyer?"

Duran's smooth baritone was no longer working on her. "It sounds like I'm being interrogated. If that's the case, I want my lawyer present. And as he is presently unavailable, I am asking you to go. Now." She stood up. "Leave your card and he'll be in touch."

The cops took their time standing. The two metal chairs groaned in relief as they rose. Duran handed her a card. She saw her fingers shaking as she took it and quickly buried both card and hand in the pocket of her khakis.

"Don't take too long getting back to us," Duran said. "Or we'll have to come back."

24

TED WAS FINISHING THE bulgogi and rice from Chung Moo and sipping a pint from the growler he'd picked up on the way home. Kenzie had barely eaten and was now trying on the three dresses her mother had dropped off.

"How's this?"

Ted looked up from his laptop screen where he was studying his notes for Tuesday's court session. "Nice."

"Too short?" The full-length mirror hung on the inside of the broom closet door in the kitchen, but in order for her to see herself completely she had to stand in the living room.

He didn't look up. "Not for me."

She ignored him. "Too short." She pulled it off over her head, dumped it on the couch, and slid into another black dress.

"Now I'm seeing Haidir everywhere I look," she said, posing again.

"But it's not Haidir," Ted said.

"Right. It's some other teenager with brown skin."

"Which pisses you off."

"My racist brain keeps filling in a person of color. Swarthy. Such an ugly word. I rode the bus with two Haidirs tonight. One of them followed me all the way to our street. And yet if the real Haidir walked in here right now I wouldn't be sure it was him unless Mohammed had him by the arm."

Ted gave up on his notes. He needed to concentrate, and Kenzie obviously needed to talk. "That dress is nice." He couldn't tell how it was different from the previous but felt he should contribute something.

"The only reason I'm getting compulsive about Haidir is because of that old man."

"And maybe you're worried that it *is* Haidir, and then where will you be?" He brought his empty bowl to the sink and gave it a quick rinse.

"I'm sure it's not him." She stared angrily into the mirror before shaking her head and stripping off the dress.

Ted had no opinion on the subject, but thought Kenzie was working hard at convincing herself of the boy's innocence. "Good. Then we can talk about something else."

She looked at him and let her shoulders relax. "Okay. How was your day? What did you do?" The third dress went on over her head.

"Lester and I wasted the day looking at a property in Red Hook."

"To buy?"

"God, no. A foreclosure."

She scrunched her face into a mask of disgust.

He smiled into it. "The guy's a crook." He nodded. "That's nice." The dress.

"You're no help. You like them all."

"I guess it's just nice to see you in a dress."

"What is that supposed to mean?"

"Nothing. You look nice, that's all."

"Nice?"

He raised both hands in surrender.

"This is a costume, Ted. Tomorrow I am going to show up looking like one of them."

He knew exactly who "them" was—the rich and mighty.

"And maybe they won't notice when I pick their pockets."

"And I will run interference for you."

"Oh, god. I need to tell you about the calendar."

"The calendar? And what was that text about access to my case files?"

"The intern. Ashley. She merged our calendars."

He shrugged. "And?"

"Can she see anything else? Emails? Notes? Whatever?"

He thought about it. Possible? Unlikely. He was not a computer security expert. But there was a firewall, wasn't there? His notes were kept in the cloud. He erased them from his laptop as soon as he saved them. Kenzie knew his password and if she'd saved it on her system . . . He shrugged again. "I'll change the password."

"Suppose she sees some of your legal stuff."

"Legal stuff. I'm crushed."

"You know what I mean."

"She's an intern. She can ask me anything about what I'm working on, and I'll tell her. Isn't that why she's there?"

"I don't know about her."

"Please. I need her."

"Isn't it too coincidental that just when you needed someone to help you, the perfect candidate *happens* to arrive at the door?"

"Yes. That is a coincidence. Practically the poster child for coincidence. And I'm happy she's there."

"Fine." It wasn't, but she stopped pushing it, which, for Ted, amounted to the same thing. Until it returned, and it would.

"Those detectives will start hounding me, won't they?"

"It is their way. Let me find you a lawyer who'll go with you next time."

"You're a lawyer."

"So you keep telling me. Me and my 'legal stuff.'"

"You know these guys."

"Yes, we have a history. I don't know that will be a help. One of them got shot."

"That wasn't your fault."

"No, but it's the kind of thing that leaves a mark on a relationship."

"Suppose we make it very informal. We meet at Gallagher's or someplace. If they're not nice, we leave." She picked up the discarded dresses and, one over each arm, took turns holding them up in front of her. "If they give me a hard time, we make an appointment to meet on their turf and then—I promise—we will bring a real lawyer."

"Somebody followed you?" It hadn't really hit him when she first mentioned it.

"I don't know. He walked the same way I did, but he wasn't hiding or anything. He stayed half a block back."

There was a limit to his paranoia. Living in the greatest city in the world meant maintaining a level of caution that might be inappropriate in a small suburban town. Muggers, monsters, and madmen were real. They were out there. But the fear must be reasonable, otherwise one would go mad or move to a gated community.

"Did he really look like Haidir?"

She considered before answering. "No. Wait. Did I tell you about the gas guy?"

FRIDAY

25

KENZIE THANKED THE HOST, the listeners of WBAI, all the contributors, and, as always, Father Byun for renting the space in his church to this worthy effort. She ended by repeating the phone number and email address for contributions. "Fully tax-deductible."

It was 6:34 A.M. and she was both exhausted and too wired to go back to sleep. Who knew if her appearance on the morning show would benefit Stop the Spike? It was part of the job. If it got one ten-dollar contribution, it had been worth it.

And it hadn't been so bad. There were no other guests, so for a half hour she'd been able to make her pitch, aided by a surprisingly well-prepared interviewer. Ashley had done good. Kenzie reminded herself to publicly thank her the next time she came into the office.

Ted wouldn't be up for another hour—at least. Friday was his sleep-in day. She could fix herself breakfast but risked waking him with the noise or the aroma. Or she could call Mohammed, go to the office, and grab something on the way. She could ask him to take Myrtle and she could treat herself to a celebratory cinnamon bun from Rudy's.

She had a plan. She made the call and got dressed.

NEW YORK RAIN IN November can produce hail or sleet, can be driven by gale-force winds, and can drop in temperature to freezing. There can be a frozen fog that leaves a patina of ice on everything from sidewalks to fir trees, making the first treacherous and the latter magical. It can rain for days until basements flood and parks become impassable swamps with mud powerful enough to pull one's shoes off. And every once in a long while, the last tropical storm comes up the coast and runs into the first polar vortex.

It was snowing. A heavy, wet concoction that was already melting to slush before it hit the ground. Kenzie kept her head down and fought the wind for her umbrella. The weather app said the temperature was forty-one degrees, but the damp wind and snow made it feel like twenty. She rushed across the sidewalk. Mohammed must have seen her coming because the rear door swung open as she reached it. She followed her collapsing umbrella into the back seat and pulled the door shut behind her with a satisfying thunk.

Mohammed had the heater on full blast, which, rather than comforting her, overwhelmed her. Between caring for her umbrella and its load of wet snow and shielding her eyes from the waves of heated air coming out of the fan, she did not at first see the figure in the passenger seat up front.

When she did, she almost gasped, stopping herself with a hand clapped over her mouth.

The man—young man, but she couldn't say why she thought so—had a dark hoodie and held himself in a stiff crouch leaning against the inside of the passenger door. He was either an angry, fractured soul with no social skills or a teenager. He was turned away and made no acknowledgment of her presence. And in that terrifying first sight, he looked exactly like the person she had seen run from the crime scene at Spitzer's office.

And instantly looked nothing like him. She flushed with guilt at her response. It was Haidir, and yet what she had seen was a hooded brown boy, and she had reacted as though he was a threat. The fact that she had not gasped or otherwise allowed herself to comment did not excuse her response.

She was mortified. She thought of herself as a woman of the world, comfortable with man or woman of any color, shape, or cultural background.

Yet, she acknowledged the fact that in twenty-first-century America there is a touch of racism in all of us. No matter one's skin color, we are all trained to fear the different. What is important is not what you *feel* but how you *behave*.

Now that she took a post-panic look at this person, she could see the differences. The brief look she'd had the other day was remarkably clear—and devoid of detail. But she was sure this was not the man she'd seen.

And that realization released her. She had a responsibility to behave normally. She did not need to apologize or to be forgiven, only to show respect and acceptance. She spoke. "Good morning, Mohammed. Thanks for picking me up. Good morning, Haidir. Are we to drop you at school?"

Haidir did not answer. Mohammed replied. "*Sabah el kheir,* my friend."

"*Sabah an-noor,*" she responded. "Though there's not going to be much light. It's a nasty New York morning."

"It will pass. The wind and rain will be gone by midday, you will see."

"From your lips to god's ear," she said. The fundraiser scheduled for that night needed a warm sunset and a wind no stronger than a gentle breeze. Two hundred people cold and huddled over a pile of slush would have a hard time signing checks.

"Haidir works before school."

"Oh? Do you work in the bodega?" Kenzie made another attempt to elicit a polite response. "With your mom?"

Haidir made a scornful sound. "Tuh."

Mohammed said something in Arabic, and Haidir, with a flash of anger, looked away.

"He works for Sri Singh." Mohammed sounded uncomfortable making excuses for the boy's rudeness.

Kenzie didn't see how stocking shelves at Manny's market could be that different from stocking shelves at a bodega. But the boy didn't want to work for his mother. Clear and understandable.

The boy sneaked a peek at her over his shoulder, turning away as soon as their eyes met. Kenzie felt goosebumps down her arms. She might think she was sure of Haidir's innocence, but her body had another opinion.

The ride to Ridgewood was slow. The weather exacerbated the increased traffic. Rush hour had become a fourteen-hour daily event since the lifting of pandemic restrictions. Kenzie tried to focus on the day ahead, but her eyes kept drifting to the silhouette of young Haidir.

They pulled up in front of the huge grocery store. The snow had turned to rain and was pelting like a cascade of marbles, making an intimate farewell impossible. Haidir popped the door open, muttered something to his stepfather, and dashed across the sidewalk.

Kenzie watched him run, her heart pounding. She was not normally this subject to wild emotional swings. How could she think this boy capable of such a heinous murder? Was this some form of PTSD? A reaction to finding the dead man? Whatever was happening to her, she did not like it.

Haidir reached the door and looked up. Someone had called him. He stepped under the awning out of the rain and waited.

A young man in a dark hoodie and black jeans ran past the car as Mohammed pulled away, stopping again almost immediately as the light changed. Kenzie craned her head and looked back.

And laughed. To herself. At herself. The young man was

older than Haidir by more than a couple of years. He was not Arab. He was Latino. And while she was certain he would still have qualified as "swarthy" according to the old Polish talent agent, the differences between the two vastly outweighed the similarities. There were, no doubt, thousands of young men and boys in Queens who could answer the same vague description. She had let her fears for Mohammed and his family bend her judgment out of all proportion.

She watched the two talking under the awning. They were arguing. Haidir repeatedly shook his head. The other was insistent. Threatening. He grabbed Haidir's sweatshirt and shook him. Haidir pushed him away and dashed inside the store.

Kenzie watched the young Latino glower at the closed door until an Asian mother pushed past him with a stroller. The man turned away and ran.

"He is not a bad boy," Mohammed said. He had not seen the altercation and was therefore speaking only of Haidir.

"No," she replied. "A teenager."

26

THE RAIN HAD SUBSIDED to a less-than-monsoon level by the time Mohammed pulled to the curb in front of the church. Kenzie gathered her bag, the box of breakfast pastries, and her twenty-ounce black coffee and scootched across the seat. As she opened the curbside door a brown delivery van pulled in behind them, sending a wash of rainwater over the curb.

Kenzie struggled out, waited for the flood to abate slightly, and with a last thank-you to Mohammed, ran for the gate. It was open. Someone was there ahead of her.

The drain at the bottom of the stairs was working today and she made it into the basement office with minimal water damage to clothes or shoes. She was greeted by both Deepa and Ashley.

"Nice work this morning, boss," Deepa said.

"You were awesome," Ashley enthused.

Kenzie thanked Deepa and delivered her best smile to Ashley, not trusting herself to respond politely to the effusion. "You two are here early."

"I was supposed to sleep? We have two hundred potential donors on a roof tonight and it's raining."

"Two hundred RSVPs?"

"Close enough."

"And how's the flowers situation?" Kenzie was also prepared to panic if the rain didn't lay off, but Deepa needed encouragement.

"Taken care of."

"See? You've got this." Turning to Ashley, she went on. "And you're here for moral support?"

"Documents are coming today, but we don't know when. I didn't want ten cardboard boxes full of paper to sit out on the curb."

"In the rain," Deepa said.

"Enough with the rain," Kenzie cried. "It's stopping late this morning. The sun's coming out and the temperature will be in the high seventies by late afternoon."

"Really?" Ashley said.

"Believe," Deepa said.

"Faith moves mountains," Kenzie said.

"Yeah, we'll see," Deepa said. "And we had a visitor already. A guy from the gas company wanted to check for leaks."

Kenzie was startled. "You're kidding."

"No. I told him *he* must be kidding. There's no gas lines anywhere in the building."

"What did he look like?" She must have spoken louder than she thought because now Deepa looked startled.

"I don't know. He had a plastic poncho over some kind of uniform. A blue hard hat. He looked very official."

"He had a mustache," Ashley offered.

Kenzie tried to remember the man outside her apartment. He had a mustache. Too big for his face. This couldn't be coincidence. It had to be the same man. But after having swallowed a lesson about young men wearing hoodies, she would not allow herself to jump to a conclusion.

"You sent him away."

"Sure. He didn't like it, but he went. I told him to call the rectory and make an appointment if he really had to get in here."

"That was good."

"You act like you know this guy," Deepa said.

Sharing her suspicions might frighten the two women and would do nothing to relieve her own anxiety. "I doubt it," she said—truthfully, if not completely.

There was a pounding on the door. "Delivery."

27

"LONG TIME, COUNSELOR," DETECTIVE Duran said. Kasabian just stared stone-faced.

"Not long enough," Ted said. He and Kenzie were facing the two detectives across a table at Gallagher's. Neither of them wanted to be there. Kenzie needed to get ready for the evening and Ted was reluctant to act as her criminal defense lawyer. And, he had not seen these two cops since witnessing a shootout on the courthouse steps that had left two dead and two wounded, one of whom was Detective Kasabian. The detective hadn't liked him before he got shot.

"You both know I'd rather have another lawyer here, but in the interest of helping the inquiry at the earliest possible moment, I have agreed to this informal conversation—off-the-record, no notes, and no recordings. If Ms. Zielinski is currently a suspect, you have to tell me now." Ted, of course, was recording the proceedings with his cell phone, but only to preclude the cops from submitting their tapes as evidence at some future date.

"If she becomes a suspect, I will tell you," Duran said.

"Then let's go," Ted said.

"How'd you know Spitzer?" Kasabian asked in a voice dripping with disdain.

"I didn't," Kenzie shot back.

"The last person to see the victim alive is always one of the first people we look at," Kasabian said, turning to bare his teeth at Ted in a wolfish smile. "She may not be a suspect right now, but she better have a good story to tell if she doesn't want to become one."

"He was dead when I got there," Kenzie said, matching his icy delivery.

"Please, please, please," Ted said, raising both hands. "Detective, please do not make provocative remarks. We've agreed to this meeting to assist you in your investigation. Period." Then turning he added, "Ms. Zielinski, please check with me before speaking. That's why you dragged me here."

"You came for the burgers," Duran said with a wide smile.

"And your company," Ted said, matching his smile.

The lunch crowd had picked up considerably at Gallagher's with the expanded menu. Lily had a packed bar. Two servers handled the floor. Zhang, who was working the far side of the room, and Huan, who had the tables and booths in back. Huan was a terrible waitress. Though she spoke excellent English with an accent reflecting both Harbin and Rego Park, Ted had never seen her smile or show interest in any patron beyond what they wanted to eat. She was also close to six feet tall with plenty of upper-body muscle. She could be intimidating.

"You want menus?" she asked, dropping four silverware-filled cloth napkin rolls on the table.

"Any specials?" Kenzie asked.

"It's Friday."

Ted turned to the two detectives. "The sushi is California rolls. There's also a hot roast beef and melted Swiss with sauteed onions on an onion roll. Lots of garlic. The soup is corn and chicken chowder."

Huan said, in an uncharacteristic display of polite assistance, "The RB comes with mashed and gravy. Whaddya want for drinks?"

It was an informal meeting, but no one ordered a beer. She

repeated their orders. "Coke, Diet Coke, seltzer with lemon, and a coffee—black." She turned to leave.

"Hang on," Ted said. "You ready?" he asked Kenzie.

"House salad. No dressing."

Duran turned to his partner. "I've had the burgers. They're good."

Kasabian nodded.

"Two burgers," Duran ordered. "Medium rare. All the way."

"I'll have my usual," Ted said.

"What's that?" she replied. It was a conversation set in stone, repeated two or three days a week.

"Pad Thai." Friday, it would be chicken.

Huan shrugged and walked away.

"Can we get started?" Kasabian asked. He brought out a small notebook but no pen.

"Here's the drill," Ted said. "One of you asks a question. I confer with Ms. Zielinski. She answers or declines. We start over. No interrupting with follow-ups, no trick questions, no argumentative or leading questions. All clear?" He waited for Duran to nod. "And no shouting," he added.

"Go for it," Duran said to the other cop.

"Why were you at Mr. Spitzer's office?" Kasabian asked in a quiet, reasonable tone. Ted was immediately on guard.

They'd prepared for this question, so he gave Kenzie a nod.

"Spitzer was handling an immigration case for a friend. The friend was unhappy. He thought Spitzer was bungling it. I found myself in the neighborhood and decided I'd stop in and have a chat."

"I'm a little confused," Kasabian said. "You're saying you didn't go there on purpose. You just happened to be on Steinway Street and dropped in on a guy you say you never met before." The tone was accusatory and unpleasant.

Ted held up a hand and turned to Duran. "Rein him in or get those burgers to go."

"Manners," Duran said to his partner.

Kasabian grunted. Ted took it for both assent and apology.

"What happened after you got into the building?" the cop asked.

"Take it back one step," Ted said. Then to Kenzie, "Tell him about getting in."

Kenzie nodded a few times, preparing herself, "No one answered the buzzer. I tried it a few times. I thought about leaving, but then I tried the door. I was surprised to find it wasn't locked."

An unlocked street-level door was an aberration anywhere in the five boroughs.

Neither cop reacted. Ted thought they must already have known.

"I went up to the second floor, found the office, knocked, and got no answer. I called out. Then I went in and called out again. There were two doors. One looked open, so I tried it. There was nobody there. I was about to leave when I saw someone dash out the front door."

"Description?"

She looked to Ted and rolled her eyes. He shrugged. Nothing about her answer could implicate her in any way.

"You have it already. My memory isn't getting any clearer. I'm pretty sure it was a man. Not big. I couldn't swear to it, but I think he was wearing a black hoodie."

"Could it've been blue?"

"Sure. Or charcoal, or maybe even deep heather gray. I don't know. It happened in a split second."

"I'm asking again, you see, because no one else saw this person leaving the building."

Ted felt Kenzie was about to erupt but before he had a

chance to stop her, Huan appeared around the partition with their drinks. She cleared the tray and dropped four paper-wrapped straws on the table.

Ted waited for her to leave before addressing Duran again. "I'm going to have to give Detective Kasabian a failing grade in Plays Well with Others. Ms. Zielinski previously told me about another witness. The talent agent from upstairs."

"Not a reliable witness," Kasabian said.

Duran put down his coffee and raised a hand to deflect some of the rising animosity. "He's ninetysomething and a bit of a kook."

"That's ageism, officer," Kenzie said.

"I'll be sure and report it."

"We both saw the same thing," Kenzie said.

"Tell it your way, all right? Give me as much detail as you can, and I will keep my partner on a very short leash."

So, once again, Kenzie told the story. Duran didn't interrupt. He closed his eyes, laid his hands flat on the table, and hummed tunelessly from time to time to indicate that he was still awake. Ted listened to her tale carefully. He was hearing it now for the third time and was concerned that it sounded like there were holes—missing moments.

"The hoodie, jeans, and black Adidas . . ." Kenzie rapped out the minimal description and paused as though expecting a demand for more detail.

Duran opened an eye and closed it again.

"I went into that room and found a man who looked very dead. There was a lot of blood. I didn't know him, but there was a brass plaque on the door that read 'Howard Spitzer,' so I made the assumption that was the name of the dead man."

Duran cracked a smile, but kept his eyes closed. Ted realized the cop was doing exactly the same thing he was—listening for the gaps in her story. He felt a chill.

"I called 911 and reported it. Then I waited for you guys to show. The end."

The food arrived and for a moment all parties concerned themselves with silverware, napkins, and condiments. When Duran had swallowed his first massive bite of burger and groaned with pleasure, he signaled for a coffee refill, then turned to Kenzie.

"So how long were you upstairs?"

Kenzie spoke before Ted had a chance to intervene. "Minutes."

"Minutes? Like three? Five? Ten, maybe?"

"Does it matter?" Ted asked.

"Background," Duran said. "I'm trying to get a feel for the whole situation."

Ted thought this was where his criminal lawyer should magically appear and give him some guidance.

Duran picked up the burger as though about to take a bite, but then held it in one hand as he spoke. "I hear you were in the front room, then for some reason you went into the partner's private office, then you saw the unknown person, then you finally went into Spitzer's office. Is that the timeline? Have I got it right?"

Kenzie looked to Ted, and he gave a nod. "Yes. That's right."

"Did you spend a lot of time in the front room? I mean before you looked into the private offices."

"No. I was looking for . . . for someone . . . anyone. Nobody answered when I called out."

Ted heard her stumble.

"Okay," Duran said. "But why did you go into the other office first? You were there to see Spitzer, but you say you looked into Hillyer's office first."

"Let's take a minute," Ted said. "I want to confer with my client."

Kenzie looked surprised. Duran didn't.

Kasabian looked like he wanted to object, but Duran answered for them both. "Absolutely. It'll give me time to finish this delicious meal."

Ted exited the booth and walked to the bar. Kenzie followed. The noise level increased exponentially to the point that two people could carry on a private conversation while surrounded.

"You're not happy," Kenzie said.

"Duran thinks you're lying," Ted said.

"About what?"

Ted almost laughed. She wasn't denying the lie; she just wanted to know where she'd screwed up. "He knows how long you were upstairs."

"Then why is he playing games? What difference does it make?"

"It's cop-think. If you lie about little things, you must be lying about the big things."

"That is so bullshit. I'm not lying. About the big things, I mean. And where do you come up with this 'cop-think' stuff?"

"*Law & Order* reruns," he said. "What is he after?"

"I don't know," she said, and he almost believed her.

"Then walk it through with me. What did you do when you first entered their offices?"

"Like I said, I called out. No one answered."

"You told me you saw some files. Mohammed's file. Where was that? Out on the desk?"

She looked away when she answered. "I guess so. I'm not sure." She was a lousy liar.

"Oh, no. You remember. Trust me. Today I'm your lawyer. If you broke any laws, we can deal with it. *I* know you didn't kill Spitzer, but *they* don't."

"I didn't do anything illegal." She looked like she was ready to deck him.

"Can you get mad at me later? Right now I need you to focus on getting Duran and his pit bull to leave you in peace."

She let loose a dramatic sigh. "I looked at the computer. The receptionist left her files open. It wasn't really even snooping. It was all right there."

"So you touched the keyboard? The mouse?"

"Yes."

"Maybe brushed against the cabinets? Or the back of her chair?"

"The goddamn plant."

"Okay, not the plant, but you may have left fingerprints or DNA on her desk?"

The music surged to a near painful level. Wilson Pickett. "Don't Let the Green Grass Fool You."

"Probably," Kenzie admitted with a rueful grimace.

"So here's the problem. We can stop the interview now and they'll go away thinking you're guilty. Of murder. *Or*, you tell them that you were checking out the files on what's-her-name's computer and maybe they believe you. And, if we're lucky, they focus their investigation elsewhere. What *is* her name?"

"DuPre. They'll think I was snooping."

"You were snooping."

"If I tell them, they'll assume I'm guilty."

"Yes. Of snooping. Not murder."

She let this sink in for a minute. Her combative stance relaxed, and the rigid line of her jaw softened. "Right," she said, switching gears. "Let's do this."

He'd seen her do this sudden reversal before. She challenged others to convince her of a course of action, but once she was on board with it, she was unstoppable.

"You good with this?" Ted knew she was, but he had to hear her say it.

"I'm good. And Ted? Thank you. Sometimes the Girl Scout in me takes over and I get all caught up in not wanting to look bad and . . ."

He let her trail off. "You ready?"

"Screw these guys. You bet I am."

They headed back to their table. Ted watched the two detectives watching them. Kasabian maintained his usual scowl. Ted thought it his resting face. But Duran had dropped his sleepy-eyed pose of *hey-we're-all-just-working-together-on-this-murder-thing* and a raptor-like stoniness had replaced it. Ted reminded himself that Duran was as dangerous as Kasabian acted.

"Ms. Zielinski would like to add some color to her story, though she believes the information is irrelevant to your investigation."

"That's our call," Duran said. "Not hers."

"She understands that." Ted gave her a nod.

Kenzie wasted no more time. "When I first walked in, I was surprised that there was no one around. I called out a few times, but no one answered. Then my curiosity got the better of me. The computer on Ms. DuPre's desk was on. I used the mouse to look at some files regarding my friend's case. That's it."

Kasabian looked disappointed. She hadn't revealed anything indictable.

Duran looked thoughtful. "Let's go with this a minute. Who's the friend?"

Kenzie glanced at Ted. He shrugged and nodded encouragement. There was no point in trying to hide Mohammed and family; it would only make them appear guilty.

"Mohammed Mahdi," she said.

"Don't tell me what you read. I'd need a warrant to see those files."

"Not legal files. Billing. Numbers."

Duran's forehead creased and his eyebrows threatened to fuse into a single line. "Why were you looking at numbers? Why do you care?"

"Because I think—*we* think," she said with a nod toward Ted, "that Mohammed is getting screwed. That's why I went there. Not only by Spitzer, but his partner too. And the secretary has to be in on it. They're running multiple sets of books."

"Isn't that all the more reason why your friend smacked Spitzer on the head?"

"But he didn't do it."

Duran smiled—wolfishly.

Ted leaped in. "She's right. He had a fare. He was driving a man from JFK to Roslyn out in Nassau County. When Spitzer was getting smacked, Mohammed was stuck in traffic on the Parkway."

"He says."

"It was an Uber ride. There'll be a timed record."

Duran shook his head, looking both tired and disgusted. "Why not tell us all this in the first place?"

Ted let Kenzie fall on her sword.

"I didn't want you to think I was snooping."

28

THE PENTHOUSE OPENED OUT onto a roof garden that faced east and, thanks to the off-kilter alignment of streets in Long Island City, slightly to the north. Sunrise would always be a touch to the right, even more so as winter approached. Long Island stretched out to the horizon, as flat and featureless as the midwestern plains beneath the waxing moon. Though the skies were mostly clear, there was a haze over the northern sections of Queens, partially obscuring the farthest reaches of the East River and the beginnings of the Long Island Sound. The phallic shaft of the Trump tower in New Rochelle poked up angrily at a line of low-hanging clouds that hugged the far shore. Ted enjoyed visiting such a view but was afraid that living with it couldn't help but transform the viewer, bestowing an exaggerated sense of self-worth.

He knew, without having to experience it, that the sunset Manhattan views on the other side of the building, Penthouse W, would be partially obscured by the young crop of high-rise buildings that, over the last decade or more, had transformed this warehouse neighborhood into the hottest real estate market this side of the river. Penthouse E was the primo property.

And looking out to Corona and the site of the proposed LBC project, a.k.a. the Tower of Babel or the Spike, Ted had to admit that the Olympian view from this vantage point would forever be lessened by that monstrosity. On the other hand, the view might easily be obliterated by the next high-rise that sprouted two blocks over, but that was a local matter.

Kevin Dehler and his hundreds of millions—he was not yet in the ten-figure set—might find a way to head off the creation of a new view-blocking atrocity in his neighborhood—or he might simply purchase the penthouse in the next building. But the black spike of the LBC tower would still be out there, a few short miles distant, piercing the sky and dominating the view. A single middle finger raised to rich and poor throughout the borough and beyond.

Though the temperature couldn't be described as warm, the tall propane heaters were keeping the frost at bay. Women carried shawls rather than wearing them. The men were in suits—though no one wore a tie. It was, after all, a casual gathering.

Kenzie was not casual. She was working hard. And looking good doing it. She didn't need jewelry; she sparkled on her own. At the moment she was beguiling Dylan Hemmings, the fourth-generation landlord of an empire that stretched from Patchogue in the east to Morristown, New Jersey, in the west. Mr. Hemmings was Hallmark-movie handsome with a deep tan (four weeks from the first day of winter) and perfect teeth, on the board of MoMA, a guest lecturer at Columbia Business School, single, and two years younger than Ted. He was glowing in the attention Kenzie was pouring his way. Ted hated him.

Ted was also here to work. He should be schmoozing someone, but his heart wasn't in it. He was three days out from having been beaten, kidnapped, and abandoned on the arctic plains of a Jones Beach parking lot. He was also worried about his friends. A murder investigation could drag in Kenzie, Mohammed, or even Mohammed's stepson. He felt monumentally inadequate, unable to offer aid or advice, or make a request.

"You've brought out a good crowd," Ashley said, suddenly

appearing at his side. Ted hadn't seen her arrive and was surprised she'd managed to secure an invitation. Only a few of the volunteers were there, all working the marks like Kenzie. Most likely, he thought, she didn't get one and decided to come along anyway. It wasn't like anyone was checking tickets at the door.

"I take no credit. I'm only a hired hand. It's Kenzie and her posse who make things happen."

"And our host," Ashley said, looking past Ted.

Ted turned and found Kevin Dehler at his side. "Kevin," he greeted him with some enthusiasm. Not only was Kevin the host and an important donor, he had also become a new friend. And he was a fellow Mets fan. They'd been to a few games together. Kevin had a daily elevator commute from his penthouse to his hedge fund offices on the third floor.

"Evening, Ted. All good?"

"Seems to be. This shindig is much appreciated. Do you know the newest member of our team? Ashley Parker. She's working with me. She seems to know you."

"Google," she said, shaking the proffered hand. "I overprepare for everything. It's a compulsion."

Kevin laughed politely. He was smooth. He made it sound genuine. "You see the news? Is that nuts or what? That kind of money for a third baseman. Do you know how many third basemen end up in the Hall of Fame?" Before Ted had an opportunity to guess at the answer, Kevin switched gears. "Come with me. Let me introduce you to some friends."

Ted followed as they passed around the party. Tech and finance outweighed the professionals. Doctors and lawyers. Most of them lived in the building. No idle rich. Ted understood it was not a cause that would attract them.

"You need to meet Andy Krentz. Brilliant lawyer. He can give you some valuable tips." Kevin guided Ted toward a threesome of dark-suited silver-haired men.

Ted realized that Ashley Parker was following close behind. It was a brash move—almost rude—to put herself forward in this power group. But sending her off for fresh drinks or a tray of canapés would be seen as even ruder. He reminded himself that she was not only a volunteer—and a woman—but an ambitious law student. Cut her some slack and see what she's got.

Krentz, mercifully, did not attempt to impart his great wisdom to Ted. His substantial legal expertise—practiced on Wall Street for thirty years—did not extend to environmental or community planning issues, or to strategies and appearances at court. His investment banker daughter owned an apartment in the building, and he was there to contribute to the effort. Her dearly bought twenty-third-floor view must be maintained. After a brief chat with Ted, he promised a thousand-dollar check.

A volunteer stepped forward with the digital pledge book, taking Krentz's name and contact information. She asked for and received his signature on her iPad.

Ashley, he noted, was more than holding her own in this moneyed group. She carried herself with an easy self-confidence rarely seen in people in their early twenties. He was impressed.

Real estate developers. A surprise to find them here. Two of them. Kevin introduced him to the young Mr. Hemmings, whom Ted found he liked in spite of himself, and a gruff-speaking, balding man in his sixties named Pachis who proceeded to tell Ted all the reasons he was *not* going to support "your little group of sob sisters." There were many, but Ted early on caught the gist. Liberty. Freedom. Let the Market decide.

Ashley asked twice why the man had come to this gathering, but he ignored her. He continued to speak to the two men. Ted gave her credit for trying. But once the man began to bring in his feelings about past presidents, going back to Jimmy Carter (bad) and Ronald Reagan (GOAT), Ted tuned out.

There was a woman with him, but Pachis had not bothered to introduce her. She was a good twenty years younger and looked like she spent her days doing Pilates or yoga, spinning, or shopping for the gold jewelry that flashed from her earlobes to her toes. She did not speak while Pachis ranted, only smiled radiantly at them while holding her untasted champagne.

Two of the volunteers were hauling out the easel and posters for Kenzie's presentation, indicating that the pitch would be starting soon. Kenzie did it well and Ted was looking forward to watching her.

Mr. Pachis drained his glass of the amber-colored liquid. Kevin rescued them by leading him away to the bar. "The speeches will start any minute. Let's get some refills."

The woman stayed behind and for the first time her pasted-on smile softened. "Hi. Nina Pachis. I'm in PR. If there's anything you ever need in that line, call me."

Ted took the card she produced. It was thick, textured, and embossed with gold lettering. "I'll pass this along. Thank you."

He must have sounded less than enthusiastic because she shook her head sympathetically. "Don't pay Artie any mind. He needs to sound off sometimes. He doesn't want anyone to know he's supporting you guys."

"Oh?" Ted was skeptical.

"Oh, yes," she stated. "He's going to write a check. Anonymously. But he's in for high four figures at least." She grabbed

Ted's wrist and leaned close. "He *hates* Ron Reisner and would love to see you guys screw him royal." She released him and turned her head to face Ashley. "Nice to meet you, Alice."

And she went to join her husband.

SATURDAY

29

KENZIE GAVE HERSELF THE morning off. She'd earned it. The fundraiser had been a moderate success—she always hoped for more—generating promised donations totaling more than the cost of one year's education for three children at one of the city's exalted private schools. That was *if* everyone paid what they'd pledged—the rich stayed that way by *not* spending. But even at the usual two-thirds, it was enough to keep the lights on and Deepa employed for the next six months. It was a team effort, of course, but Kenzie was the star attraction, and she knew she'd done well.

She rolled over to check the clock and stopped herself. She didn't need to know the time.

Ted was out early, off on one or another of his projects. She had the morning and the apartment to herself. Her first inclination, which she immediately squashed, was to get out the vacuum and dust mop as soon as she was out of bed. No. Not a chance. Today was for her. Besides, it was Ted's turn to clean house and he did a much better job at it than she. For a lawyer, and a guy, he had some surprising homemaking skills.

She reminded herself that Ted had a lot of good qualities. Sharing a life in this space was not easy—for either of them. They were both too busy. She laughed at this. Busy was an excuse. The reality was that they were both too ornery. Too independent. Too used to not having to take others into account when making plans. Only child syndrome. Taken in that context, the two of them were doing wonders in terms of making the relationship work.

But they *were* too busy. Incapable of taking a vacation or even a full day off. Like today, stealing a few hours on a Saturday and feeling guilty. She hoped he took moments like this for himself.

What would she do?

Coffee. She could make a pot or walk three blocks to the Guyanese bakery and get a butterflap—or two—with a twelve-ounce fair trade, shade-grown, rainforest cuppa. She would have to put clothes on first.

Of course, she'd have to put on clothes to go downstairs, so she might as well go to the bakery for breakfast. Decision made.

Twenty minutes later—she rarely lingered in the tiny shower; it was much too claustrophobic—she was checking her parka pockets for house keys when there was a knock at the door. A forceful, peremptory knock connoting impatience, anger, or authority. The police again? She did not want to deal with them before coffee. Or after. But definitely not before.

The front door of their apartment—the only outside door, in fact—had been the side door before the conversion of the building. It led to a narrow alley and faced the side wall of the next two-family structure. The alley was too narrow for a car and only provided access—unnecessarily—to a high-fenced garden behind their building. It was also where the garbage cans resided when they were waiting to be hauled to the curb. She and Ted did not get many random visitors. No door-to-door salesmen. No proselytizing young people in suits. The mail and deliveries all came to the porch around front. A friend would have called.

Therefore, it must be the cops.

She peeked out the tiny kitchen window, careful not to touch the curtain.

A woman in a raincoat with one of those clear plastic rain

bonnets stood on the porch, her head turned down to avoid
the clinging mist—what Ted referred to as Irish sunshine. She
raised a fist and banged on the door again.

She did not look like a cop. She looked like someone's
mother. A little old-fashioned. The raincoat a drab gray,
matching the dull color of her hair. Her makeup was severe,
not flattering—heavy eyeliner and a slash of red on her lips.
Though her knocking signaled anger, her rounded shoulders
and bowed head indicated pain or submission or both. One
thing, for sure, she did not look threatening.

Kenzie stood at the door and called out, "Who's there?"

There was a pause before the woman responded. When
she did, her words came out in a harsh rush as though they'd
been bottled under pressure and were now released through
a narrow opening. "Open the door. I want to see your face."

"Not a chance," Kenzie said. "Either tell me who you are
and what the hell you want, banging on my door, or I call the
cops." Ted kept a baseball bat under the couch. Kenzie had
thought it a bit silly. Dramatic. Right now it made perfect
sense.

The woman laughed nastily. "Call them. Go ahead. Call
them. I dare you."

Kenzie was not prepared for that response. Was the woman
a crazy lady? She didn't have that look, but what was that look,
anyway? "Go away," she called.

"I came here to talk to you, slut. Now, open this door."

Kenzie had never been called a slut before in her life. She'd
never been through a slutty phase.

There was another bang on the door, followed this time by
a loud scream. "You damn whore. Open the door."

"Go away. You're a nutcase. Leave me alone," Kenzie
shouted back. She dug out the baseball bat. She felt no safer.
She leaned it against the wall behind the door.

"Whore!"

Kenzie's phone rang. She looked. Her landlord. Amos Kennedy owned the building and lived with his wife in the other small apartment cut out of their side of the two-family. Mr. Kennedy, who after thirty years in Queens still spoke with the musical rhythms of his native Jamaica, worked shifts at Transit, often getting home to bed at dawn. He liked quiet tenants. He did not like noise—or screaming.

"I'm sorry, Mr. Kennedy," she said. "There's a crazy lady at my door."

"Who the hell is she?"

"I have no idea. I don't know the woman."

Another scream from outside interrupted her. "McKenzie Zielinski, you slut! Open the door, you damn redheaded whore."

Oh, shit. How in the name of all that's holy does this woman know me?

"Mr. Kennedy? Are you still there? Really, I don't know who she is."

"Well, she knows you. Don't you make me call the police."

This was a threat. Mr. Kennedy had included a rider on the lease. If he was forced to call the police on a tenant, that was grounds for eviction.

"Fine," Kenzie snapped. She took up the bat again, drew herself up, rolled back her shoulders, and swung it as powerfully as she could. If this was going to work she needed to be fully committed. Total berserker mode. She pulled the door open. "Shut the hell up."

The woman was startled. She saw the bat and her eyes grew wide. She opened her mouth.

"Nope," Kenzie said. "Stop your screaming. Now, if you behave yourself, I will talk to you. If not, take a hike. Your call, lady."

30

MOHAMMED, ONE HAND HOVERING over the horn, threaded his chariot through a fleeting gap between a city bus and a gray minivan with stenciled white letters on the side proclaiming JESUS IS LORD and HE IS WATCHING. There was a longtime urban myth that such vans had been used for marijuana delivery. Ted believed it, as the proliferation of these vehicles had exploded during Covid lockdown.

They parked in front of a butcher shop. Ted noticed it was halal only because there was another butcher three doors down claiming to be glatt kosher. He wondered if they were both open on Christmas.

"You know this is a bus stop," he said.

"No problem," Mohammed said, locking a security device to the steering wheel.

"Won't you get a parking ticket?" Ted asked.

"No, boss. This is a commercial vehicle, and I am delivering a passenger. It's the law."

Ted wasn't so sure this was the case, but traffic law was not his bailiwick. "Have you ever gotten a ticket?"

"No. I tell you. I am legal."

"I mean for anything."

"Before I got license," Mohammed said with a shrug.

Ted decided he knew as much as he wanted to know on the subject.

A new intercom had been installed—nothing like a murder in the building to persuade a New York landlord to perform a bit of maintenance—with crisp, clean signs unbleached by

sun or rain. The second-floor law offices were now listed as
Hillyer & Associates. Mr. Spitzer had left the building.

"Hillyer," a woman announced through the static from
the tiny speaker.

"I'm here with one of Mr. Spitzer's clients. He needs to
speak with Mr. Hillyer."

"And you are?"

"His translator." From legalese into English.

"Second floor."

The lock released with a buzz and a thunk.

Ted's first breath sent a shock through his system. His
brain fluttered through a time warp. That smell. He had not
encountered it in decades.

Ted recognized the odor immediately. The first apartment
he'd known. A tiny two-bedroom off Lefferts Boulevard
where he lived with both parents until his father left for
good. The scary old man in the street-level apartment had a
miniature farm in the back where he raised vegetables and
kept chickens. The smell, rising to Ted's un-air-conditioned
bedroom window on a humid night in late July, was never to
be forgotten.

"Chickens," Mohammed said smiling. "Like home."

And there you have it, Ted thought. The same trigger and
two entirely different reactions. The man with the abusive
alcoholic father is distressed, while the man who escaped a
famine-ravaged war zone where members of his own family
had sworn to kill him became nostalgic.

The aroma dissipated as they mounted the stairs. By the
landing, it was gone. Ted shook off the cloud of memories.
He needed to be on his best game.

31

THE RECEPTIONIST WORE OVERSIZE sunglasses that almost hid the yellow and green hues of a healing black eye. She was an attractive olive-skinned woman of about Ted's age with glossy black hair, high cheekbones, and a wide mouth. She had probably been model-gorgeous ten years earlier and twenty pounds lighter.

Ted introduced himself and Mohammed. The woman didn't bother.

"I told him you were here. Go right in." She gestured unnecessarily to the doorway on the left. The one on the right was covered in an X of bright yellow crime scene tape.

The room was dark with pockets of light—a desk lamp, a standing lamp over a side table bracketed by two leather armchairs, and the glow from a laptop that shone upward at Hillyer's face. It was a face made of rocks and planes. He was fair-skinned and dark-haired. And held himself as though waiting to quash the next challenge to his alpha status.

Behind the man, a combined credenza and bookshelf stretched four feet high from wall to wall. There was a sad-looking American flag—sun bleached and dusty. A line of brass statues two to three feet tall lined the top shelf, each one representing some roughly phallic architectural marvel. The Eiffel Tower. The Washington Monument. The Chrysler Building. Ted assumed the Statue of Liberty was still in police hands and would be for some time to come.

"I don't know how much I can help you," Hillyer said once they were all settled. "We're in disarray here right now.

Howard left us some loose ends. And our legal secretary is claiming PTSD." He gestured with his head. "Marjorie, my wife, is helping out front."

"My condolences," Ted said. "I am not acting as Mr. Mahdi's lawyer, only as a concerned friend. But, full disclosure, I am a lawyer. I don't want you to find out later and think I was pretending otherwise."

"What field?"

"Real estate. Mostly corporate." Cigars. That's what he was smelling. Expensive cigars. Ted had never been a fan, but he'd traveled in circles that appreciated good ones. Hillyer smoked good ones. Expensive ones.

Hillyer nodded. "I do the real estate work here. Mostly residential. Also estate work. Trusts. I left the immigration work to Howard. I don't have the patience for it."

Ted winced inwardly. The hope of finding some help for Mohammed or Haidir in their pursuit of citizenship was fading into the far distance. "Can you give us any guidance?"

"Let's see." He flipped open a laptop and began typing. "Mohammed Mahdi?"

"That is the name on my documents," Mohammed answered after a moment's pause.

Ted heard the hesitation and understood. When Mohammed fled Yemen for Canada, with half his family threatening to murder him, he had done what many of his fellow refugees had done—he changed his name. In Mohammed's case, he merely stopped using his family name, as it too easily identified where he came from, and adopted his father's name as his surname. Remarkably, when he arrived in New York and claimed refugee status, no one questioned it. He became Mohammed Mahdi for all officialdom.

If Hillyer noticed the hesitation, he did not react. As he kept tapping at the keyboard, his expression became more intense and baffled. "Are you a new client?" he asked finally.

Mohammed shook his head with a dark expression. Ted noted it and his concern grew.

"Here it is. Got it." For a moment his face cleared, but the confusion returned immediately. "And for some reason, your file is cloaked."

"Cloaked?" Ted asked.

More taps.

"Yeah, but that's not a big deal. It's password protected. I'll talk to the girl on Monday. She'll know how to access it." He said all this with an insincere smile. Ted found he didn't like this man.

"There's a sizable outstanding on the account," Hillyer said with more certainty. He glanced up at Ted with a salesman's look of shared understanding. "Howard has a soft spot. Had. I told him 'Always get the retainer up front.'" He flashed a sad smile, inviting Ted to join him in appreciating the vagaries of a do-gooder. "Do you have a plan for how to handle this?" Though the question was one only Mohammed could answer, Hillyer directed his words to Ted.

"Not likely," Mohammed said.

"Excuse me?"

Ted thought the response both forced and false. "I believe that Mr. Spitzer was paid."

"Cash," Mohammed said. "Every month."

"Cash? No." Hillyer kept addressing Ted rather than Mohammed. "The firm doesn't take cash. You can understand. The banks are crazy about money laundering. Why deal with the aggravation?"

"I pay cash," Mohammed said.

"My friend says he paid cash," Ted said when it was apparent Hillyer wasn't going to respond to Mohammed's claim.

"There is no record of such a payment." He opened a drawer, took out a Post-it, and with one of the decorative pens wrote something and handed it to Ted.

It was a number. A five-figure number. A number far beyond Mohammed's ability to pay.

"He had a book. He write it in a book," Mohammed insisted.

"I suggest you caution your friend about making allegations that could reflect badly on the reputation of the firm or my recently deceased partner. He was a good man."

Hillyer was overplaying his hand. Why would he not at least entertain the possibility that Mohammed was revealing something about the dead man?

Hillyer was lying.

Ted stood. Mohammed looked up with surprise but quickly followed Ted's lead.

"Mr. Hillyer, I thank you for your time, but we're wasting ours. We're here to find out where Mohammed's case stands. And that of his stepson. If you can't provide us any information right now, please tell me when we can expect it."

The man leaned back in his chair in a relaxed pose. He raised both hands, palm up. "I just lost my partner. We'll get back to you."

The receptionist—Ted now assumed this was Marjorie Hillyer—was waiting for them. She nodded her head slightly to Ted as he walked by, then stepped between him and Mohammed. For a moment the two performed an awkward dance. She stepped aside and Mohammed followed Ted out the door.

Ted checked the windshield as he approached the car. Against all reason and expectations, there was no orange parking ticket under the wiper blade.

Ted's thoughts were ranging from fact to fiction and all

points in between. He was primarily concerned that Hillyer was hiding something from Mohammed. Whether it was on the level of annoyance or catastrophe, he couldn't be sure. And so, he worried.

"Where to, boss?"

Ted climbed into the back seat. "Did you know the word 'boss' comes to us from the Dutch? The first European immigrants to these shores. It's a very New York word."

"What it means?" Mohammed asked as he stabbed the start button.

"In Dutch? Hmm. I don't know. I suppose it means 'boss.'" He caught the reflection of Mohammed's eyes in the rearview mirror. His black eyes stared.

"What you thinking?"

Ted let out the sigh that had been threatening to strangle him. "I think that man is lying. Covering up something that cannot be good news for you. I'll tell you, *sadecki*, I am worried."

Mohammed nodded. "Same, same." And after a minute pause: "*Sa-di-qi.*"

Ted repeated the Arabic word for friend—correctly this time.

"He is left-handed. In Yemen, we are taught to use the right hand. The left hand is dirty."

"I guess I didn't notice."

"No. You are the right hand."

"You're right. I don't think I ever notice."

"I always do," Mohammed said. "So, what I do with this?" Mohammed held up a scrap of paper. There was a number on it. The first three digits were 917. A cell phone number.

"What is it?"

"That woman. She gave it to me."

Ted sat forward. "Say what? Did she say anything?"

Mohammed nodded. "She say, 'Call me.'"

"Then call her," Ted said. "Put her on speakerphone."

Mohammed plugged in the numbers. It rang only once.

"I'll call you back," the voice said.

KENZIE DIDN'T THINK SHE was capable of hitting anyone with a baseball bat, even this annoying woman, but the lady had stopped screeching.

"Who are you? Start talking," Kenzie said, summoning all the authority she possessed.

"I'm his wife. And I know who you are," the woman said with a sneer. She was regaining her purpose.

"Who?" Kenzie said.

"Naomi Spitzer. You must have known he had a wife."

Spitzer. For a moment Kenzie was stunned and could not respond. Too many questions fought to be first out of her mouth.

"Howard Spitzer?" she asked.

"Oh, please," Mrs. Spitzer said with a shake of her head. "I saw you. You're all over the internet."

Of course Kenzie was on the internet. It was practically part of the job description these days. Social media was the most efficient way of communicating with her supporters. She devoted an hour or so every day to posting, responding to messages and mail, and uploading pertinent pictures, articles, or videos. But she had never posted anything remotely linked to Howard Spitzer. It was time for her to take charge of the conversation.

Ted's Irish mist was turning to a Queens drizzle. "Where's your umbrella?" Kenzie asked as Mrs. Spitzer's bonnet shed water with each movement of her head.

"What?" the woman said, obviously taken aback.

"Oh, for fuck's sake," Kenzie said. "Come in out of the rain."
The woman looked at her, stunned.

Kenzie saw the bat in her hand. She reached around and stuck it behind the door. "Get in here." She stepped back and was mildly surprised that the stratagem worked. Naomi Spitzer shook the rain off her head, came up the step, and walked into Kenzie's living room where she removed the plastic bonnet, careful to keep water from dripping on the hideous brown carpeting.

"I'm making coffee," Kenzie said. "You can hang your coat on the back of the door." She ducked into the kitchen.

The woman must have been used to following orders, for once she crossed the doorsill she became quite meek, almost apologetic.

Kenzie started the coffee machine and opened the fridge. The milk smelled fresh—or at least not poisonous. But there was nothing else that looked appetizing. She reminded herself to come back later and throw out everything that had been there for more than three days.

She promised herself a trip to the bakery as soon as she dealt with Mrs. Spitzer.

"How do you take your coffee?" she asked.

"Oh, I don't need any."

"It's made." Kenzie allowed some of her impatience with this dishrag of a woman to show.

"Oh, all right then. A little milk." A pause. "If you have it."

The woman's voice was strained. Quiet. Submissive. And phlegmy. She was crying.

Kenzie took a long, slow breath and returned to the living room. Mrs. Spitzer was seated on the couch, openly weeping. She wasn't nuts; she was grieving.

Kenzie sat next to the woman and handed her the coffee. Then she waited. It didn't take long.

"Did you kill him?" the woman asked in a surprisingly nonjudgmental tone.

Kenzie told herself to keep chill. The woman was going through a lot. "No."

"I would understand if you did. I would have killed him if I'd found the nerve. Which would be never."

The police had also assumed Kenzie was the killer—and might still. She vowed that the next time she came across a dead body she would simply keep on walking.

"Mrs. Spitzer. I never met the man."

Her head whipped around. "There's no reason to hide it. You weren't his first. I'm sure you've guessed that."

"Your husband was dead when I got there."

"He wasn't a good man. His mother knew. She tried to warn me. I thought she was interfering. A jealous mother. 'No woman is good enough for my child.' That whole thing, you know?"

"I don't know what to say, Mrs. Spitzer."

"He didn't even bother to hide it anymore. He laughed when I accused him. How could a person grow so cruel?"

"I can't say. I didn't know the man."

"Then why were you there?" she asked in a suddenly challenging tone.

"I was helping a friend. A client."

"The website said you were his paramour."

Kenzie smiled at the word. Were there still such things in the twenty-first century?

And then the import of her meaning hit.

"What website are we talking about?"

"TheWordNYC. All one word."

"Never heard of it."

"I'll show you," Mrs. Spitzer said, and pulled out her iPhone. They waited while the device searched for, and finally found, sufficient bars to operate. "Here it is," she said, thrusting the smartphone at Kenzie.

DID DO-GOODER SLAY PARAMOUR? read the headline over a picture of Kenzie borrowed from the Stop the Spike website. The article was short on hard facts, using words and phrases such as "reportedly" and "according to" while referring to unnamed sources. It was an ugly hatchet job. And poorly written, with "there" used when the writer clearly meant "their."

Kenzie was described as a radical provocateur. Another old-fashioned word. The article did not state that the man was a serial adulterer, but a reader would have to be brain-dead not to figure it out.

One major source, she determined, had to be someone on the police force. To her knowledge, Kenzie's status as a witness or subject had not been made public. Who else would have known that she'd been questioned by detectives?

The website itself was both professional and slick in appearance, but that was no indication of journalistic integrity. With the right software and sufficient time, anyone with moderate computer skills could have put this together.

"Who are these people?" Kenzie asked.

"The police are telling me nothing, so I googled *Howard Spitzer news* and this came up."

"You've never seen this website before?"

Mrs. Spitzer shook her head. "Should I have?"

Kenzie scrolled through the homepage. All the other articles were either about celebrity scandals or gruesome murders, and all cribbed from other websites. The whole effort was designed to draw readers to the main page—and this story.

The full horror came on slowly.

"Excuse me," Kenzie said, and fetched her laptop. She did a search for *McKenzie Zielinski* and the expected sites were listed. The organization website, the local newspapers like the *Courier*, the *Ledger*, *Daily Eagle*, and so on. Mostly quotes. A few photos. Nothing from the *Post*, of course—the *Post* adored Ron Reisner. (Currently. The always-fickle afternoon tabloid could switch sides faster than Mohammed changed lanes.) And there were too few mentions for the *Daily News* to show up on the first page. She advanced the page. No sign of TheWordNYC.

She started a new search. *Stop the Spike.* Their website was second on the scroll. First was the offending article. How in hell could that be possible? The organization wasn't even mentioned in the article.

Kenzie was not prone to panic. Crises energized her. But for a moment she felt lightheaded and nauseated. Her hand was shaking. Who? Who? That fool of a talent agent? Unlikely. Whoever did this had some rudimentary computer skills.

"Mrs. Spitzer, I am so sorry for what you are going through. But you have to believe me. This story is a fabrication. An evil trick. I am going to find out who did this. And I have to get started right now."

33

"SO, WE WAIT." TED absently checked his watch. A Bulova. A birthday gift from Kenzie. It was not showy or expensive. It kept time in an exemplary fashion. And, most importantly, it was not a constant reminder of his ex-wife. That watch, also not showy but much more expensive, sat in a box at the back of his sock drawer.

Mohammed started the car and the heater roared.

The first rush from the vents was a frigid blast no colder than the air outside—though it always felt that way. "You cold?"

"No," Mohammed said. "Traffic cop."

"I thought you were immune from tickets."

"Not when I have a passenger."

Ted regretted saying anything. There was a Mad Hatter's tea party quality to Mohammed's understanding of New York parking violations. And upon reflection, that may have been the appropriate response in a city that had been creditably accused by the *New York Post* of pursuing alleged scofflaws after altering hundreds of thousands of tickets that had been mistakenly filled out by police or traffic wardens and should have been invalid.

At that moment the front door of the building opened and Mrs. Hillyer, wrapped in a long black overcoat, came out and strode down the block.

"Aiii," Mohammed said.

"Agreed. Follow her?"

Mohammed pulled away from the curb. They hadn't traveled more than half a block before the woman ducked into Yasmeen's

Bakery. Mohammed hit the brakes and put on the flashers, prompting the driver in the car behind them to lean on his horn. Somehow, Mrs. Hillyer failed to notice the disturbance.

She purchased a tiny cup of coffee from the counterwoman and carried it to the lone table where she sat and took a cell phone out of her coat pocket. She punched a button.

Mohammed's phone rang.

"Are you alone?" She sounded tense.

Mohammed questioned Ted with a raised eyebrow. Ted nodded.

"I have no fare."

The horn sounded again from behind them. Mohammed lowered the window and waved the other car around.

"What happened to the lawyer?" she asked.

"Asshole!" the driver yelled as he careened past them.

"What?" Mrs. Hillyer squawked.

Mohammed raised the window. "He had an appointment."

Ted was impressed. Mohammed sounded calm, in control, and thoroughly innocent. Like most of the lawyers Ted had ever known, he had an exaggerated faith in his ability to discern when a witness was lying. Mohammed was good.

"I want you to know my husband was lying to you," Mrs. Hillyer said.

"What? What he is lying?" Mohammed let a touch of panic show in his voice.

"I can help you."

"Sure, sure. What do I do?"

"I can wipe out your bill."

Mohammed looked at Ted for guidance. Ted didn't have any—yet.

"I paid Mr. Spitzer."

"Not according to the firm's records. My husband will go after you. Take you to court. You need my help."

Ted watched the woman. She was facing the street, but her focus was on the table in front of her. Her shoulders were hunched, and she gripped the phone like a lifeline. She was agitated. Desperate.

"Find the book. The book shows I paid."

"There is no book," she sneered. "If you want to settle this, you need to listen to me."

The blatant arrogance of her approach said a lot to Ted about both her character and her desperation. It also suggested that she fully expected it to work. She was pushy, sloppy, and lacked finesse, but she'd succeeded before.

"What do I do?" Mohammed asked again.

"That's better," she purred. "Records show you owe more than forty grand. Bring me half that and I'll see that the balance disappears."

"Half? You are talking ten thousand dollars. Where do I find this money?"

The woman apparently failed to notice that Mohammed had halved the total and then halved it again.

"I'm cutting you a big break. You'll find it."

"I don't have money. I work. My wife works. Her son works. But we have nothing like that."

Ted gave him a thumbs-up. He was doing well. Ted wished he'd had the foresight to record the call. He looked back at her as he pulled out his phone.

Mrs. Hillyer was now shaking her head wildly. The sunglasses slipped and landed in front of her. She grabbed at them, but for a moment Ted saw her bright red eyeball and the bruising surrounding it. She hadn't gotten that walking into a door. Someone—her husband, Ted guessed—had hit her hard.

Ted motioned for Mohammed to put his hand over the phone. "Negotiate. See how low she'll go."

"You ask too much. I can never get that money. Some, maybe."

"How much?" she snapped back.

"I don't know," he whined. "Maybe two."

"Two! No. You need to do better. Ask your lawyer friend. Get him to loan you the money."

She had not hung up. She was willing to take less. "Tell her you have to talk to me. You'll get back to her."

Mohammed did so, with enough stammers and doubt in his voice to be believable.

"Make it quick. We need to do this right away."

"I should give the money to Mr. Hillyer?" Mohammed asked. He was enjoying himself and doing better than Ted could have imagined.

"No!" she squealed. "This is between us. I'll deal with him."

A nest of snakes. Each one ready to strike at the next. Mohammed needed a new lawyer. And Ted needed to let Detective Duran know his victim was a slimeball crook—and the rest of the clan was just as bad.

"Hang up," he said. "Let's get out of here. The stench is getting to me."

34

THEY WERE STUCK ON Queens Boulevard. Ted could see the red and blue lights flashing two blocks up. Mohammed had jumped the light and they now found themselves trapped in the left-hand lane. A few yards behind them cars were making the turn onto Fifty-First Avenue in order to come back down on Broadway and get past the accident. Mohammed could only fume.

"They should back up so we can all do that," he muttered. He put the car in reverse and edged back an inch, earning a horn blast but no movement. "Aiii."

Ted thought the man's aggressive driving might have brought this upon them. If they'd stayed with the flow, they would now be traveling up Fifty-First Avenue. He kept this insight to himself.

A question occurred to him. He rang Lester.

"Give me a sec. I gotta step outside."

That meant Lester was probably in the records room. Cell phones were not allowed. The ban included earbuds.

A moment later his voice came back. "Here. Whaddya need?"

"I want you to find a case. Unfortunately, I don't know the name of either plaintiff or defendant."

"It's Saturday, partner."

"Of course it is," Ted said, giving himself a mental face-palm. "I thought you must be in the records room because you couldn't take a call." Losing track of the day of the week was a sure sign of being overworked, overstressed, and over in general.

"I'm in church."

Ted ingested this and let it settle. "You're kidding, right?"

"What do I often do on a Saturday?"

Visit his granddaughters. Drink.

"Ah. You're watching college basketball." In a bar.

"Can this wait until Monday?"

"It will have to, I suppose."

"Give me the deets."

"I want to see if Hillyer is bent. Spitzer was a crook. Hillyer's wife is too. It's beyond belief that he's not involved in anything shady. Can you run his name and see what comes up?"

"First thing."

"Do what you can." Ted's phone buzzed. Another incoming call. Kenzie. "I gotta go. Talk later." He opened the other line. "How's your day going? Any better?"

"I need to sue a website. Who do you know who can do that for us?" Kenzie paused. "Cheap."

A great number of questions came to Ted's mind. "If it's possible, I'm sure we can find someone."

"What do you mean? If it's possible. Why wouldn't it be?"

She was already fighting mad with someone; his task was to keep from taking that person's place.

"Can we start over? Maybe you could tell me what happened."

"You sound testy. Are you all right?"

"I'm sorry." Ted didn't feel testy. Cautious. Tentative, possibly. "We're stuck in traffic." Always a good excuse for any kind of aberrant behavior.

"I had a visitor. Mrs. Naomi Spitzer."

"The widow," Ted replied.

Mohammed hit the horn again, though no one around them could move. It was an ineffectual cry for attention.

"Herself. At the door." Kenzie went on, relating the whole crazy incident.

"We could have taken the LIE," Ted said, with one hand over his phone.

"First rule of driving in Queens," Mohammed said. "Never take the LIE."

"Are you listening to me?" Kenzie asked.

"Mos def," Ted said. He listened without comment until she was done. Then, "What is this website?"

"It's all over the internet now, being reposted everywhere. Deepa says it's on Facebook, Twitter, Instagram, probably Truth Social too, but I haven't looked."

"Yeah, but . . . reposted from where?"

"Oh. TheWordNYC. I'll text you the link."

An ambulance had threaded its way through the light and now emitted two long brays of impatience. There was nowhere to go.

Ted opened the message. "I like that picture."

"Stop."

"It's very Joan of Arc."

"You know she was burned at the stake," Kenzie said.

"And achieved immortality. Name one of the monarchs involved in that war. I can't."

"Please, stop. I need your help."

"Of course. It's not true, right? You weren't having a mad affair with a man you never met."

"What? Of course not."

The ambulance let loose with an insistent howl.

"I didn't really think so. Come on, this is nonsense. I know you better than to believe this trash."

"You don't get it, do you?"

The SUV behind them angled to the left and with a sudden lunge mounted the lane divider, cruised over the

178 • MICHAEL SEARS

pedestrian crosswalk, and continued into the turn lane for
oncoming traffic. Many horns were sounded but against all
odds no cars collided. That maneuver put the ambulance
directly behind them. Ted looked over his shoulder. The letters
E C N A L U B M A filled the rear window.

"No. I don't get it. Why do we care?"

"I'm a public figure. That story is now linked to the Stop
the Spike pages. Anybody who looks for information on what
we're trying to do will see it. That's why this is a problem. It's
defamation."

The ambulance sounded off again and it was now impossible to carry on a conversation.

"Mohammed. Can't you do something?"

Mohammed glowered in the rearview but he inched the car
forward, put on his flashers, and held his hand down on the
horn. The combined cacophony had an effect. Cars began to
move, squeezing three lanes of traffic into two. Mohammed
rushed forward as soon as the car in front of them cleared
to the right. Ted could see the next driver looking frantically
to either side until finally he drove into a gap that suddenly
appeared. Mohammed sped up. And now they were rolling—the
ambulance directly on their heels. Siren still going strong. But
the lane ahead was open and Mohammed floored it. Seconds
later they flew past Van Loon Street and the two police cruisers
blocking the scene of the accident. Ted had a moment's view
of a tricked-out Maxima which had been inserted under an
Amazon tractor trailer on its way to the Maspeth warehouse.

And then they were gone. Out of the bog and racing down
Queens Boulevard at Mohammed's standard nineteen miles
an hour over the posted speed limit.

"Okay?" Mohammed turned his head to face Ted directly.
"Better?"

It had been in the top ten most electrifying eight seconds

of Ted's life. And he would have liked for Mohammed to keep his eyes on the road ahead. He was glad that Lester hadn't been there. It would have marked a permanent end to their fragile peace.

"Ted? Are you there?"

"I'm sorry. There was an accident on Queens Boulevard."

"That's not newsworthy."

"Sorry." He was using that word all too often these days. "Defamation. That's legit. It's written, so it's libel. Slander is oral. I think you have to prove actual harm."

"I would think that's obvious. Loss of new donations."

"Maybe, but I don't know how you'd *prove* it. Document it, I mean. It's not like you got fired because of that story. Or had a contract taken away."

"You don't want to fight this."

"I am fighting the biggest losing battle of my life right now. LBC will eventually crush me. The developers always win in the end. But in this case, I think we can get more out of it by using a little strategy."

"Explain."

"We need to find out where the story came from. Detective Duran didn't call up some journalist working out of a Starbucks and throw you to the wolves. This came from somewhere else. Someone with connections."

"Ron Reisner. He hates me enough."

"It has the Reisner smell to it, yes, but let's keep our minds open. There might be two people in New York who don't like you."

"In the meantime, that story is out there."

"Maybe. We can threaten to sue. See if they retract, or at least back off. Give it a week or two and the internet will be back to Trump or the Kardashians or whatever Kanye is calling himself these days."

"I want to find the people responsible and destroy them."

"Revenge? The courts rarely provide an adequate level of revenge."

"I'm serious, Ted. This is personal."

"A court case could take years. Delay is the name of the game. Meanwhile you'll be asked to prove that you weren't screwing this guy."

"What? But it's a lie. I wasn't."

"And you will have to prove that the story was meant to harm you, not just to inform the public."

"Bullshit."

"No doubt. But the story will stay on the internet the whole time. There will be constant speculation and you and I will not be able to stop it."

"Aaaahhh!" she screamed into the phone. Frustration, not fear.

"Exactly," Ted said.

SUNDAY

35

"NINA PACHIS?" DEEPA ASKED.

"Who?" Ted knew he was supposed to recognize the name but couldn't be bothered to finesse it. He was admittedly cranky. It was Sunday morning and already it had been a really long weekend.

"Wife of Artie Pachis. Contributor. Developer." Kenzie rattled off the information in an impatient machine-gun delivery.

"Right," Ted said. Gold jewelry. Boorish husband. "I remember."

Kenzie had called the meeting. Deepa, Ted, and the Preacher were gathered with her in the living room of their apartment away from any other listeners. "She's in publicity. And she offered."

"Wait," Deepa asked. "She knows about this?"

"No, no. I don't know. But she made a blanket offer the other night," Ted said. He turned to Kenzie. "Does she do this kind of crisis consulting? We don't need someone who's going to get us more eyes on the site."

"I don't know," Kenzie said. "All I know is that she offered, and we need someone. And we can't pay."

"Slander is like a scorching fire," the Preacher said, his deep bass immediately commanding attention, though he spoke softly. "Take the higher path. Turn your face and continue with your work. These attacks must not steer you from your path. They are a distraction. Their slander will bring about their demise."

Ted's inclination was to agree with him, but he held back. He knew from his own history that perception often outweighed fact, and that a negative scenario took on its own momentum. He might have weathered such accusations and shrugged them off, but this was Kenzie. She was no delicate flower—she was strong and resilient—but she was young and a woman and the face of the movement. She would be lambasted, or worse, made to look laughable. What would hurt her the most would be the effect on the organization she had built.

"My girls are already getting calls," Deepa said. "They need guidance. Reassurance. And mostly, they need a plan. What do we tell our people? Without their support we got zilch."

"Why don't I call and ask her? Either she can help, or she can't. She knows we can't pay, so she's got no reason to sell us on something she can't deliver."

No one raised an objection.

Ted beamed at her. Direct to the heart of the matter. Storm the ramparts. Damn the torpedoes. She wasn't fearless—he'd heard her late-night worries about failure—but she was brave. Fear didn't stop her.

"Can we listen in?" Deepa asked.

Kenzie nodded as she picked up her phone. She was scanning through the donor list, looking for the number, when the phone rang. Kenzie's eyes widened. "It's her. *She's* calling *me*."

"She knows," Deepa said.

Kenzie answered and put the phone on speaker. "Hi, Nina. I was about to call you."

"McKenzie, we need to talk." She made it sound like *she* needed to talk, and Kenzie needed to listen.

"So you've seen it," Kenzie replied.

"It? What?" Then in an abrupt return to her previous tone, she demanded, "Do you remember me mentioning that my husband's most generous donation *had* to remain anonymous? Do you?"

Eyes widened around the room. Nina was thoroughly pissed off and making no attempt to hide it. And the implication of her words was unnerving.

"Nina, we all knew. I'm here with Ted and senior staff. We most assuredly knew Artie wanted his participation kept quiet. What happened?"

"That's what I expect you to tell me. He called a few minutes ago in an unholy snit. Ron Reisner got in his face at the New York AC and reamed him out. Threatened him. Said Artie was a dead man. Called him all kinds of names and told him he was going to sue—though I can't imagine what for."

No one went to the New York Athletic Club on a Sunday morning to work out. They went to see and be seen by the city's power elite. The bar was busier than the lap pool. This would have been a very public confrontation.

Deepa gasped. Kenzie repeated the words, "What the . . . ? What the . . . ?" The Preacher made a sound that could have been a low growl. Ted felt a headache coming on.

36

DEEPA AND THE PREACHER left with nothing resolved. Had someone leaked the donors list? Or was this a random bit of gossip provided by any one of the more than two hundred people present? There was no way to tell.

"Want any more coffee?" Kenzie asked when she was alone with Ted. "I'll start a fresh pot."

Ted didn't think coffee would do much for his sour mood, but it might get him thinking and there was plenty to think about. "A short one," he said.

"I told you about the gas guy, right?"

It took Ted a moment to resurrect the conversation from days ago. Kenzie had been understandably upset about discovering a dead body. A visit from the gas company hadn't made much of an impression upon him. "Hmm," he answered.

"It turns out, he was over at the church. On Friday."

This brought him to full alert. "Did you see him? Was it the same man?"

"I think so, but I didn't see him. Ashley described this monster mustache."

"Did he get inside?" Ted asked.

She hit the button for robust and turned to face him. "No. Deepa told him to get lost."

"Good for her. Could he have gotten in here?"

"He was knocking on the door when I saw him." The coffee machine gasped behind her.

"Maybe he'd just come out."

"Where are you going with this?" She placed hands on hips. Her fighting stance.

"I want to know if he could have come in and planted a bug. A listening device. We were just talking about leaked information. I don't think it's much of a stretch to think Reisner sent someone around to bug our home or your office."

Kenzie's eyes widened and her mouth formed a perfect O. But her expression immediately morphed into one of iron resolve. "That bastard."

They both paused to let it all sink in. The coffee machine hissed.

"I'll make a call tomorrow and get somebody here to do a sweep," Ted said.

"They won't find anything," she said with a surety he thought more of a wish than a promise.

She poured a mug and reached out to hand it to him. There was a hearty knock at the door and Kenzie flinched, splashing her hand with fresh hot coffee.

"Fuck! That hurt."

Ted took the cup from her, and she ran to the sink.

"I'll get it," Ted said.

"I don't want to talk to anybody right now," she said, running cold water over her wrist.

"Gotcha." Ted peeked out. "I don't know if we've got a choice. It's the detective. Duran."

"Oh, wait. Him I want to talk to."

37

"**YOU'RE HERE ABOUT THAT** bogus news article, aren't you?" Kenzie asked a second after Duran crossed the threshold.

"No," Duran answered. "Mind if I sit?"

Ted gestured to the couch.

"Yes." Kenzie didn't want him comfortable.

"Thank you," Duran said, his butt already landing on the couch.

"That story's a fake. Even the NYPD can see that." She knew he was not there to investigate that offensive article: he wanted her to participate in putting some luckless soul behind bars for having murdered a corrupt lawyer who preyed on penniless refugees. Not going to happen. She'd seen nothing that might help him.

"I've seen it," the detective said. "And I agree with you."

"Do you agree that the source for that story is someone involved in the investigation? In other words, a cop." Offense was always the best defense, whether in sports, politics, or arguments.

Duran leaned forward, shaking his head. "Nooo." A longer, more emphatic response. "I'm here to question a witness to a murder."

"I can't be a witness because I didn't see anything."

"Give me five minutes," the detective said.

"Not a chance," Kenzie shot back.

"Look, Detective, maybe you don't get it." Ted said, still on his feet and now commanding the room. "Maybe you think this story is a joke. A prank. I don't know. But this little prank will hit us hard. It's personal, sure. Humiliating. But the office is getting bombarded with calls. People will believe it because people are like that. And if it makes them pull away from the organization we may as well fold up the tents and go home."

Ted was at his best—clothed, at any rate—as an advocate, fighting with words. If she were the swooning type, this would be the moment. She could now forgive him all those sleepless nights when he was in the living room watching *Law & Order* marathons.

"You're wrong, Mr. Molloy." The detective pinched the bridge of his nose and closed his eyes. When he spoke again it was with resignation. "I take it seriously. But I can't do anything about it. The leak—and I don't know that there was one—did not come from me, or my partner, or anyone else on our team."

"Can the department issue a statement?" Kenzie pressed hard, despite knowing the odds were against her. "Say just that. It's something I can show to my people that says we're working on it. We're in the fight." She could no more have held back than suddenly sprouted wings and launched herself out the window.

Duran shook his head. "There is zero chance that the NYPD will issue a statement like that. I wouldn't even ask 'cause my LT would think I lost my mind."

"Can you at least tell us who would have known?" Ted asked, dropping into his chair.

"Have you two considered that this bull pucky was created by the murderer?"

Kenzie had not. She looked at Ted. He had. Goddamn him. He was protecting her again. She hated when he did that. She should have thought it through rather than allow herself to get stuck in reaction mode.

"Is that the focus of the investigation now?" she asked.

"I came here to ask you a few questions."

"But you're following up on that idea, right?"

Duran held up both hands, whether in surrender or defense Kenzie couldn't have said. "I'm working a murder. I understand what you're going through, but I have a job to do. A man is dead."

"Do you have any suspects?" Ted asked.

"None I will discuss with you," Duran answered.

"Interested in any fresh information?"

Duran squinted at him. "You're not a witness."

"Neither am I," Kenzie reminded him.

Ted hunched forward and spoke softly, inviting Duran to listen carefully. "I visited Mr. Hillyer yesterday morning."

"Interfering in a police investigation? That didn't work out so good last time."

Ted grimaced. "And yet you got your killer. But that's not why we were there. I went with a friend. A client of Spitzer's who's afraid he was getting a runaround."

"Name?"

"Mohammed Mahdi. He's in the clear. I told you about him. He was taking a fare to Roslyn."

Duran shrugged dismissively.

Ted ignored the skeptical response. "Spitzer was cheating him, though the partner is now lying to cover it up. The partner is lying about a lot of things. If I were in your shoes, I'd take a long look at him. Check the books, too. They were cheating each other."

"I can't discuss this with you."

"The rumor around the courthouse was Spitzer was screwing Mrs. Hillyer—not exclusively—but now she's got a black eye."

Kenzie had not heard this before. She was impressed. Not

that Ted had found this out, but that he had not idly passed on gossip until it became relevant.

Duran was shaking his head. "Hillyer's got an alibi. He was in court that morning and didn't get back until after Ms. Zielinski called 911. End of story."

"What forensic evidence do you have? DNA? Fingerprints?"

"No comment."

"Surveillance?" Ted went on. "The NYPD supposedly has the best facial recognition capabilities in the country."

"You're reading the wrong magazines," Duran said with a laugh. "But that does bring up this . . ." He produced an iPad from his overcoat pocket. He spoke to Kenzie. "Can you help?"

"What do you want?" she asked, prepared to offer nothing.

"Jesus!" Duran yelled and ducked. "God help us!"

A plane was passing overhead. Close overhead.

Kenzie smothered a laugh.

"Sorry." The detective shook his head and sat up straighter. When the sound had dropped to a level that again allowed for normal conversation, he said, "Does that go on all the time?"

"A few times a year when the wind comes a little east of south," Ted said. "We must have had a wind change."

"Mother of god," Duran said.

"It's runway 13 at LaGuardia," Ted explained. "They take off into the wind, bank overhead here so they don't interfere with flight paths for JFK, then head out east to clear the area before setting course. There'll be a few coming now."

"It sounds like they're right over the house."

Kenzie smiled unsympathetically. "You get used to it." She barely noticed anymore unless she was watching *The Great British Baking Show* and missed some of the dialogue.

The iPad had to be first generation. "I brought some pictures. Stills. From two cameras across the street from the nail salon."

Kenzie froze. Suppose she did recognize someone. She didn't want to do this, but short of tossing Duran out the door, she was stuck. She reminded herself, she hadn't seen anyone.

"I saw a pair of shoes."

Duran stared hard at her for a moment before speaking again. "Neither camera is state of the art. As you can see, facial recognition isn't going to work. I'm looking for anything. An impression. An attitude."

He swiped slowly through the photos. All were gray and fuzzy. The cameras hadn't been focused on the front door to the building, but on the commercial space—the nail salon. What was caught in each case was a shadowed figure in the background entering or exiting the main door.

"No women?" Kenzie asked.

"Three. All easily identified. The secretary, what's-his-name's wife, and you."

"Hillyer," Ted offered.

"That's it. Sorry, my caffeine level must be getting low."

Was this a none-too-subtle request for a cuppa? Kenzie thought, *the hell with him.* This wasn't a social call. Next time he could bring coffee. For three.

"I don't recognize anyone," she said.

"I understand. What I want now is for you to see if any of these ring a bell. Too tall, too short, just right? Too fat or thin? You get what I'm going for?" He opened the iPad and again swiped slowly through the pictures, watching her face the whole time.

The first showed a very round man in a knee-length over-coat. "The person I saw was wearing a hoodie." She paused and thought—she almost said "kid." Why? Maybe it was the way he moved? "Wrong coat. Wrong build. No. But you knew that."

"You're doing great. Keep going." The picture changed.

She didn't want to do great. "Same guy, different angle."

"Right. Next." Duran swiped again.

"No," she said almost immediately. He had the hoodie. And he wore a denim jacket over the hoodie. A long white scarf dangled loosely down to his waist. But he was too tall. And he held himself like a dancer. "He's got to be there for the Polish talent guy."

Ted gave her a quizzical look—which she ignored. The old man. Another extraneous moment in the story of that horrendous day.

Another picture.

"Same guy. Only now he's coming out of the building."

Another plane roared past. They all waited. Ted and Kenzie patiently. Duran, a bit unnerved.

"What makes you think he's visiting the old man?" the detective asked when the roar had diminished.

Kenzie allowed herself an eye roll. "He's a dancer. The old guy books talent." She held back the "duh" that had formed on her tongue. She looked at the next picture. And froze.

The figure was slight. Not tall. The face was in shadow. The picture cut off anything below the knees, so she could not see shoes. A black or navy blue hoodie. It could be the person she had seen. And it could be Haidir.

It could also easily be the young man she'd seen arguing with Haidir. Or any one of thousands of young men—and possibly some women—from all over Queens, skin color, build, and casual dress being so similar across so many ethnicities.

Her mind was playing tricks on her.

She felt Ted looking over her shoulder.

She leaned forward and swiped to the last photo. It showed the same person, but now she was positive. This was not Haidir.

"See something?" Duran asked.

"I didn't see anything." She could understand the awesome power of suggestion. She could feel it. And she wasn't going to let herself be talked into fitting up some brown-skinned person. Duran had a job to do, but she had nothing to offer. "I didn't see anything," she said again.

Ted was now staring at her.

So was the detective. They both could see right through her.

Ted face's showed concern, Duran's projected disappointment. In her.

Fuck him. She wasn't falling for it.

The stoic, professional shield came down. Duran stood. "You have my card. Call when you're willing to help."

"One minute, Detective." Ted looked up at the man. "Let me walk you out."

Duran considered the offer. "One minute."

Ted felt Kenzie's eyes on his back.

They stopped on the stoop. The wind cut through Ted's light sweater. This would be a short conversation.

"So, tell me," the detective said, hunching his shoulders against the cold.

"Both Hillyer and his wife are lying." Ted needed the detective to understand the dynamics he'd uncovered.

"So you said."

"She tried to pry twenty grand out of my guy."

"Who might have been driving a fare out to the Island, or maybe not. The guy's got motive."

"If you want to talk to him, I'll set it up."

Duran turned up his collar. "Fair enough."

Ted wanted to finish this up and get warm again. But he needed Duran to hear him out. "This business with his legal bills? He paid cash. Who takes cash for legal services? People with something to hide."

"I'm listening."

"The guy's wife and stepson have all been going to this lawyer for years. And yet Hillyer couldn't pull up any information on his refugee case or the stepson's naturalization. Nada. The father doesn't even have a file, according to Hillyer. It looks like Spitzer took cash and did nothing. There could be dozens of defrauded clients with good motive to whack him over the head."

Duran shook his head. "My partner talked to Hillyer. He maintains Spitzer was a good guy and that the firm is legit. Everybody liked him."

"You do know that not everybody is as honest and forthcoming as I am?"

"And don't forget the magic word. Alibi. Anything else you want to add?"

"Talk to Hillyer yourself."

The door swung open. Kenzie stared at them. "You're still here? Come on, Ted. You must be freezing."

Ted looked at her. Duran knew she was holding back. There wasn't going to be a better time for her to give it up.

She looked away.

Duran watched this interplay, probably correctly filling in all the words that hadn't been spoken. Then, with a long-suffering sigh, he stepped off the stoop. But he turned back once more. "I'll be in touch."

A plane roared by as Duran walked away down the alley.

38

"CARE TO SHARE?" TED asked when he'd stepped back inside and shaken off the chill. Kenzie had to trust someone, and Ted felt he had demonstrated that he was on her side.

"That picture?" she said in a small voice.

"I know. It could have been Haidir. Only it wasn't."

"I was embarrassed. I'm not a good liar."

"That's not a bad thing." Lying did not come naturally to her; to get good, she would have to practice a lot more.

"I don't mind lying for a good cause. But I don't like being bad at it."

As an officer of the court, Ted was proscribed from knowingly stating an untruth, and so like most honest lawyers, had become adept at saying nothing.

"What do we do?" she asked. She must have been seriously concerned, otherwise she'd already have worked out a plan and begun to implement it.

"Well, we start with Mohammed. If Haidir *was* there—"

"He wasn't."

"—the police will find out one way or another."

"He wouldn't have killed Spitzer." Her spirit was coming back.

"No," Ted said, though, having been taught by Jesuits, he held the opinion that anyone is capable of aberrant, destructive, even mentally deranged behavior given the impetus. Life wasn't fair and humans were a fragile species.

"We still have a problem," Kenzie said.

"Problems. Plural."

39

THE ONLY APPROACH KENZIE knew was forward—full speed. She had a problem. She needed a fix. She called Mr. Fix-It. Her father.

"Have you seen the news?" she asked when her father picked up.

"What news?"

"On the web. There's an ugly—and fake—story going around about me."

"Nah. Your mother told me not to read it. If it's not in the *Guardian* or the *Nation*, I wouldn't see it anyway." She knew he also read the *Wall Street Journal* to stay apprised of what "the enemy" was up to, though Peter Zielinski would never admit to paying for a subscription.

"Okay, so you know about it."

"Sure, sure."

"I need to find out who posted it."

"And how would I do that?" he asked, dashing her dreams of an easy fix.

She sighed. "I don't know. I was hoping you did."

"Me? Hoo boy. It's nice my daughter thinks her old man is such a genius, but I'm a hardware guy. I don't know nothing about content. I only go online to read the newspaper—and check email. And if it weren't for the business, I wouldn't do that."

"Don't you go on computer-geek websites? I thought that's where you learned how to fix them."

"And now you know all my secrets. When are you coming for dinner?"

"Not now."

"I know Ted doesn't like me, but I don't know how to talk to a guy like that."

"Like what?"

"He's always pretending. It's like I'm supposed to guess what disguise he's wearing every time I see him."

Ted had first met her father while posing as a close friend of hers. It had not gone well.

"And he doesn't like sports."

"He does. Mets baseball."

"Baseball is boring. He doesn't like hockey, football, or basketball. What kinda guy doesn't like basketball?"

Ted did like basketball. Amateur street-rules ball. An early date had been an afternoon watching pickup games at The Cage on Sixth Avenue in the city, and a pizza dinner at John's. They'd both agreed Brooklyn pizza was better. But he didn't follow professional basketball and so had nothing to say when the subject arose.

But rather than make a pointless defense of Ted, she attacked the underlying issue.

"Dad, stop. We'll come to dinner." She'd set the date with the parent who ruled the calendar. Her mother. "Wait! We are coming to dinner. Thanksgiving. Ten days. And that's the earliest because I've got too much going on right now."

"Thanksgiving already? Fine. A week, Thursday. You know something? You're right. About those websites. There's a guy who might be able to help. I'll message him. It can't hurt."

TED HAD TO BE in court the following afternoon to demand still more documents relevant to the traffic study, even though he had not yet examined any of the files that had already been delivered. He would file a motion to challenge the credentials of the LBC expert witness—a traffic-flow maven who, if allowed to testify, would do his best to convince the judge that there would be no adverse effects from disrupting one-way streets, six-lane highways, elevated trains, and a raised pedestrian walkway connecting Corona to the biggest park in Queens. If Ted prevailed, opposing counsel would be forced to produce evidence of the man's qualifications at some future date set by Judge Bagdasian and Ted would have won another minor delay. It was the legal equivalent of death by a thousand cuts. Still in his boxers and yesterday's shirt, Ted was huddled over his laptop making notes when Lester called.

"You want good news, bad news, or today's special combo?" Lester asked.

"What's up?"

"So I did a little hunting. Mr. Hillyer seems to be legit. Most of his business here is real estate. His name shows up on a lot of closings."

"As he indicated," Ted said.

"I can't access full divorce records, but both he and Marjorie have started proceedings and then dropped them. Multiple times. Going back years. Nobody's Couple of the Year."

"Other than being both corrupt and mercenary, she seemed nice enough."

"The combo platter is interesting. Hillyer is connected to Reisner. He fronts for him, buying up properties in a blind, and flipping them to LBC right after closing."

Such operations were legal as long as there was no intent to defraud or evade taxes. Anonymity often helped a deal get done.

"Reisner needed to replace the Russians," Ted said. Corona Partners had performed a similar function for LBC before resorting to muscle rather than brains. Their banker had fled the country when the whole structure went wrong side up. He was rumored to now be living in Malta.

"Hillyer's not the only one. Reisner has lined up an army of small-time lawyers to do his dirty work."

"Bottom line. Hillyer's dirty, unpleasant, mean to his wife, and has lousy taste in clients, but maybe not a crook."

"Lie down with dogs . . ."

"Get up with fleas," Ted finished. He checked the time. He'd arranged for a home security firm to come execute a check for listening devices. He didn't think they were going to find anything, but both he and Kenzie would feel better with that possibility off the table. They were due in ten minutes. "Are you still at the courthouse? I'll have Mohammed pick you up and then come get me. Give me an hour."

"Give me time to up my insurance."

41

WHEN KENZIE WALKED INTO the basement office, she found Deepa and the volunteers huddled around Ashley, all eyes glued to whatever was showing on the laptop. She heard her own voice—somewhat stilted, formal, and uncomfortable—emanating from the tinny speaker.

Deepa reacted to her presence first, and Kenzie saw a range of emotions flash across her face. Surprise. Embarrassment. Maybe a touch of fear.

But she recovered in an instant. "You must see this."

The two volunteers stepped aside, both of them watching her warily as though she might suddenly fly around the room on an imaginary broomstick.

Ashley looked up with a serious expression. "I found this on our Facebook page when I logged on today." She angled the MacBook in Kenzie's direction and tapped the keyboard. "I'm restarting it."

Kenzie stepped forward and watched as her face appeared on the screen. She recognized the scene immediately. She'd been interviewed for the public access news channel by a grad student from the journalism school at Columbia. The young woman was prepared and enthusiastic—but unpolished.

The video had been taped last spring on the sidewalk in front of the church. Kenzie's hair, still growing out from having been chopped by the doctors who had saved her life, was shorter and the white streak was more pronounced than now.

Kenzie almost turned away. It wasn't a great interview, and

she didn't need to be reminded of it. But her head snapped back at the first words.

"How do you address the accusations that your organization is secretly funded by rival developers who only want to see Ron Reisner fail?"

That was not what the woman had asked. Nothing like it. But she was half turned away from the camera, and she held her microphone too high. It partially covered her mouth. It would have been easy for any amateur video editor to rewrite the dialogue and have words that had never been spoken come out of her mouth.

Or Kenzie's mouth. She braced herself.

"I'm not prepared to discuss the funding for Stop the Spike. Our donors are accustomed to their privacy."

Practically an admission. She forced herself to keep watching. The voice was hers though the words were not.

"Some of your critics have pointed out that this project will benefit most the working poor in Corona and nearby neighborhoods—primarily Black and Latino populations." The video cut away to a shot of subway commuters—more brown- and black-skinned than yellow or white—in early-morning light, coming up the stairs at the 103rd Street station. "Why do you favor a perverse coalition of illegal immigrants and a cabal of wealthy, white landlords and NIMBY penthouse liberals?"

The scene shifted to a helicopter's point of view of sky-scraping gardens and palatial apartments in the clouds. It was gone too quickly to be sure, but Kenzie had the impression she was seeing rooftop Singapore or Dubai rather than Long Island City.

Kenzie's voice—or its simulacrum—returned. "The truth is, Judy, that undocumented refugees make excellent tenants." Two shots came up in quick succession. The first was a line of burka-clad women with children in tow disembarking from a school bus. Who knew where? The second was more ominous; bearded men with turbans looked back at the camera with undisguised anger and suspicion. "The federal government picks up the tab for housing them. Landlords can raise the rents without fear of any backlash, and they don't have to deal with spurious claims of substandard housing conditions." The camera came back to Kenzie's face. "People who've been sleeping outside for months don't complain about lack of heat or broken toilets, they're just glad to have a roof over their heads. It's a win-win."

Now she could see it. Anyone could. Both the visual and the audio had been manipulated. The words had been strung together from other clips, or, in some cases, spoken by some actor mimicking her voice. She wanted to laugh at it, but the feeling fled as the horror of it hit her.

"Where else is this? Instagram? TikTok?"

"Everywhere," Ashley said.

"Fucking hell. How long has this been on Facebook?"

Ashley craned her head over and tapped the keyboard. "Posted a little over an hour ago."

An hour. An eternity on the internet.

"Shares?"

Ashley did not look up. "Sixty-some and counting."

It could be worse. "Report it." She turned to Deepa. "Compose a message that the group has been hacked. Post it and then change your password. Let's hope that slows this down. I'm calling Ted."

One of the volunteers—a late-thirties Wall Streeter who'd taken a year off to have her first child and was suffering badly from hormone-related acne—stared at her open-mouthed. "That's it? You call Ted?"

"We need a lawyer. It's what he does."

"How could you say such things?"

Kenzie felt a real flash of anger. "That's not me talking," she snapped back. How could any of these women think it was?

"Oh, please. It was shot right out front. I even know that blouse. You wore it half a dozen times this summer."

The other woman—a box-shaped school bus driver and mother of three adorable grade school girls—yelled over her last words. "It's a fake, sweetie. Not even a good one."

The video was still playing, and the Not-Kenzie was now saying something about Reisner being an egotistical monster. That might not have been fake. "Turn that damn thing off, Ashley!" She sucked in a breath and tried for patience. "Please."

Kenzie turned to her stalwart, Deepa. "Do you believe that's me talking? What do you think?"

"I think it looks bad, Kenzie. But, I agree. It's a fake."

"Oh, god," the new mother said.

Lisa something, Kenzie remembered.

"I know you get stressed sometimes. We all do. Maybe you thought you were being ironic or something. I wish you hadn't said it to a reporter—on camera. That's not good."

Kenzie wrestled with her panic and managed to keep it in check. This was bad and threatening to spin out of control. Support came from a surprising source.

"Stop," Ashley cried. "Kenzie's right. This is doctored. I don't know how they did it, but it is fake." She hit replay. "Here." She looked up at the group. "You don't see it? Really? It's like TikTok lip-sync. Watch."

Deepa looked at the screen. The Wall Streeter did not. Lines were being drawn. The community spirit was breaking down faster than Kenzie would ever have imagined.

The brown-eyed bus driver turned to her with sympathy written large all over her face. "I don't know, Kenzie. I know it doesn't sound like something you'd say—even tired, cross, or being ironic, but it does look like you saying it."

"Oh, for fuck's sake. You have got to be kidding me."

Lisa whirled away, picked up her purse, and looped it over her shoulder. "I'm out of here," she said. "Call me when you figure this crap out. My husband already thinks I'm nuts working here for nada. He sees this, he'll start kicking the dog."

And she was gone.

"Let me talk to her," the bus driver said quietly. She left.

"It's like that app where you put heads of your friends on cartoon bodies and they sing 'Happy Birthday' or something," Ashley said.

"This is a goddamn nightmare." Kenzie faced off with Deepa. This had to be straightened out now or never. "That's not me. Are you with me or not?"

"I know that's not you, but it frightens me. And it's not me you need to convince."

The anger went out of her. Deepa was right. She'd already lost a valuable volunteer by reacting instead of managing. "I'm sorry. What's next? What am I forgetting?"

"We got this," Deepa said. "Call your boyfriend."

42

TED AGREED WITH DEEPA; the video made Kenzie look awful. He and Lester huddled in their booth at Gallagher's watching a third replay on Ted's phone, Lester occasionally uttering harsh growls. Even if you were familiar with Kenzie, her speech patterns, her mannerisms, the package was convincing. And the quality was beyond the powers of some random nutcase who had it in for Stop the Spike or its leader. The work was professional.

Which meant it came from Ron Reisner, or someone in his employ. It was inflammatory, riot-mongering rhetoric. And in direct violation of Ted's agreement with the coalition backing the LBC project. Players in that group, and that included Reisner himself, deserved to be in jail for making or taking bribes, covering for money launderers, and ordering assaults and worse on witnesses. The fact that almost none of these people had even been indicted ate at Ted's guts. And his conscience.

Now Reisner had gone back on the deal, putting Kenzie in the bull's-eye for any wing nut with a grudge. There was only one person Ted knew who could exert any control here. The man who had brokered the agreement: Judge Cornelius Fitzmaurice.

When they had last met, Ted had willingly ceded his testimony in exchange for the promised safety of his friends. Reisner had sent his Russian accomplices to beat up Lester and murder Kenzie. They had failed—twice—at the latter, but Ted would not have risked a third attempt. It was a one-sided deal—guilty people walked away unscathed while the bit players suffered the most—but he would do it again in a heartbeat.

Ted contemplated tactics. After his divorce and break with the family, whenever he needed to speak with the Judge, for any reason, he would rely upon his ex-wife to persuade her grandfather to get in touch. But Jill blamed Ted for the disaster that left her wife confined to a wheelchair and they had not spoken in well over a year. When Jill saw his name come up on her caller ID, she would, most likely, ghost him, if he was not already blocked.

So, he borrowed Lester's phone and made the call.

"Who is this? And what are you selling?"

Ted was only slightly surprised at Jill's greeting. Telephone civility had succumbed to the onslaught of robocalls, scammers, pollsters, salespeople, politicians, and charitable organizations seeking funds.

"It's Ted, Jill. Please don't hang up."

There was a long silence, and he was afraid she had already done just that.

"What do you want?"

He let out the breath he'd been holding. "I have to talk to your grandfather."

"He's sick." Her voice made it clear she would have much preferred to say the same of Ted.

"I'm so sorry, Jill. Is it serious?"

"Pancreatic cancer."

As serious as it can get. "Again, I apologize for bothering you. I'll go now."

"Leave him alone."

"Goodbye, Jill."

Her grief spilled out in an angry wave. "He's been in and out of the hospital for months. This time they say the next step is hospice." And if she could have blamed Ted for it, she would have.

"My condolences." As he'd already made his goodbye, he said no more but ended the call.

"So, what'd you find out?" Lester asked.

Ted took a moment before answering. He and the Judge had once been close and despite their recent differences, the sad news weighed on his chest. "He's dying. Cancer. He's in the hospital."

"MSK or New York?"

"I didn't ask. Why those two?"

"They're in his neighborhood. Give me the phone." Lester hit the speakerphone icon. "Hey, Siri. Call New York Hospital."

A moment later a robot answered. Lester hit zero. And again. And again.

"New York Hospital," a female human announced.

"Good afternoon," Lester began, speaking with an Irish lilt. "I'm here in New York for the day and just found out that my uncle is there. When can I see him?"

"Your uncle's name, sir?"

Lester's eyes went wide and he looked to Ted.

"Cornelius," Ted whispered.

"Cornelius Fitzmaurice," Lester said into the phone.

"One moment."

They waited.

"Why Irish?" Ted whispered.

Lester covered the phone with one hand. "Because when I try to do 'white,' I sound like Ned Flanders on *The Simpsons*."

"Sir? Visiting with Mr. Fitzmaurice is limited to family."

"Ah, bless you, my dear. Did I not mention that the Judge is my uncle? Edward Molloy is my name."

He went on, charming, schmoozing, and cajoling in an

accent that sounded, to Ted's ears, thoroughly authentic. And in time he wore her down.

"You can see him any time up until nine this evening, but you may have to wait. Only one visitor allowed at a time."

"Saint Malachy protect you, and I am forever in your debt." He hit the red button. "Shall we go?"

"Malachy?" Ted asked.

"First native-born Irishman to be canonized. Call Mohammed."

"I'm dialing."

43

LESTER, WHO DID NOT drive and had no license, sat shotgun, so that he could "keep one eye on the road" with Mohammed at the wheel. Ted ignored their bickering and the navigational instructions from Mohammed's new GPS—in Arabic.

He owed much to the Judge. Against all rhyme and reason, the man had picked his résumé out of the pile, and after an interview that lasted all morning, had offered Ted a clerkship, the first step on his ascending ladder. The Judge had later seen Ted hired at his family's firm, and championed him when Ted began dating, and later married, the Judge's favorite grandchild. And still later when Ted's career was in decline and his marriage was in tatters, the old man had stood by him as Ted hit bottom. His counsel had come without price or demands.

But his might had always been evident—and frightening. The Judge held power and granted it. He was fair in his rulings but leaned hard toward those with wealth and connections. He kept his word and demanded reciprocity. Those who disappointed him found there were no second chances.

The cyberattacks on Kenzie violated the very private agreement that Ted had made with the Judge. Ted had to see his old mentor. He had nothing to offer, and a dying man had nothing to lose. But Ted had to try.

Lester made a sound like a throttled chicken as Mohammed aggressively accelerated through the last flickers of yellow on the traffic light onto Queens Boulevard, creating for a moment a third lane approaching the bridge. An Empire Liquor delivery truck rolled forward, and Mohammed squeezed in after it, earning an angry honk from the CVS truck behind.

"You are nervous passenger," Mohammed said, unfazed by these maneuvers. "You should ride in back seat."

"Or somebody else's back seat," Lester grumbled.

Ted was nervous. He had no idea what to expect and therefore had no plan. He had never appeared before any judge, least of all this one, without some clearly thought-out strategy.

And then it was too late to be nervous. They pulled up in front of the hospital entrance. "They're not going to let me stay long, so don't go far. I'll text you when I'm on my way out."

At the security desk, he had to attest that he did not have Covid, or the flu, and had not traveled outside the country in the last two weeks. None of those applied to him, but he wondered what the penalty was for lying.

Judge Cornelius Fitzmaurice warranted a private room with a window facing the East River high enough to provide a view of Astoria beyond Roosevelt Island. The bed was aligned so that the patient faced that way rather than the door. Ted had to come fully into the room before he saw the old man. He stopped as soon as he did. The Judge looked practically mummified with dry, sallow skin and only a few wispy strands of hair on his mottled scalp.

Monitors were hooked up to both arms, as was an IV drip and a morphine pump so he could self-administer for pain. The nurses were obviously not concerned he would become addicted. He wasn't going to be around long enough.

His eyes were closed, but he did not look peaceful. His

facial muscles ticked into a grimace, relaxed, and then spasmed again, baring his startling white teeth in an ugly grin.

Ted sat in the padded chair and waited. From this angle—and he surmised from the bed as well—the view was limited to a broad patch of sky. There were a few clouds. Maybe it was arranged so a patient would be able to stare at the firmament and envision where he or she might be in the too-near future.

There was a leather-bound book on an end table next to him. He picked it up. James Joyce. *Dubliners.* An ancient bookmark from Rizzoli marked the second page of "Clay." He put the book back on the table and closed his eyes against the light from the window.

Preparations were meaningless. He would not outsmart this man, even in this shrunken state. His plan came down to showing respect and relying on the Judge's sense of fair play. And honor.

He opened his eyes and found the Judge staring at him.

"Here to gloat?" the old man said in a harsh whisper.

"I wish you no harm," Ted said.

"But you won't be shedding any tears."

"I've never been any good at crying."

"You were the best."

"No. I wasn't born to travel in those lofty circles."

"Why are you here?"

"We had an agreement. I've held up my end."

"And now it's too late." The Judge's voice held a touch of a sneer.

"True. But I expected you to hold up your end."

"Look at me," the Judge rasped. "Who would listen to me?"

"You have commanded respect for as long as I've been alive."

"Tempus fugit."

This was a man who had built his life on a network of acquaintances, trading favors and disciplining those who failed to honor their loyalties. And in his last hours they had abandoned him. "Where are they all?"

"Jill visits. She reads to me."

"No one else? No other family members? Not friends?"

"No one."

Neither spoke for another minute as Ted absorbed this alteration in the universe and the Judge murmured a prayer. "Now and at the hour of our death . . ."

A demand for the protection he was owed was pointless. The best he could hope for now was a word or two of advice. "Reisner is playing tricks. Someone is going to get hurt. Someone may already have been hurt."

The Judge laughed. It was a croaking hack that had little to do with amusement. "It's what he does. No deal is ever final."

"Kenzie could get hurt."

A spasm flickered across the old man's face, and he reached for the morphine pump. But he stopped himself, breathed deeply, and looked at Ted again. "She's a pain in the ass."

Ted laughed. "I thought you admired that."

"I do." He closed his eyes again and for a moment Ted couldn't tell if he was still breathing. "The Russians are out."

It came out in such a reedy whisper that Ted wasn't sure he had heard it. "What's that?"

"Reisner broke with the Russians. Bought them off. He now uses a private security firm."

"Collins Guards," Ted replied. "His new bodyguards."

"Only one of their functions."

Ted had considered this but was pleased to have his suspicions confirmed. "Dangerous?"

"All-American talent. Global reach. They present cleaner,

but they're every bit as ruthless as the competition. They bring terrorist ethics to commercial negotiations." The Judge was stronger now, more alert, eyes wide open, but there was a growing edge to his voice. Pain was returning.

"I can't fight people like that."

"You don't want to." The Judge let out a long sigh, surrendering for the moment to whatever inner torment was running through his body. His eyes closed again.

Ted waited.

"Something to consider," the Judge said.

When he did not go on, Ted asked, "What's that?"

"Reisner may no longer be pulling the strings." He paused and took another long breath. "He believes chaos serves him. In the end, chaos serves only itself." His face twisted again, and he drew in air and held it. For an interminable three seconds he fought the pain, then he hit the pump, and immediately relaxed. "It comes down to this. Feel pain or feel nothing."

Ted waited for more, and when it did not arrive he gave a small nudge. "Reisner?"

"When you hire the devil, you're working for him now."

"Collins?"

"You should go," the Judge said, his voice now shrunken and airy.

Ted wasn't going to get any more. He held up the book. "I could stay and read to you."

"Those stories are fucking depressing."

"Then why have Jill read them to you?"

"I love her."

Ted could see the morphine working behind his yellowed eyes. The Judge was fading into a world free of pain.

"I'll come back to visit," Ted said.

"Don't," he said. "I won't be here."

TED'S PHONE RANG WHILE he was on the elevator. Kenzie. Two white-haired dowagers in black overcoats dared him with their eyes to answer. He took the challenge.

"I can't talk," he said by way of greeting.

"Where are you?"

"In the city. Trying to take care of business."

"You need to be here. Now."

44

FOREST AVENUE WAS A slow-go on the best of days. Today it wasn't going at all. Mohammed fumed up front as they watched the traffic light turn red for the third time without a single car having advanced.

Lester opened the passenger door and stood on the doorsill looking ahead. "There's red and blue flashing lights two or three blocks ahead." He sank back onto the seat and closed the door. "We're going nowhere."

Mohammed was stabbing a finger at the GPS screen and muttering. All Ted could see were bright red lines.

"Let's walk," he said with a nod to Lester. "Mohammed, you're on your own."

They were barely out of the car and on the sidewalk before Mohammed began a three-point U-turn that quickly became a seven-point turn. But as there was almost no traffic coming away from the roadblock ahead, Mohammed managed the maneuver with relatively little use of the horn.

"What could you see?" Ted asked as the two walked quickly toward the church, weaving through the afternoon shoppers on this rare warm day.

Lester shook his head. "Just the police block. Maybe a news van farther down."

They hustled, crossing the next intersection against the light. Cars weren't moving on side streets either.

And then Ted could hear the chanting. The cadence, at any rate. The words were distorted by distance and street sounds but became crystal clear as they came down the last block.

"Throw her out! Throw her out!" and "Take a hike! Build the Spike!"

There were news vans from all the major television outlets—channels 2, 4, and 7, of course, but also 5, 9, and 11. Reporters trailing cameramen were buttonholing anyone who slowed down to a reasonable pace. The moment anyone stopped to answer one of their questions, a screen of kibitzers jockeyed to get into the shot and achieve celebrity status for a second or two.

The protestors making the noise were a vaguely homogenous group. Mostly men, but all burly, dressed in worn jeans and work boots with yellow or white hard hats—and all wearing Covid masks. Construction workers. Ted would have bet they all worked for Reisner. They all carried a look that lent a sameness to them. The printing on their signs was identical. The wording reflected—or imitated—the chants. The sight had the staged look of a protest scene in a cheap TV movie, as though all the props had come out of the same studio workshop.

Ted was amused that the protestors had latched on to the use of the word "Spike" for the Tower. Kenzie and her group had won the branding competition, as that had always been their word for the project. The fact that it was now being used against them was testament to its acceptance.

"There!" one of the small crowd called, pointing at Ted. "That's one of them. He's the lawyer."

Ted felt all eyes on him and paused midstride. Lester grabbed his arm and pulled him toward the gate and the basement entrance.

"Get him."

Ted looked back and saw half a dozen of the bigger men running toward him. Those signs—supported by thick chunks of wood—would make formidable clubs.

Lester pulled him again and this time Ted responded. He ran. He followed Lester through the gate, and swung it closed behind him. The gate didn't lock and wouldn't hold the pursuers back for longer than a nanosecond, but it might constitute a psychological barrier. The church was, after all, consecrated ground.

They dashed down the concrete steps. Lester pounded on the metal door.

The door flew open. They fell inside and heard the jail-like clang of the door closing again behind them.

"Where the fuck are the goddamn cops?" Ted said, his fear switching in a heartbeat to a combination of outrage and relief.

"Directing traffic," Lester answered.

"They were here. Then they left," Kenzie said.

Ted took another few deep breaths and looked around. Ashley was there. Deepa, too. Two volunteers he didn't recognize.

He peered out the window, his view limited to the stairs, the gate, and a few yards of the sidewalk in front. The gate was still closed. Not one of that angry mob had dared to cross that line. The leaves on the tree at the curb presented browns and muted yellows against the cloudless royal blue sky. A bucolic vision with not a sign-wielding, pitchfork-carrying rioter in sight.

Kenzie stared out the window with him. "I had the same experience coming back from the bank. They chased me into the building. Which you'll be able to watch later today on almost any news show you want. I called the police and was surprised that they got here in under ten minutes."

"Why did the cops leave?"

"They told these people where they could walk and how close they could come to the building and what would happen if they became violent again. Then they told the news people they had to be gone by three or they'd be towed."

It was now twenty of. "Brilliant."

"Are you enjoying the irony?" Kenzie asked.

"That the woman who has organized untold numbers of such protests is now the protestee? No. I'm more than a little concerned for your safety."

"One good thing happened," she said. "The guy you hired to look for bugs showed up. We're negative."

Ted was not surprised. "The apartment, too." Lester signaled with a twist of his head that he had something to add.

"The one who pointed you out?" Lester began.

Ted nodded.

"He's the leader. His boots are brand new."

"A plant," Deepa said. "He was the one who identified Kenzie."

"This is not merely a spontaneous gathering of like-minded citizens," Ted said.

"No," Kenzie said. "This is Reisner."

"Easy enough to hire a crew of construction workers to spend a day making your lives miserable," Lester said.

"If we get proof, I'll put it in front of a judge. But the first priority is to keep us all safe."

"They'll leave as soon as the cameras are gone," Lester said.

"Let us hope so," Deepa said.

"They'll be gone by three," Ted said. "Reisner won't want to pay overtime."

45

FIFTEEN MINUTES LATER A small minibus pulled up and swept the protestors away. Deepa and the volunteers celebrated in relief, but Ted and Kenzie shared a look. The crew would be back in the morning. The protestors had a good day with both media exposure and opportunities to intimidate. They wouldn't quit until someone forced them to leave, and the police wouldn't do that until someone got hurt. Ted needed to find a solution.

While his attention was focused on the bigger, more immediate problem, he worked with Ashley on the boxes of documents, a wall of legal-sized cardboard-lidded containers. Each box bulged with manila folders filled with copies of emails, letters, memos, directives, contracts, and notes on meetings with contractors, politicians, bureaucrats, engineers, police and fire officials, and community leaders. And almost all of it was irrelevant.

They each attacked a box, scanning the pages for clues to the slightest impropriety. "Keep a stack of anything you think I should see," Ted said. They faced each other across the long table, the boxes beside them, the proposed "stack" between them. By the time Ashley finished with her first container, there were three pieces of paper on the table, and she was red-eyed and exhausted.

"I've got a class," she said, her voice straddling relief and guilt.

"We'll quit." He had almost a quarter of the box left to examine, but he couldn't face it. "See you tomorrow?"

"Sure thing."

"Early?" If they got in before seven, they might not have to deal with the protestors at all.

"Class. I can get here by eleven or so."

"Wait until noon. They'll be on lunch break. Union rules. I'll be in court, but you can get started."

She gave a half wave and left. The volunteers were gone. Deepa was packing up. Kenzie was deep in conversation on her phone, but he could see she was tired—stress showed.

They couldn't operate this way, planning their comings and goings around a commercial construction schedule, in fear of stepping out onto the street and being attacked.

"Lester. Got a minute before we head out?"

Lester had been listening to music on his phone. He took a bud out of his ear. "I know you're talking, and you're looking at me, so I figure you are saying something I might want to hear." He strolled over and took the chair Ashley had abandoned. "What's up?"

"Set up a meeting for me."

THE FENCE AROUND THE church was a late construction, dating to the mid-1960s. The church had already survived fifty years without protection, but the arrival of the aerosol paint can compelled the parish to address the nascent issue of graffiti. The additions of a fence and gate were both tasteful and effective and, combined with community pressure, had kept the building safe from vandals. Until this morning.

Kenzie got the call long before sunrise, and it was still dark when she and Ted arrived on the scene.

"We beat the protestors, at least," Ted said as they climbed out of the Uber.

There was a single police vehicle parked at the curb, lights flashing, though the crisis was long past. Two cops were watching a trio of Latino workmen wrestling the bent and mangled pieces of the fence into an organized pile for the salvage company.

Kenzie strode up to the cops and introduced herself.

"I have offices in the basement here. Can I go in and check for damage?"

"I'd say wait until the priest gets here. He went back to the rectory for coffee. He won't be long."

"What happened?" Ted asked. "Do we know?"

"And you are?"

"I'm a lawyer. I work for her."

The cop grimaced at the word "lawyer" and spoke to Kenzie. "You know a homeless guy sleeps around here? Drew?"

"Ivancic, sure. He's a sweetheart."

"He saw it. A black pickup pulls up, backs over the curb. Two guys get out, hook a rope to the fence. One tosses a brick through the stained glass. The other pulls the truck back onto Forest and the fence comes down. They take their rope and they're gone."

The other cop had seemed to be asleep on his feet but now chimed in. "The whole show took less than a minute."

There was now a plywood panel over the window.

"Did he get a license plate?"

The first cop looked at Ted as though surprised to find him still there. Neither one bothered to answer him.

No one had been maimed or murdered. Property damage like this ranked below automobile theft, and that rarely warranted a call from a detective. The police were stretched too thin to care. These guys were only there to produce a case number for the insurance claim.

"We know who did this," Kenzie said.

Neither cop seemed to notice.

The barrier was no longer there. If someone wanted to throw another brick, or chase one of the volunteers down the stairs, or cause havoc in any other way, there was nothing at all to hold them back. These guys were amping up the intimidation. The threat wasn't implied, it was being shouted in their faces.

It was time to get some help.

47

SHAKRA, TED'S UBER DRIVER, took the left at the end of Ninety-Eighth Street onto 165th Avenue and pulled to the curb by the handball court.

"This is where you want?" she asked with a touch of skepticism. The wind coming in off Jamaica Bay whistled past the car. The sky was the color of old pewter. It looked damned cold outside.

"What does it take for you to wait for me?"

"I don't get paid for waiting."

Ted took out a hundred-dollar bill and ripped it in two. He held out half. "You get the other half in twenty minutes. Or less." He thought he'd seen John Garfield do the same thing in one of his early movies. Or was it George Raft? Only it was probably a ten.

"I'll make an exception," she said, taking the torn bill.

Ted fought the wind as he pushed open his door. The heater in the car had been cranked up to an uncomfortable level, but the sudden blast of frigid air changed that in a heartbeat.

"Shut it," Shakra squealed.

Ted jumped out and the door, propelled by a fresh gust, slammed shut behind him. He pulled his overcoat up to cover his mouth and nose. His eyes teared up. He wished he'd worn a hat.

He strode quickly around the ball court and came upon the deserted tennis courts where a handsome, dark-haired young man wearing a bright yellow, neon-purple-trimmed track suit was feverishly swatting at green balls being fired from a catapult on the far side of the court. He was doing well, despite the random automatic rotation of the machine and the vagaries produced by the gusting wind.

Ted recognized him. It was the psychopath from the Jones Beach parking lot. The guy who had ordered the kidnapping. Peter Scarduzio, Lester had informed Ted, named for his uncle, Peter Scarduzio. As two Peter Scarduzios in the same power structure might have caused some occasional confusion, the younger was called Junior, though he was not a son.

Behind Junior, the squeaky-voiced bodybuilder, today wearing long gym shorts and a puffy parka, was using a broad push broom to scoot into a basket the few balls that had made it past the young man. There weren't many.

Both men ignored Ted's presence until the catapult coughed once, then again, and no balls shot forth.

"Load it up," Junior ordered as he waved his racket in greeting. "How's the head, fella? Did you see somebody about it?"

"I did, thank you for asking. I'm gonna live."

"Let's walk." Junior laid the racket against the fence and began strolling toward the water.

Ted winced but followed quickly. How could this man be so unaffected by the damp, cold wind?

"Wait," Junior said. "I'm sorry, but we gotta check you." He called to the bodybuilder. "Morey! Morey, *bubbeleh*, comeheah. Bring your magic wand." He turned back to Ted. "Maurice. He hates it. Who names their kid Maurice these days? It's kinda ethnic, if you know what I mean."

Ted did not respond. Was "ethnic" code for something racist? He couldn't keep track. He did not point out that Morey had not been given the name "these days" but twenty-some years ago.

Morey hustled over, leaving the tennis balls to get swept along by the wind until they bunched up along the net or fence.

"Raise your arms. Like this," he said in that high-pitched nasal tone. He demonstrated with hands outstretched to either side.

Ted copied him.

"You got a phone?" Junior asked. "Give it up."

Ted handed the phone to Morey and put his arms out again.

Morey took a black box from a deep pocket. Attached was a short black wire and sensor. He turned it on and ran it over Ted's arms, legs, and torso.

"Clean."

"Sorry about that. Nothin' personal. SOP. No offense."

Morey went back to collecting tennis balls.

"None taken," Ted said, though surrendering his phone had given him a jolt. It wasn't fear, but a feeling of incompleteness, as though his identity had been challenged.

"Glad to hear it. We're gonna be friends," Junior said, slapping Ted on the shoulder. "I love this view from here, you know."

The airport to the left. The back side. As attractive as any industrial park near a major city. Ahead was Cross Bay Boulevard and the green bump of the wildlife preserve, then Arverne and the Rockaways a few miles away across the bay. And Jamaica Bay itself, whipped up with whitecaps and froth as far he could see. They were standing on landfill from an early developer and looking at generations of assaults on the natural terrain. It wasn't ugly by any means, but you'd have to be a native to love it. It could have been worse. There had once been a plan to create a second shipping port here, which would have destroyed the last vestiges of natural beauty. The developers had lost that round. They hadn't lost many.

"Nice," Ted said. "Aren't you cold?"

"Nah. I don't feel it. So whaddya need? What can my uncle do for you?"

Ted could hear a jet plane powering up across the channel. Barely hear. The near-gale winds whisked the sound away. The wind giveth and the wind taketh away.

"Let me explain. I work pro bono for a nonprofit. They want to stop a Ron Reisner project in Corona."

"Reisner has a lot of friends."

"If there's a conflict of interest, forget I mentioned it."

"No, no. But it's hard to operate in Queens and not cross paths."

"He's hired a crew of beefy-looking construction workers to protest outside of the offices. They're led by a plant who I'm pretty sure works for an organization that goes by the name of Collins Guards."

"Like security guards?"

"More like a private army."

Junior nodded. "Jesus, you're shaking. I didn't realize you were that cold. Let me get you a coffee. Morey!" he yelled. "Go to Gino's and get this guy a coffee. Black? White? How do you take it?"

"Black."

"Get him a black coffee. And get me an expresso. A double."

Morey leaned the broom against the fence and jogged away.

"Hey, and *no* sugar," Junior called after him. Turning back to Ted, he became solicitous again. "Come on, we gotta get you outta the wind."

Ted followed him around the tennis courts until they were standing in the lee of a small building. Judging by the strong scent of industrial-strength cleaning supplies, the building housed the park's restrooms.

"I am *so* sorry, fella. Like I said, I don't feel it. Maybe you should think about silk underwear. Much warmer than cotton. Cotton kills. Don't get me started. It's cray-cray."

Ted thought him a thoroughly adequate self-starter on the road to cray-cray.

"So, I'm guessing you want I tell these poor slobs they gotta go back to working for a living?"

Ted nodded. "I'm worried. They're getting prepped by this guy. There's going to be violence there."

"And the cops won't intervene until someone gets hurt—or dead."

"Yes. They've come right out and admitted it. There's already been vandalism and they shrug."

"Let me axe you something. You think it's, like, a slow-down? I know the cops are all crazed over this no-bail thing, letting all the lowlifes back out on the street, but you think it's deliberate? I mean, why work hard when nobody gives a ratfuck?"

"I really don't know."

"Yeah. Me neither. But I think about these things."

"I see that."

"So, give Morey the address. He'll take care of this right away. And maybe if my uncle needs a little more time?"

"I will speak to Mr. McKinley," Ted said. "And can he do it quietly? I'm not looking to start a war. I just want those guys to go somewhere else."

"Morey will explain things to 'em. Not to worry."

"Thank you."

"You're welcome. Where the fuck's that coffee?"

Ted checked the time. The Uber driver would be expecting him soon, but it felt awkward to run off so quickly when the gangster was being so gracious. "Morey can finesse this? My impression is he's more of a muscle guy. He's done this kind of thing before?"

"That's kinda proprietary information."

Ted was reminded of the gulf between them. He didn't respond.

"Hey. Don't worry. He's good."

"I appreciate it," Ted said, looking for Morey and his cell phone.

"I tell you, working with your partner is a fucking pain. The guy is a hardhead. I give him credit—I mean that's his fucking job, right? But it is so much nicer doing business with you."

Ted shivered again. He did not want to make a habit of doing business with these guys.

"So, whaddya think?" Junior said, his voice suddenly easy. Conversational. "Mets going to be looking for a new coach?"

Ted's mind went blank. Team management might very well cashier the coach, but having this conversation with a psychotic mobster was unique.

"I wouldn't be surprised," Ted said.

"My thoughts exactly. And look who's here," Junior said. "Come on, Speedy."

Morey arrived red-faced and short of breath. He handed Junior a short Starbucks cup and Ted a tall. "There was a line at Gino's," he said. "I didn't think you wanted me to wait."

Junior nodded absently, barely acknowledging the man. He swallowed his espresso in a single gulp. "I want you to take care of a little problem for my friend." And turning back to Ted, "I'm gonna get back to practicin'. Thanks for coming out. Hey, and don't be a stranger."

There was an uncomfortable moment as Ted and Morey waited for Junior to get far enough away to plead ignorance if ever asked.

Ted explained the situation in a few short sentences. "But no violence. I'm trying to avoid getting people hurt."

Morey nodded. "I'm on it. No problem." He handed over the cell phone. "I'll call you."

"What do I owe you for the coffee?" Ted asked after taking a long, warming sip.

"Zip."

"Well, thank you, Morey."

The man's eyes went flat. "Maurice," he corrected in a chilly tone.

48

KENZIE CALLED DEEPA AND told her to put the troops on hold for a day or so to let things calm down. Then she met her father for a late lunch at Il Taverna, two blocks down from his shop. She was a few minutes late and the two men were already seated—with drinks—at a quiet table in the back.

Her father's hacker friend, Richard Pike, was a big bear of a man, dark eyed and intimidating until he smiled. Which he did often as he described how the fake news stories had been created.

He took a sip of his martini—one olive—and opened a tablet. "I can show you exactly how that first story was done. The person who wrote the original story is not a proficient technical hacker. They left breadcrumbs all over the website."

"The two stories didn't come from the same source?"

"I'll get to that," he said. He rescued the olive from drowning in vodka and popped it into his mouth. "I contacted TheWordNYC and told them I would try to convince you not to sue if they let me root around in their system a little."

"I don't need convincing. I only want this to go away."

"I understand," he said. His spaghetti Bolognese arrived— and her father's veal Saltimbocca, and her Caesar salad with fresh anchovies—and for a minute they were all preoccupied with pepper, parmesan, and fresh drinks.

"So, they got the picture of you from an old news article." He tapped the keyboard and the story appeared. "They cut you out and changed the background, using a current picture of the building, so it looks like you sneaking out the door."

He demonstrated on the tablet. It looked magical to Kenzie, but she realized quickly that it was all easily done. The average American teenager could have done it with an iPad. "They gave you the barest touch of purple tint. You come off looking shady. It took me about two minutes to track the original picture."

Pike paused to break off a slice of rustic Italian bread and mopped up some of the sauce.

"But could you trace the origin of the story? Who wrote it?"

Pike ignored her and went on with his exploits in cyber detection. "Stories that come in to TheWordNYC are looked at by an editor, but not for content or accuracy. What they check for is credit. Can the item ever come back and bite them in the butt? They want to have no responsibility for the story. It was submitted by a 'source that may or may not be reliable.'"

"So why did it go viral so quickly?"

"Picture of pretty girl. Murder. Sex." He held up a finger for each. "Also maybe it got a boost because your name pops up in local news once in a while."

Was this a backhanded compliment? She—and others—worked hard to get her name and that of the organization into the news. That was the point. This story would forever show up on any search app.

"Pretty slippery," her father said.

"But not slick. A good amateur job. The whole thing could have been put together with simple software. Then they loaded it onto a stick and took it to the local library."

"Why?" The answer was forming in her mind the moment she asked the question.

"I bought a software package from a guy at DEF CON this year that's pretty useful for this kind of thing. I was able to track the message back to the Long Island City public library. Someone uploaded it there. It would have taken them all of two minutes to do it. But there is no chance of finding out who. It's anonymous."

And brilliant. Distribution to the world and no way to backtrack it.

"Sorry, my dove," her father began. "I wish there was better news. If you think you know who did it, it will be in their computer. Forever, pretty much."

She shrugged it off. The faked interview was now the greater problem. "Tell me about the other one."

Pike ate more of his pasta, finished the martini, and patted his lips with the napkin. He looked for the waiter, caught his eye, and pointed to his empty glass.

She waited patiently. On the surface, at least. She took a long slug of water to keep from grinding her teeth.

"The other case is much more interesting," he said.

"Interesting sounds bad," she said.

"It is. The presentation is much more professional. Deep-fake. The cutting, mixing, editing. The voice! Not an exact match, but good. You don't need voice recognition software to hear the difference, but the actor does a convincing job. Possibly digitally enhanced."

"Where did this one come from? The College Point library?"

"No. From you. You were spoofed. To the passive viewer, the story looks like it was generated from your email site. But I got around that and discovered another layer. The Netherlands. From a Swiss-based company that officially does not exist."

A warren of false trails. She groaned.

"But that signature is identical to one used by a Russian group."

"I've run into badass Russians before," she said, unconsciously running a hand over the silver streak in her hair.

"Probably not these guys. They're independent, not mob affiliated. Gunslingers. Expensive. They work for whoever pays."

"You know these people?" she asked in muted horror.

"No. I know these people exist. That's as much as I ever want to know."

"Like leg-breaking, or murder?"

"Worse. Identity theft. Ransomware. You'll only wish you were dead. But they only go after people who try to go after them. Or clients who don't pay."

"Ron Reisner is known for not paying his bills. I don't know how he keeps getting contractors to work for him."

"He didn't invent that game, but he is a master at it," her father said.

"You think he's backing this?" Pike asked.

"I don't know who else hates me enough."

49

THERE WERE TIMES WHEN Ted wished he had the knack for drinking himself into a self-induced coma. Not many, but the few were choice. Strong spirits might wipe away his feeling of complete worthlessness. Beer was a joyful beverage and wouldn't do the trick. He needed oblivion. And because associating the word "need" with alcohol both terrified and disgusted him, he did not have a stiff drink. He made himself a hot tea and suffered through his memories.

"Your halo is throwing off sparks," Kenzie said, giving him a kiss on the cheek before pouring herself an end-of-day glass of wine and plunking down on the couch next to him.

Ted grunted.

She turned to look him in the eyes. "And there's a dark, sulfurous cloud around your head."

"Well earned," he said, manfully attempting to smile.

"Uh-oh. What'd you do this time?"

He almost laughed. He would have if he hadn't been so deep in self-pity.

"I see," she said. "This is a tough one. I can tell you about my day."

"Why don't you do that?" he said. He wasn't ready to reveal his mega-failure as yet.

"Well, after you left I had lunch with my father and his computer guru. Which reminds me, we're having Thanksgiving with my folks. I know that's no surprise, but I thought I should remind you."

"When's that?"

"When's Thanksgiving? Oh, you poor thing. Next week."

"Next Thursday?"

"You still got it, champ."

"What can we bring?"

"I was telling you about my day."

He sighed. "Right. The computer guy."

"Yup. He says I'm screwed. Or mostly screwed. The first story—the one that Naomi Spitzer got all nerval over—was a cheap shot, probably put together by someone with basic Photoshop credentials. Most teenagers could do it. That doesn't tell us who did it, but it makes it seem a lot less threatening."

"Which tells me the interview video has a darker back-story."

"Russians. Fake internet accounts. Switzerland. Holland. Very high quality. Probably expensive."

"Reisner."

"Yeah. And no way of tracking it. Ever. Unless you've got contacts in the CIA you've never mentioned."

"Well, that sucks."

"He's going to check our computer security systems— change passwords and stuff. We can't get the story removed, but we can make sure we don't get spoofed again."

Listening to Kenzie was helping. His head felt lighter. Maybe the cloud was lifting.

"Ready for your turn?" she asked.

He nodded. Then took a moment to organize how to tell his story without making his actions sound worse than they were, and yet convey the full impact.

"I was in court this afternoon."

"My hero."

He smiled. "I challenged one of their expert witnesses." He paused again to organize the right words. "For competence."

"Okay? And?"

"What usually happens then, is opposing counsel asks for a date to present their witness for questioning. That could be weeks away. I would get my delay."

"Do you know how hot you are when you start talking legal strategy?"

"So when your eyes roll back and you start to snore, those are actually indications of arousal?"

"Why not tackle the expert right away?"

"Those mountains of documents? I need to go through them so I can slip in questions that might trip him up or reveal something juicy."

Kenzie set her wine glass on the floor and held his hand. "So what happened?"

Ted nodded his appreciation. Her jokey, flirty early response had helped, but no longer. He needed serious, caring, listening Kenzie.

"Instead, this Phi Beta Krappa wearing a fucking bow tie got up and announced that they were prepared to answer my concerns immediately."

"Oh, shit."

"No shit."

"Did you?"

"I had to. It was embarrassing. The engineer took the stand. I asked questions like, 'And where did you attend graduate school?' And he answered, 'Harvard.' This went on until the judge interrupted me. 'Satisfied, Mr. Molloy?' 'Yes, thank you, Your Honor.' And then I crawled back to my table."

She sighed and squeezed his hand. "What kind of engineer?"

He gave her a skeptical look. Did she really care? Did it matter? She didn't flinch. "Traffic patterns," he said.

"Oh."

"It's not sexy, I know. But this is what I do. Anything to slow them down because delay costs them money. Higher interest rates also help, but I can't do anything about that."

"But you didn't do anything wrong. They came prepared, that's all."

Ted now laughed. A bitter laugh. "I pull down their pants. They don't pull down mine."

"But it must happen to everybody sometimes."

"It's like they had read my notes."

"**DO YOU THINK THEY** could have?" Kenzie asked.

"They who?" Ted was already shaking his head.

She was fuming but kept it under control. "You're not going to like this."

"No fair. I'm feeling low already."

"Reisner's people, that's who. How secure are your notes?"

"I'm convinced that any password can be beaten, but I keep everything pertaining to case files pretty well locked up."

"Suppose they had someone inside feeding them information."

He gave a lopsided grin. "Ashley? Look, I know you don't like her—"

"Funny thing is, I *do*. I just don't trust her. That's different."

"I admit it seems convenient that at the moment I needed a junior lawyer-type to help with this case, a gung-ho lawyer wannabe walks in and offers to work for nothing."

"That's not you capitulating, right? There's a 'but' clause hanging at the end there."

"First off, I felt the same way about Lester when I met him, and he's now my right hand. Two, she's competent. We've barely looked at those files, but I can already see she knows what she's doing. Three, and here you can beat me up over it if you want, but I feel for her. She's a scrapper. A fighter."

"A striver. Like you."

"Exactly. I had my luck—good and bad. But I fought for everything I got. I made mistakes and accepted help when it came with no hooks, but I earned that help with hard work and loyalty. I have the opportunity to pass it forward."

"And you are projecting all of your long-ago successes and all the subsequent stumbles onto this woman? A stranger who came in off the street."

"Whoa! Hold up. Unfair. Do you really think I'd be any less on her side if Ashley Parker was a man? Or old? Or bald?"

She was embarrassed. The reference to his "stumbles" was low. Jealousy was an indulgence of the weak. She should take the high road.

Or higher, at any rate. "But she's not. And she's here. And I don't trust her."

"And I need her."

Ted could be maddeningly stubborn at times. "Could she be passing Reisner information? Your notes? Donors' names?"

"She can't get into my files. They're in the cloud."

"We know that we're not being bugged, so how else are they getting this stuff?"

Ted didn't answer, but she could see him turning it over in his mind. Maybe she was getting through to him.

WEDNESDAY

51

KENZIE WAS FEELING NERVOUS. She did not often get that way. To find that she was being hounded from not one but two directions was confusing—and scary. And she did not look forward to facing off with those protestors again. Then there was the message she'd received: Father Byun wanted to meet with her today. His gate and fence had been torn down. A brick destroyed an almost one-hundred-year-old stained glass window. He would have every right to toss Stop the Spike out onto the street, and she had no plan B. They'd be screwed.

She left Ted snoring softly, showered, dressed, and headed downstairs where she fixed herself a breakfast of coffee and—the result of getting lost in a *New York Post* article on her phone—a piece of burnt rye toast with a smear of peanut butter. Mohammed called from out front two minutes early. She left the cup in the sink, and holding the toast between her teeth, she threw on her parka and ran out.

Haidir, again in the passenger seat up front, was as uncommunicative as ever, but her response to him had returned to normality. He was only a boy, uncomfortable with adults and covering his insecurity with a sullen indifference. He wore a black hoodie under a purple puffy vest. He did not say good morning, or anything else, for that matter. When she greeted him by name—so that he could not entirely avoid responding—he nodded.

"On your way to work, Haidir?"

Another nod.

"Then school?"

Haidir didn't respond.

Mohammed said something in Arabic, which could have been a mild admonishment, then turned to Kenzie. "You are striking cold iron," Mohammed said with a chuckle.

"Yes," Haidir said. "Then school."

"Do you enjoy school?" She heard herself from his point of view. Annoying.

He nodded. The brief foray into verbal communication had passed, leaving no evidence it had ever existed.

She couldn't help herself. She persisted. "So, you're a good student?"

Hesitation.

Mohammed was listening intently.

Then, after a quick look at his stepfather, another nod.

"He could do better," Mohammed said, putting on his blinker and slowing as they approached Manny's store.

Haidir scowled but said nothing.

There was no room for Mohammed to pull to the curb. A line of three black SUVs had taken up residence, blocking the fire hydrant and the bus stop. Mohammed muttered something else in Arabic. Kenzie didn't need a translation.

He stopped the car and rolled down his window to wave traffic to go around. Haidir hopped out with a mumbled "*Shukran.*"

"No problem," Mohammed said with a wave.

Kenzie watched the boy dash between two of the SUVs and start across the sidewalk.

Mohammed began to pull away, his eyes on the traffic.

Kenzie saw six men wearing black windbreakers with NYPD in large white letters across their backs leap out of the SUVs. They tackled Haidir and threw him to the ground. She screamed, "Stop! Stop!"

Mohammed hit the brakes and instantly there were horns blasting behind them.

Kenzie threw open the door and ran. Haidir was face down on the sidewalk with one of the policemen kneeling on his back, while two others held the boy's legs.

"What the fuck are you doing? Leave him alone," she cried, pushing to place her own body between the cops and the boy. They pushed back. She'd been manhandled by police before. She went limp. Lesson one in protest school. They threw her face down next to Haidir. They wrenched her arms, and she felt handcuffs lock around her wrists.

She began to process the voices yelling at her. Hysteria, she thought. Police panic.

"Leave him alone," she yelled back. "You've got the wrong man."

52

"NO. THEY DIDN'T. THEY got the guy they were after," Ted said to her many hours later as they rode home in the back of an Uber. "Haidir will be held in JDC until trial."

"JDC?"

"Crossroads Juvenile Detention Center in Brooklyn. Juvie."

"He's fourteen!" Kenzie cried.

"And suspected of murder," he said, cutting her off. "Can we concentrate on your case for a bit?"

"They sent six detectives in body armor to arrest a boy. Who didn't even do it."

"They should have sent two basketball coaches from the Police Athletic League to give him a good talking-to."

"Do people appreciate your sense of humor? I mean, is it me?"

"I'll get hold of Detective Duran and see if I can find out what made them go after Haidir."

"And get him out," she said.

"All we have to do is convince Duran—or the ADA—that a defense attorney could present a plausible alternative story. They'll let Haidir go and restart the investigation."

"They swarmed him. Oh my god. Mohammed. He must be going crazy."

Ted nodded. "Freaking out. Ashamed that he did nothing to stop them. Glad that he wasn't arrested along with you. Terrified of the police in general. And lawyers, courts, the government, and the universe. He is definitely reexamining his acceptance of 'inshallah.' I told him to go home and hug his wife. She's going to need it."

"What did I miss?"

"Not much. Deepa came in for a while. The protestors kept their distance." And there had been no sign of Maurice. Ted had expected a more immediate response. "I had to leave Ashley working on those documents when I came to get you. There might be something interesting there. We'll see."

"Watch her, Ted."

He wasn't yet prepared to admit it, but Kenzie's attitude toward the law student was starting to work on him. He was at the teeth-grinding stage, torn between agreeing with her and snapping back. "As for you . . ."

"Yes?"

"You will be arraigned this evening. You will plead guilty to resisting arrest. The ADA will ask for a fine. We will find a way to pay for it. Then I will take you home and we'll order in a pizza."

"With anchovies?"

THURSDAY

53

KENZIE WATCHED THE STREET, her fears split evenly between the flip sides of a single coin. If any volunteers showed up, they were bound to be harassed, or even attacked, by the protestors. If no volunteers showed she was on a path to shutting down the whole organization.

Were there more of those jerks out there today? Maybe not many more, but the crowd had grown. The chants were louder and there was a tone to them that set her nerves snapping and sparking.

Ted was burrowing in one of the cardboard boxes.

"Lose a lens?" she asked.

He sat up. He looked worried.

"How ya doin'?" he said, attempting, through diversion, to hide whatever was bugging him. She hated when he did that.

"What'd you lose?" she said, staring into the box.

"Pages," he said. "Ashley went through this box and I need to reference something from the other files. Only the documents aren't here."

Kenzie considered coming right out and blaming Ashley but shelved it. She did not want to hear Ted defending her again. The wall of boxes loomed behind him. "They could be anywhere."

Ted tipped his head to the side to indicate he was considering this possible explanation. "They should be here."

Lawyers and documents. Like misers counting pennies. "What are they?"

He gave her the look. The one that asked, "Do you really want all the details?" "Email transcripts," he said.

Bravely confronting the minutiae of legal maneuvering. "And?"

"An email conversation between two engineers, one questioning the wisdom of running a traffic study during Covid lockdown, and the other giving his opinion that the client was quite pleased with the timing. The exchange is mentioned obliquely in another memo from an LBC manager, indicating that the whole issue was not an accident." Now he gave her another look. This one said, "Happy now?"

"Exactly what you wanted to spring on that witness."

"Truth."

"I'm sure they'll turn up," she said, now eager to move on.

"Which will give me a clear win on the plea for a new study, costing LBC money and gaining us another delay. *If* I can find the offending docs."

Ashley had definitely made off with those pages. "Best of luck," she said, giving him a short wave.

Lester had his feet propped up on a folding chair, his earbuds in, and appeared to be fast asleep, though Kenzie occasionally heard emanations of soulful music.

Deepa was at the window, videoing the protestors with her phone.

"They seem angry today," Kenzie said.

"I didn't think they would be back," Deepa said.

"Wishing on a star, my mother would call that."

"There's new faces," Deepa said, zooming in on some of them.

"Seems like it. I'm trying not to pay any attention, but it's like standing in the tunnel staring at the headlight from the oncoming train."

"Oh, no," Deepa groaned. "More of them."

246 • MICHAEL SEARS

Kenzie did look this time. "Those guys aren't construction workers."

Two men in suits—white shirts, no ties—followed a stone-faced young man wearing a puffy jacket and pants. The anti-Michelin man. Frowning rather than smiling.

They stopped ten feet or so from the protestors, one or two of whom paused to have a look at this new group. One of the suits stepped forward and spoke.

The protestor with the too-new work boots stepped out of the group and faced the suited man. There was a brief back-and-forth. The protestor had the poise of someone used to giving orders—and having them obeyed.

Kenzie didn't need to hear the words to feel the tension—the threat.

The suit wasn't impressed. He turned to the Michelin man and spoke. Kenzie realized that the man's clothes were not all that puffy. The man was built in tiers of rolling muscle. Whatever was said wasn't good news. He nodded twice and took a quick look to his right.

Another crew came up the sidewalk. There were half a dozen young men carrying baseball bats.

"Jesus Christ, Ted. Look at this."

Ted was back in the box. He looked up. "What's up?"

"There's a goddamn war about to happen out here."

Deepa was still filming.

Ted joined them at the window. "Holy hell," he said. "Where did they come from?"

"Howard Beach'd be my guess," Deepa said. She spoke in a near whisper as though afraid of being overheard by either side of this confrontation.

There was something off in Ted's voice. Kenzie heard it but didn't process it. She took out her phone in case she needed to call 911. And she watched the action.

The protestors seemed to be as clueless as she. But they stopped moving. Stopped chanting. Suddenly they looked much less angry. Some of them appeared nervous and looked from one to another of their companions for guidance. A few stared stonily at the newcomers, but no one looked ready for a confrontation.

Three more men with unscuffed work boots and canvas overalls still creased from the hangers they'd hung on at the store stepped out from the crowd, lining up behind the first.

"Wow," Ted said. "It's like the OK Corral."

What the hell? He was enjoying this.

She watched as one by one men and women were peeling off from the protest line and fading away up the street. Retreat.

The head of the new-boot team had made a mistake. He should have left some of his crew toward the rear to keep the troops in line. Now his superiority in numbers was melting.

But he wasn't ready to quit the field. He indicated with a word or two and a tip of his head that he wished to parley.

"Ted! What the hell is going on here?"

He held up a hand to silence her.

She could feel his tension. He knew what was happening and was as concerned as she. The sneaky sonofabitch. What was he up to?

Or what had he done?

A suspicion began to grow.

"Ted. You know these guys. Who are they?"

He shook his head, indicating *not now* rather than *no*.

There were now only four construction workers lined up behind the four men with the clean pants and new boots—the instigators. The professionals. Facing them were Michelin man and six grinning baseball-bat carriers. The two suits faded to the side. The numbers were with the protestors, but Kenzie would have laid even odds on the newcomers. The professional protestors looked efficient, muscled, and prepared to do battle. The new guys looked like they would enjoy kicking ass. The few remaining construction workers looked a little overweight, a little over-the-hill, and a little out of their league.

Michelin man stepped forward. He had not yet smiled. He did now. He leaned forward and spoke to the head instigator. It was an intimate gesture, a private moment. New-boots considered the words. They both stepped back.

And it was over. What in hell had he said? The four men in their squeaky-clean Timberlands walked as a unit across the street where they piled into a late-model Nissan Pathfinder—no plates—and drove off. Michelin man and his followers walked away toward Myrtle Avenue.

A few aging construction workers, bellies hanging precipitously over their belts, stood looking lost and confused until they too wandered off, heading toward the Dew Drop Inn two blocks north.

Kenzie turned to Ted, staring him in the face, daring him to speak. But he merely smiled, quite pleased with himself.

54

TED SMILED AT KENZIE, proud of the result, pleased that his apprehensions that the confrontation might explode into violence had been merely petty fears.

She did not smile back. She faced him, hands at her sides, back straight, head level. Formidable. "Talk to me, goddamnit. No more games. Who were those guys?"

She had a right to know. She wasn't going to like it, but the plan had worked. Junior had kept his promise. Threats. No violence. Ted would love to know what Maurice had said.

"The only one I know looks like he lifts a lot of heavy things. His friends call him Morey but he prefers Maurice. I've run into him a couple of times."

"What the hell? Where do you meet people like that?"

"He once brought me a cup of hot coffee when I really needed it." Why was he stalling? He knew she would object to the means, but the ends were what mattered. The protestors were gone. Maurice and his crew were gone, and with any luck he'd never see them again.

"Goddamnit, Ted. What went on out there?"

"Negotiations. For today, we are ahead." A touch of appreciation would be nice, but obviously that wasn't happening. "Way ahead. Count your blessings."

"Those are your damn mafia friends."

He had no mafia friends. No one did. They were all sociopaths, as likely to kill each other as their enemies. "Not one of those people out there is a friend. My friends are here. Most of them."

"You are such an asshole," Kenzie said. "There could have been real bloodshed out there. I don't know why there wasn't. Whatever problem you think you're solving doesn't warrant a band of vigilantes. Mafia-fucking-vigilantes."

Lester sidled up, removing his earbuds. Ted could faintly hear a lonely trumpet. "If you two are squabbling, the riot must have been canceled." He looked out at the street. "Where'd everybody go?"

Ted gripped Lester's arm. "Deepa, show him your video," he said, with relief at remembering her name on the first try. And to Lester, "See if you recognize anyone."

"We will talk about this later," Kenzie said. She'd never sounded so angry. Maybe she thought she had reason to be, but there were extenuating circumstances. An immediate physical threat had been removed. Permanently? He couldn't know. But effectively.

But he needed to take her upset seriously. "I hear you," he said. When she calmed down a bit he'd have an opportunity to explain himself. "This evening? Over a glass of wine and some reheated pizza?"

"Well, we've seen this guy before." Lester held the phone up for Ted to see the frozen picture. It was one of the four professional protestors. This one had remained hidden in the crowd until the final face-off. Lester had focused in on him and expanded the picture.

"I know him?" Ted asked.

Kenzie, her eyes wide in astonishment, took the phone from Lester. "I know him," she said. "Only he was wearing a Covid mask and dark glasses. But that's the gas leak guy. Deepa?" She passed the phone on.

"You are so right," Deepa said the moment she saw the photo.

"Collins Guards," Lester said. "And you and I saw him on the television a week or so ago. Standing behind Reisner."

"The gas leak man?" Ted asked, trying desperately to catch up on these revelations.

"He came to the apartment," she explained once again. "Checking for a gas leak. Ever since those houses exploded in Brooklyn, I worry about that."

"This guy," Ted said, tapping the screen.

"It was a busy day," she said.

"Week," he agreed.

"But I didn't like him, and he wasn't concerned about the dog, and I had come from finding Spitzer murdered, and we don't have a tub."

"The dog?" Ted asked. "Are you okay?"

"Two days later he shows up here. Here! There's no gas here. They went from whale oil to electricity. Coal to oil. Gas? Never. Deepa got rid of him. And, no, I am soooo not okay. There was going to be a gang fight right out there and my boyfriend got a war party from Howard Beach to get rid of a bunch of protestors."

Ted needed to say something to stem this tirade. To reassure her. To keep her from flying off on a wave of released fear and anxiety. Maybe not. Just shut up and let her do what she needed to do.

"Baseball bats! Are you fucking shitting me? People could have gotten murdered. This is my safe place, Ted. This is. Not our apartment. Not my parents' house. Here. And I do not feel safe in my safe place."

Lester and Deepa faded to the far end of the room.

"I'm sorry. The point was to keep you safe."

There were tears in her eyes, but she wasn't crying. She wouldn't let herself. But he could feel she wanted to very badly. Needed to. He put an arm around her. She tensed. For a moment, he thought she was going to throw it off. Or slug him. She did neither.

Kenzie collapsed into his chest, and he wrapped her in his arms.

She shook. He held her. She hit him in the chest with the heel of her hand. Hard. He continued to hold her. She pulled back. Gently. He let her go.

"For a really smart guy, you can be incredibly dumb."

"I thought I was making you safe."

"See?"

He didn't, but he was trying. Maybe he'd get the Most Improved trophy.

"Working on it," he said.

"Did it ever cross your mind that I might have an opinion? Because I do."

"We needed a plan." Not an opinion.

"Whoo, boy. And your best plan was to recruit the mafia? Don't they own you now? Isn't that the way they work? What the fuck, Ted?"

"They paid back a favor. We're even. No strings." Did he believe that, or was he justifying his actions after the fact?

"What favor?" she asked, suddenly on alert again for any attempt at camouflage.

"We're going to talk later?" He took her hand. "I will explain."

"Mohammed would say, 'A man who plays with a cat will feel its claws.'"

"Is that one of his proverbs?"

"Yeah, though he mangles it half the time," she said with the beginnings of a smile.

"And that's why I prefer budgies."

She laughed. Still tense at first and then easier. She sank into his chest again. "I can be brave and strong and so you think that's who I am. But I'm only like that when I get to pick my battles."

"You're a dragon killer."

"Yes, but I get to choose my dragons."

"And angry protestors?"

"Unpleasant. A little scary. But I've organized groups like that. I know what they're like. I'm not happy they're out there, but I don't believe they're about to storm the gates."

Images of the January 6 mob at the Capitol flashed through Ted's head. But that was different. This was half a dozen big men with hunks of two-by-four chasing him and Lester into the building. She might think she had things under control, but he still believed the danger was all too real.

"You haven't dealt with a mercenary army before. Collins Guards. They're all ex-military. They work for Reisner, ostensibly as bodyguards, but they do a lot more than that."

"Hacking computers?"

"If they don't do it themselves, they'll contract it out."

"And your solution was to get in somebody even scarier than Collins Guards?"

"Mob enforcers with baseball bats?" Maybe she was right, but at that moment he didn't see any other options. "I don't know that I'd change anything I did, but there won't be a next time. Mr. Scarduzio will pay off the loan and Maurice and I need never see each other again. By the way, I don't think he will miss me, either."

She kissed him. A nice kiss. He kissed back.

"Hi, guys," Ashley said, bursting in the door. "Whoa! Excuse me." And then seeing Lester and Deepa across the room, "You've got an audience?"

55

"**WHAT HAPPENED TO THE** crazies? There's nobody out there," Ashley asked.

"A citizens committee persuaded them to move on," Ted said.

"Semiprofessional baseball team," Lester said.

Deepa and Kenzie exchanged scowls.

"Lucky us," Ashley said.

"Yes," Kenzie said, her sharp tone cutting through Ashley's good cheer. "Lucky us."

Ted felt Kenzie's eyes boring into the side of his head. He got the message. "I need your help. There are missing docs in those files we were working on."

"Oh, nooo," Ashley gasped. "Would they do that? Withhold documents after the judge ordered them to turn them over?"

Ted was stunned. Ashley had overplayed the moment. Her gasp was the tell. The words, a smoke screen.

He had no evidence. He didn't need evidence. He had his gut. Kenzie had been right. Ashley was the leak. Accusations weren't going to elicit confessions. He needed more information. Who was she working for? What had she told them? Where were the missing pages? They must be dynamite if they were worth hiding.

Ex-presidents withheld docs for no good reason simply because they could. Ron Reisner had very good reasons to play that game.

"I'm not prepared to drag them back into court just yet," Ted said. "Not until I'm positive I can get Judge Bagdasian to crucify the bastards. I want you to start looking. Maybe they're misfiled. Let's keep an open mind for now. But I'm going to want you to maintain a file on anything you or I suspect might be missing."

He turned his head and met Kenzie's eyes. Messages were exchanged. Understood.

And to Ashley, "Better get started."

If she suspected that he now suspected her, she did not let it show. Smiling with her usual upbeat demeanor, she walked away and sat down by the boxes of documents.

"Nicely done," Kenzie whispered with no hint of told-you-so-ism in her voice.

Ted walked her down to the far end of the room. "We'll get through this."

"I have to go talk to Father Byun," she said. "I'm sure after what happened that he's going to want us out of here. I need to convince him to give us another chance—and I have no idea how I'm going to do that."

"Nevertheless, she persevered," Ted said.

"Persisted."

"Oh? Is that how it goes? Well, persist away."

"You're not being very empathetic," she said.

"You got this," he said, not entirely sure that he believed it. "You perform miracles every day. Finding a new basement to run the phone bank from does not sound like a disaster on the same level as Haidir being in jail."

"That's fair."

"And the holidays are coming. If we start falling apart now, we won't get the Christmas cards in the mail until Millard Fillmore's birthday."

She was laughing again. "Thank you for helping me put things in perspective. Now I'm ready to face Father Byun. I'll be back. Will you be here?"

"I might be. I've had some thoughts about Mr. Hillyer and that alibi Detective Duran found so compelling."

"Oh?"

"Which I will explain later. I've got to do some reconnaissance first."

"Wish me luck," she said, heading out.

Lester sauntered over. He removed an earbud. No music emanated from the tiny speaker. Lester had been listening and paying attention.

"What do you think?" Ted asked.

"About time," Lester replied in a low voice.

Ted nodded, not surprised at his friend's previous silence. "I need your help."

"Tell me about it."

"Two things. First, give Junior a call and thank him. I'd do it, but I prefer a buffer. It provides some credence to any denials I may have to make."

"I believe he will appreciate your discretion," Lester said, impersonating a stuffy diplomat.

"Let him know Maurice handled things with no fuss. And I'd love to know what he said to that guy."

"Will do."

"Then I want you to come with me. I want to see Spitzer's building. Do some snooping. Are you game?"

"I'm in." He took out his phone and dialed.

Deepa was already on her phone, trying to line up volunteers for the rest of the day. Ashley was at the long table riffling through the box of documents.

Ted joined her. "How goes it? Finding anything I need to see?" He didn't want to start a conversation with an accusation. But he did want answers. He was, therefore, surprised when she addressed the issue head-on.

"Did you look over those pages I left you last night?"

"No." He was neither subtle nor smooth.

"But you got them, right?"

"No."

"The engineers? Emails? No?" She was good, he had to admit. But she was playing a losing game. Did she know it?

"No," he said again. "I didn't see them."

"Then they must still be here. Were you doing something in this box? It's all out of order. Or Kenzie? Somebody was in here."

This would be the time for the pages to magically appear.

"It was something about traffic. Not my area of expertise." She laughed.

"Hmm."

"I'll go through the box again," she said, "as soon as I get some coffee." She rose and walked slowly to the makeshift kitchen.

Giving him time to "discover" the pages.

Or was his habitual skepticism sliding over into paranoia? Had the pages been there all along?

He didn't think so.

He opened the box and pulled out the file he'd been working on that morning: "MTA Feasibility Study for LBC Corona Project." Upgrades to tracks and subway station. Never going to make the bestseller list. Though it might serve as a cure for insomnia.

Tucked inside the cover and first page were two sheets of paper. Email transcriptions. The missing pages. They had not been there a half hour ago.

He looked over his shoulder. Ashley was making a fresh pot. She would be another few minutes.

The pages appeared intact. He scanned the text quickly. Nothing jumped out at him that looked newsworthy. The two engineers seemed much in agreement. Boring. Nothing mysterious here at all.

And that was the problem. The memo he had read referred to a series of emails between two engineers disagreeing about the timing of the traffic study, one taking issue with using Covid lockdown data, the other arguing that it didn't matter, both agreeing only on the indisputable fact that management approved and may have quietly encouraged this bit of chicanery.

There was nothing like that here.

All of the documents were copies or printouts. How easy would it be for someone to remove a page or two, retype them, recopy, and return? Such a deception wouldn't stand up in court when a demand for the original document would bring down the judge's wrath, but it might pass a casual inspection by a frazzled and overworked solitary attorney.

"Coffee's fresh," Ashley said as she slid back into her chair.

"I've got to run. Something's come up."

"Okley-dokley," she said. "I'll keep plugging along then. I can leave you a file of any questions I come up with."

"Tell you what. Take the day off. We'll pick up again tomorrow." *Keep your friends close and your enemies closer.* Whether the adage originated with Sun Tzu, Julius Caesar, or Vito Corleone, the meaning was the same. He needed Ashley, if only so he could keep an eye on her.

She stared at him for a second with a blank expression. When he didn't explain any further, she nodded, hiding anything that was going on behind those eyes. She put her coffee cup down on the table. "Then I'll see you in the morning."

He stayed silent. If she was offended and innocent, he would make it up to her. If not . . .

She gathered her things and left. Ted watched to be sure she had no documents with her.

Lester, now standing by the door, watched the scene play

out, and gave Ted a nod when she was gone. "You ready to head out?"

Ted walked over. "I wanted to stay for Kenzie to get back. The priest may be giving her a hard time."

"She pays rent here. It's not a gift."

"I don't know why the church should make an easier landlord than any other in New York." He checked his watch. They could go and be back in an hour or so. "I'll leave a message with Deepa and we go."

"Junior told me what his guy said."

"Oh?" That stopped Ted midstride. "Share."

"He said, 'It's your move.'"

Ted felt a crack in his carefully constructed certainty. Maurice had been prepared to do battle. It was the professionals who had called it off.

This war was far from over.

56

"IT'S SIMPLE," TED SAID, happy that the blast of Bollywood Hindu-pop coming from the car speakers muffled their conversation from the Uber driver. "If we can demonstrate that someone other than Haidir could have committed the murder, the ADA will have to let him go."

"I kinda cringe when anyone starts with 'It's simple.'"

"Humor me, Lester. I have an idea. If it works, we have a chance at keeping Mohammed's stepson out of prison. It all hangs on whether there's another way into the building."

Lester didn't reply, but neither did he beg off.

The Uber deposited them in front of the building. Ted hustled across the sidewalk.

He tried the door. No luck. The new lock and intercom made for a sufficient barrier.

"I don't want Hillyer to know we're here," he said and pushed the button for the third-floor talent agency. "We're testing his alibi."

A moment later a plummy male voice announced, "You must call first and make an appointment."

"I'm with Global-tec," Ted said. "I need to check the building for gas leaks."

"Go away."

"There could be an emergency," Ted yelled back.

"I am dialing the politz," the voice answered, exhibiting for the first time a hint of a Polish accent.

"Don't bother. I'm leaving."

Lester stared at him. His blank expression told Ted exactly how foolish he sounded. "You want to give it a try?"

"Now that you've successfully muddied the waters? No, thank you."

"One of these stores will have access."

Lester shook his head. "I got this." He stepped back onto the sidewalk and stood for a long minute examining the two businesses. Butcher or nails? Ted remembered there was another butcher two doors down.

"This one," Lester said, nodding for Ted to follow him. Without giving any indication why he had chosen that store, he headed for the Muslims.

A chime sounded overhead as they entered the butcher shop. Three bearded men stared at them from behind a counter of display cases. Then Ted realized that only one of the men was looking at him. The other two were focused on a television screen over the door. Their eyes shifted in Ted and Lester's direction then went back to the TV.

The third man smiled. He was older with a touch of gray in his beard. His muscular bare forearms rested on the display case. His smile was warm and genuine, but his eyes held a question.

"You are looking for a chicken?" the man asked.

Ted wished they had Mohammed to finesse the situation. But Lester needed no help.

"You got chickens?" he asked. "We're here on an animal cruelty complaint." He flashed the man the inside of his wallet. Though it held no badge or official ID, Lester exuded all the authority missing.

"Someone complained about the chickens?" the man asked.

Lester nodded his head and raised an eyebrow. "People are nuts. I'm sorry to bother you, but if you let us into the building and the backyard, we'll be in and out in no time."

Overhead, a woman's voice came from the television. "You're wrong, Darcy. Mark's not the father."

A second woman's voice, harsher and arch, replied. "I suppose you think it's all for the best. But don't forget. You owe me."

The sound of an electronic oboe swelled, crept up a half step, and abruptly cut off.

The butcher's eyes flicked to the screen and came immediately back to them. "Chickens?"

"Whatever," Lester said. His attitude and body language were those of a harassed public employee, forced by the rules of procedure to investigate such idiotic citizen complaints. "I know you kill chickens here. That's not the problem. We need to see that they're well cared for before they get the axe."

"Knife," the butcher said.

"Can we get to the backyard through your store?"

The man seemed to make a decision. "Or through the building entrance. Come. I will show you."

Lester skirted the counter and followed the butcher through an archway into the back room. Ted, though used to Lester's ways, was once again in awe of his partner's ability to morph into any shape needed.

They passed a massive meat locker and behind it an area that must have been where the chickens were slaughtered. The stainless steel table was so clean it could have served in an operating room.

And then they passed out a door and found themselves in the backyard, surrounded by chickens. Ted took one whiff and felt faint. For a moment all he could see were feathers floating around him.

Lester asked about security and the butcher pointed out the surrounding fence topped with barbed wire. "But that's to keep the chickens in and the dogs out. There is a gate for deliveries."

"What about people getting in?"

"Why?"

"Someone might want to steal a chicken," Lester said.

The butcher laughed. "A live chicken? They will only do it once. Why are you asking that? I thought you needed to see the birds are well treated."

"It all goes into the report. I wouldn't worry. This is a good setup. I'm sure you'll get no trouble."

It looked like a scene from one of Dante's rings. Low-roofed coops were covered in wire mesh with straw lining the ground beneath. There were no chickens visible, as they were all huddling in the coops away from the cold. But the sound of them all murmuring, clucking, and squawking was both chaotic and ominous, as though any minute there would be a roll of timpani and a crash of thunder. Ted felt the dust and odor permeating his pores. He'd need all the hot water in the building to get clean when he got home.

"And there's access to the rest of the building back here?" Lester strolled along a path between the coops, occasionally bending to examine a chicken, as comfortable in this insane environment as any city poultry inspector.

"This is important?" the butcher asked, while Ted considered the possibility that there might, in fact, be such a municipal position.

Lester shrugged under the weight of bureaucratic minutiae. "I need to put a check mark on the form."

The butcher pointed to a black-painted fire door farther down the rear wall. "That leads to the main entrance."

"Does the other butcher keep chickens back here, too?"

The butcher found this very funny. He roared a great laugh.

264 • MICHAEL SEARS

"No. They don't have a shochet who can slaughter chickens here. They must buy from the rabbis."

"I thought the rules were the same for halal and kosher," Lester said, keeping up the gab while edging toward the middle door.

"Many people think that," the butcher said.

"I think we'll go out this way, if you don't mind," Lester said. "My partner is feeling a little woozy."

"I noticed. Is he all right?"

"He's really a beef man. Red meats, you know."

The butcher nodded as though this made sense. "But you can't get in that way."

Ted looked. The door was there, but it was a single unbroken slab.

"It only opens from inside," the butcher said. "There's a crash bar."

Ted felt the first wave of doubt. Could Hillyer have found a way past this barrier? Or did Ted's whole theory dissolve at this impasse? He needed to get away from the damn chickens and think.

TED AND LESTER WERE back out on the street staring at the entrance.

"We can't pretend we need to get into the building if we're chicken inspectors," Ted said.

"No," Lester said. "But we did learn nobody could get in that way."

"Unless they had an accomplice," Ted said, "who let them in."

"No rats. Did you notice?"

"I wasn't looking."

"No. You were turning green. I never expected you to be so sensitive."

"I would prefer rats," Ted said.

"To chickens? Yeah, they're cleaner. Do we still need to get into the building?"

"We do."

"Your turn. Try the nail salon. See if you can persuade someone to open the damn door for us."

THE SHYLY SMILING YOUNG Korean woman unlocked the door and stepped to the side. Ted thanked her again and tried to give her a twenty. She declined it and dashed back to her store.

"That was some slick," Lester said with a sardonic grin. "I like the way you handled her."

"Yeah," Ted said. "I walked in. Asked for her help. And she said yes. Fucking amazing."

"Never happen in Manhattan."

They found the door to the backyard in an alcove behind the staircase. As described, it was a solid steel structure with a crash-bar lock. Ted pushed on the bar and the door swung open.

"What next?" Lester asked.

Ted took out his bank card, pushed the back door open, and let it close again—with the plastic strip blocking the lock. The door appeared closed but could now be easily opened by someone from the outside.

"Listen," Lester said. "That's Trane."

"Say what?"

"Coltrane. On the radio. Must be WKCR. *Out to Lunch.*"

Ted took a breath and held it. He could hear music from the second floor. The law offices. Someone up there was listening to music.

"Coltrane?" he asked.

"With Pharoah Sanders. No? I swear you have to be the whitest man ever born."

"Guilty as charged. But I've figured out how Hillyer did it."

"More info needed," Lester said.

"Suppose Hillyer is our killer. He finds out his partner is pocketing the cash, cheating both the clients and the firm, and screwing his wife. That's more motive than you get on the average *Law & Order* episode."

"Which one drives him to commit murder?"

"Who cares?" Ted shot back.

"I'm betting on the money angle. Nobody cares about the clients. And you told me about the wife."

"The problem is opportunity. The camera on the street caught him going out early and coming back after Kenzie found Spitzer dead."

"Where did he go?"

"It doesn't matter. Court? What matters is that before he leaves the building, he props the back door this way. Then he goes off, takes care of his business, but when he comes back he goes around the block to the alley. He comes in the gate, past the chickens, and in this door. He waits until the secretary goes out to pick up lunch. Then he heads upstairs, goes into his office, and gets the statue. He confronts Spitzer, who's an asshole and probably laughs at him, and Hillyer whacks him over the head. He wipes his prints off Lady Liberty, comes back down, out this door, and back to the street. Kenzie said the stairway smelled strongly of chicken. That's because the door was opened just before she arrived. Hillyer waits around the corner until he sees the cops show up. Then he walks in and acts surprised."

Lester kept an indulgent smile through Ted's explanation. "That's good. No evidence, but it's a good story."

"Right. A decent defense attorney could create enough doubt to get Haidir off."

"But we don't want things to go that far. We want Haidir cleared now."

"Yes, but I can get Duran to listen," Ted said. "He'll have to release Haidir."

"Isn't he going to want a little more? Evidence, maybe? All we've got is more work for him."

"He cares about who the murderer is. I don't."

"So what do we do?"

"I tell him our story. See what he says."

KENZIE CAME DOWN THE stairs and let the door slam behind her.

Deepa looked up, startled. "How'd it go?" And when Kenzie failed to respond, "That well?"

"What's going on here?" Kenzie asked. She needed to chuck her bad mood and find some positive action that might turn her dark thoughts around.

"Ashley left early. I think she and your man had words."

"Then I'll hear about it later. Any sign of the troops?"

"No luck. I don't know how we're going to get any of my girls back. They're spooked."

"Damn. We're about shut down for now anyway. Father Byun insists we keep a low profile." The last two words came with air quotation marks.

"Until the protests started, we did keep a low profile."

"Think lower."

"Gotcha. Well, at least he didn't kick us out."

"He did that too. I got us two months by pleading that New York real estate shuts down from Thanksgiving to New Year's every year, no matter what."

"That sonofabitch!"

"Yes. Don't think I'm defending him, but I get the feeling he's being pressured from on high."

"How high?" Deepa asked, giving the impression that she could be referring to anything up to divine intervention.

"High enough. Our Lady of Hope in Douglaston is angling for a new gym."

"And?"

"And LBC may be building it. In negotiations with the bishopric at present."

"Reisner again."

Kenzie nodded. "He's like a spider. His web is everywhere."

"Two months," Deepa said, making it sound like a cancer diagnosis.

"I know at least one commercial realtor who will take my call."

Kenzie phoned and was at first pleased that the woman sounded so positive and upbeat about her chances of finding something for Stop the Spike in their budget range. She'd get right back with some ideas.

And as soon as Kenzie ended the call, she remembered that all real estate professionals spoke in a similar positive and upbeat manner. It killed them to admit defeat—or even doubt.

So, she was amazed when her phone buzzed a half hour later and the screen ID read "Lucia Parducci."

"Lucy? I didn't think I would hear from you this quickly."

"Yes, well, I don't know what to say."

"So just say it," Kenzie said.

"I ran your credit because you'd have to sign for the organization anyway."

"Okay."

"What happened?" Lucy managed to sound both disapproving and sympathetic.

"What do you mean, 'what happened'? Nothing. What's the problem?"

"Could you have been hacked? Your credit score has dropped a couple of hundred points."

"What? That's not fucking possible."

"Your report says you're in default everywhere."

"No. No goddamn way."

"And the bank stopped your ATM."

"I just took cash out." Yesterday. Only eighty dollars, but the transaction went through with no problem. How in hell had this happened?

"You might want to look into hiring an internet security service. Or getting insurance. There are people who can fix this for you."

For a price. People with money could pay to protect their money.

"We'll get it fixed," Kenzie sighed. "It's all a mistake."

"Oh, that's such a relief. Give me a call when you get it straightened out."

She ended the call before Kenzie could reply.

58

TED AND LESTER GOT the Uber to swing by and pick up Kenzie in Ridgewood. There was a plastic pandemic panel between them and the driver granting them a bit of privacy, some audio distance from Beyoncé's charms, and a shield against potential infection. They headed down Myrtle to their respective homes. Kenzie was quiet and seemed distracted as Ted relayed what he had discovered.

"I think it's solid. I'm going to call Duran as soon as we get home."

Traffic was inching along. "Soon" and "home" did not deserve to be in the same sentence.

"Or I could try him now," Ted said.

Kenzie's lack of response caused Lester to crane his head around. He raised an eyebrow at Ted. Ted shrugged and shook his head.

"I'm going to do that," Ted said. "Right now."

Kenzie looked at him with a touch of confusion in her eyes. "Okay."

He thought she had no clue what she'd agreed to.

"You okay?"

She gave him such a strong glare he thought she must be trying to send some telepathic message. But he was too thick to receive it. So, he smiled kindly and told Siri to call Detective Duran.

But getting Detective Duran on the line took more time than driving through late-afternoon traffic in the center of Queens. Ted was still on hold when they walked into their apartment.

Kenzie sat at the other end of the couch. "I need to make a call. I'll explain later."

Ted nodded agreement, keeping his curiosity in check. She made her call and they separately waited to talk to live humans.

"Ashley," Ted said into the silence.

"Deepa told me."

"Those pages."

"Is it bad?"

"No. Now that we know."

"Do I fire her?" Kenzie stretched her arm and for a moment Ted could hear the bank's hold music. It must have been designed to get people to hang up.

"I don't think so. She'll quit if she thinks we're onto her. If she shows up, we put her to work."

"We could feed her bad information and let her send it back to Reisner."

"I think that works best on television."

His phone clicked. He'd been transferred without anyone speaking to him. Should he continue to hold or start over?

"Do you have proof?" Kenzie asked. "Solid?"

"Almost."

"That's encouraging," she said.

His phone clicked again. "Duran."

Ted didn't waste time. He introduced himself, then put his phone on speaker and spun out his theory on how Hillyer could have committed the murder. Duran listened with occasional impatient grunts. Ted eyed Kenzie to see her response to his investigation. She didn't appear as impressed as he hoped. In fact, she barely reacted, leaving Ted a bit deflated. Duran wasn't impressed either.

"Don't give up your day job, Molloy."

Ted wasn't going to let him get away that easily.

"Mervyn Prestwick is Haidir's lawyer," he said with a vocal flourish. Mervyn was one of Ted's few friends from his law school days, but more importantly, he was a top-notch defense attorney working both federal and state cases. If he handled a case that went to trial, he won it. "With this information he will torpedo your case. Ask your ADA."

Again, Kenzie failed to be astonished.

Duran sighed. "I don't know why I'm doing this, but I'm gonna tell you because Prestwick will get it in discovery anyway. One. Hillyer was in court that morning. Two. Forensics says odds are the killer's right-handed. Hillyer's a leftie. And three. There's a witness."

"Wait. Someone saw Haidir hit Spitzer?"

"No. That would be too neat and tidy. She saw him in the building."

"Who?" Another "she." So, not the talent agent, then. One of the wives? The secretary?

"Four and final. The kid has no alibi. He cut school that day. According to records, he did that on a regular basis."

Ted tried a scoffing laugh. "From truancy to murder? That's quite a leap."

"We're done."

He was gone and Ted had nothing.

59

"WHAT? WHO?" KENZIE THOUGHT for a moment. GeeGee? Goth girl? She'd shown up at an all-too-coincidental time, hadn't she? But the young man—whoever he was—had been gone for long minutes when she arrived.

"You know what I know," Ted said.

The wife? The other guy's wife? "Goddamnit. This is wrong." She still had the phone to her ear and was trying desperately not to hear the monotonous hold music.

"Haidir has no alibi," Ted said. Now he sounded like he was worried about it.

She wasn't. "Why would I expect a middle school kid to actually be in school?"

"I've got to pass all this on to Mervyn," he said.

"I'd bet he already knows."

"Mohammed says he hated middle school," Ted said.

"Who doesn't? Besides, he'll be in high school next year."

"I liked middle school."

"Nerd," she said.

"Not really. More of a brownnose, always seeking approval. I didn't get a lot of that at home. Are you still on hold? Who are you talking to?"

"The bank."

"What's up?"

She waved a finger, indicating later—or never. She wanted to get a handle on the problem before sharing it with Ted. She did not want his help, advice, or recriminations. "You

know, Duran only showed me pictures of *men* going in and
out that morning."

"The bank?"

She ignored the question. "I know the secretary left, picked
up lunch, and came back. How about the other woman? The
wife? Not Spitzer's wife. The one who sent GeeGee out to
get lunch."

The hold music paused again, and she repeated the magic
word three times. "Representative." She was reassured by
the robot that the call was important to them, and someone
would be with her shortly.

"You didn't see her," he said.

She shook her head.

"Unless the mystery person was that woman."

She considered this. "Possible." That felt wrong. "Unlikely."
That felt better. A woman might have worn those shoes, but
her gut told her the figure was male.

Another memory popped into her head. "The other day
when Mohammed drove me to the church, we dropped Haidir
off at Manny's."

"And?"

"And he got stopped by someone on the street. A kid.
But older. They were arguing. From a distance, with rain,
snow, and sleet coming down, and me looking through a car
window, I thought they looked way too much alike."

"You told me."

"Listen. The other kid—young man, whatever—was wearing
those same black Adidas. Smiths?"

"Stan Smith?" Ted asked.

She shrugged. She'd never heard the name before the
policeman mentioned it.

"The tennis player," Ted said. "I hear everybody's wearing
those now."

"Everybody?" she said, surprised that Ted would possess such knowledge.

"I know. I don't get it either. The guy's got to be in his late seventies."

"I saw those shoes. I'd swear to it."

"A good prosecutor would slice and dice you and send you home in tears."

"I'm not a crier," she countered.

"I know you're not. But it would be brutal and could hurt Haidir more than keeping quiet."

"I know it wasn't Haidir," she said, digging in.

"No, you don't. You believe it, and that's different."

"I would swear to it." Was she now sure it wasn't Haidir? Or was she merely fighting against Ted's mansplaining?

"And if you did, that would be perjury. As your sometime lawyer, I would counsel against it."

"Just for a freaking minute, consider if I'm right. Can we find that guy? Haidir obviously knew him."

"Yes." Ted bit the word.

"Oh," she said, surprised by him again. "Great. Gimme a sec." The music stopped and after a brief pause a recorded message came on suggesting she handle her problem by accessing the bank's website. "Shut up," she said to the robot because it felt good to do so.

"What's with the bank?" Ted asked.

"I'll tell you as soon as I get some questions answered." She went on before he had a chance to interrogate her any further. "How do we find out about this other guy? Like, a name, for starters." The more she thought about it—talked about it—the surer she became. The young man she saw with Haidir that morning was a ringer for the shadowy figure leaving Hillyer's office.

"Do I have this right? You are looking to get one

brown-skinned kid out of jail by pinning it on another brown-skinned kid."

She didn't need to ponder the issue. "I am trying to get a friend's kid out of the clutches of the highly prejudiced legal system. As you yourself pointed out, we need to provide an alternate explanation."

"Again. By railroading some random stranger you saw on the street one day?"

"Who could be the person I saw leaving Spitzer's office. It's not about skin color."

Ted stared at her expressionless for a moment. "I thought it was always about skin color."

She heard the word "swarthy" in her head, and for a moment stopped fighting and questioned whether Ted was making a legitimate point. Was her brain filling in the outline of a faulty memory and the cloudy observation of a fleeting event? "I need to give that some thought," she finally said.

Ted nodded once. Agreed. "I'll have Mohammed ask his son the next time he gets in to see him. We can get an answer by tomorrow afternoon."

The hold music paused again. There was a moment of silence during which hope blossomed. There followed a series of clicks and, finally, a dial tone. "Goddamnit!" She did not throw the phone across the room. She wanted to.

Ted was staring at her. Patiently.

"My credit score dropped by almost two hundred points, I'm overdrawn, and my card doesn't work anymore."

"Whoa," he said.

"And my credit card account is maxed out and closed."

"You've been hacked."

"No shit," she said.

FRIDAY

60

KENZIE WAS UP EARLY. Or more accurately, she'd barely slept. Warring, in and out of her dreams, were the two forces twisting her brain into knots—rescuing Haidir and defeating Reisner and his horrible tower. And she could feel herself losing both fights. Haidir, she was sure, had not slept well either.

She slid out of bed, careful not to rouse Ted. She had a full agenda of her own this morning and needed to get started. Judging by the regular pulse of his soft rhythmic snores, he would sleep for another hour or more.

Coffee and dry toast would do nothing for the headache taking up residence behind her eyes. A real breakfast was in order. Bammy and shrimp on Atlantic Ave? A Mexican omelet at the Classic on Myrtle? Either would go far to restoring her sanity. But first, she had to prepare for the arrival of Deepa, and Richard Pike, her father's friend, coming to tackle her computer problems. She headed for the shower.

There was no bread for toast. No time to run out for bagels or muffins. She put on a pot of coffee and ransacked the cabinets. She found a box of McVitie's Digestive biscuits that Ted had bought that summer when she made the mistake of asking him to pick up a package of "interesting" cookies. "Something I've never had before," was what she had requested. She'd tried one, rewrapped the rest, and they'd occupied a bit of shelf space ever since.

They would have to serve. She arranged half a dozen on a plate and set them out on the table. The coffee maker beeped. She was ready for company.

And just in time. There was a knock at the door. Deepa came in bearing two laptops—their primary and backup—and an iPad of her own. They set up on the card table and Kenzie plugged in her own computer.

"Oh!" Deepa exclaimed. "Digestives. I love these."

"Great," Kenzie said. "I'll give you the box. Ted doesn't like them."

The computer guru arrived. Though Pike had heard it all before, he listened patiently as Deepa described all their security issues, from the leak of Artie Pachis's name to the fake interview that appeared to come from the Stop the Spike website.

"And somebody had access to Ted's pretrial notes," Kenzie added. "The other side slammed him in court earlier this week."

"And your problems with the bank?" Deepa suggested. She had polished off the cookie and was eyeing the plate again.

"I finally spoke to someone there late last night. I wasn't hacked. Brian in Mumbai told me that the information on my credit report came from some 'unrelated bad actor,' posing as the bank."

Pike was already typing, scrolling, and scanning, but he looked up briefly. "You're lucky the bank is taking you seriously. But it will be a month or more before the credit agency posts the corrections." He stopped scrolling and glared angrily at the screen for a moment. He nibbled on a biscuit, then typed furiously.

A month? And a month after that Stop the Spike would be out on the street. "What have you found?"

Pike grimaced. "Who is authorized to tweak your system?" Another bite of the cookie.

Authorized? Kenzie had never considered the question before. Herself, of course. Deepa. Ted theoretically, but he would never make the attempt. Ashley had made some changes. She supposed any of the volunteers could have discovered the password and signed on. "Just about anyone in the office," she admitted. "It's never been an issue."

Pike frowned. Deepa squirmed.

Kenzie felt a flush of embarrassment. "I suppose we look unprofessional, but internet security has never been a concern."

"No, it never is, until it is." He put the cookie down and took a long swig of coffee. "This is a professional job. Someone created a backdoor passkey. Anyone—and I mean anyone in the world—with that key can access your whole system through your router."

"Our donor list," Deepa said. "Volunteers. Contact information."

"Could this have been done remotely?" Kenzie asked. "Someone from outside?"

"It could have," Pike said, "but it wasn't. Whoever did this was logged on to this laptop." He typed and scrolled again. "A week ago. Thursday."

Ashley's first day.

"Fuck," Kenzie said. "They'd be able to see not just our work, but anyone who'd used our Wi-Fi."

"Yes, but only what was uploaded," he said. "Say, if somebody used your system to save something in the cloud, or sent in an email."

Ted's notes. Kenzie shuddered.

Deepa looked at her. Their eyes locked. "Autosave," Deepa said. "That bitch."

"So you have a suspect?" Pike said.

"Is there any way this could have been inadvertent? An accident?" Kenzie said without much hope.

Pike gave a sad shrug. "I'm afraid not," he said. "This is high-end software. Well hidden." He broke the remains of the cookie in two.

"Have you ever heard of Collins Guards?" Kenzie asked.

"That is exactly the kind of people who are capable of employing a scheme like this."

Ashley would be in the office in the afternoon. Kenzie would be there too. She'd kill the bitch and hide the body behind the boiler as a going-away present for Father Byun.

"I can reroute this," Pike said, breaking the cookie in smaller pieces while he stared at the screen. "It will look the same, but all of the information will be scrambled. Useless, for anyone you don't authorize."

"Is that difficult?" Deepa asked.

He smiled and brushed crumbs from his hands and the table in front of him. The cookie had been reduced to a fine dust. "It won't take me but a minute or two." He took a flash drive from his bag and inserted it. The machine began to hum, and a downloading message appeared. "Maybe three minutes," he said.

61

TED CAME DOWN THE stairs, unshaven in sweatpants and a Sinéad O'Connor T-shirt Kenzie had found at the church's back-to-school jumble sale. Ted had failed to see the irony.

"What time's your meeting?" he asked.

"Done and done. Ashley has to go."

"I guess I'm not surprised."

She filled him in quickly on Richard Pike's report. "The LBC lawyers didn't outthink you. They outflanked you with stolen information."

"Oddly, that doesn't make me feel any better."

None of it made Kenzie feel any better, either. They were losing. Outgunned. Outmanned. Outmaneuvered. Haidir was going to jail, Ted was losing his case, and LBC was going to build its goddamn tower.

"I'll take care of her," she said.

"And I'll see what I can do with the lawyers. I'd love to see them try to explain this to the judge."

The headache and depression followed her out the door. She needed moral rejuvenation. She needed to remind herself why she was striving so diligently. Why was she doing all this in the first place? She would go to Corona and see the community she was fighting to save and talk to Manny Singh. They'd been introduced by the Preacher, a man they both trusted. Possibly Manny could shed some light on her pursuit of the shadowy figure at Spitzer's office. It was outside his store that she had seen that young man arguing with Haidir.

A long Uber ride later, she got out at Corona Plaza. The

Sanitation Department had made another one of their peri-odic sweeps only a week ago, but already the street vendors were back. Licensed and unlicensed. Dolls—thousands of dolls in styles ranging from indigenous to quinceañera. Sports caps in every color imaginable touting shoe and clothing manufac-turers and teams in dozens of sports ranging from Vancouver to New York, Miami to San Diego—and some farther south. Stacks of perfumes, hair treatments, scarves, and charms. Hot food, raw food, sweet or spicy with roots in the Caribbean and Central and South America. This was what she fought to save.

And across the street, a Dunkin' Donuts.

Kenzie walked down Roosevelt Avenue to the proposed building site. Directly in front of her, a three-story apart-ment building stood, though it had been empty for close to two years. Graffiti tags covered the plywood over the shattered windows. "Chaco," "718," "420," "TRAP," "Che," the always popular "SHARK," and her favorite, "Corona 19," a macabre joke considering that the community had been among the hardest hit by the virus. Street graffiti had made a comeback during the pandemic.

The six-foot-wide Stop the Spike poster she'd hung on the fence was covered in a spray-painted mural of nothing but eyes, each immediately recognizable as from some distinct ethnic background. If she stuck it in a closet, it would prob-ably be worth five or six figures in a decade or two.

Pedestrian traffic along that side of the street was sparse. The locals avoided walking a block with nothing but an eight-foot-tall chain-link fence, preferring the north side where there was still a feeling of vibrancy. Industry. Possibility.

Or was it all projection? Everyone on the street held their own visions of success. There were, no doubt, laborers, con-struction workers, and others who would temporarily profit from a multibillion-dollar project here. But the entrepreneurs, people like her father, who had created businesses and livelihoods for themselves and others, knew better. Their stores, bodegas, cafés, laundromats, Santeria shops, boutiques—and electronic fix-it shops—would not survive. Outside the Spike there would be a desert. Property values would plummet. And another developer—or maybe the same one—would buy up another block at fire-sale prices and erect another tower, taller and newer, and the poor and working class would be forced to move. Again. And again.

"You are holding back Armageddon, my friend. Never doubt it."

The Preacher. He was wearing his long black overcoat and sporting a new pair of Converse.

"Do I look like a doubter?" she asked.

"Today?" He smiled sadly. "A bit."

"Nice to see you," she said. It was. His mere presence lifted her heart as it always did. He carried a serenity that soothed her, and an air of permanence that reassured.

"How have you been?"

She paused before answering as the number 7 train rattled and clattered overhead like a tube of Lincoln Logs rolling down the stairs. It drowned out any chance for conversation.

When it had passed, "It's been a terrible week. Can I tell you the truth?" she said.

"Always."

"How does one fight evil and win?"

"Trust in the path of righteousness."

Calling in help from the mob was definitely off the path. So was lying to protect Haidir.

"I have to meet Manny in forty minutes. Is there time for me to buy you breakfast?"

62

KENZIE WAS SEATED ON a short stack of LaCroix seltzer. *Pample-mousse.* Manny had the only chair. In front of him an empty OUT box sat beside an overflowing IN box, while every square inch of desktop was buried deep under towers of magazines, circulars, flyers, unopened mail, and notepads covered in scrawled reminders and to-do lists.

"Eber Lopez is one of his names. The police say he has many." Manny grimaced. "I am not usually a soft touch. You know the meaning?"

"I know you help those less fortunate, and that the Preacher thinks highly of you."

"Eber is not a good person, and yet I hired him—twice. And fired him—also twice."

"Did he and Haidir work together?"

"Sometimes. But I told Haidir to stay away from him."

"You don't have a photo, do you?" she asked, aware of how unlikely this might be.

"No. I have an address, but . . ." He shrugged.

Kenzie understood. An address was a luxury for an undocumented immigrant. It could as easily be a fiction or a memory. It was almost never permanent.

"You're sure that's the man I saw?" she asked in one last forlorn hope.

"Talking to Haidir that day? From your description, yes."

It wasn't enough. A name. Probably a false one. She needed more.

"Can I ask you about Haidir?"

"A good worker. Like his mother."

"You know the family."

"She worked for me years ago. I would take her back in a minute. But she does well with the bodega."

"And Haidir?"

"He is very smart. He will make himself a success. I know he cuts school sometimes to put in extra hours and I look the other way. I need the help and he is wasting his time in school."

Kenzie felt a sudden shock.

"He's too smart for middle school," Manny said. "But I tell him next year will be different. He agrees."

"He cuts school to work here?" she said, trying to keep her hopes in check.

"Wednesdays. Half day. Tuesday and Friday mornings he comes in early for an hour or two."

"Wednesdays? Last Wednesday?" She jumped on this.

"No. He was arrested on Wednesday."

"No. Not this week. Last week."

"There was an ICE raid on Tuesday—an annoyance—but Haidir came to work the next day."

"All morning? Jesus Christ, Manny. You're his alibi."

He threw up his hands. "Am I? The police barely spoke to me. I had no idea."

"Would you tell them?"

He hesitated. He obviously did not want his employee relations brought up in court. "Yes," he said with a reluctant air, "but why would they believe me? I have no proof."

"You don't keep records?"

"My employees don't want records. They want cash."

She had to try. "But you'll talk to the detective if I can get him here?"

Manny swallowed once before answering. "Of course."

"Thank you. Thank you. Thank you." She'd gotten more than she'd hoped. Haidir might soon be free. "I'll call you."

Kenzie was at the door when Manny suddenly cried out. "One minute. I do have a photo."

Kenzie watched him tear through the papers on the desk, mentally revising her opinion of his filing system.

"It's here." He moved a leaning tower of circulars. "Somewhere. Don't leave. I'm sure of it." He kept up these entreaties as he became more frenzied in his pursuit. Kenzie wanted to reach over and help sort through the mess.

"Ah!" Manny looked up, glowing, holding a black-and-white police photo with wording across the bottom. Aliases. Warrants. Arrests.

"That's him?"

63

THE PHOTO WAS INCONCLUSIVE. It could have been the figure at Spitzer's office—or not. She was sure it was the young man she'd seen with Haidir last Friday. A week? It had only been a week?

Much more compelling were the crimes referenced on the bottom of the page. Kenzie had to remind herself that these were accusations, not judgments. This young Latino man could be innocent of all. The list of possible aliases further clouded the picture. This piece of paper had been produced by agents of the government to provide a wide net. If it produced a dozen possible suspects, at least eleven of them would have their lives turned upside down by the experience of being arrested and charged with any of these crimes. And the police would claim a victory.

All she had to do was cast sufficient doubt on the narrative that Haidir was the guilty party. Manny's word might be enough for an alibi. It might not.

There was one more bit of detecting that she could do to help Haidir. She could get this photo in front of another witness. The next time she and Ted confronted Detective Duran they would have a viable story to tell.

The halal butcher shop was already closed for Friday prayer. The nail salon was packed with women primping for the weekend.

The new buzzer worked well.

"Go away." The old man's voice came through with remarkable clarity.

"Mr. Krzysztof? It's McKenzie Zielinski."

"You must make an appointment. I am a busy man. I don't take walk-ins."

"We met on the stairs a week ago. I'm the woman who found poor Mr. Spitzer."

A pause, then: "The red-haired girl?"

She gritted her teeth. Were red-haired men referred to as boys until they turned gray? She counted to five. "Yes, Mr. Krzysztof. I'm the red-haired girl."

"Ah, come right in, *moja droga*." The lock buzzed. She pushed through.

Chickens. Straw. Acetone. And cigar smoke. And the sound of a dozen women's voices chatting in a variety of accents, though the primary languages were English and Spanish.

She hurried up the stairs, rushing past the law offices.

Mr. Krzysztof was waiting in the doorway when she reached the third-floor landing. Today he was wearing a stunningly white silk shirt with a high collar open to a few inches above his navel, revealing a pale but muscular bare chest. His pants were stop sign red with a slight flare at the ankles, and the ballet flats on his feet were school bus yellow. His glasses were the same purple-framed rose-tinted pair she remembered from their first meeting.

"Come in, come in. Ah, *słoneczko*, you are most welcome. You know what this means? Sunshine. You bring sunshine to my castle."

He stood back to usher her into the office. It was not a castle. The front room was obviously where he conducted what business he had, but she could see through the door into the adjoining room where there was an unmade double bed. Judging by the aroma, he cooked his meals back there, too, and he liked onions.

But the office appeared to be a professional space, with an ancient oak desk that must have been a nightmare getting up three flights. The chairs and other furnishings were also old, faded, and worn, but of good quality. At one time, there had been money channeling through this business.

"Sit, please." He waved a hand at the leather couch on the far wall.

Kenzie took one of the two padded leather chairs by the desk. With only the slightest sigh of disappointment, Mr. Krzysztof sat in the other.

"So, to what do I owe the pleasure of your company? You are not considering a career in performing Polish folk dances, are you? The *polonez*? *Mazur*? I could get you work."

She was not. "I'm here trying to help a friend. His son has been arrested and charged with Mr. Spitzer's murder."

He gave a noncommittal nod.

"I think he's innocent," she said.

"This Mr. Spitzer was not a nice man. No one should mourn him."

His voice modulated across the Atlantic, sometimes Poland, sometimes Astoria, and sometimes landing somewhere mid-ocean, sounding like the actors in those black-and-white movies Ted watched when he couldn't sleep.

"Did you have much contact with him?"

"I hear them. They fight. Not disagreements. Fighting. Things are thrown. Doors slam. Both of them. And their wives. *Szalony.* You know? Crazy people."

"Did you tell all that to the cops?"

"The police were not interested in me as a witness."

"They're pushing this through without listening to either of us."

"I am used to being ignored or having my opinions dismissed. I am *odd*. A character. I have proudly been so all my life, but now I am also old and therefore not only outré but unreliable. You, however, have both beauty and youth. Why do they not pay you respect?"

"I have a history of provoking authority." She, too, was an oddity. A character. Her role in the community required it and now that mask defined her to many. Especially so to the police.

"What can I do?"

"Do you think you would recognize the man you saw leaving Spitzer's office?"

He considered this for a minute before answering. "The mind plays tricks."

"I agree, but I've brought a picture. Can I ask you to look at it and tell me what you think?"

"But of course. If it will help."

She retrieved the photo from her bag and handed it to him. "Have a look."

He stared at it for a long time. "The face is familiar, but . . . many are."

Damn. She hadn't realized how much she wanted him to back up her identification.

"If I could see him move . . ."

Of course. He worked with dancers. His whole business was watching how people moved. "Just tell me this. Is it possible this is the man? Not for sure. Just, could it be?"

He sighed.

BACK ON THE STREET, she checked the time. Still midmorning. There was a possibility that there was time to get her plan in motion. She made a call.

"Nina? Kenzie."

"I don't think we have anything to say to each other."

"Again, I am dreadfully sorry. I know your husband must

have been embarrassed. I wanted you to know we've discovered who leaked his name to Ron Reisner."

"I'm listening."

Kenzie smiled. She was over the first hurdle. "We had an intern who looked too good to be true. It turns out, she was."

"The one at the party? She was no intern."

"No. I wish we'd had your insight when she came on board."

"But I loved the little gold crucifix," Nina said, the sarcasm oozing forth. "Just like a little nun."

"We think she works for a private security firm. Probably one of Reisner's people."

"Oooh. I'd love to hear that was true. Andy would too."

"She got into our computer system. I'm on my way to confront her now."

"Well, brava, Kenzie. You go get her. And let me know if there's anything I can do to help."

"As a matter of fact—do you have a contact for that website?"

64

IT WAS LATE MORNING at the Bahai coffee shop across from the courthouse—too early for the lunch crowd and long after the morning crush. Standing at one of the two bar-height tables near the front window, Lester was warming his hands around a mug of steaming coffee. Ted got a cup of Earl Grey at the counter and joined him.

"Cold," Lester said.

"And it's only November."

"And it could be in the seventies again this weekend."

"And we are thankful to live in a place with seasons. What did you find out?"

Lester looked around the near-empty store. They were the only customers, and the two women behind the counter were busy preparing for the lunch rush. Soft jazz with an unidentifiable melody wafted from overhead speakers. No one but Ted would be able to hear what he had to say unless he began shouting out his news.

"Hillyer was in court that morning."

"Yes. But . . ."

"But the judge granted a forty-five-minute recess around ten-thirty. Opposing's witness was running late."

"When did they reconvene?"

"They didn't. When the wit didn't show by eleven-fifteen, the judge broke for lunch, telling everyone to get back by one."

"By which time, Hillyer was talking to detectives back at his office."

"Right. He called in, the judge excused him, and they finished for the day."

"The only way it works for Hillyer to have gotten his butt back to the office and do in his sleazeball partner is if Hillyer left court as soon as they first broke and never came back. Do we know if he actually came back at eleven-fifteen?"

"The clerk is hazy. It was all hurried and the judge was in a piss-poor mood. The jury had just been seated and the judge ordered them out. Then he lit into the other lawyer, broke for lunch, and stormed off. The clerk wasn't paying any attention to Hillyer's side of the room."

Ted fumed. He wanted this timeline to fit. One small shift and all the pieces would line up perfectly. But where he needed surety, there was only the muddy puddle of human memory. "We need more information. The legal secretary, Jennifer DuPre. According to Hillyer, she's home nursing her PTSD. Can you find her?"

"And if I do? What do I say?"

"I have great faith in you."

"And why will she talk to me?" Lester asked.

"I repeat, I have great faith in you."

"And what exactly are you going to be doing while I'm hunting her up?"

"Talking to Reisner's lawyers. About Ashley."

"What will that get you?"

"Forging and altering documents tends to get judges' attention. Not in a good way."

"*Didn't My Lord Deliver Daniel?*"

"Say what? Is that a question?"

"It's an old spiritual," Lester said, pointing to the speakers overhead. "*From the lion's den, and Jonah from the belly of the whale.*"

65

ASHLEY WASN'T DUE FOR another hour, so Kenzie used the time to make more calls. There were plenty of donors who needed to be reassured. One of them called her.

"You're making quite a splash," Nina Pachis said. "Have you looked online lately?"

Kenzie pulled up a news feed. The WordNYC article was getting plenty of play. EYEWITNESS SAYS COPS ARE BLIND. *Though the only witness to a brutal murder says she has identified the man leaving the scene, the cops are paying no attention, content to railroad a juvenile with an unblemished record* . . . The picture was even clearer than the copy Kenzie had sent. The article went on to list all of the pending charges against Eber. The NYPD had declined to comment. There was no mention of the possibility of another perpetrator. Haidir's name was not there, though the *"person currently being held is said to have an airtight alibi."*

Kenzie was appalled.

"Nina, that's not what I said. This isn't what I wanted." She should have insisted on a contact with a more reputable news outlet.

"Honey, this is what they do. It would have been just the same with the *Post* or the *Daily News*. They write the story that gets the most clicks. You got your name spelled right and a plug for Stop the Spike. What more could you ask?"

Truth? What had she expected? The story was not what she had planned. There was no mention of Spitzer's many faults, nor Hillyer's lies or motives. Whitewashed. Meaning anyone white got full immunity from innuendo while the brown-skinned undocumented immigrant got crucified. And it was Kenzie's fault. She should have anticipated this. "Thank you, Nina. It's going to make trouble for that young man, but I can't do anything about that now."

"Sounds like he's a wrong one. You keep doing what you're doing, hon."

One thing at a time. She would talk to Ted later and find some way of reversing this mess. Or mitigating it, at any rate. First she had to deal with Ashley.

Kenzie took up station by the window and watched for the traitor. She was going to enjoy this.

And there she was. Without the over-the-top enthusiasm Ashley usually showed, her face looked ten years older. Thirties, rather than twenties. What was it about her walk that made Kenzie imagine her in uniform?

She disappeared from view as she came down the stairs. Kenzie felt a flush of anxiety but drove it away with raw determination. She had this.

"Oh, hi!" Ashley gushed. She went on, performing her usual entrance. "No Deepa today? Is she okay? She practically lives here, right?" She bustled to the table where she and Ted had left the files stacked. "I've got to make some headway here, or I'll feel like I'm letting the team down. Oh, is there coffee? Should I put up a pot?"

Kenzie watched and waited, letting her blather on.

Ashley swapped one box of files for another, removed the lid, and began piling manila folders on the table. "I was thinking, we could invest in one of those double hot plates like they have in a coffee shop. We could use one for coffee and the other could be for decaf or hot water for tea. I bet they're not that expensive . . ."

She ran out of steam, finally acknowledging that Kenzie was staring mutely at her.

"What's up?"

"We need to talk."

Ashley did not look surprised. Resigned, at first. But she rallied quickly and plastered on that oh-so-sincere demeanor.

"Uh, sure, Kenzie. If there's a problem, let me know."

"Sit."

"This organization and the work we do has become so important to me."

Bullshit! But she was good at throwing it. "Sit down," Kenzie said, and waited for Ashley to sink into the chair across from her. Kenzie took the seat that Ted usually used.

"We know."

Ashley did not immediately respond, though her face changed. The perkiness was gone. "Maybe I should leave."

"Not without giving me some answers."

Ashley got up and began gathering her purse and briefcase.

"If you try to disappear, the police will find you. There's got to be fingerprints here. DNA? There will be a warrant."

"I've committed no crime."

Bullshit and it showed. "Really? You hacked our computers and facilitated attacks on the organization and me personally. That will all reflect badly on your employer. And be assured, I will use all of that to attack Reisner."

"I don't work for Mr. Reisner. Or his corporation."

Kenzie stood and faced her, blocking her exit. "Are Collins Guards going to keep you around after you've been outed? Arrested? Or will they say, 'Thanks and see ya'?"

"What do you want?" Ashley asked, dropping her things on the table. It wasn't capitulation; she was negotiating.

"Your testimony. Help us screw Collins. And the hackers who work for them. I'm sure the FBI would offer you witness protection."

"I'd be dead before the trial."

298 • MICHAEL SEARS

Would Collins really go that far? It was clear that Ashley believed it. "You're the puppet. I want the one pulling the strings. I want Reisner."

"I never met the client."

"But you had to know that's who hired Collins."

She shook her head. Definitively. "I feel a little bad, you know. I like you people. If I lived nearby, I'd be cheering you on."

"How did you get into something like this? You're smart, presentable, capable. You're not a criminal. What about NYU?"

"I washed out of law school first year. That was a long time ago. And it wasn't goddamn NYU!"

"And this was your fallback? Lying? Deceiving people?"

"I did six years with Army Intelligence before Collins recruited me. The pay is stellar."

"You're good." Kenzie realized she meant it, and hated her for it. "The business with merging all our calendars? Slick, but in the end, not slick enough."

Ashley scowled. "You're going to lose this fight. I don't like the way you give people false hope. You think I'm a lying cheater? I could say the same about you."

"We may yet surprise you."

"Do what you need to do, Kenzie. Call the police, or don't. I don't care. But I can't help you." She picked up the purse and briefcase again.

"I need to see what's in there." Were there more forged documents there?

"No, you don't. I'm not taking anything I didn't walk in with."

"This time?"

"See you around," Ashley said and started to step around her.

Kenzie grabbed for the briefcase. Ashley pushed her away

and Kenzie stumbled backward, surprised at the strength of the woman. Direct confrontation wasn't going to work.

Ashley rushed by her, got to the door, and swung it open.

A young man stood there, his face hidden by a Covid mask. But his eyes—burning with anger—were visible. He wore a dark hoodie, black skinny jeans, and black Adidas. Stan Smiths.

THE LAW FIRM OF Hasting, Fitzmaurice, and Barson had been the primary legal real estate advisors to LBC for three years. A record, as Reisner changed personal attorneys with the changing of the seasons. The firm had even created a satellite office in Long Island City to facilitate meetings with Reisner and other clients and managers in Queens, Nassau, and Suffolk counties, saving them all a trip into Manhattan during the pandemic.

But Ted could feel the difference as soon as he came off the elevator. The Park Avenue offices, where he had, years ago, worked on mega corporate real estate transactions, had the look and feel of an antediluvian New York legal establishment. Dark paneled walls, carpets as deep as a well-kept lawn, and a quiet that seemed to suck up and hold generations of secrets. One could imagine gray-suited lawyers from a century and a half ago meeting clients with family names such as Bayard, Winthrop, and Schuyler. Barson joined the firm early to attract the Belmonts and Goldmans. Fitzmaurice came later when political connections demanded a more democratic face. His progeny were still in the ascendant.

The LIC office had a modern look. Efficient. Computerized. Anonymous. A place where bitcoins were exchanged for analog assets with only a digital signature, witnessed by a bot.

A single phone call had been enough to gain access. The team of lawyers he faced in Judge Bagdasian's court were surprised at his request for a meeting, but intrigued. No doubt they were expecting some form of surrender. He was going to disappoint the firm again.

He felt a buzz of discomfort when the scanner immediately registered his fingerprint and the electronic gate swung open. He'd been gone for ten years and yet the firm's systems remembered. He had not left on good terms.

"Ted," a thirtyish young lawyer greeted him as he stepped through to the main hallway. Brian Carter, number two on the team representing LBC. French cuffs and pointed collars, his way of demonstrating his wild and free personality. A golfer. He had never addressed Ted by name before this, always using the formal "Counselor." He led the way into a corner conference room, much too large and imposing for the meeting Ted had planned. But the view of the east side of Manhattan was impressive from this height. "The rest of the team will be joining us shortly." This meant they were in another conference room prepping, trying to intuit whatever Ted might have brought. He hoped—for their sake as much as his—that they would be thoroughly surprised.

"Can I get you a coffee? Tea? Soda?" Carter waved a hand at an array of such liquids on a chrome and glass credenza.

"Water, thank you," Ted answered, taking a square plastic bottle and refusing the offer of a glass tumbler.

The young Mr. Carter did not allow an uncomfortable silence to develop. "I had the most extraordinary luck last weekend. An old law school buddy was visiting town and hosted me to a round at Sebonack. Have you ever had the pleasure?"

Ted understood that the conversation was about a golf outing. He assumed Sebonack was a course somewhere nearby.

"A bit cold last weekend, wasn't it?"

"Ha, ha. And a wind off the bay strong enough to hook a shot right over the dunes. But a great day. It's a Jack Nicklaus course, you know."

Ted didn't, but kept his ignorance guarded. "That's nice," he said. "Is Jackie going to be joining us?"

Despite his law school indoctrination to never show surprise in any legal setting, the man's eyes bulged for a long few seconds. "Uh, no. I don't believe so."

Jacqueline Clavette was senior partner on the LBC account. No one called her Jackie, or even referred to her that way, save for Ted, who had a reason. Jackie was married to his ex-wife and had been instrumental in maneuvering him out of the firm years ago.

"She'll want to hear what I have to say."

"I think she's tied up in meetings all afternoon."

"Well, why don't you ask her anyway. La Bella Casa is her biggest client."

"She delegates much of the day-to-day work."

"I can talk to her or I can talk to the judge," Ted said, tired of the dallying, and so delivering his best threat.

Carter excused himself and left the room.

Ted let himself take in the view. Roosevelt Island. The East River. And a mile farther on, Central Park was laid out like a miniature version of itself. A shadow swooped over the reservoir. It took Ted a full minute to see it for what it was, a flock of starlings gathering to make the next leg of their journey south. Or wherever starlings went. He didn't notice birds unless he was far outside the city. Loons at Jill's family house in the Adirondacks. Fat pelicans perched on dock pilings in St. Lucia. Those black birds drying their wings on the dive float off Eleuthera. How long ago was that? His last vacation. Three years? Maybe four. Could he ever talk Kenzie into taking a break? Going somewhere together. Anywhere.

The door swung open and Jackie—Jacqueline, he reminded himself—entered in her wheelchair followed by Carter, Carter's boss sporting a paisley bow tie, and a younger woman he'd never seen before. Most junior present, he assumed, as she carried a laptop, briefcase, and some kind of electronic device with a short antenna. This she plugged into a socket in the table while the others took seats. The unit beeped once and began to issue a slight whine. No one would be taping, or listening in on, this interview.

"You have my attention, Mr. Molloy," Jacqueline said when the young woman had finished and taken a seat.

Ted took but a moment before he began. "Thank you for seeing me, Jacqueline. I'll try not to waste your time. Do you have an Ashley Parker working for the firm?"

A blank look went around the group. Meanwhile, the junior lawyer snapped open her laptop and began typing. All eyes went to her.

"Nothing current under that name," she announced.

Ted shrugged. "I'm pleased that she doesn't work for the firm. You will be, too." The three pages of emails were folded in his inside jacket pocket. He took them out and smoothed them on the desk. "I have here three documents that your people sent over for my review. I'd like to ask you to take a look and see if these copies match your records. Identically match." He handed the pages down the table.

Carter took them and read out the identifying numbers to the young associate who typed, then swung the laptop around for Carter to read. No one said a word as he scanned the physical and digital documents. When he was done, he looked up at his boss, a child of privilege named Percy Vandeleur Walters, who was consequently known as Walt. Walt nodded, giving Carter permission to speak. "Not a match," he said to Jacqueline.

"What's going on, Ted?" Jacqueline said, biting off the words.

Ted read through the pages quickly. "Please remember. I brought this to you first, not to the judge."

Jacqueline Clavette turned to Walters. "Please excuse us. Mr. Molloy and I require the room."

The other members of the team engaged in a few seconds of flickering eye contact. The young woman lawyer looked disappointed to be sent out just when things might get juicy. Carter looked relieved. He, at least, understood that things could get messy before they got good. Walt showed no emotion at all. They all filed out.

Ted found he'd already finished his bottle of water. He went to the sideboard for another. "Can I get you anything, Jacqu . . . eline?" he said with only the barest of hesitations.

If she heard, she had the wisdom to ignore it. "Diet Pepsi. No ice, thank you."

Ted poured and delivered it, then retreated to his seat across the long table.

"What do you want?" she asked.

"Some answers."

"I would rather fight you in front of Judge Bagdasian than break client confidentiality."

"I won't ask you to. I wouldn't. How's Jill?"

"Your name never comes up," she said with a shrug. "Ask your questions."

"Collins Guards."

Jacqueline nodded, her eyes revealing nothing. "My client is LBC, which happens to be run by Mr. Reisner. I am not responsible in any way for his expenditures on personal security. He survived one assassination attempt. His son did not."

"I understand. But Collins seems to be involved in more than personal security."

"This Ashley whoever person?"

"Most likely. Those pages. She smuggled them out and replaced them with fakes."

"I'll have Carter get you originals."

"Thank you. Two engineers in a pissing match about the timing of a traffic study. We could have killed a week or two with expert testimony and bored the jury to death. But I have a feeling we don't need to do that. Redo the study."

"Delay works in your favor."

"Not always." Ted told her about the protestors, the threats of violence, the fake "gas guy," the internet smear campaign, and the latest, identity theft.

"All part of their services."

"They play rough?"

"And they expect to be paid in a timely manner. Knowing Mr. Reisner's proclivities, we advised him against engaging Collins. They usually end up with a substantial equity stake." She shrugged. "Mr. Reisner makes his own decisions."

"They operate independently?"

Jacqueline didn't say anything for a long minute. Ted waited. He'd made his play and there was nothing else to do.

Finally. "If the client made a suggestion about preparing for possible tactical moves on your part, we would have been remiss in not taking the advice."

Ted continued to wait. Silence was his only weapon here.

"You had a bad day in court this week?" She made it a question. She was asking him to fill in the blanks.

And there it was. Ashley to Collins. Collins to Reisner. Reisner to Jackie's team. All protected by client confidentiality.

"With Reisner giving all the orders."

She laughed, a surprisingly sparkling sound. "You would be

306 • MICHAEL SEARS

sued for saying those words aloud. Collins makes sure nothing they do can be traced back to a client. On paper, they are providing 'personal security' and nothing else."

"Why are they doing all this?"

"To you or to your friend?" she asked with a hint of a smirk. "You will survive a bad day in court. But Ms. Zielinski? From what I hear, the bad news is piling up."

"Why are they doing this at all? Like you say, delay works for me, not you. Each one of these incidents is another gift I can offer up to Judge Bagdasian to demonstrate the pernicious false dealing of LBC and Ron Reisner."

She waited, watching him.

He knew the answer. The chaos of the last two weeks had distracted him. Which was the point. Chaos. Reisner thrived on chaos, firing executives, accountants, lawyers, contractors, advisors, pushing anyone aside—even family—in pursuit of goals only he could see. "Chaos."

"Chaos is his comfort zone. But if he feels cornered, he smashes things."

Jackie was being kind. And that was terrifying.

EBER LOPEZ CAME INTO the room screaming.

Kenzie recognized him immediately.

"What did you do? You! McKenzie Zia-something." He was holding his cell phone before him like a vampire slayer with a crucifix. At that distance, Kenzie couldn't see the display, but she guessed what was there. The WordNYC website with the featured article she had planted only a few hours earlier.

"Hold up there," Ashley yelled. She had stepped away from the door when he burst in, but now was edging around toward it again.

Eber advanced toward Kenzie. "This says you think I killed that lawyer. Why would you say that? What the fuck is the matter with you?"

"That wasn't what I said. They fucked up the story. I'm so sorry. We'll fix it."

Ashley stopped. She wasn't leaving. There was a moment of solidarity—two women facing an angry and possibly dangerous young man.

"I saw you there. Maybe *you* killed that man."

"That *was* you I saw."

"Whaaaat?" His scream this time was a long cry of pain. "You tell these news people you saw me? But you didn't! See? You lie."

Kenzie's first response had been fear, but she got past it quickly. Eber was smaller than she remembered, and these histrionics were sad. She felt for him, but she wanted to hear some truth.

"Did you kill Spitzer?"

He puffed himself up in controlled rage. It might have been intimidating from a bigger man, but in Eber's case it merely accented how slight he was.

She kept her voice calm, in control. "Ashley, call the police."

Eber whirled on Ashley. "You do and you die." He turned back to Kenzie. "That fucking lawyer took my money and did nothing."

Behind him, Ashley dialed.

Kenzie kept her hands at her side, projecting calm, empathy, and no fear. And hoped it worked. "So, you killed him."

"No, stupid woman. I didn't kill him."

Ashley spoke into her phone. "We are being threatened by an intruder. This is an active incident."

Eber turned and slapped at Ashley's arm. She dodged, but he managed to knock the phone from her hand. It skittered across the floor. Her face became a stone mask, much scarier than the scared kid threatening them.

"Stop," Kenzie yelled. "Don't you dare hurt her, Eber. You're the stupid one. If you didn't kill him, why not go to the police and tell them what you saw?"

"Fucking *gringa*." He threw up his hands. "You know fuck all. I can't go to the police. They will deport me. Or worse, send me to Texas."

"Okay, so you didn't do it," Kenzie said. "I never said you did."

"Yeah? Look what it says here." He brandished the phone in her face.

"What I told that reporter is that the person leaving Spitzer's office looked like you, *not* like Haidir."

Ashley was watching Eber with the intensity of an alley cat focused on a rat. Kenzie tried to signal with her eyes. *Stay back. Stay cool. I've got this.* Ashley wasn't getting the message.

"Why you no tell them about the crazy lady?" Eber yelled.

"What crazy lady?" Kenzie yelled back at him. A new clue?

"The crazy lady. You saw her."

"Her. Who?"

"With the rings in her face. She talks like she eats peyote for breakfast."

"The goth girl?"

"She comes out the door when I come up the street."

"You admit you were there," Kenzie said. "Finally."

"Yes! Yes! But I didn't kill the old man. I killed nobody."

Spittle flew. The guy was so adamant she found herself believing him.

"Wait," she said, forcing herself to maintain her composure. "Tell me about this lady. Did she see you?"

"She don't like me. She never remember my name."

Ashley, still looking as cold as death, came up directly behind him. What the hell was she doing?

"Or the fat lady. I heard someone coming down the stairs, so I hid. I saw this *gordita* go out the back door."

"Who? Wait. Where were you hiding?"

"The basement stairs."

"Eber, you need to tell all this to the police."

He ignored her. "I come into the office and I see him dead." Eber was still loud, but Kenzie had him talking, not screaming or ranting.

"Oh, really?" Kenzie said. "So, why didn't you call and report it?"

"Aaagh! Because I know everybody think I kill him. Killed him!" he said, correcting himself and shaking his head. "Like you. I watch you sneaking around. Then you go into the other office, and I run out. That is what is happening." He shook his phone. "Not these lies!"

He was so angry his words ran over each other. But what

he said sounded like truth. Kenzie tried pleading with him. "Listen to me, I have friends. We'll find you a lawyer. Just tell the police about this woman. Tell them you were there. You'll be doing a good thing, protecting Haidir. He's done nothing."

"I done nothing, too, you crazy bitch. Now my name—my face—will be everywhere. I could kill you," he said shaking the phone again.

Eber must have sensed Ashley behind him because he suddenly jumped around and flew at her, windmilling his closed fists and striking nothing but air. Ashley had moved.

"Nooo!" Kenzie cried.

Eber advanced. Ashley stepped back, luring him on, and away from Kenzie.

"Stop! Both of you. Goddamnit, listen to me."

Both ignored her.

Eber had youth and energy, all passion and no finesse. Ashley had training. She was a professional.

Eber lunged, both hands out to grab her by the throat. Ashley stepped forward to meet the attack, took one wrist, and spun behind him. She threw the other arm around his throat and stepped in close, up against his back.

Eber grabbed at the arm choking him. Ashley locked her arms together and with her hand pushed on the back of his head. A "sleeper" hold. Banned in New York and more than half the police departments in the country.

Eber tried to twist away from her, but she held on.

"Stop!" Kenzie yelled. "Leave him be." She grabbed at Ashley's arm but realized immediately she was only making it worse.

Eber tried to strike Ashley with an elbow, but she swung to the side and took a glancing blow to her ribs. His face was turning white.

Sirens. Flashing lights through the window. How in hell had they arrived so quickly? But Kenzie was damned glad they had.

"The police are here, Ashley. Let him go."

A look of sheer panic swept over Eber's face. He put a hand in the pocket of his parka and retrieved a folding knife. He flicked it and a nasty-looking blade appeared.

"Oh, my god." He'd come armed, prepared to kill. This madness was all her fault. She had to stop him. Kenzie lunged for his arm. The knife grazed her hand. She gasped at the stinging pain. Blood spatters flew. She grabbed at him again. This time the knife missed but it came within an inch of her left eye. Kenzie shrieked and pulled back.

Ashley had him. She forced his head to the side, cutting off blood to the brain.

Eber swung his arm behind him blindly, stabbing over and over. But Ashley did not let up on the choke hold. He kicked with his heel. She evaded. He stabbed again. She grunted but held on. A moment later, Eber slumped and dropped the knife. His legs collapsed and his eyes rolled back. Ashley dropped him to the floor and stepped back.

"Jesus, you killed him," Kenzie said. She grabbed a roll of paper towels from beside the coffee pot and wrapped her hand around it. Damn, there was a lot of blood.

The thump of steps sounded coming down the basement stairs.

"He's out. He'll be fine." Ashley's voice was reduced to short gasps. She put a hand to her stomach. It came away covered in blood. She staggered toward a chair, but her knees gave out. She sank to the floor.

Kenzie dashed to her side and caught Ashley's head. Blood was already pooling around them on the cement floor. Kenzie could feel it soaking through her pants, warming her leg. She put her good hand to the woman's stomach and pressed hard to stop the flow.

Ashley groaned.

There was a pounding at the door.

"NYPD. Police. We're coming in."

TED WALKED OUT OF the lobby into a blast of cold wind coming off the East River. There were days in New York City when the threat of global warming didn't sound so bad.

"Siri, call Kenzie."

"Calling Kenzie. Home."

Three rings later he got an incoming call notice. Lester. He took it.

"Where are you?" Lester asked.

"Just leaving here."

"Long Island City?"

"Yeah, what's up?"

"The young Ms. D. Meet me at the Starbucks at Queens Plaza."

"There's only one?"

"Across from DD's."

TED DID A DOUBLE take. This was not the woman Kenzie had described. She was blonde. She was wearing a get-ahead-in-corporate-life suit. Her makeup was subtle and attractive. This woman sitting across from Lester at the tiny table by the window could not be the same person.

"I got you a chai latte," Lester said, waving him over. "I hope that's all right." They both had cappuccinos with extra foam. Still steaming. They had not been there long.

Ted drank coffee when he first woke up. Later in the day, he tended toward tea. Black tea. Not green. And never chai tea.

Lester made the introductions. "It turns out Mr. Hillyer

fibbed a little. Jennifer isn't angling for a disability; she's got another job. A better job."

Ted raised the tea to his lips, inhaled, and returned the cup to the table. He was stalling, giving himself a minute to examine the woman before responding. The dye job was new; the roots were as blond as the tresses. She wore a small ring in her eyebrow and a tiny dot on her nose showed where she'd recently worn a stud. The suit was new. She could have been someone's daughter from one of the ritzier enclaves of Queens.

"I've been trying to get away from those people for months. Thank god, you know?"

Ted nodded.

"And I don't have to wear a fucking costume to work."

"Oh?" Ted asked.

"Yeah. Spitzer. The guy has a problem."

"Had," Ted said. "What kind of problem?"

Jennifer gave him the *what-are-you-stupid?* look.

"He hit on you," Ted said.

"The guy had like eight hands."

"So you dressed like a goth."

"He made jokes about lesbians, but, yeah. He left me alone."

She had solved her problem by moving on. "Where are you working now?"

"La Bella Casa. It's more of a paralegal job. I don't answer phones."

LBC. Reisner. The devil.

"How'd you land it?"

"Mr. Hillyer helped me."

Ted mentally laid out the connections. Hillyer has the in with LBC's in-house counsel—he'd worked with them. He helps a problematic employee get hired there, almost immediately after his partner is murdered. And then lies about it when questioned. Ergo, Hillyer wants her out of the way.

And to top it all off, the guy has a shaky alibi.

Lester leaned in and spoke softly to her. "Like I said, we're trying to help Haidir. Do you know the family?"

She pulled away from him, just enough to indicate her reluctance to share space. "I don't really get involved with clients." She spoke to Ted.

Lester gave Ted a quick glance, clearly communicating: *This was your idea.*

Ted took over. "How about a young Latino named Eber? Eber Lopez. Did you ever come across him?"

"Oh, puh-leeeze. Mr. Spitzer had sooo many clients with names like that. I couldn't deal with it. I don't know why they kept coming to him. He made 'em pay in cash and then did zippo. A creep."

"Did you happen to see one of Spitzer's young clients on the stairs that day?"

"On the street. Yeah. I told the cop." She stopped and let loose an exaggerated sigh. "Detective," she said, correcting herself with much effort. "I told him I saw the kid."

"Kid?" Ted asked. Haidir? Eber must be close to her age.

"Well, he's not real big, you know?"

"How old?"

"I don't know. Like twenty, maybe."

Eber. Not Haidir. "Did you recognize this kid?"

"What? No. I was out the door. The detective showed me a picture and I said, 'Sure,' and so what?"

"Right," Lester said.

She ignored him.

"Would you recognize him again?" Ted asked.

"You're kidding."

"I thought you might have noticed something about him."

"He had those shoes everybody's wearing. They're like tennis shoes, but none of the people wearing them would

316 • MICHAEL SEARS

ever be playing tennis." She looked squarely at Lester. "Know what I mean?"

Lester returned the look and spoke slowly and deliberately. "I know exactly what you mean. People of color."

Jennifer smiled. "No. People of color play tennis. I'm talking about losers. Lowlifes. Any color."

Lester didn't smile back. "Tell my friend about working for Spitzer. And Hillyer."

"It was awful. Fucking awful. When they weren't cheating the clients, they were busy cheating each other. Or fighting. They fought about everything. Even the damn music I played to drown out those chickens."

"One of them liked jazz," Lester said.

Jennifer let this pass. "Mr. Spitzer fought with Mr. Hillyer. Mr. Hillyer fought with Mrs. Hillyer. Mr. Spitzer fought with her too. He fought with the clients. He was always yelling at somebody."

"He fought with Mrs. Hillyer?" Ted didn't like this young woman. How could he? She was a ditz, but an unpleasant one. But she knew something that he could use. He didn't know what it was, but when it was revealed, he'd be ready.

"When they weren't smashing in his office. That was, like, disgusting. Whenever Mr. Hillyer was in court, the wife would show up and they'd be going at it."

"How'd you know what Spitzer and Mrs. Hillyer were up to?"

"She tried to get me to call her Marjorie, but I was like 'no way.' She wasn't my friend."

"Did you hear them? See them?"

"First they'd argue. Same thing every time. She wanted him to leave his wife and then they'd be together. That was never going to happen, by the way. The wife has the money."

Lester grunted, which Ted thought was most likely a strangled laugh.

"Then they'd go all quiet. Next, he'd stick his head out and tell me to go get lunch. Sometimes the door would still be closed when I got back. Then I'd hear them. Grunting. Moaning. Slapping. Fucking disgusting."

"And then they'd eat lunch?" Lester asked. Lester didn't smirk, but his low-key delivery got his point across. The mental image of Spitzer and his partner's wife enjoying a deli sandwich after screwing on the couch was bizarre.

Jennifer shook her head. "Mostly, she left right away."

Ted's phone rang. Kenzie. Not now! He flicked the ringer to Off. "Did you tell all this to that cop?"

"Mos def."

"What did he say?"

"It wasn't . . . wait . . . wait . . . what'd he say? Pertinent. That was it. It wasn't pertinent."

His phone vibrated. He checked the screen. Voice message. Kenzie. It would have to wait. If he broke the rhythm of his questions, he could lose this young woman's assistance. And he was close. He could sense it. He turned the phone off.

"And that's what was going on that morning?"

"They quieted down, like usual, and I wanted to yak, and she sticks her head out the door and tells me to go pick up lunch."

"*She* told you. Not him." This was important, but he didn't see how. Yet.

"I almost told her to EFF OFF. I didn't work for her. But then I just wanted out of there, so I went. Even though she sent me all the way to Thirty-First to pick up."

"And that's when you saw the young man on the street?"

"If you say so."

This young woman was never going on the witness stand. No prosecutor would present the defense with such an opportunity to blow up a case.

"And, again, you told all this to the cop?"

"He had a limp."

For the briefest moment, Ted thought she was referring to the person on the street. On second thought, "The cop?"

"And he acted like I was the one who whacked Mr. Spitzer. I could never. I'm vegan."

Kasabian. A believer that there were cops, and there were criminals. Citizens were potential criminals.

"Who do you think killed Spitzer?"

"I don't know. The cop told me it was the Arab kid. It wasn't?"

"Haidir?"

She shrugged. "That's his name?"

"You never thought it could have been Mr. Hillyer? Or Mrs. Hillyer. Or Mrs. Spitzer? Or any of the people Spitzer was taking money from and doing nothing for them?"

"No. Should I?"

Kasabian had made up his mind early and buried anything that didn't fit with his view of how the murder happened. And who did it. And he gave a not-too-subtle push for Jennifer to keep her mouth shut.

"If I get another detective to listen, will you meet with him? To tell him what you told me."

"I don't want cops coming to my job."

"No. That shouldn't be necessary." He handed her his card. "Call if you think of anything else."

"Like?"

"Anything," Ted said, having no expectations. "I've got to make a call." He wanted to get all this in front of Detective Duran. He needed to plan how to present it. Oh, and he had to get back to Kenzie.

Lester rose with him. "Thank you for your time." He followed Ted out to the street. "Mohammed'll still be at prayers."

"Uber?"

Lester checked. "Traffic is bad."

Ted nodded. This was not news. "We'll take the train." He began walking quickly to the subway station, Lester a few steps behind.

"You think the M train is faster than getting an Uber?" Lester asked before swiping his card.

"No more than eight minutes," Ted countered.

"I'll take the over," Lester said.

"For a dollar?"

"Done."

"What do you think?" Ted asked when they were on the platform. There was a lot to process.

"Detective Duran isn't going to buy it."

"So you believe her?"

Lester took his time responding. "I do. She's a flake and an idiot, and a racist, too. But I think she's telling it like it is."

"Which means Detective Kasabian is off the rails."

"Surprised?" Lester leaned out and looked down the track. He must have noticed it first, because Ted could now feel the thrum of an incoming train.

"He strikes me as the kind of cop who cares more about closing cases than getting it right."

"In my experience, that's situation normal," Lester said as the train squealed to a jolting halt. He peeled a dollar bill off the clip in his pocket and handed it over.

Ted took the bill with a grin. He rarely won bets with Lester. "I don't believe that."

"You mean you want to believe that's not the case. You're a skeptic but also a good guy, sometimes disappointed. I'm more of a cynic. I'm stuck with always being right and miserable."

69

THEY CAME UP THE steps from the subway at Fifty-Fourth Avenue. Queens Boulevard was a six-lane parking lot bordered by low iron fences. Nothing was moving. Lester began hoofing it up the block toward Grand Avenue.

"Hold up, I'm calling Duran." Ted finally settled on what he would say. He passed the Chinese bakery and another of the hundreds of Dunkins that had somehow failed to drive good coffee out of the borough and ducked into the bus shelter to get out of the wind.

Lester gaped at him in surprise.

Ted understood what he was thinking. They were three blocks from Gallagher's, where he could make calls in a warm space. Also, it was Friday afternoon. The weekend. Maybe a little early for a cocktail, but sunset came before five this time of year.

"Just give me a minute," Ted said. His phone was still turned off. He gave it a squeeze and waited for it to boot up. It pinged madly with missed calls, text messages, and voicemail. All Kenzie. He'd deal with that next.

"Hey, Siri. Call Detective Duran."

For once, the call went through with minimal gatekeepers. "Duran."

"Your partner's in trouble. Care to listen?"

"Molloy? You are seriously pissing me off."

"I understand. But Detective Kasabian is burying evidence. He may also be guilty of witness intimidation."

"Those are serious charges."

"You know him best. Is it worth having a sit-down? Without him, I mean."

"If you are making accusations, he should have a chance to defend himself."

"I don't see that it's got to go that far. I'm only interested in getting my friend's stepson out of jail. If we can make that happen, I'm happy to ignore your man's overenthusiastic approach."

"Up yours, Molloy."

Ted waited. Duran didn't hang up.

"Fine," the detective said. "I'll meet you at your gin mill."

Ted didn't hide his exultation. He jumped on it. "How long?"

"Hold on," Duran said. Ted could hear the detective tapping keys. "You'll never guess who just showed up on my computer. Again. Your pal. McKenzie Zielinski. Because she was the victim of an organized crime attack, I get notified every time her name shows up in the system."

And she'd been trying to reach Ted for over an hour. "What the hell happened?"

"No details as yet. But she's a witness. Again."

70

"**THAT'S A NICE CLEAN** cut," the ER doc cooed. "Six months—a year, maybe—and there won't even be a line. Nice. What was it? A box cutter?"

"Knife," Kenzie said. They were waiting for the local anesthetic to kick in, so the doctor could sew up the back of her hand. Kenzie had already demonstrated that despite her steely resistance to pain, the very idea of stitches caused her to vomit and pass out, frustrating both the medical team and the two NYPD detectives who had been questioning her.

"Of course," the doctor said. "Same as . . ."

"Exactly," she said and mimicked his head gesture indicating the curtained alcove where many of the same team were busy saving Ashley's life. She checked her phone again. Still no response from Ted. She had to tell him all she'd learned about Ashley—and the young Latino. And he should know that she had been wounded in the confrontation.

It wasn't easy texting one-handed, and she'd finally given up. His phone was off. He hadn't simply stopped the alerts, he'd acted like a boomer and turned the damn thing off. They needed to set some basic ground rules for telecommunications.

"We're going to get started," the doctor said.

How old was this guy? Could he really be old enough to be working in an emergency room? She tried to remember the doctoral hierarchy. Were residents the same as interns? She acknowledged that Ashley's wounds required the most experienced senior staff, but hoped that this guy had done this kind of thing once or twice before.

"Are you ready?"

No. Of course not. She was goddamn terrified. The doctor was pinching her thumb. She could see him doing it. But she didn't feel a thing. It was like the hand he held belonged to someone else. Her stomach threatened to do another somersault.

"I can't watch."

He smiled. "Just turn your head. This won't take a minute."

She couldn't. Her eyes were incapable of looking anywhere but the bloody seam on the back of that hand. "Can't you just put a Band-Aid on it?" They'd already covered this. Scarring. Infection. Gangrene. She was in full avoidance mode, terrified and hating herself for being such a baby.

Where the hell was Ted?

Lester. She could call Lester. He had the good sense to answer his damn phone.

Her phone rang. Ted. She grabbed it. "Finally."

"Are you okay?"

"Ted. Where are you?"

"Gallagher's. Lester just went inside. I saw your messages. Duran said you were a witness. To what?"

"Ashley Parker is in the ER. And that's not her real name, by the way." The information poured out of her. Ashley was Alicia. Collins Guards. Eber arriving. The fight. The knife.

"Are you okay?" he asked again.

"I need a few stitches. I'm fine."

"My phone says you're in Brooklyn. Wyckoff Hospital?"

"Treating Kings and Queens," she quoted. "I was born here, you know."

"I'm coming to get you."

Wonder that he had figured out how to track her phone

met continuing monumental annoyance that he'd been unreachable. "Don't bother. The Preacher's here. Mohammed's on his way." Unlike Ted, her friends had responded to her text.

"Just another minute," the doctor said.

"We'll meet you there," she said into her phone. "At Gallagher's. If the cops are through with me. I think they are."

The doctor stepped away and an unsmiling female nurse with the forearms of a dockworker took his place.

"Is Ashley going to make it?" Ted asked.

"Alicia. Alicia. Eber stabbed her, but it was self-defense. They let the cops talk to her so she can't be that bad." She looked at her hand. The nurse was wrapping a gauze bandage around it. "I thought we weren't going to do that."

The nurse looked up at her. "Put away the phone and I'll explain to you what you have to do to keep it clean."

"But the doctor warned me about scarring if he didn't do the stitches."

"Stitches are done. Now get rid of the phone."

She gasped. She hadn't felt a thing.

"Kenzie! What the hell is going on?"

"I'll see you at Gallagher's, Ted."

71

THE FIVE OF THEM were crammed into the back booth at Gallagher's. It was designed for four, and despite the less than average size of Mohammed and Kenzie, it was a tight fit for Lester, Ted, and the Preacher.

Lester was taking it slowly, but as it was within wishing distance of sundown on a Friday, he'd begun his weekend. Vodka, rocks, no fruit. Ted had a Stella. Mohammed and the Preacher ordered Cokes. And Kenzie, with her right hand wrapped in multiple layers of bandage, was sipping at a glass of Jameson Irish Whiskey. Neat.

"Detective Duran is due here in twenty minutes and I think we have a lot to cover." Ted deferred to Kenzie. "I think you go first."

Kenzie had been released from the ER after receiving hours of questioning by police, and eight stitches across three fingers. She looked as though she'd rather go home, shower, and sleep for twenty-four hours. But she sucked in a breath and began.

"First up. Haidir has an alibi. He was at work. Unfortunately, Manny doesn't keep records for part-time staff. For part-time, read undocumented."

"Will Manny testify?" Ted asked.

Kenzie winced. "He will, but we'd rather avoid it, if possible. The repercussions could be awful for a lot of innocent people."

"Including Manny," the Preacher said.

"So what can you do?" Mohammed asked. "He is a boy. Just a boy. And he is in a bad place."

Ted administered an encouraging grip on the man's shoulder. "That's why we're here, my friend. We show the cops they made a mistake by pointing them at the real murderer." He turned to Kenzie. "Please, keep going."

"I learned a few things while being questioned. Ashley Parker is Alicia Pratt from Hudson, Ohio, according to the NYPD. She works for Collins Guards. She told police the gas guy who was also leading the paid protestors is somebody senior at Collins. She's never met him. The interview video was not their work—they subcontract all that—but she said it was probably paid for by the firm. She's ex-military, which I guess explains why she thought she could take on a skinny Latino teenager without getting stabbed. She's in intensive at Kings County."

"She saved your life?" Mohammed asked.

"I don't think so. Eber was furious, not murderous." She held up the bandaged hand. "This was the result of me trying to intervene after she jumped him. If I'd kept my distance, I'd have saved myself a trip to the ER and the stitches."

"He is a liar," Mohammed snapped.

"But I don't think he's a murderer," Kenzie said. "Or Spitzer's murderer, at any rate."

Mohammed wouldn't let it go. "Haidir tells me terrible things about this boy."

"I'm not surprised," Ted said. "But Kenzie has a point."

She made it again. "He didn't come in waving a weapon. He pulled it out only when attacked—from behind. And the only reason he was there at all was because of me. That reporter twisted the story, but I made it happen."

"Hmmm," the Preacher hummed.

They all looked at him.

"Take responsibility for your own actions, not those of others. That is as much as we can bear," he said.

"Amen to that," Ted said.

"Haidir tells me that he is a monster," Mohammed said. "The police want him in Texas. In his home, he did terrible things to a child."

Kenzie nodded at Mohammed's anger but replied calmly. "The police ran his fingerprints and shared them with Texas. They don't match."

But Mohammed wasn't done. "In El Salvador . . ."

Kenzie cut him off. "I don't know what happened in El Salvador, and I bet nobody else does either. It was my words—twisted, but still mine—that helped turn Eber into exactly what we all imagined him to be. Only, he wasn't, and now he is."

"Your heart is big," the Preacher said.

Kenzie threw up her hands. "Do we just let it go? Haidir was getting railroaded and now we're fighting for him to be free. So, Eber will get railroaded next. Only he has no one to take up his side."

"I don't think he did it, either," Ted said. "The guy needs our help."

Kenzie looked at him in surprise. He understood. He was an unlikely advocate for a man he'd never met. But Ted had been arranging clues into a pattern that made sense to him. "I have an alternate theory," he said into their silence. "Which I will share when we've all had our say on Eber. Please, continue."

"That's all I got," Kenzie said. "Anyone else have an opinion?"

"I don't like him," Mohammed said.

"Well, neither do I." Kenzie held up her bandaged hand. "But I still think we need to do something."

"Lester, my friend, it seems you are the deciding vote," Ted said.

Lester sipped his vodka, nodding his head to the music.

Something from the mid-twentieth century with a raucous piano. The song ended. He waved for a refill.

"Lester?" Kenzie prodded.

"I'm savoring the power of my position," he said. He tipped his head back and sucked the shards of ice left in the glass. "I vote aye. Eber is no doubt guilty of something besides stabbing that lady, but that's the excuse the police always use, isn't it? What next?"

"I think we have more than one possible perp," Ted said. "How about a timeline?"

Kenzie raised her eyebrows. "A timeline? Didn't we see that in one of your old movies? William Power, right?"

"Powell," Ted said patiently. "William Powell. *The Thin Man*. Nominated for an Oscar three times." He stopped and looked around the group. Mohammed looked confused. Everyone else—including the Preacher—was giving him the eye roll.

"Old ways are time-tested," the Preacher said, speaking to Kenzie.

She nodded to Ted. "The floor is yours."

"Here's how it could have happened. I need to sell it to Duran."

Huan slammed Lester's drink on the table. "I'm goin' off shift."

Ted looked down the table. "Last call?" No one responded. "I'll have another," he said.

"You could have saved me a trip," Huan said before turning back toward the bar.

Ted swallowed the last of his beer and began: "That morning, Hillyer leaves for court, planning to come back later, on the sly. He jams paper or a piece of plastic—something—into the back door latch so he can get in without being seen on the street. Lester and I looked at that yesterday. Very doable."

"Unless someone else uses that door," Kenzie said.

"Unlikely," Ted said. "It's a fire door. No one uses it."

Kenzie nodded.

Ted went on. "Mrs. H arrives sometime later, goes upstairs for her usual fight-and-fuck with Spitzer. She sends DuPre out to pick up lunch. What time?" He directed the question at Lester.

"Eleven-thirty or so."

"Hillyer cuts out of court at eleven-fifteen. It's tight, but with no traffic he could have made it in half an hour. Let's say, eleven-forty-five. Mrs. H. takes off."

"Could that be the lady Eber saw?" Kenzie said. "Not goth girl."

Ted nodded. This was possible. "Meanwhile Hillyer and Spitzer fight. Who knows who did what, but when it's over, Spitzer is dead. Hillyer leaves, going out the back door. Eber is still hiding in the basement."

"Why doesn't Eber see him?" The Preacher was looking skeptical.

"Because Eber is still hiding in the basement. He doesn't want to be seen."

The Preacher didn't look satisfied with that answer, but he merely blinked. Ted went on.

"Eber waits a few minutes until he's sure no one else is around and goes upstairs to have it out with Spitzer. Only Spitzer is already dead. The buzzer from the front door goes off and he panics. It's Kenzie."

Huan slammed the bottle of Stella down in front of Ted. "Yous needs to pay up. I'm going off shift."

Ted handed her a twenty. "That's for your impeccable service. I'll settle up with the bartender when we're done."

Huan gave this some thought, then took the bill and shrugged. "Zhang don't like that."

"I'll make it right with him," Ted said.

She shrugged again and left.

"Where was I?"

"I just arrived," Kenzie said. "Noon, give or take."

"You're there, what? Five minutes? Ten?"

"Ten," she said.

"The buzzer goes off again," Ted said. "Upstairs."

"The dancer," Kenzie said. "Only the intercom is fluky. He gets no answer and leaves."

"Right. Eber takes off. Kenzie barely gets a glimpse of him. The talent agent goes out to the landing looking for his dancer appointment and sees Eber tearing down the stairs."

"And I find Spitzer and call the cops," Kenzie finished.

The Preacher was rapt through all of this. Lester hadn't tasted his fresh drink.

Kenzie looked unconvinced. "Goth girl walked all the way to Bareburger, got the lunches, and walked back in less than half an hour? She had to have left earlier. No way could that woman move that fast."

Ted checked his watch. Duran was due any minute.

Lester swallowed some vodka. "Wait up. So who did Eber see on the stairs? I thought he was hiding. What am I missing?"

"'The fat lady,'" Kenzie said. "That's what he said. A fat lady came down and went out the back door."

"Who is that?" the Preacher asked.

"I've never seen Mrs. Hillyer," Kenzie said. "Could she be the fat lady?"

"No way," Ted said. "She's . . ." *Curvy* was what he almost said, but thought better of it.

"Curvy," Lester said.

"Might a nineteen-year-old boy from Central America think this forty-year-old woman was old and fat?" the Preacher asked.

"No," Ted said.

"Mmm," Lester said.

"Mohammed?" Kenzie asked.

Mohammed's thick eyebrows had meshed into a single line of concern. "No traffic?"

They all stared at him. No one answered.

"You said 'no traffic.'"

Ted understood immediately. This wasn't just a hole in his timeline, it was a chasm threatening to swallow all the other clues. There was never a moment with no traffic these days.

"I'll be damned," Ted said, expressing the thought all were sharing.

Silence from the rest of the table.

"I say it was Colonel Mustard in the Library with the Noose," Lester said. He waved for another vodka.

Kenzie spluttered a laugh and raised her glass. The Preacher chuckled. Mohammed had a look of utter bewilderment. Ted shook his head and raised his beer.

"Putting the 'happy' in Happy Hour?" Detective Duran asked.

How long had he been standing there?

SATURDAY

72

LESTER AND TED WERE in the back seat of the unmarked car, two detectives up front with the eavesdropping warrant. Duran and an investigator from the DA's office named O'Mara. Kasabian had not been invited.

"I'd feel better if you guys were all right outside the door," Ted said.

"I'll be right outside the door," Lester said with a chuckle. "I'm not fast on my feet, or worth much when I get there, but I'm all heart."

Duran wasn't making jokes. "We'll be on the landing. The two of you go in together. Mr. McKinley stays in the anteroom. You're there so that if they get the idea to take hostile action, they will hold back as there is a witness right outside the door. But if they do, get out of the way because we're coming in. Molloy talks to them alone, so they think they're in control. We're coming in if we hear a threat of any kind. Or, if the device cuts out. Clear?"

They'd covered all of this twice before. The ADA was in the van across the street with the recording engineer and a backup team. If some part of the plan went haywire there would be an instantaneous response, with all of it on audiotape.

"Tell me again, why are these people going to talk to you?" O'Mara asked.

This, too, had been covered in previous meetings. "Because they really fucking hate each other," Ted said. "And they both hated Spitzer. But mostly because they'll think I'm as crooked as they are."

"He's a lawyer," Lester said. "People believe they're capable of anything."

"Thank you for that vote of confidence."

"We'll be on the landing, half a flight from you if you need us," Duran said. "What's the magic word?"

"Help."

"Nah," Lester said. "It's 'chocolate.'"

"Chocolate?" Ted asked.

"Nobody ever misheard the word 'chocolate.'"

"Fine," Duran said. "It's chocolate. Let's hear it."

Ted could think of no good reason to object. "I will enunciate and speak quite clearly. Chocolate."

"Very good."

"Can we get started now?" Lester asked.

"Well, aren't you cranky today?"

"It's the weekend." Lester wanted a drink.

Ted thought that a reasonable wish under the circumstances.

73

MARJORIE HILLYER EYED LESTER with suspicion. He ignored her, which seemed to bug her even more.

"I'll be right here," Lester announced to Ted, planting himself in front of the receptionist's desk with a deliberateness that dared anyone to get him to move.

Mrs. Hillyer didn't try. "This way," she said and led Ted into her husband's office, closing the door behind him.

Hillyer was seated at his desk giving the appearance of having been interrupted at work. It was bogus. The little reading lamp was angled slightly so that anyone sitting across from him would have light in their eyes.

Ted took the seat nearest the door after tilting the lamp away. Mrs. Hillyer, with a nervous glance at her husband, sank into the other. Someone had polished and rearranged the three sculptures. The Eiffel Tower was now closest. The American flag was as dusty, faded, and drab as ever.

"Make your pitch, whatever it is," Bruce Hillyer said. "We've both got a lot to do today."

"Sure," Ted said, with his best smile. "I'm here to shake you down."

The wife started like a rat caught on the subway platform during rush hour.

"Excuse me?" her husband said.

"You're busy. So am I. So let's not waste time. Here's the deal. I want my friend's outstanding bill wiped off the books." He grinned at Mrs. Hillyer. "Your wife already offered to do that—for a price."

Hillyer opened a drawer and took out a cigar. "I am not surprised," he said coolly.

She, on the other hand, was practically squirming in her seat.

"I have something better to offer," Ted said.

"What would be better than cash?" Hillyer asked, taking a clipper from the drawer and fiddling with the cigar.

"I'm not done," Ted said. "I'm trying to help a friend, but I'm no altruist."

Hillyer looked up with the first sign of interest in his eyes. "Please go on."

Mrs. Hillyer squinted at him with suspicion.

"But I'm cheap," Ted said. "I want fifty grand. For myself. Cash would be best, but that's negotiable."

Mr. Hillyer's eyebrows shot up. "Cheap? What does your friend owe? Forty something? Do I remember correctly? Plus your extortionate cut, that comes to almost one hundred thousand. What is worth that much to me?"

"My silence. Your freedom."

The wife laughed. It was a strained sound. Forced. If she was trying for derision, she failed. Desperation was more like it.

Her husband gave her a quick glance. "You should go."

She set her jaw. "Not a chance."

Hillyer turned to Ted again. "I'm listening."

"Howard Spitzer was a terrible human being," Ted said.

"Agreed."

"He scammed his clients, you, the IRS . . ."

Hillyer shrugged, unimpressed. "Spitzer was a crap lawyer. Always. He never lifted a finger for a client unless he absolutely had to. Then he got worse. Two years ago, maybe? I was worried that the Bar Association might go after him, but then I realized they don't give a shit about immigration law. Nobody does."

"And more recently?"

"Are we up to the part where he was screwing my wife? Is that where we're headed? That would be July. Four months ago."

The wife may have been surprised at this revelation. Had she thought she'd been better at hiding her tracks? She tried a murderous look instead. It washed right over the guy with no apparent effect.

Mr. Hillyer smiled grimly. "She's a sloppy liar. Wasn't it Mark Twain who said something about how lying required a good memory? My wife doesn't qualify."

"Maybe she wanted you to know." Ted thought the plan was working. These two would soon be at each other's throats.

"A cry for help? That's good." He made a sound—more of a scoff than a laugh. He looked at her. "I promise not to be surprised when your lawyer trots that out at our next divorce hearing."

She finally rose to her own defense. "That's exactly what it was. Howard saw I was lonely and hurting, practically abandoned by my husband. He took advantage."

Every word sounded false. All three of them could hear it; if she was at all embarrassed, she didn't let it show.

"At any rate, you had motive," Ted said to the still-grinning husband. "He'd put your firm, your career, and your marriage in jeopardy. And he was robbing you—as well as the clients. I don't know what finally sent you over the edge, but you planned it and killed him."

"I was in court that day. Check. The cops have already cleared me."

"Your alibi doesn't hold up. Court let out early because the other side couldn't locate a witness. No one remembers you coming back after the first break. I've timed it. You could have made it here easily," he said, bending the truth almost to the breaking point. "You came in the door from the alley— blocking it open when you left that morning. You went out the same way. That's both opportunity and pre-planning. Murderous intent."

Hillyer's grin hadn't faded. It was an ugly smile, smug and condescending. For the first time, Ted began to doubt his plan. He wasn't getting to the guy.

The man kept up the show. "I'm insulted. You think that's the best murder plan I could come up with? I whack the guy with a statue. In our offices? While cutting out on a hearing? Of course no one noticed whether I was there or not. That witness fell asleep on the train and didn't wake up until he got to Ronkonkoma. I didn't plan that. It happened. And I know about it because I was there while the judge was reaming out opposing counsel. It was a hoot."

"There will be a witness. Or a camera caught you on the street, or the subway. Or was it an Uber? Your credit card will have a record, including time. They'll link it."

Hillyer looked down at his cigar, and Ted realized this was technique. The movement hid his eyes.

"You had it planned. When you left the office that morning you propped something in the back door so you could get back in without being seen. Or photographed. The vid-cams across the street? You came upstairs after your wife got the secretary out of the way. You killed Spitzer and then went out the same door you came in. Then you waited around the corner for the police to arrive and showed up acting all surprised."

Hillyer looked at his wife. She stared at Ted.

Ted stared right back. "Which makes you an accessory. I don't really care, you know. It seems everybody hated the guy, and he certainly did no good for Mohammed or his stepson. But the police will make another go at it."

"Enough of this crap. Bottom line? They've got the stepson for this," Hillyer said.

"You haven't heard? He's being released later today," Ted

replied. "Ironclad alibi." He waited while the two of them digested this further stretching of the truth. "The ADA has ordered the case reopened. And there's where I come in. Now, what's my silence worth?"

Mr. Hillyer was good at hiding his thoughts and feelings. The business with the cigar being one of his tricks. He managed to convey sincerity while avoiding connection. "Without new evidence they'll drop it. It's tough to make a case against a second suspect."

His wife was not as good a card player. Ted could see the gears working as her thoughts flashed across her face.

"Unless . . ." Ted said.

Hillyer cut him off. "That's a story, Counselor. And it's not worth a hundred grand. Tell you what, I'll forgive the immigrant's debt. It would cost me more in time and aggravation to litigate it. But as for your cut, not a chance."

"Pay him," Mrs. Hillyer said. "Give him the damn money."

"Shut up, Marjorie."

"Don't be an idiot. Pay up and we never have to hear about this again."

Ted felt a glow. Things were moving in his direction. "Are you admitting to anything here, Mrs. Hillyer?"

"Shut up. I'm talking to my husband."

Good advice. These two might do fine without his nudging. The cops on the landing and across the street were getting an earful.

Hillyer kept fighting. "He's got nothing. Ergo, what he thinks he has is worth exactly that. Zero."

"You are not only arrogant and stupid, which is a terrible combination, but you are also cheap. Now pay the goddamn man, Bruce!"

"Shut the hell up. You want to pay him, be my guest. Take it out of the money you've been skimming here."

"You are such a needledick."

Hillyer leapt up and roared, "I've had it, lady. I swear I'll . . ." He stopped, his voice choked with barely controlled rage.

"What? What would you love to do? Hit me? Knock me down? I'm sitting, so that's no fun. Wait. Wait. I'll get up." She pushed herself up and out of the chair and faced off against him. "Well? Howard Spitzer was a shit human being, but at least he was a man. And he never fucking hit me."

Ted watched in quiet satisfaction and prepared to yell "Chocolate!" Events were moving along nicely.

But Hillyer stepped back, rolled his shoulders, and turned to Ted. "Fuck you and your shakedown, fella. I'll tell you what happened."

"Shut up, Bruce. You wouldn't dare."

"Sorry, sweets," he said in a quick aside. "Here's another version of your story. Only this one's true. When the witness didn't show, the judge called a recess. I got a coffee, made some calls, and waited. A little after eleven, Marj called me. Told me she'd whacked Spitzer. According to her, it was an accident, but who knows, right? I told her to send the girl out for sandwiches, then to leave by the back alley. Then I went back into court and stayed there until the judge ordered us done for the day."

This sounded like truth.

"That's all a lie! He did it," the woman screamed, all pretense of believability tossed to the wind.

"And you two were willing to let this kid, Haidir, go to prison in your place?"

"Another one of Spitzer's losers," Hillyer said. "I'll testify. I'll do no time, you'll see. I'll bet you I don't even lose my license." He turned to his wife again. "Such a shame, doll. You've got a great ass."

Mrs. Hillyer pushed past Ted. But instead of breaking for

the door, she grabbed the Eiffel Tower off the bookcase and swung it. It was a three-foot-long solid brass club, and she wielded it like a medieval mace.

Hillyer ducked. The tower brushed his arm. She raised it and swung again.

The damn thing probably weighed four or five pounds. She was no baseball slugger, but she didn't need to be. Full arm extension, an unblocked arc, and a hell of an attitude were what she had, and that was enough.

Hillyer put up an arm to fend her off. The crack of his forearm breaking was a sickening sound.

Ted moved. He threw himself out of the chair and tackled her midthigh, lifting her up and dropping her to the carpet. She rolled away as he scrambled to his knees.

Hillyer huddled against the cabinets moaning in pain.

"Chocolate!" Ted said, careful to enunciate.

74

"**I CANNOT GO IN** there," Mohammed said, bringing the whole entourage to a sudden halt halfway down the block. The entrance to Crossroads Juvenile Center was a long twenty yards away.

Mohammed was pale, and despite the bitter cold wind whipping down Bristol Street in Brooklyn, sweating profusely. Panic attack or heart attack? Kenzie took one arm, and with Lester helping on the other, they lowered him to a sitting position on the curb.

"Put your head down," Lester said. "Down. Between your knees. That's it. Now try to breathe slow. Slow and deep. Better. Better."

Detective Duran and the ADA had continued another few steps and now stood waiting, not wishing to interfere—or intervene.

Kenzie turned to Ted. "Go. Take Almeda in. We'll stay and make sure he's all right."

Ted took a quick look at his watch. "Yeah. We should go."

Though she questioned his judgment at times, he was a rock. He'd be there for the woman and her family—and his friend.

Almeda wore a long light gray scarf that covered her hair, neck, and shoulders, but left her face free. She was pretty. And, Kenzie realized with a start, they were the same age. This young woman had already survived so much, had come so far, and her teenage son was about to be released from jail, no longer accused of murder. She walked on with Ted, head held high. They joined the lawyer and detective and all entered the grim building.

Lester watched her go. "I tell you, my man, you got a good one there."

Mohammed nodded, though he kept his head lowered. He pulled up the collar of his coat to block the wind. "I am blessed."

"You gonna make it? You want some water?"

He shook his head.

Lester patted him on the back, then turned to Kenzie. "Any word on Ashley? They going to arrest her?"

Ted had filled Kenzie in on the morning's excitement during the drive to the courthouse, but she'd had no chance to relay her own news.

"Alicia. No," she said, releasing a sigh that carried a bucketful of conflicting emotions. "Reisner has provided legal counsel—and claims to be paying her hospital bills."

"What about her employer? Collins Guards? They still around?"

"I don't know, Lester. Life's complicated."

"Why is it taking so long?" Mohammed complained.

Ted had explained the procedure. Once the ADA had another suspect in custody, Haidir's release became number one priority. They'd found a judge to sign the letter. Getting Haidir out and home was a mere formality at this point. As long as he was still unharmed. Bad things happened, even in juvie jail.

"We could go inside," she suggested. "We can wait in the hall."

"Where it's warm," Lester said.

"I cannot," Mohammed said.

"I understand," Kenzie said. "But you'll be more comfortable."

Together, they helped him to his feet, and, once moving, Mohammed appeared much stronger. They waited to go through the security line. She watched friends and relatives of other young men and women—boys and girls—who were unfortunate enough to have been swept into the judicial circus. All carried a stoic gloom. Some of these people were visitors, few would be taking their children home.

Lester led them to a section of wall to lean against while they waited. Lawyers ushered clients and their supporters in and out through doors that opened and closed, egesting a few, swallowing more. Time dragged on. They were not the only ones waiting in the hall. Others chose not to subject themselves to the tension, frustration, and boredom of the proceedings.

And then the door opened and Mervyn Prestwick, serious faced, came out. Detective Duran followed, stoic as always. Then Ted, looking relieved.

She felt her heart soar just a little. He was a good man. Not an easy one, but she wouldn't have wanted one of those.

Behind him came Almeda and Haidir. Jubilant.

La Bella Casa, flagship property of LBC, Ronald Reisner's real estate empire, has announced an injection of capital by the diversified holding company Collins & Sons in return for a 25 percent stake in LBC's most recent project in Corona, Queens.

Collins & Sons is the closely held conglomerate run by Calvin (Cal) Collins, creator of the multinational security firm Collins Guards, which provides cybersecurity, bodyguard, mercenary, military training, and provisioning services to individuals, businesses, and governments in thirty-four countries.

LBC owns or manages more than one hundred buildings in the greater New York area, but has struggled in the last year as construction in Corona has stalled. Mr. Reisner admitted that the project is currently beset by legal challenges. "The support of Cal Collins, with his contacts and expertise, will make an immediate contribution to our efforts to sweep away any remaining opposition by the naysayers and NIMBYs who, for reasons that make no sense to any rational citizen, wish to keep real change and economic improvement from this blighted community."

The notoriously private Mr. Collins was unavailable for comment, but a spokesman for the firm said, "When we commit, resistance melts away."